OATH
TO
HONOR

A NOVEL

TRA'VON WILLIAMS

where words connect

Published in the United States by Wordeee 2017
Copyright © 2017 by Tra'von Williams

ISBN-13: 978-1-946274-09-0
ISBN-10: 1-946274-09-7
Cataloging-in Publication data available from Library of Congress

Published by Wordeee
Website: www.wordeee.com
Twitter: wordeeeupdates
Facebook: wordeee
E-Mail: contact@wordeee.com

[10 9 8 7 6 5 4 3 2 1]

Acknowledgments

This book would not be possible if not for the work from the Wordeee staff. Special thanks to Marcia Mayne, my editor for your late-night researching and questions that sometimes did not come with an obvious answer.

My committed and beautiful wife, Dreama. You have given me everything. Through your works and faith in us, you have shown me that all things are possible. Love you so much. To my children, Quasia, Tray, Nay-Nay and Ja'lyn, its ya'll that give me life and I thank each and every one of you for just being different.

Shavone, Kenya, Adam and Kaheim my wonderful siblings, you guys Rock.

Mom and Dad the most important lesson ya'll have given me is "when life throws shade just adjust." Thanks.

Armani (Steele) Funnye, for having my back for whatever. "Loyalty isn't something that's taught, it's something you're born with."

My character as a person, as a man, was shaped in whole by my Grandparents. Rosemary Folks, George Folks, Bertha May Williams and Robert Williams Sr. (R.I.P). Miss you guys.

Special thanks to my friends at Wolfstyle clothing.

In Memory of

Michael Naughton, Neil Naughton, Karen Lisa Wright, Teresa Williams and Sharkiem (Dooley) Williams. Gone from here but forever immortalized in the hearts of the people ya'll touched.

Aunt Eva...saved the best for last. It's not said enough, but the love, respect and admiration I have for you bring tears to my eyes as I write these words. Growing up and in my adulthood, you always outlined through your actions the true bond of family. I don't know if I would ever be that shining light that you are, but you inspire me to push to those limits. Thank you for being that pillow for our family when some of us choose to lie on concrete.

Uncle Kenny and Aunt Berta, thanks for being there when it counted.

To my family, Friends and Mount Morris Park community there will never be enough thanks and appreciation for it was you guys that pushed and supported my talent.

—Bless you all.

About the Author

Tra'von Williams is a natural born storyteller. He first discovered his talent for writing in 3rd Grade but once in his teens his passion for writing and story telling took a backseat to his teenage years. Born in Brooklyn, NY, but relocating to Harlem with his Grandparents at the age of seven, this Urban writer grew up during the tumultous eighties and ninetes drug epidemic in Harlem.

Tra'von is the proud father of 4 kids and is married to his junior high school sweetheart, Dreama. He lives in Harlem with his family

OATH
TO
HONOR

(Volume One)

Several violent gangs and crews operated in Harlem during the drug epidemic that hit the area in the late 1980s to the mid-1990s. The following is the story of one of these crews.

OATH
TO
HONOR

CHAPTER ONE

"TIA STOP PLAYING and give me the keys." Tone shouted while trying to catch Tia before she made it out the door.

"Stop bitching, I'm only going to pick Jada up." Tia said as she reached for the door knob.

"Tee, you're bullshitting, you never just do one thing."

"Dang, I said I'll come right back with your bullshit ass bucket-on-wheels. Shiiiiittt, even the rims cost more than the car."

"Fuck you, Tee!" Tone shouted as he watched his sister disappear into the stairwell.

Tia stepped outside her building appreciating the semi-cool afternoon air. She scanned her block looking for Tone's 95 Maxima, which wasn't hard to find as it was the only car on the block that stood out. Tia smiled to herself as she approached the car. The black paint job was Tone's way of giving his hooptie a glossy appearance and the faded tints gave it a down-low kind of appeal. I don't know what made that fool put $1,200 dollar rims on this piece of shit! The NERVE, Tia thought as she got into the car. She put the keys in the starter and turned the ignition. Like always, she had to repeat the action.

"Damn!" She slapped the steering wheel. "Why do I always have problems starting this car?" Tia sat back, tried again and breathed a sigh of relief as the engine roared to life. "Okayyyy that's what the fuck I'm talking 'bout." She began to pull out of the parking space but stopped. *Matter-of-fact, I better call Jay first let her know I'm on my way 'cause she's forgetful as hell."*

Tia listened to the phone wailing. A male voice answered on the third ring. "Hello, who dis?"

"Who's this?" Tia responded, aggravated that Jada was too lazy to answer her own damn phone. *That Jada always has some man up in her crib.* "Let me speak to Jada."

"Hello," Jada said into the receiver with a sluggish voice.

"Do you know what time it is?" asked Tia.

"Oh shit, Tee. My bad. I was just about to…"

"Whatever, Bitch! Just be downstairs in 10 minutes," Tia disconnected the phone.

As Tia drove down 7th Avenue she noticed that 125th Street was jammed packed as always. That was Harlem for you. Harlem, though in Manhattan, was considered another world. In the mid-nineties it was a dangerous place crawling with gangbangers, drug kingpins and hustlers. There was always something going on down below 96th street and it wasn't good for the soul. Tia was bopping to the song on the radio and looking around at the throngs of people in front of her favorite store. *If it wasn't for the fact I gotta handle some business, I sure would of stopped in Strawberries and catch their midday sale.* She kept moving. As Tia rounded the corner on 115th Street coming up on Manhattan Avenue, she noticed the regular heads in front of Jada's building. The area used to be decent when she and Jada were little; now with drugs flooding into Harlem, it too was infested with a bunch of wanna-be gang bangers.

Tia parked across from Jada's building. She got out the car to ring her intercom because Jada wasn't downstairs. "Typical of her ass," Tia said loudly releasing a deep sigh and staying on the buzzer.

"Yooooo, Shortieeee," somebody shouted, but Tia did not turn around to acknowledge the individual who thought calling a female Shorty was cool.

"Ma, slow down!"

Tia heard the voice coming closer toward her. She swiftly turned around ready to put the dolt in his place. "First of all, I'm not your mother, so save that weak shit for the woman who gave birth to you and second, don't be running up on me like that." Tia said, pointing her finger in his face.

"Damn, why you acting all stuck up?"

"Listen Mutha…" Tia was interrupted by the outburst from Jada calling her name.

Tia approached Jada. "You was supposed to be downstairs."

"I know but I had to wait for C-Black to give me money."

"Oooh. So that's the niggas name that answered your phone? I don't know where you find these stupid ass dudes that be handling your bank rolls, but you better watch yourself and make sure that shit don't come back to haunt your trifling ass."

Jada responded with a smirk. "I'm not worried about that. This shit here (while patting her crotch) is like crack, one hit and you will be back." Jada was indeed a beauty. Her petite 5' frame camouflaged her deadly actions.

"Whatever, just get in the car crazy lady. Next time," Tia shouted to the man-boy, "I'll whup your ass for talking to a grown up like that."

As they drove off, Tia grabbed her cellular off the dash and began dialing numbers. The phone rang once before a dude with a deep Jamaican accent answered it.

"Ah who dis?"

"Stan, it's Tee. I'm on my way."

"Al'rite," Rude Boy answered as Tia hung up the phone.

As Tia slowed down to a red light, she turned to Jada with a serious look on her face. "Listen Jay, when we get there, wait in the car, leave it running, 'cause I really don't trust home team like that."

"I got it, Tee."

"The burner is under the seat."

"Alright," Jada replied.

"After today, we will be able to handle that situation. Stay on guard."

As Tia made a left on 161st in Washington Heights, she handed Jada a paper bag and told her to put her half of the money in the back pack on the back seat inside. They pulled up to a three-story red brick brownstone building Tia grabbed the knapsack and exited the car leaving it running. Jada was on the passenger side with a fully loaded Glock 9 tucked between her legs.

Tia walked up the three steps leading to the front door of the dilapidated brownstone and knocked on the metal-fitted door twice before she heard footsteps approaching, then the clicking sounds of the locks being opened. A dark figure with shoulder length dreadlocks stood in the doorway.

"Wah a gwan Star," Tia brushed pass Jamaican Stan. The man was beastly looking. He stood six feet tall with a heavy, raggedy beard and his accent even heavier than that. Stan was known for his variety of chebba, but his second and more profitable hustle was dealing guns. "Yah Man, come in?" Stan said sarcastically and led Tia down some narrow steps.

When they reached the basement, it was so dark that Tia had to wait until her eyes adjusted just to see shadows. When the light finally came on Tia was amazed at the artillery one person could have. If this nigga wanted, he could start his own Taliban chapter right in Harlem. Though awestruck, Tia remained silent. Her motto was to never open any doors for those whom you may eventually have to close the casket on.

"So, Star, watchyu need?" Rude Boy asked as he picked up an A-K 47 assault rifle and ran his hand over the barrel. "Dis good for distance."

Tia looked at the A-K and wondered what she'd do with his mammoth doofy-ass gun. The average nigga would probably spot the heat way before they even notice who was carrying it.

4

"Naw, Stan. I need something less obvious, but with the same kick," she said.

"A'wright." Stan moved over to the corner of the room.

Tia's eyes followed him to a crate marked "PROPERTY OF THE U.S. ARMY." Stan reached into the crate and pulled out a black Heckler & Koch automatic machine gun. She had heard about the release of this gun in *Don Diva* magazine but she never thought twice about it being on the street so soon. "Now you talkin'." Tia took the weapon from Stan and measured its weight. It was light. "How much?" Tia inquired as she handed the gun back to him.

"Fifteen Hundred, Star."

"Woha. Damn. Those shits are expensive!"

"For a reason," Stan deadpanned.

Ah fuck it, you gotta spend to earn. "A'wright Stan, let me get two, and five boxes of hollow head bullets."

Business concluded, Tia stashed her goods and walked out of the brownstone carrying the knapsack. Out of habit, she looked around to make sure everything was as it should be. Jada was now standing outside the car with a newspaper folded under her arm. Tia smiled. Her girl was on point.

"Damn, Tee, what took you so long?"

"Chill. Everything went well plus some, but wait 'til you see this shit." Tia discretely patted the knapsack. "First though, I gotta drop you off then get this piece of shit car back to my brother before he has a nervous breakdown."

"Don't let him hear you calling his car that! This piece of shit car is your brother Tone's pride and joy." Jada swore he put more money into it than he'd paid for it.

Tone, Tia smiled was a good kid. He was only 7 when their Mother had died and Ebony, their younger sister, was 5. Tia was 9. Breast cancer is what the death certificate said but Tia felt her mother died from a broken heart. After their father left them, she started to go downhill. Their Pappy was a long-haul trucker so he was gone for days, sometimes weeks at a time. But when he came home it was like Christmas as he always brought something for his "little heartbeats." That's what he called them. After he'd left for the last time, their Mother found out that he'd gotten some woman in North Carolina pregnant. She knew he wasn't coming back but he never stopped sending money to take care of them. A few years later, she found out she had breast cancer.

"I still can't believe Tone so grown up," Jada said

"After Mommie died, shit, we all had to grow up fast. As the oldest, it was my responsibility to step up and take charge but Tone really surprised me with how quickly he changed from a snot-nosed kid to responsible man. Ebony was too young but me and Tone held down the fort. Of the three of us, she had less time with Mommie and even less time with Pappy so Tone and I tried really hard to protect her as best we could and make sure she had everything. That's why that bitch is so spoiled now. We might have made a mistake."

"Nah, she just a teenager." Jada reassured.

"Yeah, and she giving me the blues. If I hadn't promised Mommie and myself that I'd do whatever it took to keep us together, I'd put her ass in an orphanage!"

"Yeah, right."

"Shit Jada can you believe? We've come a long fuckin' way from then in six years."

CHAPTER TWO

"TIA, WAKE UP. IT'S ALMOST 7:30. Don't you have to be at school?" Ebony said standing over Tia.

"Shit, why you just waking me up?" Tia answered still half asleep.

"I thought I woke you before. I guess you went back to sleep."

Tia dragged herself out of bed and went over to the dresser drawer and pulled out a white Victoria Secrets thong and bra set that she threw on the bed. She then pulled out some jeans and a Coogi sweater from the closet and padded to the bathroom.

"Come on, Tone," Tia banged on the bathroom door, "get out of the bathroom already," she shouted.

"Hold on!" Tone yelled back.

"Damn, Nigga, you act like a damn chick. Ain't that much grooming yourself in the world."

"It's yours," Tone yanked open the door and pushed her out of his way.

"Thank you."

Tia was half finished with her shower when she heard a knock on the bathroom door. "Yea," Tia shouted.

"Can I come in?" Ebony said already walking into the bathroom.

"What's up, Eb?" Tia asked as she turned off the shower.

"I need $70.00."

"Hand me a towel," Tia reached out and took the towel from Ebony.

"What you need $70.00 for?"

"I wanna get this outfit to go with the boots Ike bought for me."

Tia stepped out of the shower and sat on the toilet to dry her feet. "Who's Ike and why didn't't Ike buy you an outfit to go with your boots? Matter of fact, why's he buying you clothes? Don't we give you everything you need?"

"Tee, are you gonna give it to me or what?" Ebony asked getting flustered.

Tia let the matter drop but made a note to find out who Ike was. "If you weren't my baby sister I would juggle it to you. Interest would be high."

"What's juggled?" Ebony asked, confused.

"Ah, never mind." Tia continued to dry off, realizing the street term to loan money at high interest rates was not in her sister's vocabulary. She never told her siblings that the money that helped support them since their mother died six years before, came from the streets. She was planning to get out of the game as soon as she'd made enough money or the moment she could put the business degree she was working on to work. "Just take it out my drawer and take your ass to school."

"Thank you," Ebony said enroute to Tia's bedroom.

"I hate these rush hour train rides," Tia mumbled, elbowing her way through throngs of people waiting for the 2 train. It was bad enough to have to wade through the long ass walk from the A to the 2 train at 34th Street and she was tired of the long ass commute. Plus, everybody was all up on each other and nobody seemed like they could smell the aroma of funk from all the homeless stragglers and druggies and the cheap perfume the patrons wore. Then there was always the mutha fucker who'd purposely brush up against you for a free feel and then try to apologize like it was an accident. She again elbowed her way into the sardine packed 2 train when it pulled into the station. Tia was trying to be lost in thoughts for the rest of the train ride, but somehow, she had an odd feeling that she was being watched. She could feel the eyes on her back and it made her uncomfortable. It was probably some old perverted white guy staring at her ass. *I won't even turn around and make eye contact, because he might feel I'm flirting with him and I don't feel like going to jail today.* She clamped the Motorola headphones into her ears.

"JAY STREET, BOROUGH HALL," the train conductor announcement blared through her music. Tia's stop. She, and it seemed, the hordes of people on the train began to squeeze through the tiny cracks between bodies to exit the train. When Tia finally got off the train and onto the platform, a passenger bumped into her and knocked her carry bag to the floor spilling all its contents.

"Ah, shit!"

"Pardon me, Ms.," a brown skinned brother in a two-piece suit said, bending down to help her retrieve her belongings. "Let me help you with that," he offered picking up four textbooks. He handed them to Tia. "I'm really sorry."

"Thank you. You did enough already," Tia was annoyed and aggravated that he was hovering over her.

"Miss, I said pardon me."

"You're pardoned," Tia huffed, "now go and enjoy your newfound freedom," she said sarcastically.

"Oh, we have jokes," replied the stranger.

"Not if you're the only one laughing."

"And sarcastic, too. So, what's your name?"

"Late." Tia said hurriedly making her way out of the train station.

"Wait...wait. Ms. Late!" The stranger shouted as he picked up a text book Tia had left behind. The man caught up with her on the escalator.

"Didn't you hear me say wait?"

Frustrated with the man's persistence, Tia turned around to give him a piece of her mind but found he was only handing her the Business Science text book she'd left behind. "Thank you," Tia took the book but never waited for his response. The stranger watched the woman he deemed perfection, vanish through a cloud of commuters

BROOKLYN DA'S OFFICE

"Morning Mr. Adams." His secretary said as he came into the office. "I have the files you requested on the Park Avenue robberies. Also, the 32nd Precinct faxed the ballistics for the Rodney Jenkins shooting."

"Thank you, Linda. Oh, by the way, congrats on your engagement."

"Thank you, Sir," she said, handing him a manila folder.

Sean Adams flipped through the file and skimmed the ballistics report. *I'm tired already. I should have gone into private practice instead of taking this damn Assistant District Attorney position.* Aggravated as he was, he knew that somebody had to do this work. New York needed more black ADAs and he owed it to the community to seek justice for the underserved.

Sean sat at his desk. He rested the folder on top and sat looking out the window. How did he get here? That was simple. His father's love. Sean began thinking of his life now and it brought his past into view. Sean's father was a preacher of note who was active in the church and in the Harlem community. He'd raised Sean singlehandedly after his wife died during childbirth, and he'd kept him sheltered, as much as he could, from the harsh realities of Harlem's streets. He'd also taught him the importance of giving back and sent him to the best schools to give him an advantage most would never have. Sean excelled under his father's watchful eyes and with his father's guidance he'd conquered the streets of Harlem. Determination had willed his heart and he'd stayed the course. Now, here he was working in the Brooklyn DA's office, handling federal cases. It was a long way from Harlem but Harlem was in his blood. He had to do what he could.

A familiar voice on his intercom interrupted Sean's thoughts.

"You have a call on line two from Ms. Daniels."

"Yes. Put her through," Sean picked up the ringing phone as soon as it chimed on his desk. "How are you doing Ms. Daniels?"

"Fine, and yourself?"

"I'm well. What can I do for you today?"

"You told me to call when or if I remembered anything else about that night. You know, the night of the murder."

"Yes, I do recall," Sean said as he pondered what new information Ms. Daniels may have to help him close his case.

"Well, it's funny. I do remember something strange about that day."

"That's tereffic. Would you like to come down so we can discuss this further?"

"Alright."

"I'll see you then," Sean said and hung up the phone.

CHAPTER THREE

"J ADA, I'M ON MY WAY HOME FROM SCHOOL. Have Kaisia, Toya and Rich, meet us at the Honeycomb," Tia spoke softly into the phone's receiver. She was referring to the other members of her ride or die posse. Tia knew that the life they were living was not the life they should have chosen but circumstances dictated play. They had to live the way the die fell. She couldn't have a better crew by her side. They were practically family.

The Honeycomb was an apartment they rented, illegally, at the Drew Hamilton Housing Projects on 142 Street. They paid the superintendent a couple dollars on the side to look the other way. Her crew were friends she'd made from the hood or school who had been into credit card scams, boosting, short cons and pick pocketing until Tia showed them how to go after bigger paydays so they could get out of the game faster.

"I got you, Tee."

"Oh, and remind Kaisia to bring the info from her cousin."

"Got it."

"We'll talk when I get there."

The 2 train pulled into 135th Street. Tweet grabbed Ebony's hand and tried pulling her along. "Come on, Ebony, Jean's ain't gonna stay open for us. Let's hurry." Tweet was tugging at a loitering and resistant Ebony. "Let's hurry,"she tugged harded. "I really want to catch the store before it closes. It's the last day for the sale."

"Tweet, hold on. I'm tryna to wait for Ike. He said to meet him here."

"Damn, Bitch, homeboy got you open and you'll ain't even fuckin'."

"Tweet, you just burnt 'cause I ain't gotta spread my legs to get what I want," Ebony said walking to the corner of 135 and Lenox.

"No. I'm mad 'cause I'm waiting here with you to wait for some man when I *need* them damn jeans."

Tweet reluctantly followed Ebony toward the corner. Before they got to the corner, a red Range Rover pulled up alongside them.

"Shorty, what's up?" The man inside the vehicle said to Ebony.

"There he go," Ebony made the statement more to herself than for Tweet.

"Damn, who ride is dat?" Tweet asked as she walked over to the truck with Ebony.

"It's his," Ebony whispered with pride.

Ike stepped out of the truck and stood next to Ebony. "Eb, who's your friend?" He asked.

"This is Tweet, my best friend. Tweet, this is Ike," Ebony said in formal introductions.

"Pleased to meet you," Tweet extended her hand. This Ike was a looker. How the hell did Ebony catch his eye?

Ike looked Tweet up and down, and although she was no comparison to Ebony, Shorty definitely had an apple bottom and cute face. Them jeans were hugging her ass like they were painted on, plus Shorty had a serious gap which meant she was fuckin'. He had to pass but he was gonna put one of his mans on her. "Get in ya'll so we can get up outta here," Ike said as he climbed back into the truck.

The women followed suit and they sped off down Lenox.

Brooklyn DA's Office Later that Afternoon.

"Ms. Daniels, are you sure the information is accurate?"

"Sure, I am sure. I could never forget that scar."

"Well," Sean said, excitement in his voice. "If what you just told me pans out, we'll bring this individual in. We are going to need you to identify him in a line up though."

"Wait a minute! Ain't nobody say nothing before 'bout me pointing near person out!"

"Ms. Daniels, this in only…"

"NO, FUCK THAT," Ms. Daniels shouted, getting up to leave. "Ya'll ain't gonna have this lunatic after me because ya'll laws or procedures couldn't hold his ass."

"We will do everything in our power to make sure that never happens," Shawn got up from his desk and walked over to Ms. Daniels. He rested his hand on her shoulder to reassure her. "He won't actually see you until trial when, and that's if it goes that far."

"Wow, Cowboy, I didn't say I was testifying!"

"But it's your testimony that will send him away for a long time."

"Hell no! Matter of fact, thru' all this here confusion, I forgot what he look like."

"Ms. Daniels," Sean pleaded, "don't be irrational." Sean felt like he was fighting a losing battle because he knew the law of the street ruled over the law of the court: snitches got punished. He didn't blame the woman but he really needed her testimony.

"No, Mr. Adams. Irrational was bringing my black ass down here in the first place."

"You are aware, Ms. Daniels, that we can subpoena you?" Sean knew he was using the last card in his deck to get her to cooperate.

"No disrespect Mr. Adams, but I'm 37 years old tryna make it to 47, by the grace of God. I'll damned if I'm a have my picture as the latest victim being shown on the local news and have people, I don't even know, tellin' some newscaster that I was a God-fearing woman. So, Mr. Adams, you may subpoena me if you like, but know this, Sir, I'd rather be locked in a cage than to be in a coffin. Have a nice day."

Ms. Daniels, stood up, smoothed her skirt and walked out of Sean's office. Sean stood in the doorway, shaking his head.

UPTOWN AT THE HONEYCOMB

"Who is it?"

"It's Tee."

"The queen liveeesss!" shouts Rich as he opened the door to the Honeycomb.

Tia stepped into the apartment they used as a stash house, a place for meeting up, a place where they could think or for just chilling. Rich, the only guy in the crew had become one of Tia's best friends when he moved to Harlem from Queens. Like Tia, Rich was taking care of his younger sister, Tweet. Their grandmother, who had been the stablizing force for her trouble proned daughter suddenly died and that triggered their mom descent into alcoholism and drugs. Rich and Tia bonded over their similar struggles--life without parents. Tia trusted Rich and he was the only crew member who had a key to the apartment. Rich had suggested getting copies of the key made for the rest of the crew but Tia had been against the idea for more reasons than one. First, was the accountability factor and second, she didn't want anyone using the Honeycomb for purposes not intended.

"What's up Rich, baby?" Tia said, entering the apartment.

"Ain't shit but ahhh dolla," Rich replied locking the door. "You know me, gotta stay with ah hustle."

"I know that's right," Tia said removing her jacket and putting it on the arm of the couch. Tia looked around the modest, yet well-organized apartment and as always was impressed with the work they had put into their little establishment. Headquarters central was decked out. Two side-by-side wall units matched the black and gold coffee table and the entertainment system which was equipped with duplex flat speakers for surround sound. The windows were covered with heavy, dark drapes. Though they had put a little something into the living room, the rest of the apartment was pretty much left as it was, empty. "Where's everybody?" Tia asked.

"Oh, they went to get something to eat because it might be a long night."

"True dat. So, Mo-Mo what's good with you?" Mo-Mo's what Tia called Rich when he was dressed in drag. And she was the only person he let call him that. Rich was petite, a bit over five feet. With smooth, brown skin, oval face, high cheekbones and arched eyebrows, he was gorgeous as a woman. He looked exactly like the R&B singer, Monica, when he was in drag.

"I just got back from Binghamton last night. Boosted two short minks."

"Word! So, hook ya' girl up!"

"Can't do that this time. Those go into the collection."

Tia already knew it was a shot in the dark asking Rich to come off a mink. Rich had a fetish for furs and had a variety of colors and cuts in what he called his 'pet closet.' As they were catching up on the latest gossip, they heard *the code* knock on the door. Rich answered it.

"What's so funny?" Jada asked Rich, pushing past him into the apartment, Kaisia and Toya, the other members of the crew, stepping in right behind her.

"I was just laughing at something Tia said," Rich replied closing the door behind the last of the crew.

"What's in them bags?"Tia followed them into the kitchen to see what they'd bought to eat because she was hungry.

"We just picked up something from Ma'Ma's Fried chicken," Kaisia answered.

"Yumm. That'll hit the spot, baby," Tia devoured a chicken thigh throwing the bone in the trash and everyone dove in following suite. After they were done Tia tied up the trash and leaned it against the front door. Critters in Harlem were serious.

"Let's get down to business then," Tia opened the conversation with the first item on their agenda and the reason for them being at the Honeycomb. "Listen up. We got business to take care of and I gotta make sure that everybody is on point. Toya, did you get the rental?"

"Of course, but they don't do one day rentals, so I had to get the ride for two days instead."

"Kaisia, how is it looking on your end?"

"My cousin Fat-Steve got us a key to the lobby, plus he informed me that the security guard takes fifteen minute breaks every two hours. He comes on duty at 4pm so we can make our move at 6."

"Good. But what did your cousin say about the number of heads in the crib?" Tia asked. She was breaking her cardinal rule of never involving family but the prospect of getting out of the game faster was too much to pass up.

"He said on average night there's three. Two lieutenants and the chief but being that today's Friday the traffic may be a little heavier with workers picking up their goods and stuff."

"Alright. We just gotta move quick, in and out. Mo-Mo, you got the wigs?" Tia picked up the knapsack containing the guns she had stashed after meeting with Jamaican Stan.

"Yeah," Mo-Mo answered.

CHAPTER FOUR

SEAN LOOSENED HIS TIE AS HE walked into his condo on the Lower West Side and tossed it and his briefcase onto the sofa. It was good to be home. He was drained. He needed a drink. He went to his well-stocked bar that boasted a variety of alcoholic beverages and poured his usual drink - a shot of cognac with one ice cube. He put the glass to his lips and felt the warmth from the cognac move slowly through his body as he flopped down in the leather reclining chair. He looked around the living room, taking in the view from the bay window that framed the lights of the city beyond. He switched on the TV, put his feet up on the ottoman and thought about the day's events. It was a habit he'd learned at a young age from his father. By rewinding the events of his day, he benefited from seeing things from a different perspective. Sometimes, he recalled details he didn't even realize he had seen or heard.

Sean sipped his cognac thinking he should have offered Ms. Daniels a more reasonable option instead of legal blackmail. Maybe if he'd tried harder, he probably could have persuaded her to, at minimum, view the line-up. Shit, sometimes his mouth acted too quickly. He'd call her on Monday to see if she had a change of mind.

Sean flicked the channel. Same ole, same ole. Nothing but mayhem in New York City. He took another swig of his drink and continued scanning his life from the previous eight hours. What really stood out and had him in awe was the brown-skinned sister with the oval eyes who he immediately noticed when he had gotten on the No. 2 train at 34th Street. The striking colors of her sweater complemented her skin to perfection and her fitted jeans hugged the hips and curves of her figure eight body like a glove. There were no vacant seats and as more passengers entered the crowded car, he moved closer to where she was standing. She was so close he could smell the light floral aroma of her perfume. The woman was phat! He could tell that she took real pride in her appearance. Just looking at her back tickled his imagination. He'd hoped she'd turn around, but she never did.

Sean grimaced as he remembered that in his eagerness to connect with her when they exited at the Jay Street Borough Hall station, he'd knocked her book bag out of her hand. She hadn't even looked up as he tried to help her pick up the books that fell to the ground. She shot him the strangest look when he caught up with her on the escalator to give her the book she'd left behind. In fact, she seemed downright pissed. Maybe if he had been on his game, he could've turned the disaster into pursuit. The pressure in his loins snapped Sean out of his revere and he realized he had a throbbing erection. Sighing, he downed the rest of his drink, sat the empty glass on the side table and went to his den.

Sean pressed the flashing button on his answering machine to check his general messages. His cell number was reserved for very few. Beep, the machine came to life...'you have two new messages. First message. Hey, this is Kev, we're still on for tonight? Call me." (beep)'

Damn! He'd forgotten that he had promised to meet Kev. It was good too, he looked down at his pants, he needed to relieve some tension.

(beep) "Sean this is Monique. Why haven't you called? Anyway, call me when you get in from work." (beep).

Sean walked into his room, sat on the bed and pulled off his socks. It'd been more than a week since he and Monique last spoke and it was all her fault. If the woman wasn't so damned controlling and spoiled, her ass could have been over giving him what he needed right now. He looked at his pants and sighed again. Man, he'd better get these thought out of my head before he called that woman and regretted it in the morning. Sean threw his clothes into the hamper and headed to the bathroom for a quick 'cold' shower. It did the trick. He put on a black, cotton turtleneck and jeans and headed to his usual Friday night hangout, a bar on 28th Street.

HARLEM

"Tone, it's Friday and I'm not tryna' be cooped up in this house all night."

"Ebony, I need you to be here when Uncle Robbie stops by to drop off our check." Uncle Robbie was their Mother's younger brother and their legal guardian. They'd found out after her death that she'd saved all the money that their Father used to send her for the children. Since Uncle Robbie was the executor of her estate, every month, he brought a check to help with the rent.

"Why can't you be here? He'll want to see you anyway."

"Because I'm DJ'ing the pool party in Esplanade Gardens, that's why!" Tone poked Ebony in the forehead, fed-up with her lack of responsibility and spoiled way. He blamed Tia. "Listen Eb, you're seventeen yet you still act like you three years old or somethin'. You gotta' start takin' on some responsibilities around here, because me and Tia ain't always gonna be around to hold your hand."

"Whatever, Tone. How come all of a sudden you the most wise, huh? You're letting local fame blow your big head up and you need to stop frontin'."

"Eb, you are just like your sister. Ya'll always gotta have the last word, but you know what? I ain't got time for this dumb shit. I gotta go. Oh yeah, when Uncle Robbie comes by tell him I'll holla at him as soon as I get in. Eb, Eb are you hearing me?"

"Yeah. Damn. What you want me to do acknowledge you every time you speak?"

"Forget it Eb. Do you need some money?"

"Naw, I'm straight."

"Alright, I'm out." Tone pulled the door to the apartment shut, his chest poked out cause it's not often that he beat either of his sisters in the verbal game they often played. He wondered why Eb made him win so easily.

Tone stopped at the red light and thought of his sister. Why did he keep arguing with Ebony? She was still too young to understand the realities of life or the responsibilities and the sacrifices he and Tia had made to keep a roof over their heads and food on the table. Although their mother's death had rocked their foundation, they had had each other and Tia, especially, had been determined that their mother's death would not change Ebony's life. She'd worked extra hard to make her comfortable but it seemed more and more that Ebony was being ungrateful. He blamed Tia for using money as a means of controlling her. A blaring horn brought him out of the frustrating memory.

Ebony sat on the couch in mid-thought. They always do this corny shit to me, especially on Friday nights when they knew Uncle Robbie was coming. It's like they don't want to see him. Their mother had left him in charge of her estate until Tia was 21. Ebony wondered why Tia hadn't taken over the account and made a mental note to ask her. Ebony's thoughts were interrupted by the ringing of the phone. She picked it up on the third ring. "Hello."

"May I please speak to Ebony?" The caller asked.

"This is her," Ebony said, excitement spreading though her body when she recognized the familiar male voice as Ike's.

"What's up, Shorty?"

"Ain't much. Just house sittin'."

"Word. Damn I was gonna ask you if you wanted to ride out to Jersey with us."

"I can't today."

"Don't worry about it. We'll do Jersey some other time."

"Alright, Ike. Do your thang," Ebony said. She was disappointed.

"Naw, baby. It won't be the same without you. Besides I'd rather chill with you."

Ebony was pleased that Ike was willing to change his plans to be with her. She felt obliged and happy to give him some of her time. "Ike, check it. Ain't nobody here. Why don't you come by and chill with me for a while."

"That's what's up Peep Game. Give me your address. I'll be over in like thirty minutes. I'ma stop by the smoke shop."

"Aright. My apartment's on St. Nic's and 145th Street, No. 4. See you then."

This was a big move for Ebony. She and Ike had never spent real time alone, except for a brief five minutes at his house that almost cost her virginity, but Ike's homeboy's knock on his door saved her. "Well," Ebony said as she looked at herself in the mirror, "if today is the day I'ma gonna lose my virginity, I might as well freshen up." Ebony smiled to herself at the thought of losing her virginity. Tia would be livid!

THE BRONX

"Toya, pull up right here. This way I can see the guard and you can watch the front without looking too obvious," Tia said. Then she turned to Rich who was in full drag regalia. "Mo-Mo, what time you got?"

"Ten on the dot," said Rich.

"Okay ya'll. Security should be bouncing any second. Everybody check ya'll hammers."

The building, in the Wakefield section of the Bronx, was a moderate six story apartment duplex with little to no traffic except for a couple of elderly people who were probably going to check on their lottery ticket stub wins. The lobby area with the security desk was clearly visible through the clear glass wall. There was one guard on post.

"Tee, he's getting up," Jada said.

"Okay, ya'll, it's show time."

Kaisia exited the car first as she had the keys to get into the building. Tia was on her heels followed by Rich and Jada. As they entered the building, Jada immediately took her solo post in the stairwell. The target's apartment was directly on the lobby floor, which meant they had to move fast. When they reached the apartment, Tia and Kaisia pulled down their skull caps which transformed into a mask. Kaisia pulled her Glock from her waist and Tia followed suit. Rich reached into the Roc-a-Wear duffle bag and pulled out one of the Heckle & Koch machine guns Tia had bought from Jamaican Stan.

Rich and Kaisia both looked at Tia for the go ahead. Tia nodded and Rich knocked twice on the door then stepped out of range of the peep-hole.

"Who's dat?" a male voice from inside asked.

Rich answered in his deepest male voice, "The Super." At the sound of the door un-clicking, Rich put his hand on the knob. As the door opened cautiously, Rich rammed it forward knocking the occupant on the other side to the floor. Tia and Kaisia rushed into the apartment leaving Rich to man the door and handle the knocked-out gangsta.

"Get on the fuckin' floor!" Tia and Kaisia shouted with their guns leveled at two individuals seated in the living room. As the two occupants obeyed the gun-women's command, a half-naked young girl, no more than eighteen years old came running from the back room. Kaisia, in one stealth move, stopped the redbone in her tracks, leveling the Glock's nuzzle between the girl's eyes.

"Listen, Bitch," Kaisia said, her voice deadly serious, "you're in the wrong place at the wrong got-damn time, so you gonna do yourself a favor and park your hot ass in that corner and don't make a sound. Do we understand each other?"

Redbone nodded her head in agreement. Kaisia lowered her gun, but kept it pointed at the girl as she found a corner in the living room and tried make herself as invisible as possible.

Rich threw the stunned door opener onto the floor in the middle of the living room.

"You broke my nose, Bitch." The door man stuttered as he squeezed his fingers to stem the bleeding.

"Make sure the back rooms are clear," Tia beckoned to Kaisia. Then turning her attention back to the pussies on the floor she asked, "Which one of ya'll is the chief?" Tia brought her face close to the men and scanned their faces. No one answered. "Ya'll niggaz is tryna' make this shit bad, so I'm gonna try another approach," she said screwing the silencer onto the muzzle of her gun. "Now, I'm gonna pick a candidate to run for office in hell," Tia stepped over the guy who opened the door and headed for a fat nigga' laid out prone on the carpet. Tia bent down and put the silencer against his temple. "Fatboy," she said, "you probably was never picked for anything in your life but today you're my first pick and I hope and pray you play fair, 'cause if not by this time next year your fat ass will be all bones."

Fatboy recoiled, his body going tense. He knew the crazy before him wouldn't hesitate to kill him.

"Now, I'm gonna ask you once more and your answer better be accurate. Who's the chief?"

Fatboy pointed to the incapacitated door opener as Rich grabbed him by the collar and dragged him over to the couch.

"Damn, what are you--a super bitch?" asked the chief.

Tia was in front of him in two steps, her full palm connecting with his face before she grabbed him by the throat. "How much shit you cooked up today?" Tia squeezed hard before letting go of his throat.

The chief was coughing and spluttering for a minute before he could answer. "A half a brick."

"How much raw is left?" Tia asked.

"A bird and a half."

"You're doin' good pretty boy. Where is it?"

24

"It's in the safe."

"What's the combination?" Rich asked.

"I don't have it, I swear!"

"Who has it then?" Tia asked, rubbing the silencer against the chief's cheek.

"He do," the chief shouted looking in the direction of a dark-skinned brother wearing a mint green Sean Jean velour suit. He was lying next to Fatboy.

Tia looked over at the dark-skinned guy. He had to be the lieutenant.

"Ain't nobody back there," Kaisia walked back into the living room, "but I found a safe in the room by the bathroom."

Tia nodded to Rich and he stepped over to the lieutenant. "What's the combination?"

"FUCK YOU, FAGGOT!" the lieutenant said staring Rich down with pure hate in his eyes.

"Oh, so you're a thug, huh? A real live wire." Rich was shaking his head. "I got something for tough guys like you. "Throw me the bag," he said turning to Kaisia. He removed a roll of duct tape from the bag and began taping the lieutenant's wrist together. Then he slapped a strip of tape over his mouth. "I see you got a fresh mouth." Rich planted his full weight on Dark Skin's back and began pulling down his velour pants.

Dark Skin was tryin' to struggle but the weight on his back was too overpowering. Rich pulled a dildo out of the bag. "Want some of this," he flashed the dildo before sodomizing the too talkative lieutenant.

Dark Skin tried screaming but the thick tape covering his mouth muffled his sounds. Rich continued to humiliate the lieutenant until he felt Dark Skin's pride and self-esteem had been broken. When he eased up off the fool of a man he smiled at seeing this one-time tough thug in tears.

Rich reached across his faced and ripped the tape from his mouth. "Now Playa, do we understand each other, or do we go for seconds?"

Dark Skin was sobbing now, shaking his head, snot covered his face. "I.I.I.IT'S TH-TH 30-16-01-23, pleeeease do…don't put that in me again….pleeeeease."

Rich looked down at the hopeless coward and shook his head.

Get that," said Tia looking towards Kaisia.

Rich threw Kaisia the duffle bag to retrieve the contents from the safe.

"Duct tape them," Tia ordered Rich, walking over to the Redbone in the corner who was now crying a river of tears. She looked about the same age as Ebony. "Listen, Shorty, you're young and obviously stupid. I assume you're fuckin' one or both of these kats, if not all of them, but I'm gonna give you some advice. You can ignore it or apply it to your twisted perception of life. These niggaz don't give a fuck about you. You're just pussy to them and they, to you, probably represent success. Either way, there's no future in this life for you. Today you go home to your family but the next time you may not be so lucky. Do you understand what I'm sayin' to you?"

Redbone nodded her head without making eye contact.

Kaisia walked back into the living room and nodded, patting the duffle bag. "Come ya'll, I got it."

"Everybody taped up?" Tia asked.

"Yes," Rich answered looking at Tia, "but what about her?"

Tia looked back at Redbone balled up in the corner. "Naw, leave her. Let's go." By the time the naked girl got dressed they would be long gone.

As they exited the apartment, they threw their guns and masks into the duffle bag and took off down the deserted street.

CHAPTER FIVE

Harlem

"WHO IS IT?" asked Ebony as she made her way to answer the door.

"Ike."

Ebony opened the door and stepped aside as Ike walked in.

"What's up, Shorty?"

"Ain't shit," Ebony replied.

"Damn, Girl, your spot is laced. I knew you were living but damn you're doing it way big."

Ebony blushed at Ike's compliment. "It's alright, I guess. Listen, Ike, take a seat. I'll be back in a second." Ebony turned to leave but Ike grabbed her and threw his tongue in her mouth. Despite trying to play cool, Ebony responded to Ike's kiss with hunger. Ike released her and watched as she exited the living room.

Ebony picked up the phone receiver which she had intentionally left off the hook. "Tweet, he's here. I'ma call you back later."

"Eb, don't do nothing I wouldn't do," Tweet laughed.

"Whatever, Ho. Bye." Ebony hung up the phone, checked her appearance in her dresser mirror and returned to the living room. When she reentered the room, Ike was looking at her family photo.

"Who's this in the flick with you?" Ike asked standing in front of a picture in the wall unit.

"That's my sister, Tia."

"Damn, ya'll could pass for twins."

"I don't know if I should take that as an insult or compliment," Ebony twisted her face in a smirk.

"Compliment. So, what's our plans for tonight?" Ike asked.

"We could chill and watch *Juice* on CD. I heard Omar Epps did his thing in that flick," Ebony said praying she didn't sound lame.

"That's peace, and you know I brought that sticky with me."

"Well, roll something up while I get you something to much on. By the way, what are you drinkin?"

"Naw, Shorty. I don't drink."

"What? You don't drink soda or soft drink?" Ebony joked at the fact that he thought she was talking about alcohol. She was underage.

"Oh, my bad, Beloved." Ike said with a sheepish grin on his face. "I'll take whatever you're having."

Ebony sashayed toward the kitchen and Ike could not take his eyes off her ass until she vanished around the corner. The girl was fine and her sister was fine. Ike pulled out Shine smoke papers and sat lazily on the recliner. He was recalling the woman's tight, white shorts that hugged her hips. For a 17-year old, Shorty had it going on. Her body was slammin' immaculate and perfect. Her fine features and long black hair added to her perfection. She was definitely wifely material and hopefully tonight they'd make that official. He wondered if she was a virgin. That would definitely make her more wifey material.

"Here you go, Boo," Ebony handed Ike a Pepsi. She placed a bowl of potato chips and dip on the table and sat beside him. Ike lit up the joint, took a drag then passed it to her.

"Dis smoke is right," Ebony inhaled and then took another drag on the blunt before passing it back to Ike.

"Yeah, Ma', I only purchase the best. Listen, Beloved, are we gonna stay posted to the living room or are you gonna show me where you rest?"

Ebony knew this moment of reckoning was coming. She just hoped she was able to hype herself up enough before they took that walk. Now that the time had come, her heart was jumping out of her chest.

"Listen, Shorty, we don't gotta rush things. There's plenty of time in the near future to indulge." Ike played the gentleman even though he really had no intention of waiting for the future, especially since the moment was here and now. Being locked up for five years didn't make a man patient, especially one who had been reading all sorts of books, including romance novels, so he could learn how to cater to women's needs.

After his release, Ike had returned to Harlem and quickly went back into the game. He'd set up a stash house in the Bronx and in Harlem and went into partnership with Ice, an ex-con he'd met in jail. He was making cake for sure but what he really wanted was a nice, young girl, who wasn't in the game, at his side. Ike was 10 years older than Ebony and ruthless. Jail hadn't taught him a thing but how to be more ruthless.

Ebony grabbed Ike's hand as much in consideration of his needs as her desire, she lead him to the bedroom.

"You da Queen," Ike said taking in the room. Wine colored velvet carpet that matched the drapes complemented the walls that were a light shade of pink. A comforter in a deeper shade of pink covered the queen-sized bed that was against the far wall, and a wall-to wall entertainment system held a high definition, smart hub TV. "Shorty, you really got style with you," Ike said.

"It's alright," Ebony was trying to sound modest.

"You pitch, Ma," Ike smiled at his comment and Ebony's facial expression.

"Naw, I got people who love me. It's just us, me, my brother and sister. Our Moms died when I was 5, our Pops left when I was a toddler so I don't even remember him. Before Mommie died, she told us we should stay together and take care of each other. We could have moved in with our uncle but we wanted to stay together and even though my sister is only 4 years older, she took charge. She and my brother make sure I never need anything."

Ike was touched by Ebony's story. His mother was still alive but he hadn't seen her in years. He didn't want to think about her either. Let's just say shit happens in the Ghetto.

He stepped in front of Ebony and placed his hands on her hips. "Can I ask you a question?" he leaned in and nuzzled her neck running his lips over her ears.

Ebony nodded. A heat was creeping up her toes and spreading through her entire body.

"Can I be the one who loves you now?" Ike pulled Ebony's body to him in a swift move his face close to hers. He lowered his head and allowed his lips to meet hers.

As their hunger enflamed them, their mouths devoured each other in a passionate embrace and deep kisses that made Ebony forget her nervousness and insecurity about her first time. Ike moved his hand further down her body and felt the tight, young ass that threatened to drive him crazy. Unexpectedly, he pulled back from the kiss and looked deeply into Ebony's wanting eyes. "Shorty, I'm really feeling you but I want to know if I can trust you."

Ebony, love intoxicated, gazed into Ike's black masked eyes. Even thought she was unable to pulse his thoughts or glean his morality, she whispered, "Yes," against his lips. "Yes."

Ike held her gaze and looked hard into her eyes for any sign that would betray her words and therefore him, but found none. His desire for her flared. He took Ebony's hand and placed it over his chest. "Do you feel that?"

"I do," Ebony removed her hand and replaced it with her head.

"Yours and my heart now beat as one solid tune. Only you can make it stop."

Ike took her hand and placed it over his crotch. "Do you feel that?" The blood was pulsing as his erection grew larger and stiffer. Ike began moaning as he moved Ebony's hand quickly up and down.

"Yes," Ebony whispered, her heart doing a slow mambo.

"It will bring you pleasure and pain. Do you still want it?" he asked groggily.

Ebony didn't answer. Instead she allowed him to guide her hand until she released the object that would forever steal her innocence.

Ike laid back on the bed and closed his eyes as Ebony massaged him to total erection while he circled his middle finger over her budding womanhood.

Ebony was sucking hard on Ike's neck to fight back the impulse to cry out. As their breaths caught in raspy ecstasy, it seemed as though time had stopped.

Ike unbuttoned Ebony's shorts and slowly slid his hand over her soft public hair. Ebony removed her hand from Ike's pants and wrapped her arms around his neck leaning heavily into his chest and resting her head on his shoulder. Instinctively her legs parted allowing Ike full access to the nexus of her pleasure.

"Damn, Ma', you're so wet."

Ebony bit down on Ike's neck as he gently worked his finger inside her.

"Do it hurt?"

Ebony was too far gone with pleasure and pain to answer. Ike pushed at her hymen, gently at first then harder and faster as she moaned in delight. "Oh God. Oh Ike, your finger feeeels soooo good."

"You kitty itch, Baby?"

"Yeesss," Ebony was writhing with desire.

"Want Daddy to scratch it?"

Ike thrusts his finger deeper into her and felt her womanhood give way. Ebony, enraptured, almost lost her balance, but Ike held her waist so tight she knew she would never fall.

Ike removed his finger slowly, undressed her and laid her on the bed. This time when he entered her, she was beyond rapture. Finally, she was a woman. Ike's woman.

THE BRONX RIVER PARKWAY

"Toya, stay on the Bronx River 'til we get to the 161st Street Bridge," said Rich.

"How's the duffle bag feelin' Kay?"

"Dis shit is heavy as hell."

"That's a good sign," said Tia, reaching under the car seat and bringing out an empty book bag. "Here Jada, open this bag and put the guns in there."

Jada took the bag and did as ordered.

They got off the freeway at the 155th Bridge and drove down 8th Avenue until Toya parked in front of Rucker Park, a popular basketball court located at 155th Street and Frederick Douglass Boulevard. Kaisia passed the duffle bag to Jada and grabbed the book bag containing the guns.

"Listen Kaisia, soon as you drop the bag off, meet us back at the Honeycomb," Tia said.

"Got you."

Toya pulled off once they saw Kaisia enter Building Three of the Polo Grounds.

"Toya, you got your phone on you? I need to make sure the home front is still standing," Tia said.

"Yeah. It's in the glove compartment."

Tia pulled out the phone and dialed her house number. Ebony answered on the second ring.

"Eb, what's up? This is Tia."

"Stupid, I know who you are," Ebony said sarcastically.

"Anyway, Smartass, everything's alright?"

"Yeah, Uncle Robbie just left. He dropped off our check and told me to tell you to call him."

"Where's Tone?"

"He said something about DJ'ing a pool party. I forgot where."

"Alright, I'll be home in like three hours or less, so don't wait up for me." Tia ended the call. There was something different about Ebony's voice tonight.

"How's your sister?" Toya asked.

"Still grown as hell."

"Oh shit, Tia, you just reminded me," said Rich. "Tweet told me Ebony is dealing with some kat that's like 10 years older her. It's probably just a fling, but I thought you should know."

"That's good look out, Rich. I knew her ass was up to something with all the new shit she was bringing into the house. I guess she can't be a baby forever."

"If you want I can find out who kat daddy is," Rich offered.

"Yeah. Do that and get back to me. The main reason I give her whatever she needs is so some knucklehead doesn't tempt her with shit. I know these streets and don't want her out here. I don't want her even near the game."

"I hear you," Rich agreed. "I try to do the same for Tweet as I don't want her out there either but I think I'm losing that battle."

Toya pulled into the parking lot of the Drew Hamilton Houses.

"Jada, pass me the duffle bag so you won't look conspicuous going into the building with that load," Rich said.

The posse walked into the building just like any other day; Rich fishing for the keys.

"Come on, Rich, hurry up and open the door. I gotta pee bad as a mutha fucker," Toya said while doing the pee dance.

Rich opened the door and Toya rushed past him into the dark apartment to get to the bathroom. Rich hit the light switch and stood frozen watching what seemed like a thousand roaches scatter across the kitchen counter.

"Got damn, fuck! Where did all them damn roaches come from?" Jada asked, removing her jacket.

"I don't know but I'm glad them fuckers disappear every time them lights come on," Rich grimaced.

"Toya, hurry up, I gotta go too!" Jada shouted sitting on the couch.

"Tia, you wanna start counting the money now?" Rich asked.

"Naw. That bag doesn't get opened until Kaisia gets here."

"Damn, Bitch, 'bout time," Jada hurried into the bathroom.

"Well, what you want me to do? I said I had to pee. What' in this here fridge?"

"Left over from yesterday."

"Yesterday? We haven't been here for over a week."

"So, what does that tell you?" said Rich.

"I'm not even hungry anymore," Toya said and stretched out on the couch.

"Who got the smoke?" Rich asked pulling two White Owl cigars out of the candy dish.

"It's in the jewelry box," Jada yelled from the bathroom over the sound of the toilet flushing. Everybody burst out laughing.

Jada came out of the bathroom rubbing her belly. "I don't know what I ate but that shit got me f-up."

"Maybe you shouldn't smoke it may upset your stomach more," Tia said stifling a smirk.

"Naw, Tee. The only upset in dis bitch is gonna be me if Toya don't pass the haze."

Toya took another tote on the blunt before passing it to Jada. "Here, Bitch."

"Toya, been meaning to ask. What's up wit' Kato?" Tia asked.

"They came down hard now. Tryna offer him 8 ½ to 16 years, but he alright."

Kato, Toya's man, was the leader of a crew that operated in the 115th Street area. He had been arrested on drug and gun charges and was in jail awaiting trial.

"What the fuck is that, a cop-out?" Tia asked. "Those fuckers put so many years on the table then expect mutha' fuckers to jump on that shit?"

"He might as well go to trial with them big ass numbers," Rich added.

"I told him whatever he decided, I'm riding wit' him. Death before dishonor."

Tia thought back to the days when everything wasn't peaches and cream between Toya and her. In fact, Toya and Tia were enemies in high school. They were forever vying over their looks and bodies. Toya was thicker than Tia but with her 5' 6" stature, zero-inch waist, her silky red hair and stunning green eyes, she was a knock out. Shit, Toya could have been the stunt double for the girl who played in the Players Fight Club, Lisa what's-her-name.

Their fights were legendary. They fought at least once a month. Their disputes became pretty much a ritual that the entire student body of Fashion High would show up for. Everyone would meet in the parking lot on the 1st and the 15th to see if they were hammering on each. The boys showed up mainly to see them rip each other's clothes to shreds. It was on that very battlefield that they formed a great friendship and Toya was now her girl.

Tia closed her eyes. She was tired and drained. She really loved her girl. She didn't even remember how their rivalry started or ended. All she knew was that one day, a girl from another school called her out to fight. She thought Tia was messing with her man, though there was no truth to it. Tia had scoffed at the accusation. She'd never been or would ever be a punk-bitch so she had accepted the challenge. When she got to the parking lot, she realized that word had spread because it was packed to the gills. Tia walked into the crowd with confidence because she was on home turf. But she was also totally caught off guard by the Amazon-looking bitch asking her if she was Tia. Before she could answer, the bitch hit her with a rock-hard fist that floored her and started stomping on her. A single kick to her face took the fight right out Tia. Still, her so-called friends stood by and did nothing. A few girls joined the Amazon and began stomping but all hell broke loose when one of the girls, a shard of glass hanging from her skull, ended up on the concrete next to Tia. When Tia recovered, she saw Toya holding a broken 7-Up bottle. She looked over a Toya. She felt her pain. She was one woman who loved her man Kato. This had to be harder than she was letting on.

A code knock on the door roused Tia. She had drifted off. Rich answered and Kaisia walked in.

"It's about time. What took you so long?" Jada asked.

"I had to take Dakota over to my Mom's crib because her punk-ass father decided at the last minute that he needs to go outta town so he couldn't keep her for the weekend."

"That's fucked up, Kay," Jada said.

"Yeah, I know, but fuck him. He'll get his in the end. Besides, we got important business to attend to, so who want to talk about his punk ass?

It was Rich's turn to catch some shut eye. He stretched out in the spot Tia had just vacated. When he woke up, the women were still at counting money. "It's two in the morning and ya'll still counting?" Rich asked, pulling out a chair and taking a seat at the table. "How much so far?"

"Two Hundred, and still counting," said Tia.

"Wow, that's serious paper for one night and whoever money this is, is gonna be mad as hell," Rich whistled.

The women continued to count paper until Tia finally said, "We're done. Total count is $220,000.00."

"That's what I'm talkin' 'bout!" Rich rubbed his hand together.

"So, Miss Mathematician, how much is that six ways?" Tia asked while looking at Jada for an answer. Jada was really good at Math."

"What you mean six ways? There's only five of us," Jada said.

"Did you forget who set this up?"

"Oh, yeah, my bad, Kaisia, I forgot all about your cousin."

"Don't worry about it, Jay. Just tell us how much we taking home tonight, Wizard."

Jada began calculating the figures in her head.

"Well," Tia chimed in. "By my calculation, we each get a little over $36,000. Rich, as far as the coke, what we looking at?" Tia asked.

Rich removed the coke from the bag and put it on the table. Of the three bags, one was packed in the shape of a brick, the other two were in zip-lock bags. Rich lifted the brick. "This is a key, street value is $28,000 but it's worth a lot more once broken down."

"Kato used to break it down to bundles," said Toya.

"But won't it take too long to get rid of it like that?" Jada asked.

"Yeah, but we can't fuck with this kind of weight in the city. It will draw too much attention to us," Toya said.

"She's right. We need to be as low key as possible with this," Tia agreed.

"Well, I got family in D.C. that would probably take all this off our hands for a cut back," Rich said juggling the kilo in his hands.

"Naw, you know the rules…no family. But we still might be able to use his advice so contact him soon and set something up," Tia said.

"I'm on it."

"Okay, Everybody, ya'll know the procedure. Lay low for a while until we know what the streets are saying," said Tia as Jada handed out everybody's share of the heist.

"So, everybody straight?" Tia asked.

Everyone nodded in unison.

"Okay. Before we part ways, Toya lead us in payer," Tia said.

Everybody grabbed hands and bowed their heads as Toya opened in prayer. "Oh Lord, please forgive is for our sins for we are not perfect. Oh Lord, please continue to keep a steady hand on our shoulders so that we may never stray from our true goals. In the name of Jesus, we pray. Amen."

CHAPTER SIX

DAMN, I HATE WAITING for the train. Something told me to take a cab this morning. Wish I'd learn to listen to my intuition more often. Tia looked around contemplating taking a seat on one of the hard benches that dotted New York subway stations. Maybe not, she thought. Who knows who had made it a bed last night, especially at Penn Station! Tia tapped her feet impatiently. To her great relief, she heard the rumbling of a train, walked to the edge of the platform and looked towards the sound. She was disappointed to see that it was not her ride. Finally, she decided to sit on the bench come what may. She'd barley shifted her butt into a comfortable position when a voice asked, "Is this seat taken?"

What the fuck? Tia thought. Why would anyone ask if a public subway station seat was taken when it was empty? Did the fool think it was a communal restaurant? She looked up to make a sarcastic comment and recognized the familiar face of the stranger who had knocked her book bag out of her hands a week or so ago. "Oh, it's you again?"

"I see you have a good memory," the man took the seat next to Tia.

"Well, it's not every day a girl gets her books knocked out of her hand by a brother in a Giorgio Armani suit."

"And you have a good eye for fashion."

"No. I just know what type of clothes high-class losers wear."

"Ohhh," the man grabbed his chest as though he was having a heart attack, "now that was an insult, but I'm going to chalk that up to a misunderstanding between two people who have not been formally introduced. So, tell me Miss, Late Again, what can I do to make this right?"

Tia liked his style; he wasn't a thin-skinned loser. Mr. Armani-Suit was approximately six feet tall and about 200 pounds of pure muscle. His face was pleasant, his complexion light brown and he had the quick smile of someone who'd never had a bad day. Today, he was just as impressively dressed. "Ha, ha," Tia chuckled sarcastically. "I see you got jokes now."

"Well, every good laugh deserves another. Listen," the man hastily added before smart-mouth responded, "we got off on the wrong foot. Let's start all over," he said, sticking out his hand to Tia.

Tia hesitated and then offered her hand. No point in being stuck-up or disrespectful to someone who was trying so hard. Besides, she thought, the brother was definitely fine as hell. When she finally took his hand, it was soft and warm.

"My name is Sean. Sean Adams."

"Tia Davis."

"Do I see a smile?" He didn't miss the cute dimple that appeared on Tia's right cheek.

Tia's face felt flush. She was blushing a little too hard and turned away.

"No, please don't turn away. Your smile is removing this dark cloud that was over our heads."

"Mr. Adams."

"Please, call me Sean. Adams sounds too formal and inappropriate for friends," he smiled, beguilingly.

"Okay. Sean. Do you come on to every strange woman you meet in the subway?"

"Only the ones with smiles like yours."

Tia hoped he wasn't going to get too corny.

The rumble of the train was welcomed. She couldn't get involved with anyone at the moment.

"So, do you have a phone number?"

"What? I can't hear you," Tia jumped up as the No. 3 train approached. When the door opened, she bolted into the car. "What did you say?" she mouthed.

He put his thumb to his ear and his pinky to his mouth. "Digits?"

"If it's meant to be, destiny will find us again," Tia waved as the door of the train closed. It wasn't even her damn train. Now she'd have to trek a little further to get to her campus. Damn man! But Tia thought as she found a seat, she had to admit, he was one fine brother. The smell of Sean's cologne still lingered in her nostrils. Delish. She should probably have given him her number but she needed no new baggage right at the moment. That brother sure did have his shit together though, just the way she liked her men, tall, well dressed and smelling like success. If he was that successful why was he be taking a train? No chauffer driven Escalade meant no Wall Street titan. Or, maybe wifey had the car. What the hell was she even thinking? This was New York City. Anyway, she didn't see a ring, which in today's day and age really meant nothing.

Tia cut her eyes at the fat ass girl trying to squeeze into the seat beside her. The girl could have cared less and ignored her as she squished back into the seat. Tia went back to ruminating. Maybe Mr. Man was just efficient. As pretty as his ass was he was probably a closet homo trying to play straight? Why the hell was she going there? Whatever the case, Sean Adams damn sure got her attention. She could feel it in her loins and her mind was definitely heading into the gutter. Tia almost missed her stop. That would have been a catastrophe as she had an exam in less than an hour. She was already three credits behind and didn't need to fall behind any further, especially since she wanted out of the game badly. She wished she had enough money to leave school and the game and have a legitimate business. Then she could be more confident talking to a man like Sean Adams.

CHAPTER SEVEN

BROOKLYN DA'S OFFICE

"SO, WHAT IS THE DEFENSE SAYING?"

"It seems they are prepared to go to trial," Sean's co-counsel, John, replied.

"God damn!" Sean banged his fist against the bathroom stall. "That corrupt blood sucker they got as an attorney knows we are not ready for trial. We got nothing! The witness we have isn't even solid enough to turn state's. What evidence do we have except a fucking gun with three different fingerprints on it, none of them belonging to the defendant? The state can't afford to take this to trial."

"We can put an offer on the table dropping the charges to manslaughter in the first. Hopefully, with his record, he'll snitch."

"John, do you hear what you're saying? You want to drop premeditated murder to the lowest count?"

"Well, Sean, what do you suggest based on the turn of events?"

"I don't know." Sean was beyond annoyed. "But I refuse to believe Lady Justice is a whore," he said as he exited the bathroom.

Back in his office, Sean buzzed the intercom for his secretary. "Ms. Jackson, please get Det. Burk on the line."

"Yes, Mr. Adams."

Moments later she buzzed back. "Mr. Adams, I have Det. Burk on line two."

"Thanks. Put him through. Detective, Sean Adams here from the DA's Office."

"How are you doing Mr. Adams?"

"I'm well, thanks. You?"

"Good enough,"

"I'm calling about the Rodney Jenkins murder. You're familiar?'

"Yes. We are well aware of the case. It's big news around here. A local star athlete taken out by a local drug dealer is a big thing."

"I'm sure it is."

"So, what can I assist you with on the case?"

"I need a run down on any and all females Rodney Jenkins was seeing."

"You think this murder is sparked by a crime of passion?" Burk asked.

"That's one theory I'm working to uncover."

"Okay, Mr. Adams. I'll hit the streets and see what I can find out."

"Thanks, Detective."

"No problem. Besides that, the faster you boys downtown finish this case, the quicker I'll be able to get the chief off my back."

Sean hung up the phone and chuckled. Someone is always on someone else's ass.

"What was that all about?" John asked.

"Think about it, John. Rodney Jenkins was a star athlete for the Rice High School basketball team, an honor student who did charity work in the children's ward at Harlem Hospital. Why would a local drug dealer with a criminal record as long as the Brooklyn Bridge want Jenkins dead?

"Jealousy? Envy?" John answered.

"Exactly what I'm thinking. If we can find a girl in this picture then a missing part of the puzzle may fall into place. We may be able to link the defendant to a motive."

"You may have outdone yourself again, Sean. I like it. So, here's a plan. While you work on this idea, I'll stall defense. But Sean, I hope you're right because if this backfires, I'll have no choice but to cut the defendant loose," John said.

"I hope I'm right too."

LONG ISLAND UNIVERSITY

Tia stuffed her books in her bag. She knew she failed that test. She could barely keep her eyes open. All that late-night studying for nothing. Why her damn life gotta be so hard? And she always seemed to make things harder that they had to be. She'd taken a simple-ass assignment and made it into a project. Life was so much simpler when her mother was alive. She'd only have had school to focus on. If her Mother was here now, she'd have kicked her ass into tomorrow for messing up. Tia felt unfamiliar prickle behind her lids. She's been gone six years now but it still felt like yesterday. She still couldn't get used to the fact that gone meant forever. Tia missed her Mother every single day but she was really missed her today for some reason. Though her Mother wasn't an educated woman the woman knew how to get things done, how to look at the big picture and what to focus on. She was always making order out of disorder. Day by day Tia felt her life moving more and more into the direction of chaos. She was having doubts about hitting the spot they did. That much money and brick was sure to bring some heat. They really had to lay low and hoped no one could connect them to the robbery.

"Tia, how's everything going?"

Tia looked up. Her friend Jackie was walking toward her. "Oh, Jackie, what's up? I was just thinking about this test I took."

"Word, you too, huh? I just took my midterm science exam and I'm still stressed the fuck out," said Jackie.

"Get that. So, where you going to lunch?"

"Nowhere special," Jackie answered.

"Walk with me. I'm going over to the Starbucks on Church Street," Tia said, slinging her book bag over her shoulder.

"That's cool. I've been meaning to holla at you anyway."

As they walked along, Tia thought about how she and Jackie met at LIU in their first year. Although they never hung out beside at lunch time, they shared a personal bond of wanting to better themselves and a lot of personal information, though nothing too serious. For a chubby girl, Jackie was real confident and regardless of her size, baby girl was cute as all get up and could dress her ass off.

"So, Tee, what really good with you?"

"Same shit and same dirty-ass toilet. Just tryna graduate on time."

"I know that's right," Jackie replied as she pulled open the door of Starbucks.

The women joined the long-ass line to order their designer drinks to match their designer outfits.

"I'ma take an iced caramel macchiato," Jackie said.

No wonder the heifer's so chunky. "Give me a hot Chai," Tia said.

The women picked up their drinks at the other end of the counter, found a seat and sat facing each other. As they sipped their drinks, Tia could see behind Jackie's usual laughing eyes that something was bothering her.

"So, Jackie you said you wanted to holla at me. What's up?"

"My brother just got locked up in Boston."

"I'm sorry to hear that, Boo."

"It's alright. Ain't his first time. That's part of the game. Besides, that's not what I wanted to talk to you about."

"So, what then?"

"My brother had a couple of spots in P.A. that were doing numbers and basically I want to snatch 'em up before the wolves realize it's open season on a goldmine."

"Jackie," Tia sipped her drink and watched the girl over the rim of her cup. "I feel you, but what does any of this have to do with me?" Tia watched her body language to better understand her intent.

"Tia, let me get straight to the point 'cause you know I ain't no bull shitter. When we first met, we clicked and not too many people are able to win me over on the first day...hell, not even the first month. I know I can trust you and I know there is more to you that all this Gucci and Prada shit. I sense the hustler in you. Stop me if I'm wrong, but if I'm not, I want you to be my partner in this move."

Tia thought of the brick they were sitting on that they couldn't move in Harlem. She sized up the girl once again and said, "Jackie, what you're asking me to do is to make a serious move with you and, not for nothing, we're playin' with a serious situation and serious situations require trust. Trust extends deeper in this filed for the sole purpose that not too many people can be trusted on that level. You know the consequences of broken trust?"

"Tee, I know that. What I asking you is real and believe me, I wouldn't be risking my shit if I felt that you were the wrong person to come at. Feel me on this."

"Jackie," Tia leveled her eye to eye. "I'm gonna be honest with you and I want you to grasp what it is I'm saying to you. Currently, I'm dealing with a lot on my plate and I rarely have time for games. But I want you to understand something. If I chose to entertain the thought of your proposal and enter into this move with you, my involvement goes no further than this table on your part and I decide when and where we move. Is that a problem?" Tia knew there could only be one boss or the shit was over before it started.

"Alright with me," Jackie said noting that Tia had taken on a no-nonsense demeanor she had never seen. She hadn't just found a partner, she found the boss lady!

"I'ma gonna sit on the thought for a few days. "I'll get back to you before the week is out."

"No problem, Tee. I expected you to give it some thought but now that that's over and cleared up, can we eat for real? My fat ass is hungry."

The women broke into laughter as Jackie got up to get a sandwich and another macchiato. The only difference between them, Tia thought, was the fact that Jackie was from Brooklyn. At that moment, they clicked even more than they had before.

On the way home, Tia's thoughts shifted from the good-looking man that morning to serendipity. It's so damn funny how life works. Opportunity just drops in your lap when you least expect it. A new thought invaded. The posse won't like it. How would she bring Jackie into the circle? Her Ride or Die family had been proven over and over; their loyalty demonstrated many times. It was going against the rules and it was gonna be tough. Maybe if she tested her in front of them and she passed they would welcome her. But if she failed, what then? Home-girl would know too much and they lived and died by the motto of the Japanese Samurai. "May disloyalty meet death a thousand times and one, and may a pure heart never know my sword." She didn't know about pure, maybe they should substitute true of heart. Still it was a good option to move the shit they were sitting on.

"Excuse me, Miss. May I sit here?" An older lady asked.

"Oh, pardon me," Tia retrieved her book bag that was resting beside her and scooted over a bit. "Yes. Ma'am."

CHAPTER EIGHT

"MA! I'M TAKING DAKOTA SHOPPING with me. I'll be back in a couple of hours," Kaisia shouted from the hallway. Why her mother was always locked up in that room was a mystery. "Dakota, get your coat and come on."

"Okay, Mommyyyy," a delighted Dakota squealed, running to get her coat.

Her daughter was too much, Kaisia smiled, watching the imp scamper away. Hearing her daughter call her Mommy made Kaisia realize just how much she loved her little girl and what lengths she'd go to make sure she was happy. The game was not the way to keep her clothed and fed but for now it allowed her to keep Dakota close to her and provide the love that her father did not or refused to provide. She wanted Dakota to always feel loved and cared for.

Kaisia too was an only child but her parents were too self-absorbed to love her past their basic responsibilities. She always felt they did what they had to and not a single thing extra keeping her at arm's length and emotionally starved. Everybody said she resembled her father and she did, but that was a far as it went. She'd never felt his love. In fact, she felt so distant from her parents that when she was 9, she'd asked her mother if they had adopted her.

Her mother's face had crumpled like she had been punched in her gut. "No, she'd said, "you're our baby." But no matter what Kaisia did, she never felt love or caring, not even from her mother. Her father, a janitor at one of the apartment buildings in the West 90s, would be gone from early morning till late night. As she got older, Kaisia suspected – though her mother denied it - that her father was doing something on the side. Left to her own devises by the time Kaisia was fifteen she was no stranger to the streets and was doing her own thing. It was in the streets that she met Ty, and with the little attention he gave her she realized how hungry she was for love. She was now truly running the streets as Ty introduced her to the game.

Her father died two years later, the very same week she'd found out that she was pregnant with Dakota. At her father's funeral she sat in the back of the church with the strangers who seem to find their way to any funeral. She'd been a Stanger to her parents her whole life so it made no difference, neither had her mother come looking for her. Kaisia never told her mother that she was creating her own family. Now six years later, with that tired ass Ty flaking out, she was living with a mother who never left her room.

Dakota was running back toward her, wearing a light, spring coat. "You're ready baby?" Kaisia kneeled to zip up her coat. Dakota nodded. She was the spitting image of Kaisia, right down to the light brown eyes, a family trademark inherited from their Irish descendants.

"Mommy, where we goin'?"

"We're going to get you and me some nice shoes and summer clothes"

"Ha-raaaaay!" Dakota bounced up and down.

"Be still so I can zip up this coat," Kaisia laughed. Damn, the girl was as excited about clothes as she was even now. They were just too much alike.

Kaisia's cell rang.

"Hello Boss Lady."

"Kay, what's up?" Tia asked.

"Nothin'. What's going on?"

"Auntie Tee! Auntie Tee!" Dakota was shouting trying to get the phone from her mother. Kiasia's and Tia's friendship went back to first grade and when Kaisia found out she was pregnant, she told Tia she would be her child's godmother.

"I know that's not my baby I hear," Tia said.

"Yup. She up here acting a fool trying to get this phone out of my hand."

"Put my ragamuffin on the phone."

"Hi, Auntie Tee."

"How is my little princess?"

"Good. Guess what?"

"What?"

"My mommy takin' me to get some shoes and some summer clothes, and some ice cream," she added.

"For real?" Tia sung into the phone.

"Yup."

"Okay, have fun Miss Thang. Now put your mommy back on the phone."

"Okay. I love you, Auntie.

"I love you more," Tia said, a smile dotting her face. She did indeed love that little girl.

"Mommy, Auntie wants to speak to you."

Kaisia took the phone. "What'd I tell you? Miss Thang is growing up."

"And damn Kay, the girl loves shopping like her mama."

"Who you telling?"

"So, where ya'll heading?"

"We're going to Old Navy on 34th Street.

"I'm in the area now anyway so I'll meet ya'll down there."

"Alright."

"I'll watch out for you. Call me when you close and I'll come on over. Stand by the front door."

"Okay."

"See ya'll." Tia said and hung up.

"Huh," Kaisia thought, Miss Thing had something on her mind.

Rich stood at his bedroom door and watched as his sister rifled through his closet. When the hell did she get so grown? The outfit she was wearing was too tight and too revealing. Rich knew that Tweet was heading down the dangerous path of many of the girls in the 'hood but he didn't know how to stop her. She was getting older and with him constantly on the move, he couldn't always keep an eye on her and he wasn't exactly a good role model. Moving from Queens to Harlem didn't make life any better. Their life had always been shitty even when they lived with their mother and grandmother in the Fort Projects in Queens.

Their grandmother pretty much raised them after their father was killed in a hit and run when Tweet was a toddler and Rich was about 6. Though their mom worked two and three jobs taking care of old people, money was always tight even with their grandmother pitching in and taking care of them while their mother worked. Their grandmother was a domineering woman, who raised eight children of her own and who was the thread that held the family together. When she passed, it was a little too much for their mother to bear and her occasional Friday night, end-of-week drinking turned into every day. Rich and Tweet would come home from school and find her passed out on the couch. Things got from bad to worse when she replaced the bottle with drugs and strange men started coming regularly to their home.

"Watchya doing going through my things? " Rich grabbed the sweater from Tweets hand. The damn girl was stepping over the line searching through his possessions.

"Rich, Stop playin'. Let me hold that hot pink D&G sweater." Tweet said as she's going through her brother's wardrobe. Why can't I wear it? It goes perfect with my hot pink Gores. Pleeeeasse, Rich!"

"Stop beggin', Bitch! You got a whole closet full of shit you ain't wear yet. Plus, I just picked you up four Polo sweaters and two Coogies. What are you doin', trickin'?"

"Don't play yourself, Chicken. Besides it's too hot to wear that shit you bought and none of 'em have pink in them," Tweet said as she turned to face Rich.

"Don't give me that corny-ass look. You lost that touch years ago, Sister."

Forget it then," Tweet threw the pink sweater on the bed. "I'll just wear something else."

Rich laughed at his spoiled-ass sister. No wonder she and Eb were such good friends, he thought. "Okay, listen up. I'll give you the sweater but you gotta do me a favor. I need you to find out everything you possibly can about this kat, Ike, that Ebony is messin' wid, as well as who his people are."

Tweet stared at her brother, a confused look on her face. "Why you wanna know all that?"

"None of your business."

"Well, if it ain't none of my business, why should I care?"

Rich held up the sweater. "Do we have a deal or not?"

Tweet grabbed at the sweater. "Yeah. Now can I have the sweater?"

"Come get it, Thirsty," Rich held the sweater over his head. He knew his sister's weakness: boys, clothes and money. He wondered what he could have done differently to spare her from the streets. He was barely coping himself. His childhood had not left him unscarred. Rich remember how they had been forced to hide out in their room, sometimes for days when their mother and company were consorting. Rich's efforts to protect his sister from the unsavory men made them close. While he tried had to protect his sister, he couldn't always stop the creepy men who would find their way into the room to talk to him. Rich would always pretend to be sleeping and sometimes he actually fell

asleep pretending. On one of those nights however, his sleep game didn't work and he was left with a secret that only two people other than himself knew, the man in his bedroom and his confidant, Tia.

It was rigt after that that Rich struck out on his own. He was eighteen and his who he took with him was thirteen years old. They bummed around for a while...staying at a few friends here and there until they eventually ended up in a shelter. A year after leaving Queens, they were approved for public housing and moved into the two-bedroom apartment in the St. Nicholas Housing Projects on 127th Street in Harlem. Rich claimed Tweet as his daughter and lied about his age. He enrolled Tweet in one of the local junior high schools and himself into high school, but he needed money to maintain their life and school wasn't helping to pay the bills so he dropped out and went back to what he knew...the streets.

Rich always had a talent for blending in and stealing, so it was a trade he took up when his mother became a whore addict. It was in Harlem that he met Jada, his female counterpart and extended his talent to boosting, short cons, picking pockets and credit card scams. Although it wasn't an honest living, it paid the bills and provided a decent life for him and his sister. But it was when through Jada he met Tia, that he learned the art of the heist.

CHAPTER NINE

"DAMN, IKE, THAT ALBUM SOUNDS crazy with those woofers," Iceman said.

"You know I only cop the best, Daddy," Ike said turning right on 7th Avenue.

"So, what's up with the Ohio move?"

"Iceman, we got product, but who we got to move that much weight?"

"Peer game, Playa. I got a couple mules I use in V.A., but it gonna cost," Ice said.

"Cost what?"

"Depending on the amount and means of transportation," Ice replied.

"Fuck it, holla at them and see what's good. Hopefully, we'll be OT by Thursday."

"A'wright. Let me get on that." Iceman retrieved his cellular and began dialing as Ike crossed 110th Street.

Ike's phone rang. "Whasup Playa? What did you just say? " Ike hollered into the phone, the vein in his neck popping out. "WHAT THE FUCK YOU MEAN YA'LL GOT ROBBED?" His eyes were now bulging out of his head. Iceman clicked off his phone and tuned into Ike's convo.

"WHO ANSWERED THE FUCKIN' DOOR?" Ike was screaming.

"I,I,I,I thought it was the super. We'd called him to fix the leak in the bathroom," the voice on the other end of the line belonged to Mike.

"I'm on my way over there. Don't fuckin' open the door unless I give you the signal."

Ike turned to Iceman. "The joint got hit. Who the fuck would be brave enough to hit my joint?"

"A dead man walking." Ike stashed his phone. If the stash was gone there was no need to complete his call.

Thirty minutes later Ike and Iceman were seated in the apartment in the Bronx. Ike got up from his seat clutching a Browning 9-millimeter and stepped to Mike. "Come again? Repeat exactly why you opened the door."

"I thought it was theeeee..." Mike stuttered.

Ike smacked Mike to the floor before he was able to finish his sentence and shoved the barrel of the pistol in his mouth. "Nigga, I SHOULD LEAK THE BACK OF YOUR FUCKIN' SKULL!"

"Mummm...I..." Mike was mumbling, tears staining his face.

"Nigga, I'd sweat if you wasn't my first cousin, I would put your punk-ass under the dirt and pay for the funeral. GET THE FUCK UP, PUSSY!"

Ike stepped over Mike on the floor as he tucked his gun into his waistband and began to scan the faces in the room looking for any sign of betrayal. "What's your excuse Dav-o, and how the hell did they get inside the safe?" Ike asked.

"They were gonna kill us dawg...them broads were crazzy!" Dav-o immediately realized he'd slipped up and let the cat out of the bad and the entire room fell mute.

"Broads? As in bitches with pussies?" Ike asked in total disbelief that his spot was robbed by chicks.

"I think one of them was a dude in drag," Mike was desperate to save a little face.

"So ya'll tellin' me that ya'll...fuck that. I was robbed by a couple of bitches and a fuckin' lizard? Two hundred plus grand of my money and two birds in the hands of some hos?"

"Ike, it was…."

BLOCK! BLOCK! BLOCK!

The whole room froze as Dav-o's corpse slid down the wall leaving spatters of blood and flesh behind. Ike stood motionless with a smoking gun at his side. Iceman lit a cigarette.

Brooklyn DA's Office

Mr. Adams, you have Det. Burke on the line."

"Put him through, Rebecca, and hold all my calls except those to do with this case."

"Yes, Mr. Adams."

"Hello Det. Burk. What good news do you have for me?"

"Well Mr. Adams, we don't have anything solid. Just he-say-she-say from the streets.

"Anything's better than zero," Sean said.

"Okay, then. Our informant on the East Side says our boy was creepin' through Washington Heights to see a Maria Gonzales. We ran her name through the system and check this: she is 21 years old with two priors, assault and a weapons charge. I'll fax you all the information on her."

"Thanks, Burk."

"Don't thank me yet because the next lead isn't so great. Our sources on the West Side said the Jenkins boy was definitely spending time with some redbone who hangs out downtown. Other than that, we have no name or presumptive address."

"That's alright Detective. You were very helpful. I hope one day I can repay the favor."

"No problem. Anything for Lady Justice."

Unlike many, Sean believed that: Anything for Lady Justice. He hung up the phone and thought about what his next move concerning the Rodney Jenkins murder case should be. He called Rebecca.

"Yes, Mr. Adams."

"Get Morris in Investigation on the line right away."

34TH STREET

The only place worse that 34th street madness was 42nd street. Tia wished they didn't have to make the trek downtown to get their stuff but nothing was happening up in Harlem most of the time. Tia hoisted Dakota up on her hip.

"You want me to carry her 'cause I know how heavy she can be," Kaisia offered.

"Don't be silly. How you gonna do that with all them bags ya carrying that's probably heavier than her no how. Let's just catch a cab Kay, so we can get outta this zoo."

"Let me look for a Gypsy cab."

While the women waited, Tia informed Kaisia that they needed to start moving the package and that she might have a sure way of doing so.

"Yeah?"

Tia didn't answer right away. Instead she was staring at a Dakota wondering why life couldn't be as peaceful and innocent as a sleeping baby. "Kiasia," she finally said. "You know I love you like a sister and would never do anything to put us in harm's way, right?"

"I love you too," Kiasia looked at Tia with concern in her eyes. "But where is all this coming from?"

"Sometimes I just feel like I'm leading ya'll in the wrong direction. The idea of losing anyone of you'll to this bullshit is..."

Kaisia didn't let Tia finish. "Stop, Girl. Don't say all that shit." Doubt was a mutha and they couldn't afford all that. "We came in this together. Nobody forced us. Ain't like we all weren't doing shit, but circumstances shifted for us. We all in the same spot, Tee. We all have nobody but ourselves to look out for us and it's better to act as one body and one mind. Every day I get on my knees thanking the Lord for blessin' me with loyal and dedicated friends. If it wasn't for ya'll I probably would of fell apart when Ty left me with all the weight of raising Dakota. Just tell me what's on your mind, Girl."

"Don't you every just want to get the hell outta New York and start over? "

"Everyday, but where we gonna go? If one goes all have to. I know Toya aint leaving her man."

Kaisia noticed a cab and put out her hand. When they got in the car, Tia looked at Kaisia and then at Dakota who was not fully awake and smiling at Tia. Tia smiled back then turned to look out the window of the cab into a world of uncertainty. Maybe not much longer now, she thought.

HARLEM

Ike dropped Iceman back at his ride and then called Crime. "Ayo Crime, I need you to meet me in the vacant lot on 116th in 15 minutes," Ike was saying into his phone.

"I'll be there, Dawg."

As Ike drove through Harlem to meet Crime he again wondered who would be bold enough and stupid enough to hit one of his spots. And that wasn't even the insulting part…whoever it was had the nerve to send in a couple of bitches to do a man's job. That fuckin' hurt. Whoever it was was tryna to make a point but he was one dead mutha. His team was gonna eat their asses up…whoever they were. Ike pulled up into the lot next to the cherry red BMW X5 and motioned for Crime to get into his Rover. Crime was what the average street hustler would consider a square. His constant attire was a solid red dickey button-up, beige Dockers and some red and white Air Force Ones. At 5' 8" with his tan complexion and swagger, the average woman could consider him attractive. His only flaw was the five-inch cut scar that ran from his left eye to the back of his ear, a scar he acquired as an adolescent in the infamous 4-Building on Rikers Island

"What's the word?" Crime asked sliding in beside Ike.

"A couple nights ago, one of my main spots was hit. I'm thinking it's them niggaz from Webster Avenue, but before I jump the gun and spill blood I wanna be certain it's them. If

I'm wrong I wanna make sure the right person or persons pay for this with their lives."

"Dawg, you ain't gotta say no more but dig...I'ma holla at whoever was in the spot when the shit went down because it could of been an inside job, FEEL ME?"

"Yeah. But I don't think then bitch-ass niggaz are built to pull off some shit like that and be bold enough to stick around afterwards."

"I hear you on that but temptation is a mutha fucker and we all got dicks," replied Crime. "Who was there?'

"My dizzy cousin, Mike and Fat Steve and oh yeah, Dav-o but he no longer wid us," Ike made a cross on his chest as a wide grin betrayed his sincerity.

"Can't cry over spilled milk. Anyway, what did they tell you?"

"They said they think it was bitches who robbed them."

"What? What? They let some punk-ass niggaz get your stash?"

Ike realized Crime did not understand him when he said bitches robbed him. He could hardly believe the mutha himself. "Naw, man...not dudes, actual females."

"Bitcheeeess!" shouted Crime.

"Yeah Nigga," Ike was angry all over again. "I need you to hit the blocks, clubs, whatever and I don't care if you have to lay a couple of niggaz down, just get me to **whoever pulled** this shit off. Here's $20,000 now. $20,000 more when it's done." Ike handed Crime an envelope.

Crime stuffed the envelope in his pocket. No need to count it, he thought. If it was Ike, it was on point.

CHAPTER TEN

HARLEM

TIA OPENED THE APARTMENT door to find all the
lights off and complete silence. She figured Tone went to the
studio but where was Ebony? She was usually home already
watching 106 and Park. She decided she wasn't gonna sweat it
'cause she could do with some peace and quiet.

Tia went to the bathroom and turned on the shower. She
checked the water temperature and then went to the bedroom
while the water cleared the junk out of the pipes. Maybe she
should take a bath, she thought as she headed back to the
bathroom...nah...she was too tired. A quick shower and she
was calling it a day. Nah, she'd take a bath. She plugged up the
tub and walked back to her bedroom.

Seeing her unmade bed was a signal to Tia that her mind
was not at rest. It reminded her that her messy and
complicated life was causing chaos in the place she needed it
most. She had so much on her plate - staying vigilant after the
Bronx heist and now, after her conversation with Jackie, she
was sweating about how to bring her into the crew, even for a
limited time. Then there was Ebony and this man she was
messing with. With her life was so messy and complicated, Tia
needed her surroundings to be impeccable. She quickly made
the bed, picked up clothes off the floor and put them in the
laundry hamper. She took one look around the room and

sighed. This is one thing she could control, she thought. Tia walked over to her nightstand and punched up the answering machine. No messages. Music to her ears.

"Oh shit!" Tia said loudly running into the bathroom just in time to save a major accident. She turned the tap off and drained the tub a bit. The last thing she wanted were the neighbors downstairs getting in her face. She squeezed a generous amount of Jasmine bubble bath into the water, removed her clothes and put one leg in to test the temperature then lowered her body into the tub.

Man, if this is what heaven feels like, death might not be so bad, she thought. But was she going to heaven or to hell? Tia shrugged off the morbid thought, leaned back against the tub and switched her thoughts to Mr. Armani Subway man. When was the last time she had some nookie? Shit, that was over six months ago and it wasn't worth remembering. Playa had a head on his shoulders but his second head failed him miserably. Thank God for other muscles. Now Mr. Armani Man, Tia thought, closing her eyes and letting her hand find her womanhood, do some work. Tia began stroking herself and her mound responded immediately. "Mmmmmm, damn," She groaned as she circled, slipping a finger inside her and biting her lips to contain the rising passion. Her body jerked and she spread her legs further apart to gain full access to her yearning. She moved her fingers rapidly in and out circling her clit until her body began to spasm. "Ahhhh...ummmmmm!" she threw a leg over the rim of the tub. She was fully exposed now and as she sunk her finger deeper into her body, hungrily trying to fulfill her desire, the tub water splashed over the rim. She masturbated herself to a breath-taking climax. Tia stared at the ceiling, metering her breathing as the climax subsided, but her inner soul still very much yearned for a real man. A man like Sean Adams.

Tia washed her body, stepped out of the tub and dried herself with a fluffy towel. As she was walking into her room the phone rang.

Brooklyn DA's Office

Sean sat at his desk nursing the two-hour old cup of coffee. He should have been home but instead he was doing overtime on a Friday night staring at a computer screen with the picture of a dead 17-year-old boy on it. It was a shame how the youth were being wiped out, dropping like flies. Many of them had so much talent they wouldn't ever live long enough to find out they had and even if they did know not long enough to fully develop it. Yes, indeed, the ghetto was full of talented people and society was only too happy to blame them for their own destruction.

The cards were stacked so high against them to begin with and the American society was forever putting the guns to their heads and daring them to pull the trigger. Many argued, of course, that it was the responsibility of the adults in their lives to steer them in the right direction. To remove the proverbial bullets from the guns before they pulled the trigger so to speak but too often, those very adults too were victims of their own environment and societies dumping ground the ghetto. "Ah shit!" Sean said aloud. This was a never ending circus.

Sean looked again at the photo of Rodney Jenkins and thought of himself at that age. If it wasn't for his father and the church community right there in Harlem, he could have ended up like Rodney. But people like his father were hard to find in lives crippled by hopelessness and frustration. Yet, it was people like Rodney that gave him a reason to put up a good fight. The average ADA would have simply gotten rid of cases like this with a cop-out, especially if it wasn't a high-profile case with political benefits. But Sean Adams was not the average ADA and though this was indeed a high-profile case, Sean had no aspirations to be in the political spotlight. He wanted to solve this case for the family of Rodney Jenkins to find peace and justice. Sean was one of the few truly talented and committed attorneys who hoped that one day power would truly rest in the hands of Lady Justice and not in the hands of political manipulations and rewards. He wanted to be one of those who furthered that cause.

Sean rocked back in his chair and thought about his father. He wished he was alive to see the man he'd become and to offer some advice. His father was always giving advice. "Boy," he'd often say, "a black man's strongest asset is his voice. Without it, he is a nigger. With it, he is a carrier of justice." His father indeed, used his voice as a preacher to advocate for education as the way out for many black kids. He, the preacher's son had chosen to advocate for his people thorough the law. He used his voice as an attorney to battle the corruption that was intended to keep his people slave to a system that did not serve them at all. But even after three years in the DA's office, Sean was still floored by the continuous and systematic efforts to keep his people hopeless and defeated. He could not ignore the cries for justice for a mother in agony who'd lost her child to the evil and wickedness of circumstance. Beyond volunteering twice a month to offer legal advice at the outreach office at his father's old church, Sean wondered whether he could ever do enough. He wiped moisture from his lashes and looked at his watch. It was 10:00 p.m. and still he hadn't heard from the investigator. He'd probably gotten sidetracked, he speculated. He thought about calling it a night then decided to wait another hour.

Sean swiveled his chair to look out the picture window of his office. The Manhattan lights burned bright. He thought of that goddess of a woman who called herself Tia Davis and wondered if she was listed. He grabbed the phone and dialed information.

Harlem

Tia grabbed the phone. "Hello."

"Yes, may I speak with Ms. Tia Davis?"

"This is she," Tia replied, curious about who was calling.

"Oh, hello," Sean said, thankful it wasn't another old lady who picked up this time. There were a few Tia Davises listed in Harlem. "Is this the Tia Davis that I bumped into in the subway?"

"That depends. Are you a stalker or a crazy lunatic?" Tia asked. How incredible that the thought of this man had made her just pleasure herself and here he was calling. Was destiny at work?

"Neither," Sean said, leaning back in his chair, glad he'd hit the jackpot. "But I'm a good role-player if you're into that kind of stuff."

Tia laughed. "How did you get my number?"

"You are listed along with four other Tia Davises. They were all too old, none sounded like you."

"So, Mr. Adams now you found me what?"

"I told you my friends call me Sean."

"Okay, Sean. What can I do for you?"

"No, sweetie. I was wondering what it is I can I do for you?"

Spank me, Tia thought but said instead, "What are you offering and why are you offering your services to me?"

"For one, I think it's appropriate to extend kindness to those who capture my interest and two, to me, you are very interesting."

"You don't even know me, so your basic perception of me is an assumption. A flattering one but an assumption nonetheless," Tia was enjoying the catch-me-if-you-can game.

"Tia, I usually don't chase anyone who doesn't want to be caught. But let me be honest, I find you original and I hope we could be great friends. Please don't get me wrong here, I mean nothing more than friendship, if that's where you are."

Tia pressed her lips together. She had to give it to him. The brother had courage in addition to being well put together. "Sean," Tia said, "I'm not tryin' to be rude, but friendship on any level comes with responsibilities and I hardly know you enough to accept your friendship."

"So, allow me the opportunity to introduce myself on a more personal level by taking you to dinner. And, before you say no, I assure you that I am a true gentleman."

"I'm not worried about that. I keep my blade on at all times," Tia laughed. Little did he know how true that was! She should give the brother some slack.

"I'd love to take you out tomorrow, if you're not busy," Sean said.

"I'm going to take you up on your offer, Mr. Persistent, but I get to choose the place and time…is that going to be a problem?"

"Not for me. I love a woman who takes charge."

"I'm glad to hear that so let's plan to meet at Justin's at 9:00 p.m., sharp, okay. I hate late so if you're a minute late I'll be dining alone," Tia warned.

"Fine…But I'm happy to come and pick you up so we can arrive together," Sean offered.

"No. That alright. Besides there is nowhere to park and the "A" train is on my block," Tia joked. The "A" train goes anywhere right?"

"Ha, I see we have managed to find your funny bone," Sean laughed at her reference to the Duke Ellington song, Take the A Train. It had been a long time since he'd laughed.

"Just had to get you back. Anyway, do you need direction to the restaurant?"

"Not at all. I'm familiar," Sean said. Justin's was on 21st just a few blocks from his flat.

"Well then, I guess I'll see you tomorrow."

"For sure. Goodnight and I'm looking forward.

"Have a nice night, Sean. Goodnight." Tia hung up the phone and felt her face stretch into a smile. The smile factor. Always dangerous. She got between the covers. Maybe this was the beginning of a new life.

The sound of the front door being unlocked jolted Tia out of her sleep. She looked at the nightstand to see the clock. It was 5:30 am. What the fuck? Tia climbed out of bed, grabbed her bathrobe and walked quickly towards the darkened living room.

Ebony was trying her best to open the door quietly but the locks were like burglar alarms the way they sounded when unlocked. Ebony was easing the door behind her so it didn't slam just as Tia flicked the lights on. Startled, she let the door go and it slammed shut.

"Ebony…where have you been?" Tia asked. "It's almost six in the morning and you are just coming in? You still have your damn book bag on?"

"I stayed over at a friend's house," Ebony said, hoping the lie would send Tia away.

"You know the rules, Ebony. You're supposed to check in first before you venture off, but that's not the point. Why are you getting in this late?"

"Nobody was here," Ebony was defiant. "I called like three times and left a message on the phone."

"Don't even try that," Tia said. "I checked the messages on the damn phone. Anyway, you still have to be in this house before 2:00 a.m. on non-school nights."

"Why ya'll treat me like a fuckin' child? I'm not twelve no more. Those days are long gone and ya'll still can't seem to comprehend that I'm no longer in diapers," Ebony said tears rolling down her cheeks. She loved her sister and was more upset that she'd upset her because she had sacrificed everything to keep them together and given her whatever she wanted. But she wanted Tia to treat her like the woman she had become though she knew that if Tia knew she was no longer a virgin, she'd probably stroke out.

"Who treats you like a child, Ebony? I barely say anything to you. I have always given you space and respected your personal life. Now if you're talkin' 'bout Tone then that's something ya'll have to work out…but as long as you walk this earth you are my responsibility and my worry." Tia flopped down on the couch. She was feeling guilty that with school and her 'business' she didn't have much time to spend with Ebony.

"That's what I mean, Tee. You can't be responsible for me my entire life. I am able to take care of myself now."

"If that were so, we wouldn't be having this conversation and you wouldn't be walking in this house at 5:30 a.m. like some got damn lost child." Tia got up and flicked off the lights and left Ebony standing in the living room. She hoped she would reflect on the sacrifices she and Tone had made for her.

METROPOLITAN DETENTION CENTER, BROOKLYN

The Metropolitian Detention center in Park Slope, Brooklyn could be mistaken for a modern office building but is housed some of the most dangerious criminals, both male and female. Kato Pascal had copped some hard time in the pen casue his partner betrayed him and even now it irked him to no end how the shit went down. Kato flapped out the grey one-piece jumper.

"Yo, Kato, I'll have my girl give your girl a hundred and fifty after the V.I. (visit)." An inmate was saying.

"Naw, Dawg," Kato protested as he slipped on the one-piece grey suit assigned to all inmates receiving visitors. "I don't involve her in this shit. Just bring the stash back and tonight meet me at medication."

The prisoner agreed to Kato's terms then proceeded to the Bubble. The Bubble was the glass enclosed area where an officer could observe an inmate getting a bucket to put his personal belongings before going up to the visitors' floor.

A Corrections Officer stepped into the prisoners' waiting area and began shouting out the names of the inmates who could proceed to the visiting floor. When Kato heard his name, he stepped over to the officer to get checked off before proceeding through the gates of the visitor holding area.

Toya greeted Kato with a warm smile. She missed him. Toya and Kato had been together since they were fourteen years old. They pretty much knew each other their entire lives as they grew up on the same block, attended the same school and hung out at all the same spots. They were practically inseparable. Their street family considered them soul mates and nicknamed them "Bonny and Clyde." The name was appropriate as those who crossed them would find out that they were extremely dangerous.

But it wasn't until five years into their relationship that people came to understand how deep and deadly Toya's love for Kato really was. It was the summer of 1995. For several days straight the temperature hit or surpassed 90 degrees. In the concrete jungle the boys in the hood were playing street ball. A basketball fanatic, especially of street ball, an aggressive-style of basketball played in any open space, Toya was sitting in her favorite seat in Rucker Park. She was rooting for the 40 Wolves, her brother's team at the Celebrity Basketball Competition. The Wolves were playing the previous year's champions, The Bronx Bombers. Anticipation for the game was at an all-time high as the Wolves had lost the tournament by three points to the Bombers and was hungry for a win. There must have been over 5,000 people in the park on that hot, sticky day. Local news vans took over the sidewalk outside the park including reporters from ESPN and other local television stations. The black urban magazines and newspapers were on hand as were about 30 police officers.

Toya was decked out in a solid, white D&G crotch shorts, white DKNY wife beaters, DKNY visors, and her dragon tail braid was cascading down her back. On her tiny size five feet, she wore a pair of crispy white Air Force Ones. Toya was definitely representing Harlem's ghetto fabulous stars. Eyes ogled her but she was far more interested in her man, Kato who stood at the entrance of the park with a couple of local ballers. Kato was rocking an oversized New York Knicks jersey, white jeans shorts and Gucci visor, perfect for the sweltering day. In Toya's eyes, Kato was the shit of the night. Not only was he dapper than most, he was fine as hell with style left over. His lean frame had zero body fat.

Toya turned at the tap on her shoulders. It was Rich all dressed up wearing a pleated short skirt, tank top and laced boots. Those who didn't know him as Rich would be convinced he was a she.

"What's good, Girl?"

"Oh, shit, Mo," Toya jumped using the name Tia called him when he was in drag, "you frightened me! Nothing much, just checking out my man over there," Toya licked her lips. "That man keeps me horny." She was already getting wet, she added, just thinking about how she wanted to make love with him right then and there. "What's up with you?"

"Ain't shit, just out here to be out and I don't mean out the house, but don't you call me Mo no more," he winked and a wicked grin spread across his face.

"I hear that shit," said Toya turning back to the action.

The court announcer came on the microphone. "Playas and Playettes! We have a treat for ya'll today! We were just informed that a new player has been added to the Bronx Bombers roster. Ya'll may know him from the Philadelphia 76er'ssssss!"

The crowd erupted into cheers as the announcer introduced A.I. As the audience clapped, Toya booed but her disappointment was drowned out by the dick riders and groupies. When the Park finally settled down and the announcer began introducing the teams and players, Toya looked toward the park entrance to see if Kato had entered, but to her disappointment, he wasn't there. She looked in all directions hoping to spot him before the game started. She spotted his burgundy Navigator where he had parked by the newsstand near the Polo Grounds Projects but Kato wasn't there. He can't be far, Toya thought because he'd never leave without it. Toya's head snapped back to the action when the announcer called her brother's name. She jumped up and began clapping as if her brother was a professional and not a local street baller. To her, he was the shit.

The game started with one of the players from 40 Wolves slamming a half-court alley-oop. By half time, the Wolves were behind eight points. But Toya was distracted because she still hadn't spotted Kato. She felt butterflies in her stomach. It wasn't like Kato to just vanish, especially knowing that she was there.

As Toya was trying to shake off the feeling of doom and gloom, she spotted Rich racing through the crowd with an anguished look on his face. She didn't even realize he'd left.

Toya knew immediately that something had happened and it had to do with Kato. She sprinted towards Rich. "What? What's going on?"

Without saying a word, Rich grabbed Toya's arm and rushed her out of the park. They went west towards Bradhurst Avenue?. Toya saw a small crowd of people, an ambulance, several uniformed officers and detectives at the scene and her heart sunk to her feet. She tore off toward the scene. As she got closer, Toya saw the red police do not enter tape and a sheet thrown over a body on the ground.

"Please, God," Toya cried out in anguish. "Don't let it be him."

A uniformed officer stopped Toya as she tried to walk through the police line.

"Ma'am," says the officer, "you can't go there. This is a crime scene."

Frantic, Toya began attacking the red tape trying to reach the man on the ground. Rich grabbed Toya by the waist and pulled her back but she was kicking and screaming at the top of her lungs, "Kato! Kaaaato!"

"Calm down, Ma'am," the officer said, trying to keep the peace but Toya was uncontrollable.

A detective noticed the commotion and went over to the officer. "What's going on?" the detective asked.

"I have no idea," the officer replied. "Maybe she knows the victim."

"You think?" the detective replied sarcastically. He wondered how this officer made it pass the Academy.

The detective walked over to Toya and Rich. "Ma'am, can you please calm down. I'm Det. Burk and I'm going to take you over to ID the body."

Toya looked at the detective and nodded her head. As Rich released his hold on her, Toya ducked under the red tape and ran towards the body on the ground, the detective on her heels. Burk signaled the crime scene investigator to let Toya view the body. Toya stared at the blood riddled sheet as the investigator pulled it back, gasped and covered her mouth.

"Ma'am," Detective Burke said, scrutinizing Toya's face for a sign of recognition, "Do you know him?"

Toya shook her head and turned to leave. "I was mistaken. Sorry."

Rich met her as she walked back from the other side of the police tape. "Toya, what happened?"

"It's not Kato...it's Tue'Gee," She said, wiping tears away.

Rich looked at Toya. "You mean Kato's best friend?"

"Yeah."

"Excuse me, Ma'am," Det. Burk calls after her. "What is your name?"

"Lisa. Lisa Watts," Toya said. Kato had taught her the three no's when dealing with cops: Don't say shit, don't sign shit and never give them your real name. Let them figure it out.

"Thank you, Ms. Watts." He approached her, "Here is my card if you happen to think of anything that may be helpful."

"Thank you, Detective," Toya said. "By the way, Detective, what happened?"

"We're baffled ourselves. But we figured the individual murdered and the individual shot were together."

Toya worked overtime to stay calm and show no emotions when she heard the last statement.

"Someone else was shot?" Rich asked. "How are they doing?"

"He was pretty banged up when he left here. They took him to Harlem Hospital."

"Thank you, again," said Toya as she and Rich walked toward 8th Avenue. As soon as they were out of sight, Toya took off, Rich right behind her toward where Kato truck was parked.

Det. Burk knew a liar when he saw one. That girl was lying her ass off, he thought. He knew she was not a part of what happened but she was somewhere in the picture. He decided to keep his eye on her. Lisa Watts, indeed.

"Listen up, Rich. I need you to find out whatever you can about what went down on Bradhurst. Also, call peoples and put them on point. I got extra keys to the Navigator so I'ma go to the hospital to see what's up."

"Got it," Rich said. "Yo, Toya, hit me as soon as you hear anything."

Toya nodded and climbed into the truck. Four minutes later, she was at Harlem Hospital asking the receptionist if they had a Kato Parker or Pascal admitted and to where. Sometimes Kato used Parker, but his real name, the one the government had, was Pascal.

"He was brought in a half-an-hour ago. He's in IC…"

Toya was at the security before the receptionist could finish. She filled out the visitor form and raced down the hall toward the ICU. When Toya entered, she was surprised to see Kato's sister, Janet, already there.

Janet quickly approached Toya. "He's a'right," she reassured a wild eye Toya. "He's in critical but stable condition, the doctor told me. The bullet broke his right ribs and lodged in his hip. They've stabilized him until they do surgery."

"How did you find out so fast?" Toya asked.

"Greg called me."

Greg was Janet's man and Kato's silent partner in a number of operations. It was Janet who introduced them. Toya never understood what Janet saw in that old ass Greg to begin with but she wasn't getting a good vibe. Toya flashed back to the faces she'd seen with Kato earlier at the park. There was Tue'Gee, Greg, two other men whose faces she knew and another man, whose face she didn't know. Although it was at a distance and she couldn't see his face that clearly, she'd peeped the one thing that stood out - a scar on the left side of his face."

"Where Greg now?" Toya asked. She also wondered where Greg was when the shit jumped off.

"He didn't say. All he said was that he'd see me later."

Toya immediately got the feeling that some snake shit went down, but she wasn't about to say that to Janet. Instead she said, "Okay. I'm glad he fine. Do you want anything from the vending machine?" She needed to be out of there to think for a minute.

"No. I'm fine."

Toya headed down the corridor away from the fuckin' vending machine. She needed somewhere private to call Rich.

"Hey, Rich."

"Toya, everything okay?"

"Yeah. Kato's in surgery, but check it. I need you to find Greg and keep an eye on him. Something' ain't right. I'll call you back later."

Something, for sure, really stunk. As she clicked off the phone, Toya thought about how she would execute her next move.

Later that night, the posse gathered at Rich's crib. Rich, who had been tailing Greg, reported some shady shit going down. "We ready to ride," Rich snapped his finger.

"No," Toya said to the crew, "I gotta do this alone. That punk-ass bitch Greg tried to make a statement by crossing Kato, so I gotta make a statement that my man isn't to be crossed."

"We respect that, but we…"

Toya cut Tia off. "Then please honor my wish to do this alone."

Everyone nodded their heads in agreement to Toya's terms.

Rich drove Toya to 129th and Lenox and parked across the street from the Juice Bar Greg owned. Toya had on all black fatigues with an extra black Discus sweater and black Chukka boots. She sported dark shades but didn't hide her face because she wanted those who knew her to know why she came.

Toya cocked back the 16-shot 9-millimeter Ruger and placed it on her waist, looked at Rich and exited the car. The Juice Bar was packed as usual with the who's who of the game, gold diggers and local hustlers all socializing and trying to outdo each other. Toya's stride was steady and purposeful. She moved with stealth precision through the wannabe patrons swarming around.

The VIP section was towards the back of the Bar so Greg could do his business in private. When he had a meeting, he pulled the horizontal blinds to cover the glass panel. He didn't this time and from where Toya stood, it looked like he was wrapping up a deal. Greg was at a table with four other men, all decked out in name brand suits. Cigar smoke curled above their heads, polluting the air. Greg appeared to be very attentive to an older gentleman who was holding sway over the group. They were all laughing at something he said. Greg reached into his blazer pocket and removed a pen. He put the pen on top of a paper that was in front of the older man. Toya didn't have to be close to hear him ask, "Well, gentlemen, do we have a deal?" It was written all over his pussy-ass face.

A heavy set, light skinned dude who was sitting directly across from Greg said something she couldn't hear. Greg didn't reply but she knew that look. He was confident, like he knew he had what they wanted. He was in the driver's seat. That punk-ass bitch! He knew he had something they wanted and he was sure they would agree to his terms. If not, he would just take his business elsewhere.

"Yeah. We have a deal," the older gentleman picked up the pen while puffing away on his cigar.

"Good," Greg smiled as he extended his hand to seal the deal. "Now, Gentlemen, let's celebrate." Greg waved his hand to get a waitress' attention. Toya was careful to stay out of view.

The waitress, who smiled widely at Greg was only too happy to trot over.

"Bring us a bottle of Grey Goose, make that two," Greg said, smiling at the heavy-set guy.

This was the move Greg had been waiting on. Now he could really retire early. The game was a rough place to be all your life, he'd tried to tell Kato that and he hated that he had to do him dirty but Kato was young and hardheaded. The more Greg wanted out of the game, the more he and Kato bumped heads and, lately, they had a lot of issues. What Greg saw as means to profit Kato saw as preservation. The partnership was a disaster from day one but Kato had something he'd wanted and that was to control of 115th to 120th Street. Plus, Kato's sister was his woman.

Engrossed in ego talk and gloat, no one observed Toya fall in line behind the waitress. Both figures moved as one-- as a shadow. Just as everyone was relaxed and waiting to be served, Toya pushed the waitress aside, the tray with two bottles of Grey Goose falling to the floor. Greg looked up and immediately let out a blood curdling scream, the cigar falling onto the floor. His eyes met ones as cold as steel as he stared pleaded for his life.

"Kato send his regards."

Recognition dawned on him; he knew his assassin very well. He also realized at that very moment the Juice Bar would be closing early.

BLOCK! BLOCK! BLOCK! BLOCK!

"You need anything, " Toya asked Kato.

"No baby, I'm good. How are things on the outside."

"Same ole. Same ole. " She never told him she was fully in the game now.

CHAPTER ELEVEN

"Jada, HURRY UP! I'M NOT GONNA BE WAITIN' on no line all night to get into no club."

"Pat, chill!" Jada yelled from the bathroom. "I know security. Besides, when have you ever waited in line when you're with me?"

Pat could act like a real chicken head at times but she was good people when it came to hangin' out. Jada would much rather be with her peeps but everybody had some kind of issue tonight. Kaisia was playing mommy and constantly going through it with her good-for-nothing baby father. Toya's man was facing wild numbers with the law, and Rich was probably out husslin' some shit he'd boosted. Tia, between school and caretaking never had time to hang out anymore. The five of them who used to stick together like Lego blocks but only got together of late when money was involved. Still, a girl had to get her party on so Pat had to do.

Jada was the social butterfly of the three women in the crew. With no steady man or kid to hold her down, she was always out and about. She knew all the hustlers and all the hustlers knew her. With smooth chocolate skin, short-cropped hair and a 5-foot frame, she looked like a mannequin and used her good looks to her advantage.

"Jada! Come on!"

Jada walked out of the bathroom looking fly. "Let's go, Chicken Wing."

They were checking out this new club that had opened up called the Crystal Palace.

HARLEM

Ebony was laying across the bed at Ike house. He seemed preoccupied but so was she and she need to vent.

"I gotta get outta there and find my own place. They treat me like a fucking child. I'll be eighteen in six months and graduating this year." Ebony continued to talk and Ike pretended to listen. At this point he really didn't care about Ebony's domestic problems. His only concern was finding the faggot mutha fuckers who robbed his coke spot.

"Are you listening to me?" Ebony asked, aggravated at the blank stare in Ike's eyes.

"Yeah," Ike replied, having not a clue in the world what she was talking about.

"So, what do you think?" asked Ebony.

"You're right. I think you're right," Ike responded, figuring out that was the best answer to give as she seemed to want to be right about whatever it was she was yakking on about.

"So, you think I should get my own place?" Ebony said with excitement, knowing that if she had his approval he would help her out.

"Why get an apartment when you can just stay here with me?" Ike, deep in his own thoughts, was even surprised at his response.

Ebony jumped on Ike with excitement. "You're serious, Ike…you wouldn't mind?"

"Of course not…you're my bitch," said Ike jokingly.

Ebony punched Ike on the arm and then kissed him on the cheek over and over. He grabbed her as they started play wrestling. He could at least ease some tension.

"Ike, I love you," Ebony confessed as Ike had her pinned to the bed.

"Tia, I understand she has a location where we can move the coke but can we trust her?" Kaisia asked concern in her voice. Tia, Kaisia and Toya were sitting in Jada's living room discussing Jackie's proposal.

"That I'm not too sure about. That's why I'm bring her to ya'll attention. You see, I thought about all that. That's why I'm hesitant to just bring her into our circle. She seems on the up and up but assumptions only lead to fatal mistakes."

"So, whatchaya have in mind? How you know she's built for this shit?" Kaisha said.

"That's where you all come in at," Tia replied grabbing her jacket. "I gonna invite her over tomorrow, but until then, Ladies, I have a date with destiny."

"A date with who?" Kaisia asked, collecting her belongings also. "Don't hold out now, Miss Full of Secrets."

"Damn Kay, let her have her moment," Jada said

"Shut up, Bird, you know your nosy ass wanna know too!" Kaisia stopped her friend's pretending behind.

"You got me there," Jada grinned sheepishly.

"Shut up both of ya'll. Anyway, remember the brother I mentioned that I kept running into at the subway?"

"Who? Dark and Crazy? I thought you said he was too conservative for you," Kaisia's eyes widened.

"He is, but after last night…"

"Last nighttt? Oowwww, you freak!" Jada howled. "What happened last night?" She moved in for the juicy details. No wonder you couldn't come to da club."

"Nothing happened last night other than him calling me. And Jada I never go to da club."

"Nothing happened? Oh," Jada, disappointed, slumped back into her chair.

"As I was saying, he called and we had a pleasant conversation. He seems down to earth so I agreed to going out with him on my terms."

"Well it's about time you made a move. I was beginning to wonder if you lost your appetite for brown men," Jada walked Tia and Kaisia to the door.

"Ha ha, very funny Ho," Tia said reaching for the door knob. "I'll see you tomorrow, Jay."

Kaisia waved and stepped out the door with Tia.

JUSTIN'S RESTAURANT

Tia exited the cab at 21st Street. She was wearing a stylish champagne colored two-piece Channel suit replete with a purple scarf that complemented her silk Donna Karan blouse. Her three-inch heels extended her shapely legs. None of Justin's diners, she bet would believe that the sophisticated-looking woman in their midst, was the leader of a ruthless Harlem gang.

The line to get into Justin's snaked out of sight so she was glad she had made a reservation. Tia loved the restaurant and admired Sean Combs for making it a first-class establishment. She entered and approached the hostess.

"May I help you, Madam?"

"Yes. I have reservations for two under Ms. Davis. 9:00 p.m." Tia glanced around to see if Sean had already arrived. She didn't see him. She kind of expected that though she had told him not to be late, he didn't seem the type to be intimidated.

"Would you like to be seated while you wait for your guest?"

"I would," Tia said following the hostess to a corner table that was perfect for private conversation. It also had a clear view of the entrance and the bonus of being close to the restrooms.

"You can look over the menu while you wait." The waitress handed her the Carte.

"Thanks," Tia took the menu and glanced at it. She checked her watch and wondered what excuse Sean was going to use to justify his lateness.

"Excuse me, Madam. Is this seat taken?"

Tia turned to see Sean standing behind her, a wide smile on his face and what appeared to be a dozen roses in his hand. Pink. Friendship. She like that. She didn't need to grab her belongings after all, she thought.

"For you." Sean placed the bouquet of flowers in her hands. "I'm sorry I am," he looked at his watch, "two minutes late but you know how challenging parking in Manhattan can be. I hope you didn't wait too long." He grinned.

Tia was beginning to like the guy more and more. Fine and a sense of humor. A deadly combination. The flowers definitely put the icing on the cake. Sean was wearing shark skin grey slacks, button down black shirt and a fly sports jacket. "Well, Mr. Adams, you are right on time. I just got here myself. The "A" train was slow," Tia grinned.

The woman was strikingly beautiful and when she smiled, a one-side dimple punctuated her right cheek. "Good," Sean said unable to take his eyes off her. "By the way, you are looking most elegant this evening."

"Thank you. You are not too shabby yourself."

"Drinking?" Sean asked and Tia nodded.

Sean sat across from her and signaled the hovering waitress. "A bottle of Veuve Clicquot, please. Rosé."

"Man in charge, I like that." Tia smiled again.

"Have you had a chance to look over the menu?"

"Yes. I think I'll start with the French salad."

"Make that two," Sean said to the waitress. "We'll order later. I figure we have the entire night to get full. Besides, I am really hoping we can get to know each other a little better before we eat."

"Alright. So, what would you like to know?"

"What do you do for a living? Do you have a man, and are you happy?"

Sean's rapid-fire questions caught Tia off guard but she found it attractive. "Well, let's not waste any more time getting to the answers. I am in my third year of college studying for my B.A in Business. Marketing. If I had my act together I would have been finished last year, but life...I fell behind, a little." Tia looked over at Sean to see his reaction. Would he judge her? He didn't seem to be. "I am happy enough and if I had a man I wouldn't be here answering your questions."

"That's admirable. I admire a woman, especially a sister, who refuses to dumb herself down and defy the quota society deems appropriate. You seem like the kind of woman who pushes real hard to get what you want." Sean held her gaze and Tia blushed. She was not only beautiful, she was ambitious and he really liked that.

Tia lowered her eyes first, not because he said the wrong thing but because he seemed to be reading her soul. He was right: she was that woman. A woman who would let nothing get in the way.

"So, how did you come up with all this with the little information I gave you?" Tia folded the napkin on her lap as the waitress returned with the Champagne, flutes and French salads. She poured the champagne and disappeared.

"What shall we drink to?" Sean asked, a twinkle lighting his eyes. "New beginnings?"

Tia tipped her glass slightly, meeting Sean's at the center of the small table. "Yes," she agreed, taking a sip, "to new beginnings." The Champagne tickled the back of her throat, flowed through her body and made her tingle. Yes, new beginnings.

"Cheers!" Sean added with a smile.

"Cheers," Tia smiled back and took another sip. "So, tell me," she asked again, "how did you get all that information?"

"My father used to tell me that I had a real talent for reading people. I guess that's why I became a lawyer."

"Ah, so you are in the profession of law. That explains it. What area?" Tia asked very interested in this new development.

"Yes. I am a lawyer. I usually don't advertise that."

"So, what made you advertise it tonight?" Tia asked.

"It just came out. Many women are not too excited about having a lawyer boyfriend and others are only too eager as they see dollar signs."

"Where I'm from here, there's a name for the second kind of females."

"Oh yeah. What might that be?"

"Bitch. Pardon my French." She bet he expected her to say gold digger but Tia was testing the waters.

"Don't worry. I speak fluent French," Sean smiled and poured more champagne. "Shall we toast to getting to know each other."

"Sure. So, what kind of lawyer are you? Entertainment, civil, criminal?"

"I'm a criminal attorney. A lawyer for the people."

"So, you're a city employee?"

"Some people call it District Attorney but I guess city employee is suitable. I'm in the Brooklyn DA's office. Does that make me less likable?"

Tia took a sip of her drink to fight back the urge to cry out, YOU'RE A BLOOD SUCKER! "No. I just wouldn't have guessed you to be a criminal attorney."

"Are you alright?"

"Of course. I was just thinking about how all this came about. I mean us bumping into each other the way we did. Now here we are sitting in an upscale restaurant having dinner. Doesn't that seem odd?"

"Odd? I think a better word for that is fate or serendipity or just meant to be. What would you like it to be?" Sean leaned over and touched her hand.

"Fate, huh? I don't really know. I haven't had much use for it. Everything I've wanted I had to work for." If he only knew just how hard she had to work he'd be putting her in handcuffs instead of buying her dinner.

"What about passion? Could fate be a kind of passion?"

"I guess they could go hand in hand since in both cases, we are not in control. When two people are attracted to each other and they share the same dreams and desires, that's fate and passion working together. So yes, I suppose fate could be a kind of passion. But to have both working in harmony one must first know who they are, know their deepest desires and wildest dreams."

Sean could listen to Tia's sultry voice all night. She mesmerized him, this woman. There was something about her that was different from ever other woman he'd ever been with and it wasn't just a sexual attraction, though he couldn't deny that. It was something much deeper. A feeling he couldn't touch.

If Tia knew what was good for her, she would have cut the conversation short and found a way to end the evening. But the more they talked, the more she realized how comfortable she was with Sean and it made her nervous. No man had ever had this effect on her. It made her wish her life was not such a mess. She was treading on dangerous ground. This was not a man she could predict. She couldn't tell what he'd do next and the idea of being unprepared for anything scared the shit out of Tia.

"Ready to order?" Sean asked.

"Why don't you order for me? I need to go to the ladies' room and somehow I trust you will order just what I want," she raised from the table and did her best not to bolt out the door.

Sean was by her chair pulling it out.

Was this man about to fuck up her life, Tia thought, as she walked confidently to the restroom.

Sean watched the sway of her hips. She was a one-of-a-kind woman.

HARLEM

"Bet the whole ten!"

"Naw, Nigga, get it like I got it...on the floor."

The gambling spot on 8th Avenue was packed to the gills with hustlers looking to blow the bank up. Crime walked in and began to scan faces. He was looking for Dollar Bill. Dollar Bill managed the gambling houses on the avenue and he knew all the willies, hustlers, roosters, friends and stick-up kids and killers in Harlem and beyond. He knew their habits to a tee and if anyone was spending more than usual, Dollar Bill would know. Crime was looking for every, and anybody over the past week who seemed to have made a quick come up overnight.

Crime spotted Dollar Bill by the craps table talking to an old man with salt and pepper hair. Man, he should be home! He ain't doing this shit when he get that old, Crime thought. "Dollar, what's up?"

Dollar Bill turned at the sound of his name. "Crime, my boy, long time no see. Dollar excused himself from the old head's company and escorted Crime to the bar. "Brenda, let me get a 151 and give the man whatever he wants."

"I'm alright," Crime replied.

The bartender returned with Dollar's drink. Dollar picked up the half shot and threw if back in one gulp as though the 151 Proof Vodka was water. "This must be business 'cause you tryna stay sober." Dollar put the empty glass on the bar.

"Yeah."

"So, what can I do for you?"

"Listen, Dollar. I'm in need of some information and I willing to pay for it if it's useful."

"Lay it on me, Young Blood."

"I'm looking for some new or old faces that may have hit the jackpot overnight, especially females."

Dollar stared off into space as though he was trying to remember something. "I didn't hear of anyone lately making a fast come on, but I'll keep my eyes and ears open. If I hear anything, I'll holla at you."

"Good look, Dollar." Crimes said as he got up from the bar. Dollar gave Crime dap. "Ayo Crime, stop acting like a stranger. Come through and spend some of that bread before them young hos' get cha."

They bumped fist and Crime walked to the exit.

BROOKLYN

Tia kept her word to get back to Jackie by the end of the week.

"Jackie, my people are ready to make a move and like I said we are sitting on two birds. We're gonna go over the rest of the details when you get uptown, plus I wanna introduce you to the family. You still got the address I gave you, right?"

"Yeah. I'm good."

"Okay, then. Everything is all set. By the way, call when you get in range so I can meet you downstairs."

"Listen, Tia, I might be an hour or so late. I gotta drop off my son at the sitter. You okay wid that?"

"Don't worry about it. Take care of your business first." Tia walked with Jackie to her car and waited until she pulled off before heading to the subway.

LOWER WEST SIDE

Sean didn't really didn't like the upper west or east side. He toyed witht he idea of Midtown but couldn't find his stride there. He'd even toyed with living in Riverdale but that was just too much. Now he could think of living no place else but downtown. At first he had misgivings about moving into the neighborhood but now he was a full fledged resident!

Sean was in unlocking his front door when he heard his phone ringing. He quickly juggled the lock because if it was Tia Davis, he sure wanted to speak with her. He really liked the woman but he got the distinct impression she was holding back. Call it lawyers intuition. He sprinted to the phone and grabbed it on its fourth ring. "Hello;" he croaked a little out of breath.

"Sean, why are you avoiding me?"

"Monique, if you're calling for this, you're wasting your time. I am busy."

Monique was a fellow Attroney. They'd met on the job a few years before and he'd ignored his own caution never to date a co-worker. But more than a co-worker she was the daughter of the a well respected Judge.

"Busy doing what Sean?"

"Busy being busy."

"You must have decided to go back to the hood. I guess you got back with one of your homegirls? Is that why you are brushing me off?"

Sean felt his temper flare. He was tired of Monique's demands and her jealous ways. He wanted to say yeah, you're right. Once you go black you can't really go anywhere else. Monique was the typical white woman. The problem with white women was that think they own the black man they are dating. He had no idea why but America's racial hoax. "Listen, Monique. Why don't we let all this alone. It was fun while it lasted but I think we can cancel this now…If you will excuse…"

"Are you fucking crazy? You don't just cancel me like some fucking hooker. If it wasn't for me you wouldn't be where you are. I helped you get there. Don't forget." Monique was screaming.

"You didn't do a damn thing," Sean yelled back. "I've worked hard for my success and I alone will take credit for my achievements, so back the fuck up."

"You alone? You alone! You project reject. Don't forget who pulled the strings for your black ass. That was my father who did that. How the hell do you think you get the big cases that put your ass on the map?"

"That's called mentoring. Yeah, his influence helped open some doors for me but I walked through those doors and did all the work necessary to stay in those rooms. It's all the hours I work, that you complain about mind you, that got me there. It's all the years of college. It's all the brains I have in my head that should have known better. Don't get me wrong. Your father is a good man and I respect him a whole lot and he respects me but don't make the mistake of thinking he is the reason I am where I am now."

"Ha, do you really believe my father respects your black ass? Think again." Monique was laughing. "He didn't even do it for you. He did it to make you respectable for me because I went slumming. You were fucking his daughter. Yes, Sean you were fucking the daughter of a well-respected white judge. That's how you got where you did."

"Monique, I think you should stop now before you say something stupid. Don't…"

"Furthermore," she spat, ignoring Sean's warning, my father was politically hindered to keep balance with the thoughts of his colleagues. In other words, all you ever were to him was a charity case. Another black nobody put in a position where he can be controlled."

Sean balled up his fist at his side. It's a good thing the woman was nowhere near him. God knows what he'd have done. Those were fighting words and he was not going to let it slide. Sean sat at the foot of his bed. The words Monique just spat reverberated. I made you. Another black nobody in a position only to be controlled!

"So," Sean finally said. "Why are you getting so upset about a black nobody? This black nobody does not want you evil white thing." And hung up the phone.

Was she right? Had he let his dignity slip by stepping out with Monique? Had he been a puppet on a string for white justice? A charity case upholding the laws of white supremacy while his people were being annihilated? Was he that deaf, dumb and blind? Was he really the ultimate sell-out, Uncle Tom nigger - porch monkey? Was he or could he ever make a difference when the law of the land was meant to protect the elite few? Sean wished he could have had his Dad around. He would have helped him put this all into perspective. But his father left him with one thing: his voice and he intended to use it. The whole race shit in America wore him out.

CHAPTER TWELVE

Harlem

Was it difficult to find the building?" Tia asked as she and Jackie walked up the ramp to the Honeycomb.

"A little," Jackie said. "Seems like all Harlem blocks look the same, but it was the block numbers and avenues that confused the shit outta me."

Tia laughed. "We get that from all outta towners."

Jackie followed Tia and as they entered the building she felt in familiar territory. Groups of people were hanging out the hallways, drug deals going down near the staircase, and seven or eight guys were rolling dice by the mailboxes. All New York City Projects have exactly the same feel, she thought, regardless of the borough.

"The way of this world," Tia punched the elevator button and looked up to see what floor it was on. "So, did you make it to the babysitter alright?" asked Tia.

"What?" Jackie turned to Tia. She'd been busy watching the project action.

"The babysitter," Tia repeated.

"Oh, yeah. But he went crazy when I was walking out the door."

Tia smiled. "That's kids for you. Can't live without them and damn sure can't leave 'em anywhere."

The elevator opened and Tia and Jackie stepped in. Yeah, it was a project elevator.

Inside the apartment another conversation was taking place. "Is Tia sure she knows what she's doing. I'm just saying. I don't doubt she has the best intentions in the world and our money interest at heart but to fuck wit' an outsider is something I never thought she'd ever consider," Toya said.

"I feel what you're sayin', Toy, but it's like this. We're not gonna be able to move that much product in the city. It's too risky. Besides if home girl got an outlet we can use them, why not take advantage of it? Kaisia answered, dumping tobacco from her blunt into the ashtray.

Toya looked out the window, praying and hoping and trying to convince herself that Tia knew what she was doing, but she just couldn't shake the uncertainty she was feeling of dealing with a stranger, someone they had no intel on. Greg, Kato's business partner and sister's boyfriend had betrayed him…what might a complete stranger do?

"Here, Toya," Kaisia handed her the blunt. "Spark this up and relax."

"Naw, ya'll go ahead. I'm good."

Jada looked at Kaisia and shrugged.

There was the coded knock on the door.

"That's them. I got it," Jada got up to answer the door. She opened the door and stepped aside as Jackie and Tia walked into the Honeycomb.

Jackie followed Tia into the living room. "Hey everybody, this is Jackie. Jackie this is Jada, Kaisia and Toya.

Jackie smiled. An all-girls stealth posse. Impressive. Jada and Kaisia shook hands, Toya nodded her head and turned back to the window.

"Let me get your coat," Tia said to Jackie. "Do you want something to drink?"

"No, I'm fine, Tee," Jackie answered. Nice crib too, she thought. They got to be doing well.

"Alright. Listen, just make yourself at home. You're around family. I'll be right back." Tia took Jackie's coat and walked into one of the back rooms.

"Sit," Kaisia offered moving her jacket from the couch. "Here you go, Jackie."

Jackie took a seat beside Jada who was rolling a blunt.

"Do you smoke?" Jada asked.

"Who don't?" Jackie answered.

"I like you already," Jada smiled at Jackie.

"Toya, come here for a minute," Tia yelled form the bedroom.

Tia was on the phone when Toya entered and she took a seat in one of the folding chairs.

"Yeah. She's here," Tia was saying. "Yeah, give it about two hours. Okay, I'll see you then." Tia hung up the phone and told Toya to close the door.

"What's up, Family? Your vibe seems off tonight. I know you way too long so don't keep me in the dark. What's wrong, Toy?"

Toya got up and sat on the bed next to Tia. "Tee, I understand what you're trying to do here, but I ain't feeling this."

"Feeling what, Toya? You gotta be more specific because when I brought the situation to ya'll's attention last week you didn't feel this way. Now all of a sudden you're not feeling this. I mean is it just tonight or is it the whole situation?"

"Tee, I don't know what it is. Maybe cause I just went to see Kato. I'm probably just overstressed with the fact that Kato is locked up fighting for his life, but whatever the case I've been having butterflies all day and I can't shake this shit, Tee."

"Toy, ya'll my family first. I would never do anything on my own that deals with us. If you don't want to fuck with her then I'll find an alternative solution. We still got Rich cousin in D. C. We could fuck wit…"

"Naw, Tee. The rule is no family. Tee, you know I have all the faith in the world in you. You know you're my sister. I just wanna be sure that you're sure about this because no matter what, I'm riding with you."

"Toy, I'm gonna tell you like this. It started with five and it's gonna remain five. I not tryna add nobody to our circle. This move I'm tryna make will hopefully put us on track and allow us to leave all this bullshit alone. Right now, she's the key and we need her."

"Yeah, I hear you. Alright Tee, let's go through with it but I can't front up in her face and smile."

"Toy, I would never ask you to act other than yourself. In fact, it's a good idea that you don't get close to her. That way you can watch her when she thinks nobody's watchin'."

The long-time friends looked at each other and smiled. "Now that that's taken care of, let's get back out there before they think we forgot about them." Tia put a hand on her friend's shoulder. This life was not for the fuckin' faint at heart.

Jada was being the inquisitor. "So, Jackie. What part of Brooklyn are you from?"

"I'm originally for the Sty but I moved to Brownsville after my son was born and my baby father got murdered."

"Sorry to hear that," Kaisia said. In the 'hood, death was a way of life. No point getting too emotional about it. Kaisia thought too about her baby father and although he was still alive sometimes she wished he was dead for real instead of being just a deadbeat.

"Do you know this guy outta Howard Projects named Devine?" Jada asked Jackie.

"No. I really don't deal with too many people out there, but if you want me to I'll inquire about him. I can do that for you."

"Don't go through the trouble. He just one of my one night stands with paper."

"Damn, Jay, you're too much. How many men you have?" Kaisia asked.

The trio was laughing when Tia and Toya walked back into the room.

"What so funny, ya'll?" Tia asked,

"Just Jada reminiscing on one of her many ho escapades," said Kaisia.

Toya went back to her window seat. She wasn't in a jovial mood.

"Damn, Jay. What you gonna do, sit on the blunt all night?" Tia said

Jada passed Tia the blunt and lit another.

"I'ma gonna order out so tell me what you'll want," Kaisia said.

"Get some KFC. I gotta taste for chicken and them butter biscuits," Jada replied.

"Chicken for everybody," Kaisia said as she left to get the food.

The conversation drifted from one small talk to another while they waited on the food. It took Kaisia longer to pick up the order than it took them to eat. When they were finished eating Tia and Kaisia took the trash to the kitchen and dumped it in the brown paper bag she retrieved from under the sink, and then tied it up in a sturdy heavy duty plastic bag. They didn't need to encourage Harlem cockroaches.

"Kay," Tia said, "what do you think? I know it's too early to get a general opinion on her but I need to know how her vibe is to you."

"Shorty seems level-headed to me. I mean I like her. She seems pretty stern, and she don't seem too relaxed or too eager. Like she be checking us out too. I like that. I think though, that she is struggling with some personal shit. I don't think it's nothing, maybe 'cause the baby daddy got killed...I don't think it's nothing because we all have our inner demons and I guess she's just trying to deal with hers, like we all are."

Tia thought about what Kaisia said and although she never brought it up to Jackie, she always felt that Jackie was keeping something from her.

"So, what did Toya have to say?" Kaisia asked.

"How you know we were talking about Jackie?"

"Shit. Tee, I know you, but more important is I see how Toya looks at Jackie and my mind detects all ain't well with her. I feel the vibe as well."

"Well, if you are assuming Toya don't like her, you are right. Toya's reasons are her own, but she is down with what we're trying to do."

"Toya like that. She don't trust nobody especially after what happened to Kato."

"Yeah, you're right about that but right now let's get back in there and handle our business."

Tia walked back into the living room and put the coke on the table.

"Damn that's a lot of coke...and you say you have more?" Jackie exclaimed.

"Yup. This ain't shit but check it...I'm willing to bring a half a brick out there just to see how fast we can move it. If all is all on this upcoming trip we'll flood the town and look for other potential investments," Tia said.

Jackie was awed. She had suspected Tia was down and had something to contribute to the move but she didn't know she was such a balla. She couldn't believe the amount of product she was packin'. Jackie began to appreciate just who she was dealing with.

"So, Jackie. What you think?" Kaisia asked.

"I feel we can get off this. If it's quality, we'll be knee deep in clientele. The only dilemma I see is how we're gonna distribute it. I mean, we can break it down, do what locals are doing, selling twenties and fifties, or we can do it by weight," Jackie said.

"What was your brother' operation?" Tia asked.

"My brother was dealing with this girl out there called Diamond. She was a stripper until he pulled her off the track and made her a runner. Anyway, he has two houses in her name that we can use while we're out there. Plus, she's good people. She knows what's what."

"Jackie, no disrespect but we're not dealing with her on that level. We'll find out what we need to find out while we're

out there. Definitely snatch up one of them houses. Tell her
it's for you and that you're coming out to Maryland to just get
away from the city. Tell her nothing else," Tia advised.

Jackie agreed. She drew a map of the area and handed it
to Tia.

"What about the competition, if any?" Tia asked.

"There was a problem once with my brother and some
guy from a few blocks over on Main Street. It eventually died
down and I heard nothing else about it."

"How do you know so much about your brother's
business?" Toya inquired, looking hard at Jackie as she spoke.
To her, this was suspect as Kato never discussed this side of
his business with her and although it wasn't a secret, he never
wanted her to be a part of it.

"Me and my brother are very close. In fact, he is my best
friend. He always told me that if you can't trust your own
flesh and blood then you might as well be afraid of your own
shadow."

Toya turned back toward the window accepting Jackie's
answer for the moment but the butterflies still did not go
away.

"Tee, how you wanna arrange transportation? It's
obvious we ain't taking any chances with Greyhound," Jada
laughed.

"Give me a second on that, Jay. First of all, we're going to
need identification for each of us. We can't chance going out
there barefaced. Can you handle that, Jay?

Now about the transportation. We need to rent two
whips and we need them for two weeks at the most."

"I got that," Toya chimed in for the first time. "Kato got
some friends in the Bronx that got a car lot. Anything specific
you want in the car, Tee?"

"Yeah, make the suckers roomy," Tia laughed. "If
possible, try to get at least one SUV and two police scanners.
Jackie, when the time comes, I'm gonna need you to make
reservations for two in separate hotels, but make sure the
hotels are within a one mile radius of each other."

"Alright," Jackie nodded, an took the joint Kaisha handed her.

"Shiiit.That haze got me bent. Jay, where you get this shit from?" Kaisia asked.

"145th and St. Nic...them dreads stay with butter!"

"I need to take some of this shit back to Brooklyn with me," Jackie said, passing the blunt to Tia.

Tia held the blunt to her lips but did not inhale. She needed her head clear. Just as Tia was passing Jackie back the blunt, there was a knock on the door.

"I got it," Jada said climbing off the couch. "It's Rich. He called to say he was on his way."

"Aright, " Tia said. They had to be authentic. Jackie would know they wouldn't open the door for just anyone. "So, Jackie," Tia said feigning being high, "you ready for our mid-terms? I know I'm not but I need to pass so I can complete them damn credits."

"I'm in the same boat, but I do get a little time to myself to study 'cause the babysitter knows my situation and so she keeps my son on extra days when I ask."

Jackie was droning on when she saw the stricken look on everyone's face. She looked up to see Jada being held at gunpoint, tears trickling down her face."

"Get on the floor bitch," yelled the gunman shoving Jada to the ground. "And all you hos need to do the same."

"What the fuck is up?" Kaisia whispered to Tia.

The gunman was so swift on his feet he was in front of Kaisia in a second; a backhand connected with her jaw and rocked her to her knees.

Everyone hit the floor. They knew the gunman was serious.

Jackie looked over a Kaisia who had blood coming from her lip.

"Ya'll bitched-robbed the wrong Nigga but I'm here to collect and probably take a little extra and some," he bent down and ran the gun barrel between Jada's breast.

"We don't know what the fuck you're talking about," Tia shouted.

The gunman stepped over Jada and made his way to Tia. "Bitch, you know very well what the fuck I'm talking about and, if I'm wrong then I apologize, but near one of you bitches will be walking outta here alive."

"At least tell us what it is?" Tia said.

"The coke, Bitch, and I'm not talking "bout Pepsi either."

"You've got the wrong people. We don't fuc..."

The gunman grabbed Tia by the hair and leveled his barrel under her chin. "You must think this gun is plastic or I'm stupid, but I'ma show you how serious I am." He released Tia and stepped to where Jackie was laid out. He snatched Jackie by the back of the hair and pulled her to her feet. "I'ma make you the first victim if I don't get my answers." The man held Jackie's hair so tight she was on tippy toes trying to lessen the pain.

Jackie's eyes started to fill with tears and the room watched as her face flushed red, and veins popping out on her forehead.

"So, Beloveds, you have two options. One...you can tell me where my shit is or die. Either way, I'm not leaving empty handed."

Jackie could not believe this was happening. Just her fuckin' luck. She thought about her son. What would happen to him if she died? Jackie couldn't bear the thought. Even if she knew where the drugs were and told him, he'd probably kill them anyway. "I honestly don't know what you're talkin' 'bout. I ain't even from around here!" She held her own.

The gunman released his hold on Jackie and threw her onto the couch. She heard her head dent the wall. The gunman stepped back and aimed the gun point blank at Jackie. She covered her head with her hands as if her arms alone would stop a bullet.

"Wait. Wait!" Tia yelled, jumping from the floor her arms above her head. "It's in the kitchen. "I'll get it."

The gunman spun around and pointed the gun at Tia.

"Walk, Bitch," he said as he grabbed Tia by the neck and put the barrel of the gun against her cheek. "You try anything heroic and I'll guarantee you a spot on the 11 o'clock news. Now," he shoved her, "go get it!"

The gunman stood between the kitchen and the living room so that he could have a clear view of both areas. Tia returned from the kitchen holding a brown paper bag.

CLUB PARADISE

Ebony wasted no time moving in with Ike. She was his woman now, practically wifey. When he told her to get dressed they were going on a date, you could have pinched Ebony black and blue and she wouldn't have felt it.

Ebony and Ike pulled up in front of Club Paradise in his new black 7201 Benz. Ike exited the car, walked round to the passenger side, opened the door and took Ebony's hand. He wanted to make her feel like a woman in every way. They strode pass the losers waiting on line and everyone turned to look at them. Both were dressed in black. Ebony wore a black cat suit, with silver bracelets, belt and 3" strappy heels and Ike was in black slacks and a light turtleneck. He held Ebony slightly by the elbow and as they stepped into the club, he slapped the bouncer's hand in a dap then led Ebony to the VIP lounge. There were a few familiar faces and some women who knew Ike more than Ebony would like to know. They looked so jealous and angry, as though they wanted to beat her to a pulp.

The VIP section was decked out with carpet and each table had a complimentary bottle of Hennessey. It had an unobstructed view of the dance floor—a necessity for us guys who wanted to spot the babes. Everyone, even the stars, and there were a few, greeted them, some standing to bump shoulders with Ike. Ebony and Ike sat at the far corner of the room, more out of security concern than privacy. Ike hated being in crowded spaces, especially ones with only two exits.

"Boo, this club is nice," Ebony was awed. "I've never been to any place so nice, so sophisticated."

"Yeah, my man put a lot into this joint." Ike scanned the dance floor to check out what was happening and caught sight of a couple of bitches he'd fucked and kicked to the curb but avoided eye contact. Those hoochies had no pride, he thought. No matter how much dirt you do to these bitches, they'll keep coming back just as long as they know you're getting cake.

The music was blazing and the DJ was spinning straight fire. Usher's "Let it Burn," came on and the crowd oohed and aahed. The dancers' gyrations left sweat dripping off their faces. Ebony couldn't tell if the Hispanic girl a few feet from their table was dancin' or fuckin.' It was shaping up to be a great evening and Ike knew Ebony was enjoying herself immensely.

"Ebony," Ike tapped her on the shoulder. Ebony turned to see a tall man standing with Ike. "Eb, this is my man I was telling you about. Ice, this is my lady, Ebony."

"Ebony shook Iceman's hand. He was drop dead handsome. Six feet, brown skin with slick back hair. He had Indian blood. He wore a cream, crushed linen pants and shirt with beige suede Dior shoes. Iceman's whole aura spelled success and sex appeal in bunches. Ebony realized she was staring and quickly turned away. She knew that it was impolite to stare at her man's homeboy...no matter how fine he was! And there would be no way that she would trade Ike for a Nigger.

"So, what'd think?" Iceman asked. He had an accent.

"It's fire, Playa. Shit. When you first came to me with the idea for this club, I wasn't really feeling it but now that it's off the ground I would have regretted not going in with you man."

Ebony stared at Ike. "You own part of this? You didn't tell me!"

Ike and Iceman smiled.

"Yeah baby. Your man gets around. I wanted to surprise you. Didn't want to jump the gun until everything was done."

98

"I had to literally convince him this would be a good investment for his future," Ice smiled again.

Ebony hugged Ike. "Boo, you are full of surprises."

He pecked her cheek and said, "Iceman and I have some business to talk about. I'll be gone for a minute. You'll be alright?"

Ebony shook her head.

"It was nice meeting you, Ebony," Iceman said. "Hopefully we'll see each other more if Ike decides to stop hiding you."

"It was nice meeting you too," Ebony extended her hand and smiled.

Ebony watched as Ike and Ice disappeared up the stairs then turned her attention back to the dance floor. It was raging.

"Damn, Baby Boy, you got this office lookin' like you're the CEO of Rock-A-Fellers, or some shit," Ike said.

"Naw, Baby, this is just for show. You gotta paint the picture before you can sell the art," Iceman smiled.

Ike retuned the smile. "So, what's the deal?"

"Everything as we discussed. I got two broads from outta Queens that's willing to transport a half a bird a piece. One of them got a connect with a limo service that's reliable. We have enough stuff, right. The robbery didn't put a dent in our stock, right?"

"We a'right. Okay on the mules," Ike nodded in agreement. "So, what time Thursday can we expect them?"

"We will deliver to them Thursday night at the Crystal Hills Motel in New Jersey, and they will leave immediately afterwards for Ohio."

"That's peace. This will give me additional time to get my workers out there."

"I'ma make reservations tonight at the local Holiday Inn in Columbus for this week, so you won't be far from the action. Also, inform your workers that they should not approach the mules. They deal strictly with you."

Ike was always impressed with how Ice moved. They'd met while serving time in federal prison. Iceman, a Trinidadian transplant was an agent for rappers until he caught a bullshit drug beef. Rappers weren't Alter Boys so he understood how that could have gone down. Ike respected a man who copped to his responsibilities. Ice it seemed took the rap for one of his clients and true to his name he was cool as cucumber and the model prisoner while serving his time. Although he'd been released two years ahead of Ike, he'd kept his promise to Ike about staying in touch and even sent his a few bills to maintain. Ike liked that kind of loyalty.

Once Ike was released, Ice had already set up a connections but it was Ike who expanded the business multiple folds…and made Ice a much wealthier man. It was also Ike who was responsible for killing any competition that stood between them and their money.

CHAPTER THIRTEEN

TIA WAS THE FIRST TO RECOVER. Everyone in the apartment was shaken and it was so quiet you could hear a pin drop. The gunman had grabbed the bag Tia held and bolted out the door. It was obvious he wasn't the king pin and was trying to undo his oversight before the big boss found out. They realized they were lucky this time. Tia was the first to break the silence.

"Everybody a'right? Listen up, ya'll we gotta keep our cool about this till we find out more."

"Fuck more, Tee," yelled Kaisia. "Let's air some shit out right here, right now!"

"And who do we aim at, Kay? We don't even know who the fuck is behind this shit. You want to twist any nigga to fit the part?" Jada said.

"Fuckin' right. We can't just sit here blowin' smoke out our asses in the hopes that the mutha fucker will come back wit' our shit!"

"We can't just go out shootin' innocent people on a just-because either," Jada said.

"Just be easy, both of you," Tia screamed. "Ya'll missing the point. We alive. First of all, he only got off with a hundred grams of cook-up. We still got a key and a half of coke. We can't focus on this right now, but I promise you it will be dealt with. I understand this shit is dictating ya'll thinking and clogging ya'll judgment but you gotta keep ya cool."

"You're right," Kaisia agreed. "Now what?"

Tia turned to Jackie. "You alright?"

"Yeah, just a little shook up but my nerves coming back together."

"Listen ya'll, I'ma walk Jackie to her car. By the time I come back, everybody needs to be focused and on point."

Tee and Jackie left the apartment. "You sure you're alright to drive, Jackie," Tia asked.

"I'm good. I just didn't expect to be getting jacked in Harlem. In Brooklyn, yeah," Jackie smiled and got in to her car.

"Yeah, I know what you mean. Harlem can be just as grimy and cold hearted, but don't worry about that. We'll handle it."

"Tee, don't think I can't hold my own weight. If shit needs to be done, I'm down for the long ride. And remember, I'm not from around here so I can do my dirt and disappear."

"Jackie, I feel you on that and I respect that you are ready to ride with the people, but we got bigger plans and I need you to focus on the O.T. move if you wanna fuck with us on that level."

"Of course, why wouldn't I? This shit that happened today just woke me up from my slumber. Being away from the game so long I forgot how fast shit can happen but I woke up and I ready for whatever. I need to make some real paper and get my kid far away from this shit…but I'm ready to ride for now."

"Okay. So, like I said, we'll be ready as soon as you inform us everything is set. Hopefully we'll be pulling out this week," said Tia.

Jackie nodded her head. She started the car. Tia tapped on the side of the car and made and an imaginary phone with her hand. "Call me when you get home."

Jackie gave dap and drove off.

Tia waited until Jackie's car was out of sight before she started walking back to the Honeycomb. As she was about to enter the building someone pressed a gun to her back and ordered her to keep walking. Tia kept walking toward the Honeycomb. Jada, Kaisia and Toya were waiting for her to return and if she screamed they could hear her. Tia quickly turned and kicked gunman in the knee, knocking him to the ground. Jada, Kaisia and Toya heard the commotion and ran out to help. They pinned the gunman to the ground as Jada tried to pull his mask off.

"Alright! yelled the gunman. "I can't breathe."

The ladies released the gunman and watched as he stood and pulled of his mask. Rich had the biggest smirk on his face. He was laughing so hard the ladies had to join in.

"So, am I a good performer or what?" Rich asked as he tried to catch his breath.

"Yeah, Nigga. Too good. You almost broke my damn arm," Jada punched him.

"I had to make to look real good," Rich rubbed his arm. "Here, Tee," Rich handed Tia the brown paper bag. "You're gonna need these."

Tia removed the contents from the paper bag and looked at Kaisia, busting out laughing.

"Tampons!" Kaisia touched her sore lip. I got my lips busted for tampons!"

"Shut up, Kay," Tia looked at her lip. "It ain't that bad.

Kaisia cut her eyes at Rich who shrugged. "Authenticity. So, what's the verdict? Is she good or what?"

"She held her ground. Man, she was down and kept a straight face."

"Yea, she really did. I was sure she was going to crack when I put the gun to her head. The Bitch covered her head with her hands. Chick acted like her hand could stop a bullet!"

"Naw, she did alright. Well, I can at least say she passed the test with flying colors," Kaisia said.

Tia looked over at Toya in the recliner. She could tell Toya was not convinced by the staged test that Jackie could be trusted.

Tia's cell phone rang. It was Tone.

"What you mean she didn't come home last night or this morning?" Tia yelled into the phone. "Whatever. I'll be home in a second." Tia grabbed her jacket.

"Tee what's up? Is everything alright?" Kaisia asked.

"My stupid-ass sister didn't come home since yesterday morning."

Tia was close to tears and it took the posse off guard. Kaisia had never seen her near to tears in all the years she'd known her except when her mother passed away. Ebony was Tia's heart and she cherished her sister and would protect her with her life. She had sacrificed a lot to give her a more stable life and a chance to get the hell out of Harlem. She wanted her to go to Spellman or some such fancy school...Anywhere but Harlem. Tia's love for Ebony was like the love of a mother to a child – strong and committed.

"I'm out," Tia said as he headed to the door.

"I'm coming with you," Kaisia grabbed her sweater.

IKE'S CRIB

The night had been perfect and Ike was perfect. Ebony didn't think she could love anyone more than she loved Ike. She really wanted to please him and she was trying her best.

"Who taught you to ride dick like that?" Ike was on his back drenched in sweat."

"Practice makes perfect," said Ebony kissing his lips. "I'm getting a lot of practice with you, Ike and I love it," she climbed off him and grabbed the wet towel of the side table and began wiping herself and him up.

"Oh, last night was close to perfection and here I was thinking you were still in the kindergarten stage," Ike said as he got up to take a shower.

Ebony threw the rag at him but it landed on the floor.

"You're nasty bitch," Ike said jokingly as he wrapped a towel around his waist and disappeared into the bathroom. As Ike stepped into the shower, he thought about how lucky he was to have a pretty, young thing at his side, money in the bank and niggas who respected and feared him at the same time. Life was good and it had only taken him two years to reestablish his kingdom after five years of doing time in federal prison. His luck was in season and he was having a good run. The only fly in the ointment, his major setback was that one of his stash houses got hit. He wondered again who would have the fuckin' never to hit his spot. He was anxious to hear what Crime had found out.

When Ike came out back into the bedroom, Ebony was right in front of him naked and horny again.

"Baby, where you going?" Ebony licked her lips disappointed she wasn't going to get more until Ike returned.

"Ike palmed her tight, round ass and pulled her towards him. "Listen, Shorty, I gotta take care of some business. I'll be back in due time. There's some money in the dresser draw. Why don't you go out and buy something nice? You moved everything from your sister's?"

Ebony loved Ike and she loved the way he made her feel. She couldn't get enough of him, and best of all, he didn't treat her like a child. He treated her like a woman. Ebony felt herself get wet all over again as Ike rubbed her ass. "Uhuuu," she slipped his finger inside her. "Why can't you stay with me and take care of business later?" Ebony said, ready to ride Ike's manhood again.

Ike didn't want to but he slowly released my finger. He knew if he stayed, he would end up fucking Shorty for the rest of the day and night and not take care of business. He began to get dressed as Ebony watched.

"I'll see you later," he slapped her butt playfully.

"Where you going?" Ebony asked, disappointed that she wouldn't be getting more nookie until Ike returned.

Ike thought about the twenty-one questions Ebony was asking and realized that that was one bad habit he'd have to break her out of. He kissed Ebony's cheek. "I'll see you later," and smacked her butt again, "and I'll bring bad boy back with me." He grabbed his crotch

TIA'S HOUSE

Tone was frantic. I called everyone. No one seen her. Been trying to reach Tweet, but she ain't answering."

Tia dialed Rich. "Rich, where's your sister?" Tia asked.

"She's in the room, why?" a sleepy Rich asked. There was concern in his voice.

"I think she knows where my sister's at. She didn't come home last night."

"Hold on. I gonna wake her."

Tone came into the room with a worried looked on his face. "The Po-lice said she's not officially missing until 72 hours. We can file a report then."

"I don't even know why you called the cops, Tone. Them bastards don't give a fuck about a missing black girl. You'd be better off telling them Dunkin' Donuts ran out of Krispy Kreme," Tia said with bitterness. "I hated the fuckin' useless cops!"

Hello, Tia," Tweet said sleepily.

"Yeah. Where's Ebony?"

"She moved in with Ike."

"Ike? Who the fuck is Ike?"

"That name sound familiar," said Tone.

"Whoever he is, I'm a blow his old ass up for fuckin' with a 17-year-old," Tia snorted. "Where that sucker live?"

Tweet gave her the location but said she didn't know the building number but that Ike lived in the only red building on the block.

"Tweet, put Rich back on the phone."

Rich came back on the line. She says she think the address might be 151 St. Nic's place. Tweet said his apartment is on the third floor. The first door as soon as you get up the stairs."

"I'm glad her memory came back," Tia huffed. "Thanks Rich. And tell Tweet I said good look."

"She owes me that much. Do you want me to meet you there?"

"Naw, I got Kaisia with me."

"Alright, but call if you need me."

"Alright...peace."

"Come on, Kay. Tone I need your car."

"I'm coming with ya'll," Tone said.

"Naw, I need you to stay her in case she calls or comes home."

Tia tore down St. Nicholas Place as though she was about to pull off a drive by.

"Kay, look for the red building."

"There it is," Kaisia pointed.

As they were pulling over to the curb, a red Range Rover pulled out. Tia parked the car in the spot it had just vacated and took the steps two at a time. She banged on the door.

Why's Ike knocking down the door? Ebony wondered. She smiled. Maybe she had won the seduction battle and he'd come back for more. "Hold on, I'm coming,"

Tia looked at Kaisia and shook her head.

"You left your keys?" Ebony asked pulling open the door as she let the robe she had wrapped around her body drop to the floor. Her face spread in surprise when she saw Tia and Kaisia standing in the doorway. She sure wasn't expecting them but she was a woman in my own house. She felt brave. "What do you want, Tia?"

"Ebony, I don't have time for this shit. Get your stuff and let's go."

"Tia, I am not a child. You can't just keep hunting me down every time I don't come home anymore."

"You think because you are shacked up with a man twice your age that you're grown?"

"First of all, he only 28. And how would you know what I think? You lost that ability a long time ago, Sister Dearest. Remember those days you left me in the house? Well I've been growing. What, you thought I would be your baby sister forever?"

"Why you persist on running that lame-ass story? I'm not, shit-face, trying to justify your actions, and yes, you will always be my little sister. Now get your shit and while you're at it, tell that coward-ass nigga to come to the door."

"He ain't here and I'ain't going anywhere. This is where I live now and you might as well accept it."

"Bitch!" Tia hauled off. "You think this is a fuckin' game?" Tia yelled and grabbed Ebony by the hair. "You're coming if I have to drag your stupid-ass outta here myself."

Ebony tried to pry Tia's hand loose. She was sobbing and pulling Ebony by her hair. Kaisia watched the struggle between sisters refusing to get involved.

"Let go of me, Tia. You're hurting me," Ebony sobbed. She was holding on to the door know for dear life, pulling backwards as Tia pulled forward.

"You think that hurts, Bitch," Tia pried Ebony's hand form the doorknob. Ebony fell backwards, Tia still gripping her hair. Tia dragged Ebony a few inches before Ebony started kicking and screaming.

"Get off me!" Ebony wailed.

"I'm gonna call the po-lice," someone called from inside an apartment. Neighbors stepped into the hallway to see what all the commotion was about.

"I should have her call the Po-lice so they can put your jailbait boyfriend in the fuckin' pit. Back up!" Tia screamed at the neighbors. "It's none ya'll business."

Kaisia peeped the scene and knew it had gone too far. "Tee, let's go." Kaisia begged.

"Fuck that! She's not going back in there!" Tia shouted, tears running down her face.

"Look, Tee, I know. But this isn't how you should handle it. You gotta let her go," Kaisia tried to pry Tia's hands from Ebony.

"Why are you doing this to me Ebony?" Tia cried. "All I ever tried to do is to be there for you, to make you safe and happy. Do you know how much I have had to sacrifice for you, Ebony?"

Ebony jumped up as soon as they disentangled, pulled the robe to cover her nakedness and quickly ran into the apartment. She slammed the door and bolted it."

"Kay, why is she doing this?" Tia sobbed. "What are you looking at?" She shouted at the faces watching her from the hallway.

"Tee, I don't know, but you gotta get yourself together. I've never seen you like this," said Kaisia helping her friend down the stairs. Tia didn't reply.

Kaisia took the wheels on the way back home. She watched her friend, pained with an agony she never knew possible. Kaisia knew that Tia adored and loved her sister, but the scene she witnessed went deeper than love. There was an inner battle going on within Tia's heart that was far greater than any emotion built from love - and she was losing.

Tia stared into space watching cars go by. She had a single thought: Ike turned her sister against her and for that, he would die.

CHAPTER FOURTEEN

JADA, IN THE AFTERGLOW OF HER orgasm lay under C-Black breathing hard. C-Black rolled off her and Jada pulled the cover up over herself while he went to the bathroom. She reached for the blunt in the ashtray by her bedside. That man was a mutha fucker in the bedroom. She was reliving the massive orgasm she just had when the phone began ringing.

"Hello," she said as she grabbed the memory interrupter.

"What's up, Baby Girl?" replied the familiar voice on the line.

"Boo, what's up?" Jada answered in a seductive voice. "I thought you forgot about me."

"How can I forget about you, Baby? That's like forgetting dick need pussy."

"Yeah, well you don't act like it. I mean, you've been frontin' on me comin' to see you and shit," Jada reminded him.

"You know shit is hectic right now. Besides, you know my situation. How long we been doing this?" Big Joe, one of Jada's many men, fled south and was laying low after he almost got pinched in a drug bust. He was the only one of his crew that didn't get locked up and he feared they thought he had snitched.

"You're right but I miss you and it's been a minute since I seen you."

"I know but you gotta be strong. You can't break down on me now. I need you. Do you understand that?"

"Yeah."

"Okay, so is everything alright?"

"Yeah, I'm cool." Jada lit the half blunt.

"Well, check it. I need you to go pick up the same thing you picked up for me last month and drop it off with the same person."

"Why can't she?" Jada cut the conversation short as C-Black walked back into the room.

"Alright, I got you. Listen, I gotta go. Speak to you later." Jada hung up the phone and looked up at C-Black and smiled. She was gonna need him to do what he did before 'cause that man on the phone made her longing unbearable.

For the next few days Tia resisted goink over to Ike and scattering his fuckin' brains against the walls. She couldn't believe he let a seventeen year old just move in without even reaching out to her. He had to know she had peoples. He was a dead man walking but she had to bide her time.

Tia took a cab to 125th Street hoping a little shopping would clear her mind. "Pull over right here," she informed the cabbie, handing him a ten dollar bill. "Keep the change," she said as she exited in front of Apollo Express, the only top-of-the-line boutique in Harlem. It was also information central as it catered to all the hustlers too lazy to get their merchandise from downtown.

"Welcome, Beautiful," a handsome brother in his mid-twenties greeted Tia. "What's up, Tee Tee?" he swished over and grabbed Tia's hand.

"How you doing, Mark? I see you still got your swagger."

"Girrrl, you know I gotta stay on top of my game. You never know when the right person may pop in."

Tia smiled at Mark's comment because she knew that the right person was Rich. Mark was obviously still waiting. Tia thought they made a great couple, but like everything else, anything too good in the hood don't last long. Plus, Mark was such a gossip queer and that didn't fly in their kind of business. The gossip part, though, was what brought her to see him.

"So, Tee Tee, what brings your ass down to mi casa?" He walked Tia over to the Chanel section. "New arrival?" he winked.

"This is nice," Tia ran her fingers over a pink and green number. "A little shopping and a little information," Tia said, holding the outfit up to her body.

"If I got it, you got it," Mark said picking out the perfect accessories for the outfit.

"I need to know about a kat named, Ike."

"The only Ike I know is the Ike that gets money uptown."

"That's him," Tia said hoping that it really was him because she had no intel on the kat.

"Like I said, he definitely got cake. He fine as hell too. He just came home a couple of years ago from a FED beef. His brother use to get crazy cash back in the days before he got murdered. You probably know him. His name was Spice."

Tia thought about the name for a second but it didn't ring a bell.

"Anyway, back to Mr. Ike. He hangs out at Cherries on 23rd and Madison. I'm tellin' you, Tee, if you tryna to holla at him he's definitely a good catch."

"Yeah, I damn sure wanna holla at him. Anyway, Mark, good look out."

"No problem. You know you good peoples. Speaking of which, tell Rich I said come through sometime."

"I'ma do that," Tia said and continued shopping.

As Tia rode the cab back home, she thought of Ebony. What kind of position did that damn girl put her in? Ebony was fuckin' with a man twice her age, and a drug dealer to boot! It wasn't that she minded Ebony dating. If she was seeing someone her own age and someone far away from this certain-death-life, she'd have been cool. Why couldn't Ebony see that she wanted only the best for her? That she'd been working hard to prevent her from taking the path so many young girls did in the projects? They got pregnant, became junkies, got used by men to do their dirty deeds or become ill with diseases because their niggas couldn't keep their dicks in their pants or in one lane. Why did Ebony want to learn all this the hard way when Tia had sacrificed so much? She should have moved them outta Harlem when she started making cake, she thought, but that would have been a dead giveaway. She was going to fight the good fight for her sister. As it was, Tone was already not speaking to her because he thought she spoiled Ebony. All they had was each other and she wasn't about to let go of her family. I may have spoilt her, Tia said under her breath, but it was that good-for-nothing nigga, Ike who polluted her sister's mind and turned her against her own flesh and blood. That was a costly move on his part.

Tia snapped out of her thoughts when, from the cab window, she saw Tweet standing on Lenox Avenue.

"Pull over here," she instructed the cabbie. Tia got out of the cab and called out to Tweet.

"Tee, what's up?" Tweet approached her.

"Not much," Tia said looking around to see if Ebony was with her.

"I heard what went down. Are you alright?"

"Yeah, I'm good. Did you hear from Ebony?"

"Yeah, we talk almost every day. She asked about you, Tee," Tweet lied.

"Word. Tweet, do you know why she's bugging' out?"

"Tee, you know how she is, all stuck in her ways. Ever since that incident with ya'll she hasn't really been out. I go up there to hang with her for a while. Other than that, she's outta sight, outta mind."

"Tweet, do me a favor. If you hear from her or see her, tell her I said to call me. It's important that I speak with her."

"Tweet. What's up?" A girl called out.

"Joy, hold up. I'll be there in a minute."

Tia instinctively turned around to see who had called out to Tweet and was shocked to see that the girl Tweet called Joy was the same young girl from the apartment they'd stuck up a month ago. The only difference she was fully dressed.

Tia turned back to Tweet. "Tweet, you're like my second little sister. I don't wanna hear no bullshit in these streets with your name all up in it."

"Naw, Tee, I'm chillin'."

Tia went into her pocket and handed Tweet a fifty dollar bill.

"You don't have…"

Tia cut Tweet off mid-sentence. "Just put it in your pocket. You might could use it later."

Ike's cousin Mike was coming out of his house. He'd been making himself scarce since the robbery and had even though of going down to Atlanta. He turned when he heard his name.

"Ayo, Mike. Let me holla at you for a second," Crime leaned back in the driver's side of his M5 as Mike walked toward his car.

"What's up, Crime?" Mike stood by the passenger window looking inside the car for any signs of danger. Mike knew that Crime was Ike's enforcer and ever since the incident with

Dav-o, he was trying to keep a low profile. Even though Ike was his first cousin, he knew he was not exempt from Ike's murderous ways.

"Take a ride with me," Crime said, looking straight ahead.

This wasn't good, Mike thought. Mike tried to formulate an excuse in his head to tell Crime but he knew if he refused, the odds were that he'd made him get in the car by whatever means Crime had at his disposal. Mike climbed into the back seat and Crime pulled off.

"What dis about?" Mike asked, hoping that Crime would show his hand.

Crime continued driving, ignoring Mike's question. He made a right turn on 145th Street and Convent Avenue and parked in an isolated area across from City College. Crime shot

Mike a look through the rearview mirror that sent him chills. "Mike, he finally said. "I'ma need you to be honest with me." Crime never took his eyes off Mike as he spoke.

"Alright, Dawg, but what's dis about?" Mike asked, not sure he really wanted to know the answer.

"You were in the spot when it got hit…right?"

"Yeah, I was there but so was Dav-o and Fat Steve."

"Yeah, but Dav-o no longer with us, is he?" Crime said as he spun around to face Mike. "And who's Fat Steve?"

"He's one of Ike's runners. He do pick-ups and deliveries."

Crime thought about the conversation he had with Ike and didn't remember him mentioning Fat Steve so he figured he'd get as much information as he could from the pussy Mike. "Why was Steve up in the spot if he's just a runner?" Isn't that position usually just in and out?"

"Yeah, but the spot in the Bronx is his last drop off, so usually he chills until shift changes and we all come back uptown together."

"Does Ike know homeboy usually lay-up with ya'll in the spot?"

Mike thought about his next answer. He wondered how much information Ike gave Crime because the truth was that Ike didn't know Fat Steve hung out there, although he knew Fat Steve was there when the spot got hit."

"Naw, Dawg, Ike didn't know Fat Steve hang around after deliveries, but Fat Steve ain't no problem. He's cool, matter of fact. I hand-picked him myself and introduced him to Ike."

"So, by your answer, I can see that you trust this kat. Am I right to assume that?" Crime asked.

"I'ma sayin' Dawg, who can you really trust in this game?" Mike asked, thinking it was the best answer, especially if it turned out that Steve had something to do with the heist. He didn't want to be guilty by association.

Crime smiled at Mike's cleverness to delete himself from being involved with Steve should this shit blow up. At the same time, he didn't respect Mike's bitch-ass for feedin' his man to the wolves. Disloyalty was a deadly crime. "Check it," Crime smiled again, no joy reflected in the smile. "Check it. I'ma need to get in touch with homeboy, so make sure I have that information before the end of the day. Get out," Crime said, as he pulled over. He lit a Newport and watched the bitch-ass snitch walk away.

IKE'S CRIB

Ebony was a a wreck by the time Ike made it home. As soon as he'd hit the door she'd fallen into histrionics. Now a week later and she was still going on about the same thing over and over again. "Why are you stressin' this shit? I mean ya'll had a fall-out. That's life. If your sister can't accept the fact that you wanna live your life, then FUCK HER!

"Ike, you don't know her like I do. She's spiteful and I know she's just waiting for me to pop up somewhere," Ebony said staring out the window.

"Look at you! You haven't been out this fuckin' house for days. You act like she got a hit on you and shit! Listen Eb, it's not that serious. You got to get your shit together before you go crazy in this fuckin' house." Ike went over to Ebony and looked her in the eyes. He realized, at that moment, just how much he really cared about his Shorty but in order for them to make it through the storm, she would have to have a backbone and this scary cat shit wasn't the move. He also realized how young she was and that this was her first time away from home. Ike began rubbing her shoulders.

Ebony began to relax a bit under his soothing touch. She knew she was acting too nervous, maybe, even over-reacting. Tia was her sister and in her heart, Ebony knew Tia wouldn't hurt her, but that day when Tia came to the apartment, she had seen a rage in her she'd never seen before. For some reason, it scared her.

"Listen, Boo. I got something in the works right now that's gonna put us over the top. I wasn't gonna tell you until

116

it was done but it makes sense to tell you now. Once I take care of that we're outta here. I already got the first payment on a family house in Long Island."

"Baby, you serious?" Ebony turned to face Ike. "We're really gonna move?"

"Yeah. I'm serious. Why wouldn't I be? Listen Boo, you deserve the best and I wanna give you not just my heart but my time as well. Besides, I wanna get fat and raise some crumb snatchers."

Ebony's eyes glistened. She looked tenderly at Ike and though she'd never thought about having a family of her own, she wanted to have a family with Ike.

"Why you crying now?" Ike asked. Women puzzled the heck out of him.

"Because," Ebony sniffled, passing a hand over her eyes. "Because I was thinking about how happy I've been these past few weeks with you, Ike. I was thinking about us."

"Matter of fact, I bought something for you the other day and I want to see if it'll fit." Ike went to the dresser and returned to Ebony who was still crying. His hand was behind his back.

"What you hid...?"

Before Ebony could finish her sentence, Ike held up a velvet box containing a 5-carat diamond engagement ring.

Ebony covered her mouth in astonishment as tears gushed, her vision now blurred, she sank to the floor in tears.

Ike would never understand women as long as he lived. He raised her up, brought her right hand that was covering her mouth down and placed the white platinum ring on her finger. "Boo, I know we've been together only a few months, but these months have felt like a lifetime to me and I've never been happier. I want you to be my wife so we can continue to further our life as one. Will you marry me?"

Ebony just kept nodding her head up and down because words were lost in her throat. Ike lifted her in his arms and carried her to the bed.

CHAPTER FIFTEEN

JUST AROUND 9:30 P.M., Crime pulled his car into an empty spot opposite the Drew Hamilton Project Complex. From where he parked, he could see the interior of the lobby clearly. The dark provided the cover he needed to move around without being noticed. Plus, except for the small-time dealers, there were only a few people around or near the entrance of the building. He shifted his attention to the fifth-floor window on the left side of the building where Mike and Fat-Steve lived. The lights were on and someone, he couldn't figure out who, was moving around the apartment. He didn't know if anyone else was there so he sat tight. If there was a kid there, he didn't want that on his conscience, he would never be able to justify why a child's blood was on his hands. He would wait for Fat-Steve to exit the building. He didn't know if he had anything to do with the stick-up but Crime was damn sure going to apply enough pressure to find out. And he didn't give a damn if anybody saw him put Fat-Steve into his car because even though his ride was tagged, the license wasn't registered.

Crime took out a Newport, lit it and blew a cloud of smoke out the driver's window. Two guys exited the building and walked down the ramp towards the street but neither fit the description Mike had given him. Fat-Steve was fat. The time ticked by slowly and he started to think Fat-Steve might not be home. He lit another cigarette and glanced at his watch. An hour passed. Then from the corner of his eyes he saw a fat dude talking to one of the kats that was slinging in the building. He knew immediately that was his target.

Crime got out of his car and walked over to a pay phone so he would be able to watch the other side of the street without drawing too much attention to himself and hear what was going down.

"It can't be that slow. Ya'll keep running back and forth to get packs," Fat-Steve was saying.

"Dawg, that was about nine. It's like eleven now so shit is slowin' up. If you don't believe me all you gotta do is stand here a while," said the worker.

"Naw, Nigga. That's why I pay you. Check it...just give me whatever cake you got on you and put the rest of the work in the stash." Steve took the money that was wrapped in a rubber band and stuffed it in his pocket. "Listen, call me Thursday. I'm in the midst of getting some fire. We're about to turn it up out here." Steve gave his worker dap and continued down the ramp.

Crime watched the whole exchange and wondered why Mike didn't tell him homeboy was doin' his thing. Mike was probably in the blind. It didn't matter too much because a lot of nigga had side hustles, but it still didn't seem right.

Fat-Steve was now headed in Crime's direction. Crime thought this even better now that he didn't have to stalk the nigga. Steve went into the weed spot right beside where Crime was posted on the phone pretending to talk. Fifteen minutes later, Fat-Steve walked out of the spot cracking open a blunt with a razor. Crime placed an unlit Newport in his mouth and approached Steve.

"Excuse me, Playa...you have a light?"

Fat-Steve never saw the .40 caliber at Crime's side as he searched his pockets for his lighter.

"Don't worry about it, Fatboy, just get in the car," Crime said as he pressed the barrel of the gun up against Steve's love handle.

Steve dropped the blunt and razor out of shock. For a second, he thought he was going to have a heart attack. Crime escorted Steve over to the driver's side door and held it open, the gun aimed at Steve. "Slide your big ass over."

The apartment Crime took him to was empty except for a few chairs. Fat-Steve didn't struggle as Crime taped him to a chair. He noted the windows were spray painted black. At first, he thought it was a robbery but when the guy with the scar on his face only checked his waist for a burner, he knew it was something else.

After Crime finished restraining Fat-Steve, he pulled up a chair and sat facing him, one hand holding the gun against his thigh. He wanted to look Fat-Steve in the eyes. He wanted him scared. Without saying a word or taking his eyes off Fat-Steve, Crime lit a Newport and blew the smoke in his face. Crime laughed as Fat-Steve, unable to protect himself, coughed.

Beads of sweat started to form on Fat-Steve's face. The man in front of him was dangerous. The fact that he didn't cover his face to try to hide his identity was a big enough indication that he might not walk out of the room alive.

"What, what, what you want, Black?" Fat-Steve stammered. "You want the shit? Take it!"

"I hear that you involved yourself in something; that was outta your league and I only need some information from you. So, if you can help me, I can probably forget that we even met," Crime said.

"Black, I don't know what you're talkin' 'bout." Steve avoided making eye contact with his capturer.

"You know something. In fact, you're knee deep in it and the longer you play games, the shorter my patience will run. So, I'm going to ask you one more time, who struck Ike's spot?"

"Dawg, I was there. Me, Mike and Dav-o. I swear I don't have nothin' to do with dat. I would never cross Ike."

Crime got up from his chair, circled around Steve and brought the butt of gun on the top of Fat-Steve's head. He continued hitting him until Fat-Steve's chair fell over. He hit his head hard. Crime bent over Fat-Steve and pressed the barrel of the gun against his jaw.

"Open your mouth!" Crime screamed, releasing the pressure of the barrel.

Fat-Steve obeyed and Crime forced the barrel into Steve's mouth as he held the back of his neck.

"I tried being reasonable, but I see you don't understand that language, so we gotta do this in a language you're familiar with."

Fat-Steve tried to fight back tears but they betrayed him as they ran across the bridge if his nose."

"Who was down with you?" Crime asked, as he released the back of Fat-Steve's neck in preparation to blow his head off.

Fat-Steve mumbled incoherently.

Crime removed the gun from Steve's mouth, grabbed his shoulders and sat him upright once again.

"Now," Crime brought his face within inches of Fat-Steve's, "what were you saying?"

Ike was standing in front of a carwash on Lenox Avenue talking to a brown-skinned honey who caught his attention as she passed when his phone rang. "Pardon me, Sweetheart," Ike said as he turned his back to her and walked over to his ride. "Yeah, what's up?" Ike said into the phone. "Yeah, he told you all that?" A smile spread across Ike's face as he listened. "Make sure you get an address. Naw, don't make a move until you come see me. I'll be at the spot about 6. Matter of fact, make that seven. I gotta take care of something first." Ike couldn't believe his luck. Not only was he about to make a power move but he was going to take care of a situation that had been bothering for far too long. "Him? Naw, fuck him! He served his purpose. I could always get another runner. They come a dime a dozen. Yeah. Do him dirty."

Ike clicked off his cell and walked back over to where the honey was waiting for him. He smiled at the sight of her because baby girl hadn't moved a muscle. Time for some honey! The girl was a freak, Ike thought as he escorted her to his ride.

"I just got off the phone with your boss and he told me to tell you that he appreciates your honesty but you really disappointed him." Crime said as he removed his gun from his waist.

Fat-Steve gave up on trying to hold back his tears. "Please don't kill me. I'll give you my whole stash. I'll move to another state. Pleeeeeeease."

Crime grabbed the duct tape from the small table that was behind Fat-Steve and stuffed the gun back into his waist. "I'm not gonna shoot you," Crime said. "That would make me a cold-blooded killer."

Sweat mixed with the tears as Fat-Steve listened to the movements behind him for clues to Crime's next move. The hair stood up on the back of his neck when he heard Crime ripping pieces of duct tape. Fat-Steve wondered what he was going to do with more tape. Before Fat-Steve could settle his thought, Crime's turned and covered his mouth with the duct tape.

Fat-Steve felt relieved. He thought his captor was going to leave him there until somebody found him, but Crime started wrapping more the tape around his face. Steve began to struggle, moving his head side to side aware now, that Black was going to let him suffocate but it was too late. Crime covered his nose then stepped back in full view of Steve to admire his work. Steve's eyes pleaded with his captor.

Crime brought his face close so the pussy could look squarely into the eyes of his murderer. "It won't be long," he smiled at Fat-Steve. "They say the average person can go for two minutes without oxygen to the brain. After that, the lungs will start sucking in what's not there and until they collapse. By the way, the name isn't Black, it's Crime."

Crime watched as Fat-Steve struggled for air, his eyes begging him to spare his life. He watched as Fat-Steve's complexion began to turn and his struggles turned to convulsions. He watched as his eyes rolled behind his eyelids. There was one final kick for life, then silence.

CHAPTER SIXTEEN

SEAN ENTERED THE COURT room decked out in a gray two-piece Armani suit, white shirt and lilac-colored tie. He always made it a habit to be well-dressed in any situation but he'd dressed carefully today because the judge, who would be sitting in on his case, was Judge Miles. Her colleagues nicknamed her "Mrs. Holiday" because she was the spitting image of Billy Holiday. Judge Miles had a reputation of favoring young attorneys and Sean intended to use anything and everything to his advantage.

As Sean hurriedly made his way to the plaintiff's table, he noticed Rodney Jenkins' mother along with two of her other children sitting in the spectator's seats. He smiled when their eyes made contact. She shook her head and continued to look past him.

"Damn, Sean, I thought you were never going to get here," John said.

"John, have I ever let you down?" Sean asked, setting his attaché case on the table.

"You look spiffy this morning, but I only hope you have more than good looks and fancy clothes to get around this 440 Motion to Dismiss that the defense attorney dropped on us," John said, a look of concern in his eyes.

Sean, ignoring John, organized his papers and motioned for Mrs. Jenkins to approach him.

"Good morning, Mrs. Jenkins," Sean said, noting her tiredness. He could tell she'd been having a lot of sleepless nights since her son's murder seven months before.

"Good Morning, Mr. Adams."

The weariness was in her voice as well as her body. "Mrs. Jenkins I am going to ask you a question about your son's...well errr...how can I say this?" Sean was trying to find the right words so he didn't sound disrespectful or offensive to this grieving woman.

"Mr. Adams, if what you need to ask will allow my son to rest in peace then I advise that you ask," Mrs. Jenkins said. There was so much sadness in her voice that Sean almost choked up.

"I regret to ask but I need to know about your son's sex life."

"If you are asking if my son had sex, I guess my answer is yes. Like for most teenagers, sex is unavoidable around them. We talked about it once or twice and he assured me he was using protection. I had no reason to doubt him. So, yes, I know but he was a good boy, Mr. Adams and he so loved life."

Sean handed Mr. Jenkins his handkerchief as her tears fell and waited until she was more composed to ask his final question.

"Did you know that your son might have had a son?"

Blood drained from Mrs. Jenkins's face. She looked confused and shocked by the news Sean just shared.

"A son? No, Mr. Adams, that's not possible. Rodney had plans for his future and..." She broke into a sob her body going limp. Sean escorted her to a nearby seat and waited until she stopped crying. He was about to leave when she grabbed his hand.

"Who is the mother of this child?"

"Crystal Yates," Sean answered. Mrs. Jenkins threw her hand over her mouth.

"Your Honor," the defense attorney was saying. "The people have failed to produce any evidence linking my client, Mr. Dwayne Chambers, to Rodney Jenkins or his murder.

Furthermore, counsel has yet to show why my client is still sitting on Rikers Island after six months with only three appearances before a judge."

Sean smiled. He was waiting patiently for his turn to drop the bomb on the defense.

"Why are you smiling?" John whispered to Sean. "Do you not understand that we may have to let this one go?"

"The defense moves to have this case dismissed on a lack of evidence."

"Do the People have anything to address?" Judge Miles looked at Sean.

Sean rose and buttoned his jacket.

"Yes, Your Honor." Sean faced the defense table. "Your Honor, it is true that the defendant's prints were not on the gun. It is also true that most of our evidence against Mr. Chambers is hearsay, but to paraphrase the words of Malcolm X, 'A cat that gives birth to kittens in an oven does not make them biscuits.' We know that the obvious is not always obvious…"

"Objection. This is not a trial, it's a motion hearing!" the defense proclaimed.

"Overruled, Counsel. You are right. This is not a trial but a motion hearing. However, one thing it is not is a one-way argument. The charge of murder is very serious and therefore in order for me to make my decision, I must know the facts from both sides. Please, hold your objections and allow me to do my job. Continue, Counsel."

Sean smirked. He paused slightly allowing the defense to fully appreciate his round one knockout.

"Thank you, Your Honor. In a January statement the defendant made he said, and I quote, "I only knew Rodney Jenkins from around the 'hood and watching a few of his basketball games. Other than that, we never spoke or crossed paths…." This statement was made nineteen days after Rodney Jenkins was murdered on the very street he grew up on." Sean produced a document of the recorded statement.

"This is Mr. Chambers' arrest sheet. I will read a list of prior charges, dates and locations of arrests. May 3, 1990: arrested on 133rd Street and Lenox Avenue for loitering. August 15, 1993: arrested on 135th Street and Lenox Avenue for criminal possession of a controlled substance for which the defendant copped to a sentence of 3-6 years. On May 9, 1998: consistency in format in sentence the defendant was arrested for aggravated assault on his girlfriend. Charges were later dropped as his girlfriend refused to testify. On October 1, 1998the defendant was involved in a domestic dispute with the same girlfriend, this time charges were not dropped and the defendant served nine months for violation of parole."

"Counsel, where is all this leading? If there is a point, I wish you would get to it before I change my mind," Judge Miles snapped.

"I apologize, Your Honor. The point is, Jenkins was murdered on the very block the defense had most of his prior arrests yet he claims to have been neither associated nor communicated with the deceased. I find that rather odd. What also disturbs me is that his girlfriend lives in the very building where Jenkins was gunned down. Is this also a coincidence? No, Your Honor. It was jealousy. A jealous rage that was the act of a coward," Sean turned to look at the defense. "The defendant's girlfriend is Crystal Yates. She is also a cheerleader for the Rice High School basketball team, the same high school Rodney Jenkins attended. Not only did she attend the same school with Rodney, she was also his best friend since she was nine years old until his death. What I have here," Sean said, holding up a paper, "is an affidavit that was signed by Ms. Yates making these facts known, including the fact that the two had an intimate relationship that produced a child."

Sean looked over at John, who had a big grin on his face. The defense team, caught off-guard, was whispering amongst themselves, no doubt trying to regroup. Judge Miles perused the affidavit Sean had just handed her and Rodney Jenkins's mother was still trying to comprehend what had just happened.

126

"If there are no further entries, I will retire to my chambers to assess these findings. Court will be adjourned until 2 p.m." Judge Miles said.

Sean felt a rush. He always felt a tingle when he won a case but today was different. Today, he broke out of the shell that justice had kept him in. Today, Sean had entered the court as ADA, and left the courtroom as Mr. Sean D. Adams, lawyer for the people.

HARLEM

Tia sat in the Honeycomb with her home girls and Rich preparing for their trip to Baltimore the following day. She liked the way everything had come together and especially because Jackie had come through. Toya had managed to get two whips fully equipped with police scanners and hidden compartments. Jada had come through with the IDs. They'd cost an arm and a leg, but worth it. Jackie got reservations at a motel right outside of town and close to the house her home girl was going to let them use.

"Check it, ya'll," Tia said to the crew. "This is going to be the driving arrangements. Jada, you are going to be pushing one of the rentals and Toya, you're going to push the other. I'ma gonna flood your whip with the work and the heat. Jada, you're gonna be decoy for Toya just in case somethin' goes wrong and she gotta blow it on the highway. Me and Jackie will ride together in her car. We'll be the lead car. Jada you'll be right behind us, and Toya you'll be in the back. I'ma give each of you a walkie-talkie once we pull out tomorrow. I'll also have one. This way we can keep each other on point. Kaisia and Rich are staying back so we can Western Union back the money instead of travelling with it."

"Kaisia, I thought you were rollin' with us?" Toya said.

"I was, but my mom's is going to New Jersey. Her uncle passed away this week and I don't have anybody to keep Dakota."

"I'm sorry to hear that. Give your moms my condolences," Toya said.

"Ya'll take care of business and get back safe so we can party."

"Yeah, that's what I'm talkin' 'bout," Jada shouted doing a whipping movement.

"Matter of fact, Rich. I'ma gonna need you to do me a favor from time to time when I'm gone. I'll need you to get in touch with Ebony for me and try to talk some sense into her," Tia said.

"No problem, Tee. In fact, I'ma have Tweet take me over there so I can talk to her face-to-face."

"Rich you don't gotta do all that," Tia said. She didn't want Rich to cop a beef with that dead-man-walking, Ike.

"Don't worry, Tee. I'm not gonna start no shit. I just wanna vibe with her personally and I don't think I'll be able to do it over the phone."

"Alright, Rich but if she starts acting funny and shit just pull back and I'll handle it when I get back." Tia didn't really want to get Rich in the middle of her drama but she had to keep the idea of family on Ebony's mind while she was away. Plus, she needed someone she could trust to look out for her.

"We'll ya'll it looks as if everything is on point." Tia knew, though, that nothing was final until it was complete.

BROOKLYN DA'S OFFICE

Sean sat at his desk going over the Rodney Jenkins case. Although he had won the hearing a few days before, he still needed to iron out his facts because there was no telling what kinds of tricks the defense attorney would pull out of his bag. That was his advantage as a lawyer, a good one always prepared for surprises and he was a good lawyer. Sean's thoughts suddenly wandered off track and ended up on Tia. It had already been almost a month since they'd seen each other and he was, well, missing her company. He must have it bad because he barely knew her but he was smitten. Sean looked at his watch then at the phone. He decided to call her.

The phone rang three times before the voice mail came on. "Tia, this is Sean. I just called to see how you are doing. I'll be at the office late tonight so if you want to call me, the number is 555-2081. Bye." He hung up the phone, DISAPPOINTMENT sapped his joy. Sean felt as if he had just placed a desperation call to Mother Theresa. The phone on his desk immediately rang back. Excitedly, he grabbed it.

"Yeah, John," Sean slumped back in his chair.

"You don't sound too happy to hear from me?"

"What do you want, John?"

"Oh, I see it's that time of the month, huh?"

"What time of the month? John, what are you talking about?"

"Let me know when the bleedin' stops and I'll call then, Partner," John laughed.

"So now you got jokes. You really need to work on them. So, what's up? And, please don't tell me any bad news about the Jenkins case."

"No, Partner. In fact, it's great news and I felt I should be the one to deliver it to you."

Sean sat forward in his chair. John had his full attention.

"Are you familiar with the drug bust that brought down the Dynasty Crew?"

"Yeah, it was all in the papers. You mean the drug raid from 115th to 120th Streets, right? Why? What about it?"

"Well, the DA wants you to handle it."

"WHAT?" Sean screamed into the phone.

"You heard me right, Man. He liked the way you performed on the Jenkins case and he assigned you to handle one of the biggest cases out of Harlem. Are you up to it?"

Sean was shocked. He sat still to soak in what he'd just heard.

"Hello…hello? Sean, are you there?"

"Yeah…yeah, I'm here. Just digesting what I just heard. It's a surprise. That's all."

"Well, Buddy, get to digesting because you have a lot of work to do on this one and I mean a whole lot," John said, putting emphasis on the words whole lot.

"Okay. I'm ready. Just point me in the right direction and I'll take it from there."

"Listen, Sean a few things you should know. Pay close attention. This case has over thirty-four co-defendants. Thirty-three of them are just pawns in the DA's eyes. He wants the top man and he wants him like yesterday. Your goal is not so much the organization, although that is your calling card but your target is Kato Pascal."

CHAPTER SEVENTEEN

TWEET WAS THE FIRST PERSON Ebony called to share the news about her engagement to Ike. She screamed with excitement, "We have to celebrate!"

Ebony declined, at first. She was still sad about her fight with her sister and though she believed Tia was wrong, she missed her.

"Bitch, is you crazy. You just got engaged! "

"Okay," Ebony said, "let's meet at 34th Street later. We can shop and celebrate."

Ebony got dressed. She wore something silvery to match her new ring. Who would ever have thought! She met Tweet at the 34th stop. There usual spot.

"Let me see. " Tweet grabbed her hand. "That shit ain't no joke, huh. Who's gonna be your maid-of-honor?" Tweet asked, as they strolled down the avenue looking into department store windows.

Tweet's question caught Ebony by surprise. She had been so wrapped up in the excitement of getting engaged, she hadn't started to think of those details. She stopped in front of a shoe store display window, not to admire the shoes, but to think about Tweet's question. When she was fifteen, she used to imagine getting married. She and Tia would to sit up late into the night going over every detail imaginable. They would laugh and playfully rehearse the ceremony. Tia would always tell her that when she found Mr. Right, she would spare no expense and go all out for her wedding. Ebony found it strange for Tweet to ask her that question. She blinked back tears. The only person in her life that deserved that honor was her sister, Tia.

"You still didn't answer me," said Tweet, standing beside Ebony with her hands on her hips.

Forcing a smile, Ebony looked at Tweet. "You know it's you, Chicken."

"It better be or I would whip your ass right here on 34 Street in front of all these white folks."

"Shut up and let's go inside and try on these shoes." Ebony stepped into the shop, with Tweet following her.

Ike was beside himself with anticipation as he jumped into Crimes car. "What's the word, Gangsta?"

Crime crushed his Newport into the ashtray and cranked up the radio to drown out the conversation he was about to have with Ike. "The word is the word. It was an inside job. The fat mutha fucker had eyes that were bigger than his intelligence. Not only was he stupid but he was bold enough to get down with a couple of bitches." Crime adjusted his chair so he could lean back in a more comfortable position.

"So, did he reveal who these bitches were or are you going to keep me in guess mode?" asked Ike, not feeling the fact that Crime was keeping him in suspense.

Crime smiled. It always tickled him that no matter what position a person had in life, you can always find something that people wanted and needed. "Yeah, I got the wire on one of them Shorties. The other he didn't know but that shouldn't be a problem once we holla at homegirl."

"Who is she?" Ike asked as he motioned to a guy standing by a building to come to the car.

"Who's that?" Crime said, sitting up as the stranger approached. He did not like strangers.

"He's a nobody who knows some people. But anyway, go ahead and finish what you were saying."

Crime checked out the person who was by now standing at the passenger window talking with Ike. Crime didn't like coming into contact with strangers, especially ones he knew nothing about, but he knew Ike wouldn't put him in a situation without an explanation. Now he'd just wait to see what Ike was talking about.

The stranger nodded his head, agreeing with something Ike ran down to him and then walked off as if he was given a direct order.

Ike looked at Crime. "There's one of my soldiers, I just put him on standby, but anyway, as you were saying."

"Oh yeah, I got his cousin's info. She's one of the broads that was down with that. Her name is Kaisia. Do you know her? She lives right in the Polo Grounds.

Ike sat awhile pondering. He picked his brain for any memory of a Kaisia but could find none. "Naw, Shorty don't sound familiar but that doesn't matter because when I'm through with here, she's gonna always be remembered."

"So, what's the next move?" Crime asked.

"Just be on standby. I may not need you past this point," Ike reached into his pocket and handed Crime a manila folder. "This is the rest. I'll get at you in a couple of days." Ike gave Crime dap and stepped out of the car.

Crime opened the envelope and flipped through the many bills. Crime liked Ike because he always paid in full. As Crime watched Ike walk away he wondered just how much cake his operations made. Crime turned on the engine, lowered the music and pulled into traffic.

HARLEM

"I'ma gonna be outta town for a few days, Tone. I need to get away and clear my head," Tia said. She was packing clothes and a few personal items into a duffle bag.

Tone stood by her bedroom door. He felt completely estranged and shut off from his sister. He understood what Ebony must have been feeling to make such a big move. Things were so much simpler when their mother was alive. All the good times and laughter had seeped out of their lives with her death. Tone did not want to go down memory lane because the regret and pain was too much to bear. Not just for his mother but also for whatever it was that was driving him and his sisters further and further apart.

"Tee, it's not helping anybody if you just keep running away from problems."

"FUCK TONE, YOU KNOW ABOUT RUNNING. DO YOU?" Tia knew that Tone didn't deserve her anger but she was tired, just plain tired of always being the one in control and ending up as everybody's fall guy. Her entire life was one of constantly being strong; the role model. Her mother used to tell her, 'since you're the oldest, you have to set a good example for your siblings to follow. There'll be a time when I might not be here to watch after ya'll.' Tia still couldn't believe how prophetic those words had been and they haunted her. She was doing what she had to do. Tia looked at Tone, though she did not apologize. "Listen Tone. I'm not running. I just need some me time. I know it may seem as though I'm taking the coward's way out but that would never be the case. I just need to do me for a minute." Tia turned and walked over to where Tone stood. "Tone, I know shit seems crazy right now and everybody's been buggin' out, but I want you to know I love you and Ebony more than life itself. That is why I gotta step off for a while. Everything will be alright once I get back. That I promise."

"Tee, I know you got a lot on your plate. I see it every day and I also see that it is weighing down on you emotionally, and although I say and do things that may seem as though I blame you for what's going on I want you to know that I would never hold you responsible. If anything, you have done more than your share to make sure that we were alright and for that, I will forever be in your corner. I just don't want to lose another sister."

Tia couldn't hold back years of suppressed emotions. It felt as though she drained her heart out in tears as she threw her arms around her brother's neck and fell against his shoulders.

Tone embraced his sister, stroking her hair in comfort. Tia lifted her head and smiled at her brother. His warm smile back reassured her that everything would be alright again.

"Listen," Tone wiped a tear with his finger. "we gotta get you packed and ready for your trip because the faster you're out the house, the faster I can get my groove on." He once again smiled at his sister and then kissed her forehead. "I love you back, Big Sis."

LOWER WEST SIDE

Sean sat in his home office going over the details of the Dynasty Drug case. New York's finest, with help from the Feds, did a good and thorough job on the case. It seemed like an open and closed case, so why did the DA give it to him, Sean wondered. He studied the photographs of every single co-defendant in the case. He compared them to the pyramid listing of everyone, from runners to lieutenants to the head nigga in charge, Kato Pascal. Sean stared at Kato's picture. He was his target. He flipped through the report of Kato's priors, and noted that he was dismissed on everyone, even for an attempted murder of a police officer. The guy had some serious lawyers working on his behalf. He'd surely have to ask John about that the next time they met. His phone rang interrupting his review of the report.

"Hello. You've reached the Adams residence. Who is calling?"

"You sound so professional over the phone. I take it as a sign that this is a good time to call."

Sean grabbed his phone and went to the bedroom. He wanted to be comfortable while talking to the girl with the voice of an angel who was blowing up his mind. "I was beginning to wonder if I'd blown my chance with you on our date." He hoped his attempt at being funny was not actually the case.

"No, Honey, I'm not a one-night stand kind of girl. Besides, if I felt that way I'd have, at the least, called to let you know things wouldn't work out."

"So, is this the call in which you tell me it didn't work out?" Sean braced himself.

"In fact, just the opposite, Mr. Adams. I was wondering if I could see you again."

Sean damn near dropped the phone. The girl was bold, large and in charge. He knew these days women had no qualms about making the first moves but...

"Does my directness intimidate you?" Tia asked.

"No...in fact, it turns me on a great deal. Plus, it gives me a chance to play possum."

"So, what does that make me, the wolf?" Tia had turned on the seduction.

"No. You more of a wild cat that sneaks up on its prey. Truth be told, I wouldn't mind if you caught me in those claws of yours. If you want, you can take advantage of my inability to escape."

"Purr." Tia felt the lining of her panties dampen. Her heart was racing a mile a minute and she wanted to catch him in her claws if only for the night. Tia, who had little interest in being coy with men somehow felt she could be natural and herself with Sean. It seemed that they had known each other for ages and though he was an ADA blood sucker even that she was willing to ignore. At least for tonight. "You still didn't answer my question, Sean. When can I see you again?"

"As soon as possible or is that too soon?"

"No, I'd say that's just right. Too bad I'm going out of town tomorrow and won't be back for a few days."

"Is the trip business or personal?"

"It's a little of both, but more personal."

"Would you like to come to my place tonight?" The words fell from Sean's lips before he could sensor his thoughts. "I mean we can just hang out and watch a movie. I'll even cook. I know how to make the best steak in town."

Tia laughed at Sean's clever way of covering up his true intent. "Sean, you are a crazy man but you don't have to go through all that trouble. I'll tell you what. It's a deal, but only if I can cook for you and I won't take no for an answer."

"Well, I'm not going to argue with a pretty woman. Besides, I would have really hated myself if I messed up the steak."

They both laughed at the same time.

"Where does a girl go to cook steaks?" Tia asked.

Sean gave her his address and she informed him she'd hop in a cab and be there shortly.

"I'll be waiting for your downstairs," Sean replied, clicking off and doing a celebration dance.

"I'll call you when I'm five minutes away."

Tia freshened up wondering why on earth she was messing with an ADA. She chalked it up to the emotional rollercoaster of her confrontation with Ebony and then her meltdown with Tone earlier. Maybe that was why she'd called him in the first place because somehow she knew she could find comfort there. She needed someone to love her, if only for tonight.

The cab pulled up and, as promised, Sean was waiting to greet her. He opened the car door and then leaned in to pay the driver.

Tia stepped out of the cab. "You didn't need to do that I have mon…"

"I am sure of it. But let me be the man I like to be. As long as you are in my presence, your money is no good."

"Thank you," Tia said and fell in step as they walked toward his condo.

Sean's unit was huge, almost twice the size of the apartment she shared with her siblings. You'd have to be making good cake to get an apartment like this in the city, she thought. The foyer opened into a spacious living room. The pine floors were so highly polished, she could see she reflection. It was like looking in a mirror. The curtains were drawn against the evening dusk and dimly lit candles gave the living room a warm glow. Sean took Tia's bag as they descended three steps into the living room. He spun a dial and flooded the room in lights.

"Make yourself comfy and I'll drop these in the closet," Sean reached for Tia's bag and jacket.

Tia stood in front of the display cabinet that held various awards and citations. She read one that said, "For upholding justice and continued excellence in serving your fellow man, The Bar Associations awards this honor of Excellency to Mr. Sean Adams." Next to the award was a picture Tia assumed was his graduation from law school. Beside it, a picture of an older man that looked so much like Sean she had to do a double take. It was his father, who had passed away, she recalled. She could like this kind of respectable life. Was she crazy to be up this man's house when a man like Sean was off limits for so many reasons? Tia looked at the picture again and sighed. Immediately, she realized that Sean was standing behind her. Out of habit she spun around quickly. "Do you always sneak up on unsuspecting women?" She laughed, toning down her usual reflexes.

Instead of answering, Sean wrapped his arms around Tia and pulled her into an embrace. Tia closed her eyes and allowed herself to be drawn into his warmth. She wanted this life that Sean represented; she just didn't know how she could ever have it. She stayed locked in his embrace because she knew that this was the man and the moment she'd been waiting for her entire life. She looked up and Sean was searching her eyes as she much as she was searching her heart. If he could read her mind, she wondered what he would do. She tried to read his thoughts but his warm lips found her eager and wanting lips. Tia surrendered to the moment and responded hungrily to his tender kiss. Her legs went limp but his firm grip kept her from falling. As much as she knew she was dancing with fire, she did not have the will to break the connection and the fire that was rising inside her. The very fire than could consume her. Maybe not having true love was the price she'd have to pay for the life she'd been forced, by circumstance, to live.

Sean raised his head from her lips though his arms still bound her to him as if he was afraid to let her go. "I'm sorry. I didn't plan this. I didn't intend for this to happen. I don't know what has come over me but I've never felt so connected and deeply attracted to any woman before. I know this sounds like a really bad pick up line, but Beloved, I've wanted to do that from the first day we met." He released Tia who did not step back.

"Why be sorry? I'm not, so let's make it happen again," Tia threw her arms around Sean's neck. The kiss they shared this time was searing and passionate and only teased the fire burning in them both. "Aren't you hungry?" Tia whispered against his ear.

"I am." Sean said, his hand moving swiftly to her button.

"What do those have to do with steak?" Tia asked seductively as she pushed his hand away. The way to a man's heart is in the kitchen, she thought, and if this man could ever have been hers, the kitchen was her best shot. "Point me to the food," she smiled.

"Okay," Sean replied reluctantly as he rose to show Tia to the kitchen. He pointed out where everything she would need was stashed. While it wasn't very large, the kitchen was laid out efficiently with enough counter space to do multiple things at once. Tia felt at home in the kitchen and wanted to be in this kitchen cooking Sean's meals, taking care of him.

She brushed aside the feeling and went to work quickly to make the steaks. Her mother used to make steak with peppers and onions on special occasions for her father and she'd shown Tia how to make them. She decided to make it for Sean.

Each time he came into the kitchen, Sean put his arms around Tia and asked, "Are you finding everything you need?" After the third time, she told him he was making her nervous.

Tia felt good fixing Sean's meal. It felt normal to her. That's what she should be doing, not running the streets. When the meal was ready, Sean set the table. As they sat down to eat, Sean held her hand in prayer. She was too through. This was the final confirmation they were meant for each other.

"I haven't had a meal like this since the last time I went to Sunday dinner at church. I have to do that more often now that you've reminded me what a good home cooked meal taste like. You must be a country girl because you sure cook like you've been raised on a farm. Maybe even butchered the cow yourself?" Sean eased back in his chair and rubbed his overstuffed stomach.

Tia began clearing the table and Sean immediately rose to help. "I can handle this alone," Tia removed the plate from his hand. "Why don't you go start the movie? I'll be there with you soon." What the hell was with this Donna Reid shit, but she really liked it.

Tia smiled at Sean and thought again how wonderful it was doing something so normal and simple. "No I'm not from the country," Tia said putting plates into the sink. "I was born and raised in Harlem."

"Me too." Sean said. "I told you we have too much in common."

"How did you end up down here?"

"Closer to the office and Harlem got way too crazy. I almost ended up in Riverdale but you need a family for that. I

139

love it down here but I miss the people of Harlem. Glad I found you."

Tia joined Sean on the couch just as the movie was about to start. He'd chosen the movie, Soul Food. He dimmed the lights and lit a few candles. It was romantic.

Tia moved closer to him. "Dessert?" she teased as she turned the volume down a tad.

Sean couldn't care if she'd turned it off. He'd seen the movie a thousand times and with her beside him on the couch, he was unable to concentrate on anything but her beauty. She was a very beautiful woman who was always well put together. Tonight, she was wearing a plain white T-shirt that matched her ankle socks and hugging hipster jeans. Sean moved a strand of hair that was covering her right eye and she turned to look at him. What, he wondered, was responsible for the melancholy behind her beautiful eyes? He continued to stoke her hair again sensing her deep sadness and his heart ached for her. *Dear God, if you let her accept me on the inside I will do all I can to help remove the deep scars this woman bears alone.*

Tia wasn't convinced that love at first site existed but she couldn't deny the enormity of the feelings that was growing inside her for this man she hardly knew. Life could be so cruel. If Sean got a chance to know who she really was, he'd pivot on the spot and run like hell. Her past and her present did not allow for a future with Sean. Tia felt so comfortable she was tempted to tell him the details of her sordid life. But they lived diametrically opposite lives and in completely different worlds. He would never be able to truly understand her struggles. Her lover could, in fact, be her capturer. Tia stared at him intensely and as their eyes locked, each in their space of need, Tia brought Sean's head down and met his lips with a kiss. Unlike the soft and tender kiss of before, this was a kiss of need, yearning and the desire for him to erase her past and fill her with a future. "Make love to me," Tia murmured through stifled tears.

Sean lifted Tia from the couch and took her to the bedroom.

HARLEM

"If this is the same Kaisia from Polo Grounds, I know her for sure. Her baby pops is a kat named Ty. He gets his money in P.A. but homie is a bird. I don't think he and Shorty even pump like that no more," said one of Ike's young soldiers, as they sat in the back of a bodega where Ike had called a meeting.

"Do you know where this kat stays at because we can use him to get at her even if she's not feelin' homes, she's still gonna feel compassion of his punk-ass just because she got seed with him. So, find out what you can before this week is out and get back to me."

Ike walked over to a mid-weight girl in her early twenties named Mika. He always used her for getting accurate information. She was one of them hood-rats who had a gift for talking her way into everybody's business and a talent for details. "I need you to hang around the projects and do you, but what I really need you to do is find out what Shorty's about and who she fucks with on the R.B. (regular basis). Don't ask too many questions for whomever these chicks are, I don't think they're stupid."

Mika nodded her head in agreement. What she really wanted to ask was why Ike didn't give her the okay to air her out—problem solved. Mika held her trap because she knew it wasn't in her best interest to tell Ike what to do. But she'd do anything for him. If only he could look her way once.

After Ike had everybody on the same page regarding the Kaisia situation, he redirected his attention to the out of town move they were about to make. "While I'm gone, Baby-J will be hittin' ya'll with regular packages and if I hear any shit when I get back, I'm going to deal with it personally. Also, when I get back I'ma call a meeting the day after because there's gonna be a few changes in how we do things. We were vulnerable once and I don't have any plans to let that shit go down like that again." Ike looked around the room to make sure that everyone clearly understood. Ike's cell rang just as he was about to close the meeting. Ike hit the answer button. "Ice baby, what's up?"

Ike spoke briefly to Iceman and then turned back to the meeting. "Okay, ya'll, we're done." Ike walked out the back door of the store and was gone. The others filed out one-by-one as per their precautionary procedure so as not to draw attention to themselves.

LOWER WEST SIDE

Tia head was rested on Sean's bare chest. She twirled his chest hair through her fingers. If she could bask in this memory forever, it would've been alright with her. She closed her eyes, not from tiredness, but to relive the moment they came together as one. Sean's touch had been as soft as a feather as he undressed her. She in turn had undressed him. When their naked bodies touched and molded to each other, it was like the missing party of a puzzle had finally been found. Sean had traced her body with his soft lips nudging, probing and teasing her to the brink of ecstasy. She'd held him close, nuzzling as close as she could get. He'd tasted salty and spicy at the same time, how symbolic. They hungrily explored each other's bodies and when Sean had finally entered her, it was like she'd lost her virginity for the very first time. This was what making love when being in love felt like, she'd thought; tender, fulfilling and emotionally consuming. When Tia had climaxed, tears from nowhere poured down her face and she'd clamped her legs tightly around Sean because she never again wanted to let him go. She felt so incredibly happy, she had to bite down hard on the satin pillow to stop herself from cooing the forbidden words, 'I love you.'

"You're okay, Beloved?" Sean interrupted her flashback with a kiss to her forehead.

"Yes," she murmured. "I never understood the meaning of making love until now."

"I know what you mean. I always thought sex was just sex until tonight. Thank you."

Tia remained silent. She couldn't risk speaking and betraying her true feelings. Sean had her nose wide open and it scared her. He was sharing her thoughts, her interests, her body and was on the same page with her emotions. They even had compatible zodiac signs, he a Capricorn, she a Virgo, no surer sign! Though in her heart Tia knew there was no other perfect match for her than the man whose arms she laid it, she was only too painfully aware that they had found each other too late and at the wrong time. In another time and space, this was the life Tia would have chosen. Today, it was too late to turn back the hands of time and her very soul ached so badly.

Tia caressed the taut muscles of his stomach. "Sean."

"Huh." He sounded as though he was drifting into sleep.

"Do you ever think about just leaving? I don't mean just New York but everything. Your job, your family and everything you know and just starting over with a new identity?

"Yeah. Once when I was younger, I wanted to run away from home. Typical teenage angst when no-one-understands-you kind of thing. After my father's death, I guess I lost the desire to run away. I was now man of the house and as such I had to uphold my family's values. My father passed away when I was sixteen. He never got a chance to see me go to law school but it was his voice that was constantly in my head that kept me pushing forward. If I had given up on life even when I felt like it during law school, I would have been giving up the man my father raised me to be the man I am. Life is like that. Filled with scars and pain. You just have to go through it. Tia," he said his voice so genuine that she might have started crying again. "I am here for you."

Tia buried her head in his chest. She wondered if Sean had pulsed how stuck she was in this life. She knew that he understood something was amiss in her life. Maybe from the question she'd asked but she could see it in his eyes way before that he was trying to understand just who she was as a woman. Actually almost from the day they'd met, she felt that he was ready to be concerned about her scars and pain. Tia looked at the man who could have made her whole and said to herself just one more time…just one more, for if she stayed with this man she would have revealed who she was and watch him walk out the door. "I bet you can make this pain go away," she reached under the cover for the thing that was making a tent in the sheet.

"Make it go away?" Sean rolled her over and positioned himself on top of her.

"Yeah, baby make it go away," Tia whispered.

CHAPTER EIGHTEEN

"DAMN! YA'LL GOT THIS PLACE LOOKING CRAZY," Tia walked into the room, Jackie trailing in behind her.

"Hey Jackie," Kaisia walked over to her and gave her dap. "What'd you expect? We movin, ain't we?" She turned to Tia.

"No doubt. " Tia greeted the rest of the Posse.

Jackie waved to everyone. All waved back except Toya, who it seemed was still not feelin' her.

"Tee, can I see you for a minute," Kaisia said. The women stepped into another room. "I've been trying to call you all night. Did you get the messages I left on your business line?" Kaisia said nervously.

"Nah, I wasn't home and I didn't stop back at my place. I came straight from where I was here. Why? What's up?" Tia sensed something was very wrong. Kaisia, what going on?" Tia pressed. Is Dakota alright?" The last time Tia had seen Kaisia this distressed was when Dakota was admitted to the hospital.

Kaisia nodded in affirmative. "They found my cousin," Kaisia's voice broke, as she tried to continue.

Tia didn't quite understand what Kaisia was trying to say. "Sit down Kaisia and catch your breath." Tia pushed her into a chair and pulled up another one beside her. She took her friends hand in hers and said, "Now tell me what's wrong, Kay. What about your cousin?"

Tia watched tears cascade down Kaisia's face landing on her leg. This was serious Tia thought and was glad Kaisia was not on the drive.

"They killed him. They murdered my cousin. Fat-Steve is dead Tee." Kaisia leveled Tia with a look.

Maybe it was a dream but when Tia saw the look in Kaisia's eyes, she knew this was a real as it came.

"Who killed him, Kay?"

"I don't know. Homicide found him last night. Somebody put his body in a plastic bag and left him in Morningside Park.

Tia got an instant headache that threatened to muddle her thinking. But she had to stay focused. The murder could probably be a coincidence because Fat-Steve was involved in the life and in this life nothing was guaranteed. Still, she wasn't ready to rule out the possibility that his death was somehow connected to them. "Did you tell the peoples what happened?" Tia asked hoping she had not.

"No. I didn't want to take them off task and get them overly concerned." Kaisia said. It was only half the truth. The other half was that she didn't want them to see her fall apart. She was a soldier. Kaisia didn't mind falling apart in front of Tia because Tia had seen her vulnerable too many times to count but the rest of the Posse depended on her strength.

"Kay, you did right not telling them. I'll holla at them but you got to listen to me. Until we find out the deal, I want you to go somewhere else besides your mom's house. I'm not saying that this has anything to do with us but we can't take those kinds of chances. I'ma gonna call Rich and put him on point as well. I want ya'll two to stay in contact at all times. Do you have heat?"

"Yeah. I got the Ruger," Kaisia said.

"Okay. Keep that on hand and at no time are you to leave without it." Tia really thought it would be best for Kaisia to ride with them but it was impossible because they couldn't bring Dakota on such a trip. The risk was too great. "Kay,"

Tia switched subjects. "What's up with Ty? You said he'll be outta town, right?"

"Yeah, that's what he told me but you know that nigga be frontin' just so he won't have to be bothered with being a father."

"Maybe so, but that's not the issue right now. We gotta get you and Dakota somewhere other than your current residence. Did Fat-Steve know where Ty stayed?"

"He didn't too much like Ty so he never inquired about him. Besides Ty is never in one place long enough for anybody to keep track of where he lay his head."

Tia didn't like Ty either but she was thankful that homeboy had sense enough to keep his residence low-key. Do you think he'll let you stay at his crib for a while or at least until we get back?"

Kaisia really didn't want to be bothered with Ty but she wasn't ready to risk having her daughter caught up in some shit because of their differences. "I can probably convince him to let us stay there for a while. He maybe a deadbeat but I doubt he'd rather me walk the streets with his child."

"Okay, Kay. You'll be al'rigth. We'll be back as soon as we can." Tia reached over and touched her friends face, wiping away the tears that clung to her lashes refusing to fall. "And don't worry about nothing. I'm going to break it down to the girls. You just get yourself together and come back into the living room when you're ready."

The crew began moving out for their departure. Jada was standing next to Tia loading Jackie's car with duffle bags of clothes.

"Fat-Steve is dead." Tia said to Jada.

"What? Do you, do you think, Tee? I mean, is there any reason to think Fat-Steve got murdered because we hit that spot?"

"It's too hard to call at this moment, but there's a strong possibility. I just hope that if it is the case, Fat-Steve didn't blow Kaisia up. That's my main worry right now." Tia said.

Jada slammed the car trunk. "She really ought to be coming with us while shit might get hot around here."

Tia looked over at Kaisia who was talking to Toya by the one of the rental cars. Toya looked over at Tia and briefly nodded her head. Nobody noticed the exchange except the person who was supposed to see it. Tia nodded back her recognition to the fact that she knew about Fat-Steve's death.

Like Tia, Toya also knew that Kaisia was trying to be strong. Shit, this was a right fuck-up. This was the reason for their "no family" rule in the first place because there were risks when lines were crossed. It was not Tia who brought Fat-Steve into the game. But Kaisia. She had convinced them that the large amount of cake involved was worth the risk and would probably be enough to put then on the straight and narrow. They had taken a vote and although Tia had the last say, she was a democratic leader and had gone along with the plan.

Tia too was regretting her decision. It was a grave mistake and the last of its kind she'd ever make. Tia knew that even if Fat-Steve's murder didn't involve them, they were still obliged to go all out to find out who had murdered him. If not, there would always be a question mark over their heads and Kaisia would never rest until the right amount of blood was spilled. And if it did involve them they had to have a plan.

"Is everybody ready?" Jackie asked as she came from across the street where she'd gone to buy a couple packs of cigarettes. She climbed into the passenger side of her car. Tia and Jada went over to where Toya and Kaisia were talking.

"Toy, you ready?" Jada asked.

Toya nodded and turned to give Kaisia a hug. Toya, not the emotional type wanted to remember this moment if shit went south. "Hold your head, Girl. We'll be back in a few." Kaisia looked at Toya and smiled as she got into her car.

Tia reached into her pocket and handed Kaisia the keys to the Honeycomb. "Remember, Kay. Rich is only a phone call away and hopefully Ty will let you stay at his crib. Just chill while we are gone. Lay low. If shit don't work out check in at the Honeycomb but I'd rather you not be alone."

Tia, Jada, and Kaisia all hugged, then parted. Jada waved at Kaisia as the cars got ready to pull away and watched with sadness as she flagged down a gypsy cab. Jackie's car pulled out first followed by Jada and then Toya, as planned. Tia sat back and prepared for the long three-and-a-half-hour ride to B-More but her mind lingered heavily on Kaisia. She felt as though she was abandoning one of her closest friends.

CLUB PARADISE

Ike stepped into the plush office and although the club was empty, he knew that later that night it would be packed with the usual club crawlers. It had been a little over three months since the club had opened but it was already returning a profit on his investment. Ike thought about making a long-term commitment and even spoke to Ice about opening a chain of clubs. Ice agreed but suggested that they wait to see how the out-of-town business panned out before he made a decision. Ike respected Ice's input because he'd proven to Ike on countless accounts that he was a great thinker and good businessman. His instincts were spot on.

Iceman stood up from his desk as Ike entered. The men shook hands and Ike took a seat across from Ice. Ice walked to the mini-bar and poured himself a shot of Hpnotiq. Ice didn't offer Ike a drink because he knew he didn't drink. "I just got in touch with an old friend who has some friends in Ohio that are looking to cop some heavy weight." Ice took a sip of his drink and walked back to sit at his desk.

"How much weight we talkin' about?" Ike figured it was major or Ice would not have told him about it.

"For now, we are talking about five keys and if the product is any good they are willing to deal with us as their suppliers. I have other people who would be interested in this come-up but I wanted to come to you first."

Ike estimated that he could easily add another three birds to their shipment but he also weighed the risk should something go wrong. If something did go wrong, that would mean not only would he'd be assed out of the Ohio move but he'd jeopardize his current operations in the city. The risks were there but he wasn't in the business to turn down money. "Alright, set it up but give me a couple of days to load up. I gotta change some things around being that the situation changed."

Ice agreed. "Don't worry about the mules. I'll cover any extra fees that may attach, being that they got more stuff to carry and all. I'll also call the hotel to change your reservations. Just let me know when you're ready to roll."

Ike stood up and reached across the table to shake Ice's hand. "Playa that was good look out. I owe you one."

"Don't even worry about it. As long as you keep doing business with me, I'm gonna make sure you're first priority. By the way, if you're not busy tonight why don't you and your young lady stop by the club? We got a couple of performers coming through. There's a couple of heads I wanna introduce you to," Ice said. He rose and walked Ike to the office door.

"I'm not going to make you no promise because there are things I gotta take care of while I got the time to do it. What I may do is send my girl through with a couple of her homegirls."

"Okay, do that and don't worry, she'll be in good hands. Oh yeah, congrats on your engagement."

Ike turned around to face Ice. He'd never mentioned his engagement to him. "How did you know that?" Ike seemed curious.

Ike didn't mind that Ice knew about his engagement. In fact, he'd have told him if so much stuff hadn't been going on. Still, he would have to have a talk with Ebony about the importance of silence. Ike looked at Ice and patted him on the arm. "Listen, Playa, I'll see you later." With that, he turned his back to Ice and walked down the stairs.

Kaisia watched Dakota as she played in the small kids' park in the projects. It was a nice day so she didn't mind being out early. She was on guard and her nerves were on edge. She was waiting for Ty, who was late as always, to come by and drop off the keys. When she'd mentioned that she needed to stay with him because she and her mother was beefing, which was about the only reason he'd let her stay, she was lying. If she'd told him about Fat-Steve his need for self-preservation would have kicked in and he would never had let her stay. As it was she had to go through the 411. First, he'd asked her why she didn't just stay with one of her friends until her moms calmed down. To that Kaisia had copped an attitude and told him that Dakota wasn't one of her friend's responsibility. She hated using her daughter as a weapon but drastic times called for drastic measures. He agreed reluctantly.

Kaisia sat on the bench watching every corner of the park, especially for faces she didn't recognize. She kept her purse on her lap and her hand inside it on the butt of the gun. The Ruger was warm to the touch and she felt a little reassured. Kaisia thought of her cousin and blamed herself for his death. He was so young, she kept saying over and over to herself. She was thankful that his mother, her aunt, had passed away for this would have surely killed her. Kaisia snapped to attention when she heard Dakota calling.

"MOMMY, MOMMMYYY!" Kaisia sprang into action, ready to do battle with whatever had her daughter's attention. She ran to Dakota.

"Mommy, look at me!" Dakota said as she swung from the monkey bars.

Kaisia breathed a sigh of relief. She moved closer to where her daughter was playing and close to the Park entrance. Somebody walked by and said hi to Kaisia. She turned to see who it was but didn't recognize the chubby girl who sauntered by looking as if the whole world should be watching her. She watched her enter into the building her mother lived and figured homegirl knew her from there. Kaisia turned her attention back to Dakota not realizing that the very girl was now watching her from the lobby window. Kaisia heard a horn beep and looked out at the parking lot where she spotted Ty's white Infinity.

"Come on, Dakota. Your father is here." Kaisia held out her hand to Dakota as she came running up from the monkey bars.

"Where is my DADDDYYY?" She kept asking, grabbing her mother's hand as they walked toward the parking lot.

When Kaisia reached the car, she opened the back door and allowed Dakota to climb in and leaned in to put on her seat**belt.** As she closed the door, she felt the hairs on the back of her neck stand up. She felt as though she was being watched and spun quickly around but there was no one there. She brushed it off as her imagination, climbed into the passenger side of the Infinity and closed the door. She knew Ty was watching her but she wasn't in the mood for him right now so she buckled her seatbelt and continued to stare straight ahead hoping that it would be a quiet ride to their destination. She didn't feel like talking.

SOMEWHERE ON I-95 S

They were only an hour inside New Jersey but already Tia was feeling fatigued. She couldn't get Kaisia out of her mind. If she'd let Jackie drive she could try to get some shut eye. She stared out the window trying to shake her ominous feelings. Traffic was slowing down.

"We can't be in rush hour at this time of day," Jackie said.

"Yeah, for some reason I kind of figured luck wouldn't be on our side the entire trip."

They had just passed a sign that said 37 miles to Delaware. They wouldn't hit Delaware for another hour and half at the rate they were going. Tia looked out the side window to make sure Jada was still behind them. Jada waved and Tia relaxed into her seat. They'd just have to haul ass the best they could.

"Jackie, I've been meaning to ask how your brother was doing." A little conversation would take her mind of Kaisia, Tia thought.

"He a'wrigth. They still didn't offer him nothing yet. I sent him a couple of bills just to hold him down till I get back. They did move him from the facility in Maryland to one in Utah. I was hoping to visit him while we were out here but I guess that ain't gonna happen. Oh, this is my new favorite song. You heard it yet? *Weak in the Knees* by SWV." Jackie was groovin' to the song.

Tia nodded her head and as the smooth sound oozed from the speakers, her mind shifted to Sean. Like the song said, she didn't know what he had done to her…If only he could see her now.

Toya was also listening to SWV but her mind was on Kaisia. Something about her cousin's murder wasn't fitting right in Toya's mind. Tia had explained how they found him and, to her, it seemed too dramatic even for a murder. Toya didn't like the fact that they were on the road instead of being with Kaisia, where they belonged. Even though she tried to convince herself that Kiasia would be safe, she still felt that prickly feeling and felt their place should be beside their friend in this kind of situation. Toya had had the same feeling the day Kato had been shot at Rucker Park. She'd been overwhelmed by the nagging feeling that all might not be well and as she thought, something bad did happen. Toya had the same feeling when she'd hugged Kiasia in the parking lot and it weighed heavily on her mind.

At that very moment, Toya had the urge to tell Tia they should turn around and head back but if she was really being paranoid because of what happened to Kato, it wouldn't be good. Plus Toya couldn't help feeling that the bad luck followed Jackie and because of her dislike for her, she'd do anything to get away from her, including abandoning this trip.

Toya took a deep breath. Maybe it had nothing to do with any of what she was thinking. She was losing her center and when that happened Kato always knew what to do. She missed Kato like crazy and the fact that her man might not be coming back soon was taking its toll. She felt like she was giving up on herself. Maybe it was time to put a halt to all this shit and focus all her attention on Kato instead of trying to be so many people in one body. Toya looked ahead and saw flashing lights just as her walkie-talkie buzzed in. She needed to chill.

Jada and Toya tuned into the walkie-talkie. "It seems there is an accident up ahead," Tia was saying. "I can't really see the extent of it so just be on point. Also turn you'll police scanners and radios off until we get pass highway patrol. We don't want them going off unexpectedly. Toya pull back a few more feet from Jay just in case you gotta burn rubber."

Jada clicked the radio off. She looked to her right and saw an opening to a dirt road.

Toya's radio buzzed.

"Toy," Jada was on the line

"Yeah?"

"You see the gap to your right just ahead of the car in front of you?" Jada asked. She figured Toya could more than blow in that direction should push come to shove on I-95.

"Yeah, I see it." Toya answered.

"Use it if need be. I'm gonna cut off traffic once you make a move."

Toya looked again at the gap. It wouldn't be difficult for her to get through. She turned off her radio and concentrated on the commotion up ahead. Shit just wasn't vibing.

Tia continued to observe the highway patrol officers. She needed to pulse what caution level they were on. As Tia steadily drove forward she was able to get a better view of the red Camry that had turned upside down after being broadsided by a commercial van. The police were on traffic maintenance patrol duty waving cars over to the next lane. Tia looked back giving Jada the sign that everything was okay. Feeling relieved, Tia relaxed once more, thankful for the distraction from worrying about Kaisia.

They pulled over at the first rest stop and she changed drivers. Jackie now took the wheel. As they drove off, Tia pushed back the passenger seat and said to Jackie, "Wake me up when we reach Delaware."

CHAPTER NINETEEN

BROOKLYN DA'S OFFICE

"WHY ARE YOU JUST NOTIFYING me that this guy Pascal has one of the meanest defense teams in Manhattan?" Sean looked at John as though he betrayed him. "So, this is the reason the DA gave me this case. I'm to be the fall guy because he's scared to take this to trial and lose, especially with elections right around the corner. He needs me to be the scapegoat on this one huh?" Sean was fuming. *God damn these white folks! He was being used once again. He was to fall flat on his face to keep another politician's record clean.*

"Sean, I swear I didn't know myself until this morning. I really thought the same thing you did that this was going to be a clear-cut case. A slam dunk. I wouldn't have brought it to your attention and I wouldn't have been so excited about you getting this case if I knew all this."

Sean looked at John. He wasn't sure what to believe. John and the DA were both Jews and Jews were bound by the same cloth. He just had to accept that he'd been blindsided. But this time he made up his mind, he'd use this case to make fools of all those who though just because he was black that he could be used and controlled.

"Listen, John, I am not blaming you. What's done is done. Now we gotta focus on the case." Sean sat atop John desk intending to milk this cow for its full worth. "I'm going to need you to get me the full federal investigation on the Dynasty Crew. Also, get me all the names of any co-defendants who're vulnerable, by whatever means necessary."

The DA wanted him to focus on Kato Pascal but he'd be damned if he wasn't going to do it his way. Instead of focusing on the boss, he was going to apply pressure to every single co-defendant. That way, Mr. Pascal would feel the pressure not only from the prosecution but also from his crew. Even if he was unsuccessful at taking down Kato, he'd have succeeded at bringing down one of the biggest kingpin organizations in Harlem leaving Mr. Pascal with nothing.

Sean left John's office with a fully formed game plan. He felt on top of his game and he was going to play it close to his belt. He always considered John a friend but he had no intention of revealing his plan, not even to John who might himself be suspect in his motives.

Sean walked to the employee's cafeteria to get a fresh cup of coffee and a bagel which he probably wouldn't eat. This was his quirk…he hated ordering only one thing. As Sean waited in line, his mind drifted to Tia. She'd only been gone three days but to him it felt like forever. They'd spoken briefly when she called to let him know she'd arrived safely but couldn't talk long as she was walking out the door to an appointment. She'd promised to call at 8 p.m. and he had planned to be home well before then so he could relax and talk to her from the privacy of his home. Sean paid for his coffee and bagel and went back to his office.

When Sean returned to his office, his secretary was holding up the phone. "Good timing. I'll put it through," she said.

"Sean Adams here."

"Hello Mr. Adams. This is Mrs. Jenkins. Rodney's mother."

"Mrs. Jenkins, how good to hear from you." He could tell from her voice that she was doing much better. "How are you doing, Mrs. Jenkins?"

"Oh, I'm well. I just wanted to call and personally thank you for all you've done for my family and for my Rodney. It's good to know we have you in the DA's office looking out."

Sean held on to her words not just because they were spoken from a mother who'd lost her child but because she represented a nation of women whose homes had been stricken by such tragic events in a system that largely ignored them. Sean finally grasped the meaning of his father's words, "A black man's greatest asset is his voice." He was a voice for his people and today that statement couldn't be truer.

"I'd also like to thank you for uniting me with my grandson. It doesn't replace Rodney but I have a small part of him. I don't know how I could have missed something so important in his life. I guess I was too busy being his coach instead of his mother. I regret that Mr. Adams," Mrs. Jenkins said.

"Mrs. Jenkins. I have to say if more of our children had mothers as dedicated as you, many generations would stand a better chance." As he was saying the words, a though popped into his mind. He wondered what kind of mother Tia would be.

"Thank you again, Mr. Adams. I'll let you get back to work."

Sean said a few more words before hanging up the phone. He couldn't believe his mind had drifted. Never had he thought of a woman as the mother of his children. This was serious! He had to force his mind to focus on the matter at hand. The next time Sean looked up from the Dynasty paperwork, the clock over his desk said it was 4 p.m. He rose from desk and stretched. He still had two hours before he would leave the office. The last time he had requested something from Investigations they took their own sweet time with the information. Rule number one never make the same mistake twice. He decided to take a walk down to Investigations.

BALTIMORE

Jackie's brother's split-level, wood frame house was located on a quiet street just outside Baltimore. As Tia sat on the covered porch with Toya watching two little girls jump rope, she thought of Dakota. She relaxed because she'd spoken to Kaisia earlier and she said everything was okay and that Ty had come through for them. Toya had also spoken to Kaisia but her feeling wasn't the same as Tia's. Toya still felt they were supposed to be with Kaisia back in the city.

"Did Jada take care of that stuff this morning?" Tia asked Toya.

"Yeah, I drove her myself to Western Union. We called Rich when we got back and let him know that it was waiting for him. He called back an hour later and said he got it." Toya said.

It had been three days since they'd been in Baltimore and Jackie was right. There was definitely a gold mine in Maryland. The day they arrived, they went straight to the hotel where Jackie placed a call to her homegirl. She met Jackie at a nearby Hooter and gave her the keys to the house. When Jackie returned, they all went to check out the house and stash the drugs. They left their guns in the hotel safe because Tia didn't want everything in one location. Later that night, they rolled out to town where they set up shop. At first sight, Tia thought the place was a middle-class ghost town where deliveries had to be made but Jackie informed her that most of the deals were done out of the houses and usually the heads drive up to cop. Tia was used to the city where everything happened out in the open. The arrangement seemed far safer in her eyes.

Jackie talked to a couple of heads who she remembered that her brother used to deal with and they arranged to get

158

them a spot in a red brick house down the block that belonged to a friend named Tracy, a white middle class woman who appeared to have her shit together. Even the house was decent. She had no kids but she lived with her boyfriend. Jackie told Tia that they would rent the house for fifty dollars a day plus a few pieces of boozka. Tia looked at Jackie like she spoke in tongues.

"What is boozka?"

Jackie looked at Tia and smiled. "Boozka is crack."

In one day, they had a spot and a sure customer. Now all they needed were workers. By the second day, after Tracy had made a few sells and the quality was vouched for, they gained a bunch of new clients. Tia also found herself overrun holding interviews with local youths looking to make some quick paper. From the group, Tia only kept three on board, until things started to pick up. Two of her workers were cousins. Both in their late teens and both looking like boys next door. Tia refused to hire anyone who stood out or drew too much attention to themselves. Red and Dee seemed calm but what interested her was that they both drove and both only lived a few minutes outside of town. The third person was Toya's hire. Her name was Nee-Nee and Tia's first impression of her was that she looked like Tatyana Ali, the actress who played the little sister on the Fresh Prince of Bel-Air. On close inspection, she looked a lot more like Chill for the old group T.L.C., the one Usher had dumped. Tia asked Toya why her. All Toya said was, "Don't she remind you of Kay?"

Tia didn't see any resemblance so she chalked it up to Toya being home sick.

By the night on their second day, they had the block jumping. All three of their workers seemed to be natural hustlers. That one night, they brought in over Twelve Thousand Dollars. They were running through the rock so fast they had to cook something up. Luck was on their side because Tracy's man was one helluva chef.

Tia stepped off the stoop so she could feel the sun's rays. She looked around at the nice homes that sat peacefully on their properties and thought that it wouldn't be so bad to live out here, but the thought vanished immediately when she realized that she wouldn't be happy without Tone and Ebony.

One of the little girls jumping rope smiled at Tia. She waved and wondered would she ever have time to settle down and have kids of her own, and with whom? Tia looked back at Toya, who was also watching the little girls. Tia watched Toya closely, wishing she could read her friend's thoughts. Toya had crawled into a shell. That was clear to see, but why? Toya was always the one who mostly kept to herself but not to this extent. She hadn't been the same since Kato had been locked up. It wasn't a surprise to Tia that Toya could be mute for hours but these spells were happening more and more. She was sure that as Kato's trial came closer, the fact that he could be looking to do a lot of time was becoming real to Toya. Or maybe this life was beginning to take a mental toll on homegirl. Tia had been feeling too that it was time to get out of the life before it was too late. That was one of the reason she'd made this move so that they could get on with their lives and never look back. There was a thrill and a reward and it seemed the further they went after paper, the deeper they got in.

"Toy, let's go out tonight. I mean it don't make no sense to just sit around here. I mean, while we're out here we might as well live it up." Tia didn't care what they did as long as they could move around a bit. She knew that, like her Jada and Toya, they needed a change of atmosphere. "So, what's up? Whatcha think? We could find a little club tonight and do us New York Style."

Toya didn't really want to go out but she damn sure didn't want to be cooped up here either so she agreed. She continued looking at the little girls realizing for the first time they were twins. One just had longer hair than the other.

HARLEM

Kaisia had been in the house for two days and she was beginning to feel smothered. She would probably have felt more comfortable if something in the house was familiar. Everything felt foreign. She stood looking out the window watching people move about as if they didn't have a care in the world. If only they really knew how short life was. She thought about her cousin and felt a deep sorrow enter her heart. She wanted to go into the room to wake Dakota just for company but she knew Dakota would be cranky the entire day if she disturbed her rest. She walked over to the couch, flipped on the TV to BET. Free and AJ Calloway were prancing around the stage of 106 & Park before they introduced the next music video. When Tia called, it was a relief just to hear a familiar voice. Tia said that everything was alright but she already knew as Rich had given her a heads up. Kaisia wanted to keep Tia on the phone as though she already knew everything she allowed Tia to ramble on, giving her the full-page layout of the B-More operations. Kaisia wished she'd been with them. Anything was better than being cooped up in this stranger's apartment. The damn man was such a liar. If he had not lied about being out of town just to keep from watching his own daughter she could have been with her friends. Kaisia couldn't, for the life of her, understand why a father would not want to spend every chance he got with his own child. She'd so hoped to give Dakota that - the father she never had. Now here she was repeating history. The least she could have done was give her daughter a father who would accept responsibility. Maybe there was something wrong with her for not seeing the bullshit because even after her breakup with Ty every man she dated was not father material. Maybe girls without fathers were at a disadvantage in reading men, especially trifling ones. She was now just tired of men altogether. One night stands for hormonal prosperity were enough for her.

Ty had stayed the night and it had seemed so natural. Dakota was happy to be around her father. That was the way it was supposed to be, Kaisia thought. His company had given

Kaisia some time to herself and as he and Dakota played on the living room rug, in her heart she knew that this was how she wanted her life to be every day. But knowing and living it were two different things. Ty's presence was only temporary but it was one she welcomed as long as her daughter was happy.

When Dakota had finally fallen asleep, Ty had carried her into the room. He must have fallen asleep with Dakota she thought as it was over two hours ago. Kaisia felt loneliness creep up her spine. It was resurfacing with a vengeance. This time, it had a face and a voice. When Ty finally came back into the living room, she hoped he wouldn't come near her and just go about his business. Her hopes faded when he sat beside her on the couch. She looked at Ty. She hated the man he'd proven to be and that hate had taken a toll on her heart. She sure wasn't in love with him but hate may be too strong a word. To say she didn't care about him, though, would be a total lie.

Ty didn't say a word as he sat beside her. He just looked back at her with those light brown eyes that had attracted her to him in the first place. In their younger years, those eyes represented love; now she knew the difference. Over the years, the eyes had represented manipulation and distrust. Kaisia stared at the TV though Ty continued to stare at her.

Finally, she looked back at him with the hostility and bitterness she felt. She wanted to say what was really on her mind but knew it would cause an argument and she didn't want to wake Dakota or risk having nowhere to go. Instead she rolled her eyes.

Ty moved closer to Kaisia, so close he was brushing up against her. She used her elbow to push him away but he kept coming closer. Kaisia sat still. They were that way for four or five minutes before Ty made his next move. He ran his hand across her bare legs. Kaisia blamed herself for sitting up in his house with a T-shirt and thongs. She rose from the couch to get dressed but before she could get very far, he pulled at her

T-Shirt, probably catching a glimpse of her thongs and a full view of her bare ass. The tug landed her back on the couch.

"Ty, why don't you stop being an ass and go find one of your bitches to play with?" Kaisia spat, lasering him with a look that said she was serious.

"Kay, why are you always acting so uptight and shit?"

"Because, Ty, you are a piece of shit and you know it. You're out here running around like you don't have a daughter who needs you. I'm saying, it didn't work out with us and I'm cool with that 'cause that's life. But why take it out on Dakota?"

"I don't take nothing out on her. You act like I don't do shit for her. Tell me once when she needed anything?" Ty asked.

"Oh. So, you think just because you give me money for her that automatically makes you a father?" Kaisia laughed in his face. "She doesn't care about money and neither do I. She cares about you. I don't know why but that little girl in the room asks about you almost every day, as if you bring some imaginary joy into her life by just thinking about you." Kaisia, feeling her emotions rising, looked away.

"Kay, when you was pregnant, I told you that I wasn't ready to be a father. I never threw a skirt over your eyes. I painted the picture perfectly clear yet you still decided to have the baby. Even though I didn't agree, I made sure Shorty was alright. I never denied you shit for that child. Not a damn thing. Now you want to hold me responsible for not being there enough when I do try to be there when I can. You're the one who's full of shit." Ty rose from the couch and walked into the bedroom. Dusk was beginning to fall and it made her even gloomier.

Ty's words stung. He was right. She knew his position all along. He'd begged her not to have the child but she and her selfish-self wanted a child to fill the void in her life. She was the one who'd forced him to be a father and in the long run, she'd only hurt her child. Kaisia buried her hands between her knees and rocked back and forth. She felt like her whole world was crashing down. She felt that she should at least acknowledge that he was right so Kaisia got up from the couch and walked into Ty's room. The door was slightly open but the lights were off. From the streetlight, she could make out that he was lying on the bed fully dressed, his right arm covering his face. Kaisia sat on the bed, crossed her legs and looked at Ty. "Ty," she shook him lightly. "You're right. I was wrong to put you in a position you weren't ready for but I was young and hurting. I thought having a baby would help me heal my scars and Dakota has done that for me in many ways, but I was wrong. I was selfish and headstrong and I am only now realizing that the choice I made means Dakota will inherit all the pain I tried so hard to bury. I was too selfish. I'm sorry."

Ty removed his arm from his face and looked at her. "Kay, I'm not perfect and I know that you aren't either that's why I didn't just leave you cold. It's not that I don't want kids but I knew I couldn't have kids while I was still running the streets. I know too many guys like me who are dead or in jail because of the life. They had kids. Those kids are suffering. I didn't want my child to suffer like that. I don't know what tomorrow will bring for me but I tell you this, ever since Dakota has been born I've been playing the game with much greater caution. I love that girl, Kay, but I will never be the father you want me to be just because you want it. It won't happen until I am ready." Ty sat up and looked into Kaisia's eyes. "I hope that will be sooner than later."

Suddenly, the Ty she knew seven years before was sitting in front of her. If they could have communicated like this instead of all the blame and hostility, their daughter might have had a chance. "Let me say 'sorry' the way I know how," Kaisia moved closer to Ty.

They made love that night and though they had shared intimate thoughts and feelings, Kaisia knew they could never get back to the way it used to be. Too much history had been laid down. The least she could do was pretend one more time. She looked at her watch. It was eight p,m., and Dakota was still asleep. She'd make them dinner...and like a real family they would sit down to a family meal.

Crime was in the van along with one of Ike's soldiers. They had been posted by Colonial Houses for about two hours. Ike had called and told Crime that he needed him to take care of one last thing. Crime agreed to handle the matter for the same price. Ike had also informed him that he'd be sending someone along with him to do the deed. Crime protested but Ike had explained that the kat was the only one who knew what Ty looked like. They needed him to lead them to this Kaisia bitch. She with him now. Ike wanted to know how Ike knew she was with him.

"I just do," Ike had replied. Crime knew better than to press the issue.

"Alright," he responded, accepting home-team's company. He made it clear to Ike that if shit didn't go right he was gonna have to lay home down because he couldn't afford to have a co-defendant.

"Don't worry about all that. He is replaceable." Ike replied. He was one cold mutha. Crime knew Ike was cold but he found out that moment that the mutha was also foul. Crime continued to stare out the van.

"Are you positive you know what he looks like?" Crime asked home-team not really feeling this stakeout shit.

"Yeah, I know what he looks like. I used to work for him." Crime looked over at homeboy and thought about killing him for the hell of it just because he was a grimy snitch.

Crime watched as a car pulled into a parking space next to the supermarket. Homeboy leaned in just a little too close to check out what Crime was looking at. "What's up?" Crime gruffed, irritated the homeboy was all up in his space.

"I think that's him right there," homeboy leaned in a little closer and pointed to the guy walking away from his car.

"You think that's him or you sure?"

Shorty squinted his eyes. "Yeah, that's the mutha fucker right there."

Crime screwed a silencer on to the muzzle of his gun, tucked it in his waist and stepped out of the van.

Kaisia had dinner ready. For the past few days Ty had dropped by and things were okay. She'd cooked enough just in case he stopped by today. While the dinner was finishing up, she decided to call Tia and the crew to let them know things were better than she expected. Kaisia cocked the phone to her ear and turned the chicken. The phone was answered on the fourth ring. "May I speak to Tia?"

"Chicken," Jada said. "Is that the only person you call for?"

Kaisia laughed. "Naw, Heifer. I'd get around to your crazy ass. How can I live without your wise ass comments?" Kaisia laughed. "Anyway, Boo, I'm sorry. I thought for sure you'd be out chasing tail feathers."

"Yeah, right, Chicken. But you are right about one thing, we're about to step out," Jada said.

"Word, where ya'll headed?" Kaisia was missing her friends terribly. Right now, she missed them more than ever because when they went out as a group they turned it out!

"Some spot Jackie said was jumpin' out here but I gotta see it to believe it because as far as action in this sleepy hollow town, it's deader than a mutha fucker!"

"Jay, you're just used to city life so everything is gonna seem dead to you. You might enjoy yourself tonight in Sleepy Hollow so watch out."

"I doubt it but I'ma damn sure turn these backyard niggas out."

Kaisia smiled. She could clearly visualize Jada out there acting a fool on the dance floor. "So, where's everybody?"

"Tia is in the shower and Toya's downstairs. Do you want me to get Tia?"

"Naw, just let them know I called and I'll call back tomorrow. Have fun tonight, Sleigher."

"T'ght, Kay. I'll holla at you later."

Kaisia had just clicked off the phone when she heard the keys in the door. She walked toward the door to tell Ty his timing was perfect as she'd just finish cooking. She gasped and covered her mouth as his corpse with his face blown off fell forward onto the rug. Kaisia stood motionless, not believing her eyes. Her mind kept trying to tell her to go get the Ruger from her purse but her legs refused to move. She watched as a figure stepped into the apartment, a gun leveled at his side. The man used his foot to kick the door shut and stepped over Ty's dead body toward Kaisia, who by now was trying to reach for the hot chicken grease to throw at the intruder but he reached her in time to knock the frying pan off the counter. He grabbed Kaisia by the back of the neck and put the gun muzzle directly at her temple, dragging her across the carpet and over to the couch. He put his knee in her back and bent her backwards still holding the gun to the back of her head. Kaisia was crying softly, her face smudged and scared. Her mind and heart were racing a thousand miles a minute. She was thankful that Dakota had not awakened and that the gunman had not looked in the other rooms.

"Where the fuck is my shit, Bitch?" he barked as he applied more pressure to her back.

"I don't know what the fuck you're talking about," Kaisia tried to be the soldier she was and did her best act of being convincing and fearless. But she knew she wasn't doing too a good a job, because her voice quivered.

"You know what I'm talking about. You and a few of your friends hit one of my spots. Now I'm here to collect my stuff."

"I don't have nothing here but I could get it for you," Kaisia offered. She had no intention of leading him to her people but she did want to get him away from this house before Dakota woke up. "I got it at another house. This is my baby father's house. I don't keep nothing here."

Crime swung Kaisia around to face him and then hit her in my face with the butt of the pistol. Blood rushed from her nose and my lips split open where the gun hit.

"Bitch, you must think I'm stupid. But here is what you're going to do if you want to live past today. You are going to tell me where I can find your friends." Crime put the muzzle back to her temples.

Kaisia eyes flooded with tears as she pictured the faces of Tia, Jada, Toya and Rich. She closed her eyes and pictured the sweet face of her laughing daughter. This was it. Her time had come because she would never give up her friends. She smiled.

Crime pressed the muzzle deeper into her temple. She wanted to scream but she would never give the mutha fucker the satisfaction. Better to die with honor.

"WHERE THE FUCK ARE THEY?" he screamed.

"Kaisia closed her eyes and said a quick prayer for her soul and for her baby's. Then she opened her eyes and with brute strength managed to turn to her captor. "Fuck you!" she said as she spat in his face.

Kaisia's head jerked upwards as the slugs connected with her head. Crime released her as she fell backwards and stared at the hole in her forehead. He wiped blood, brains and bone from his face with the back of his hand. He looked up from the corpse into the eyes of a little girl standing by the bedroom door.

CHAPTER TWENTY

JADA WAITED OUTSIDE IN ONE of the rental car for Red and Nee-Nee to come out from their spot. She was eager to go and pick up the rest of the cake she'd had waiting at other spots and deliver some work. As she waited she lit up a blunt. Tia told her not to be messing around while they were doing business but the working hours were long on this mutha fuckin' trip and Jada wasn't tryin' to hear. She felt jittery for some reason and need to chill. After this run she was only dropping off and wouldn't be out long. She took a strong pull on the blunt and held the smoke in her lungs as long as she could to induce a quick high. She hated this out of town weed. It was trash compared to New York butter. Jada took another toke and then put out the blunt. She reached into the glove compartment and grabbed her cell. What the fuck was taking Red so long. She dialed his number and waited for him to pick up.

As Jada held the phone to her ear she noticed a group of about three guys hold up on the corner. The sight of them ordinarily would not have interested her back in the city but for some reason here in the boonies that just didn't sit well with her. A bell went off. Something didn't seem right. Jada wasn't no fool. She'd been in too much shit not to know when someone was scheming. They probably didn't know that she was there especially since she had parked on the opposite side of the street. Jada was about to hang up and call Tia when a male voice answered.

"Red, I've been out here for twenty minutes waitin' on you. What's up?"

"We're on our way out," Red said.

"Alright." Jada said and hung up. She kept her eyes on the group wishing she had brought some heat. Then she heard tapping on the glass on the passenger side and saw Red and Nee-Nee. She unlocked the door and they climbed in.

"Jay, what's up?" Nee-Nee asked.

Jada liked Nee-Nee but it was only a week and already homegirl had broken down her name. Shit was too familiar. "Ya'll tell me. Ya'll was supposed to have been out here when I first called and told ya'll I was on my way." Jada didn't try to hide her displeasure as she handed Red the brown paper bag.

Red took the bag and transferred the content of his carrying purse. Nee-Nee pulled out a roll of cash and handed it to Jada.

"Yo, my cousin finished his shift too but he went over to his girl's house. He should be back in an hour," Red said.

Jada took the money Red handed her and threw it into the glove compartment. "Well I'm not gonna wait here for no hour. Just tell him I'll be back later tonight and the next time he decides to step out he needs to leave the cake with either you or Nee-Nee, if he plans on being around." Jada didn't press the issue further as they always made sure that the money was right. "Check it. Has anyone been coming through here lately besides the regulars?"

"Naw. I haven't seen nobody. Why what's good?" Red asked.

"Naw, it ain't nothing. I just saw a group of Kats up on the corner a little while before ya'll got here," Jada said. She looked down the street and realized they were gone.

Red and Nee-Nee got out and went back into the house. Jada sat in the car half-expecting the group to return but after about twenty-five minutes there was no sign of them so she pulled out.

While Jada was out and Toya was asleep, Tia and Jackie went for a ride. They tooled around to check out the joints before returning to the house. Jackie dropped Tia off then left again. It was a little after 4 p.m. when Jackie came back to the house and informed Tia that one of her contacts had put her onto an area that was sure fire. At first Tia refused to go along. Finally, she asked, "If they are on fire, where they're at?

"Let's go check it out."

Tia decided to go along to calm Jackie's interest. It was a little over a week and they'd made well over Thirty Thousand. Tia knew they would need a new connect soon and although they had enough work to get them through another week after that they'd be dry. They had to get rid of the shit.

As they drove along, Tia wondered about the Dominican kat Rich said he'd got plugged into. She had told Rich if the product was good she was not concerned with the price he was asking because they would make that back and then some. Rich had put her mind at rest when he said he was going with a friend to test out the product.

Tia stared out the window. Her thoughts were miles away from where her body. All she could think about was Ebony and Kaisia. She just could not get them off her mind especially since Kaisia was supposed to call back a few days ago and hadn't. Maybe it wasn't so strange since they were on the move a lot and usually silenced their phones on the job so she could have missed the call but wouldn't she have left a voice mail? She wanted to call Kaisia at that moment but Tia didn't want to talk in front of Jackie. The moment they returned from this run she'd make a point to call Kaisia.

"Tee, what's up?" Jackie asked. "You've been quiet this whole trip."

"I'm good. My thoughts have been wandering but, Girl, I'm still here with you." Tia reached for the radio dial. A little music would be a good distraction for them both. "You still haven't told me who told you about this fire town," Tia said, as the raspy voice of Nas street anthem, *Illmatic* came on.

"You sure. I thought I already did. Anyway, I was hanging with a couple of heads I knew when I used to come out here with my brother and they mentioned an enclave full of big spenders."

Tia gave Jackie a look that said, …you can't believe what mutha fuckers be saying out their mouths… Jackie caught the stare and smiled.

"I know it might be just a bunch of talk. That's why I brought you here with me to check it out. If it turns out to be nothing then we'll just chalk it off to an excuse to get out of the house for a while. Cool?" Jackie smiled.

Tia smiled back and cranked the music full blast.

HARLEM

Ebony sat on the bed braiding Tweet's hair and watching Ike pack. Ike had just gotten in in the wee hours when both Ebony and Tweet were asleep. Ebony didn't beef with him because he'd called earlier to say he wouldn't be in and that she should get Tweet to come over and spend the night. Ebony did just that the moment she hung up from Ike. Ike had been busy lately and though she didn't show it she missed his attention. She was lonely. Still, Ebony had nothing to complain about really because he always left her enough money to do whatever she wanted. She and Tweet usually went shopping and to the club but all that was wearing off. She wanted her man by her side. Now he was going out of town for an entire week. Ebony glanced at Ike. She hoped he'd look up from his packing and acknowledge her so she could be reassured.

"Aw!" Tweet yelled. "Damn girl, you are pulling the shit out of my hair!"

"I'm sorry," Ebony rubbed Tweet's head before looking back at Ike, willing him to look at her. He was now going through the dresser drawers. "What you looking for, Boo?"

she finally asked. She didn't care what the heck he was looking for but she did care that he was not paying her much attention, especially since he'd be gone a week.

"I can't find my Rolex. I thought I'd put it in the drawer."

"Which one are you lookin' for? If it's the steel one. That's in your hat box. I put it there because I found it under the bed."

"Platinum, Baby," he said walking over to the closet. As he tried to pull out the hat box another box fell and spilled its content. Both Ebony and Tweet looked in the directing of the sound, and then looked quickly away at the sight of two guns.

Like it was the most normal thing in the world, Ike picked up the contents of the box, put both the boxes back in place and headed to the bathroom.

"What's up with ya'll?" asked Tweet.

"Nothin'. Why you ask?"

"I never seen ya'll so quiet around each other. Usually a bitch gotta squeeze between ya'll just to get you apart."

Ebony really didn't feel like having this conversation with Tweet, but she needed to get a few things off her chest as well. "I think Ike's been having some mornin' sickness." She whispered in Tweet's ear so Ike wouldn't hear if he unexpectedly walked back into the room.

Tweet spun around to look at Ebony, not sure she heard right. "Morning sickness? How the hell?"

"Shhh," Ebony put her finger to her mouth. "You're too loud."

"Alrigth, Chicken, but what does that have to do with anything? Only females get morning sickness when they're pregnant!"

"You're right. But sometimes the man can have symptoms too," Ebony said.

"Yeah, but that would mean...you're..." Tweet jumped up and put a hand to her mouth and just stared at Ebony. Ebony smiled. Tweet hugged her so tight she thought she'd break.

"When did you find out?"

"I don't know for sure yet. I'm just guessing. I missed my period last month and it hasn't come this month."

"Why you didn't tell me sooner?" Tweet asked, a touch of hurt in her voice.

"I didn't want to jump to any conclusions. I wanted to be sure first. Plus, if it is the case that I am pregnant I wanted to tell Ike first, but he's been in and out so much lately that by the time I say 'hi' to him I'm saying 'bye' again and he's gone."

"I'm gonna go over to Met Foods and get you one of the pregnancy tests so we can find out together."

Ebony didn't want it to be like that. She loved Tweet and considered her a sister but she wanted to find out with Ike. For sure when she found out, she wanted Ike to be right beside her. She wanted to give her man his rights and the joy of knowing he was the second person to know that she was pregnant.

Ebony and Tweet looked at each other as Ike walked back into the room. Ike looked at them as shook his head.

"Why you'll two look like you up to something. And why you'll looking in my direction like I'ma a bail you out or something?" said Ike lifting his duffle bag. "Baby, I left money in the drawer for you. More than enough. Tweet, are you chillin' with my baby while I'm gone?" Ike asked.

"Of course, I am. Who else is gonna take care of her?" answered Tweet.

Ike stepped over to where Ebony was sitting. He bent down and kissed her on the lips and then moved down her neck. Ebony started laughing. "Don't start nothing you can't finish," she said.

"Oh, I could finish. It's the start off that worries me," Ike said smiling.

"You'll need to stop that," Tweet said.

Ike and Ebony looked at Tweet. He kissed Ebony once more before grabbing his luggage. "I'll call once I get there," he said and walked out the door.

The Baltimore Posse was not feeling New York.

"I'm sayin' what it look like. We could get them folks right now and shit. I don't see why we gotta wait?" said a dark-skinned brother with deep, dark eyebrows and deep waves.

"Ya'll don't move until I call it. I'm the one that put you all nigga on to this so this is my show and ya'll just along for the prize money. Besides they suppose to be re-ing up. It don't make no sense begging them now and all we get is a few thousand and a couple of ounces. So just be patient."

"I'ght, we'll do it your way but while you're caking' off, fuckin' wid them bitches what the fuck we're suppose to do?" Dark Skin asked.

"Nigga, do what ya'll was doin' before U found ya'll asses on my gig. I don't care what you'll do. Go rob a store or some shit, but just don't come creepin' around here again. Ya'll nigga almost blew it hanging out in front of their operations. We don't want them getting nervous and decide to take their business someplace else."

"Yeah, alright. We'll fall back but know this... I got something good for them New York hands. They think they can just come out here and make money off our shit and we don't hear." Dark Skin said, as she patted his waist and got up to leave.

When Jada walked into the house, Toya was sitting on the couch watching TV. "Where's everybody?"

"I don't know. I was sleeping. I just got up a little while before you walked in. I thought ya'll were together."

"Naw. I went down to meet Red and Nee-Nee. Something up with them two." Jada sat down next to Toya and kicked off her boots. "While I was out I stopped by the bar to see what's good for tonight. They got all-nighters going down today. Ya'll wanna roll over there and see what's up?"

175

"I don't care. Ain't shit else to do around here. Don't somebody gotta be around for the second drop-off though?" Toya asked.

"Yeah. But we can handle that and do us at the same time. I mean it only takes a few minutes to stop by the spot although today I was like out there for an hour."

"Damn. What you doing there for so long...pitchin?" Toya asked.

"Ha-ha. Real funny, Bird. Naw. I was waiting on Red to come out and check it. It may be nothing but I peeped these kats hovering around the area and I'm not feeling Red and Nee-Nee right now."

"Word. Did they look familiar?"

"Naw, I never saw them before but then again I was parked a distance from them and couldn't make out their faces but they looked like they were up to something. That old New York instinct kicked in right away."

"Even so, did you put Nee-Nee and them on alert?"

"Yeah, but I think we should give them a burner," Jada said.

"Naw. Everybody ain't built for that kind of action and hell no if you ain't feeling them. Besides we don't need one of them doing no dumb shit and putting us out there. I'll talk to Tia. Maybe it would be best if one of us is out there with them for a while to see what's up." Toya said.

"Yeah. That would probably be best. Damn, I'm hungry as hell. You didn't cook?" Jada got up and headed to the kitchen.

"Cook! Bitch you better order out," Toya turned up the TV and her attention back to the screen.

The area was upscale and seemed too quiet for Tia. Rows of stately homes lined the streets. The little Mom and Pop antique shops along the avenues probably hadn't seen any business since the Great Depression. All of the whips parked in the driveways or along the curb cost about Sixty Thousand or better. To Tia this area didn't look like a place that you would find drugs, unless they were the prescription variety. It seemed that a street like this was reserved for doctors and lawyers. Tia looked at Jackie, "Can we go now? I think I've seen enough."

Jackie too didn't expect it to be this dead. Maybe she got her information twisted, Jackie thought, but realized that it was impossible being that she paid close attention as she was getting the details.

"Yeah, I guess this was bullshit," said Jackie.

As she was about to pull off, a white male in his early forties tapped on her window. Jackie looked at Tia then rolled her window down. "Yes?" said Jackie looking directly into the man's blue eyes.

Tia looked at him, untrusting. He had the appearance of a New York City detective yet a deeper look into his eyes told Tia that he wasn't. His eyes had friend written all through them. "Open?"

"Naw, we ain't open yet," said Tia, thinking on her feet. "But we will be shortly. What are you looking for?"

Blue eyes went into this pocket. Tia not understanding his movement immediately reached between her seat and closed her hand around the Browning 9-millimeter she carried. He stuck his hand into the car revealing a knot of cash.

"What will this get me in cocaine?"

Jackie took the money and began counting. "Four thousand," said Jackie, trying not to sound surprised.

"That will get you two and a half ounces. But like I said we're not open yet," replied Tia.

Jackie handed him back the money but he declined. "Hold on to it. You both have honest faces. Besides, I don't want to make another trip outside unless I have to. So I tell you what, why don't I just give you my number and you give me a call when you will be swinging back through tonight. This way you could drop it off and I'll have a few buddies over to get some."

Jackie looked at Tia for confirmation as to the next move. Tia took the phone number. It wasn't a New York number. "Alright. We'll call you in about an hour or so. We'll tell you where to meet us since we don't do home delivery, if that's alright with you."

He nodded and walked off as though he had not a care in the world. Either he was one stoned mutha, crazy or the heat. Tia smiled before pulling off. Either way, they would be on high alert.

HARLEM

Ike got out of his truck down a block away and walked to the gambling den where Crime said to meet him. He'd been in this particular gambling den countless times. It was a good source of information and a good way to blow off some steam, though he wasn't a gambler per say. Tonight, he was in a hurry but he was a man of his word and was meeting Crime to give him the Twenty Thousand Dollars he owed him.

As Ike entered the establishment, Tiny the 6' 6", three hundred pounds bouncer met him at the door. Ike gave him a fist bump and continued moving through the shallow hallways until he got to the main entrance. The air was saturated with weed and blunt dust. The room was about the size of a gym and was wall to wall with every kind of street niggas and the groupies who leeched off them. Ike saw a lot of familiar faces but he did not stray from his mission. Tonight wasn't the night to shoot willy-bo-bo. He had business to take care of, then he was out there. Ike made his way through the throng of people until he reached the back booth which was a private space off limits to other patrons. Inside, Crime was waiting for him. Ike didn't bother to sit down, instead he reached into his duffle bag and threw a manila envelope on the table. Crime picked it up and set it beside him on a side table. He didn't bother to count it because Ike was always on point.

"Playa, I apologize for not getting you any information but the bitch stuck to her guns. Shit, I hated the fact that I had to kill her because these days you can't find niggas that loyal," Crime said.

"Life's a bitch sometimes, but at least somebody paid for my shit. Look at it like this, I didn't get my money or coke back but somebody will be missing something far greater and I believe their loss will be bigger than mine," Ike said turning to leave.

Crime looked at Ike. One cold mutha. "Wait, Dawg," he stopped his exit. "So that's it. We are done wid them bitches?"

"Yea, we're done. I consider that whoever they are they will respect the fact that I let them break even."

"Alright," Crime said. He was half expecting to see this thing through but then again it wasn't his money to spend and he was not into doing freebies. Besides he had come out ahead, with a little more cake than he expected.

"By the way, Playa, what happened to the soldier I sent you?" Ike asked, already knowing the answer.

"Well, let's just say he was in the way," Crime answered, lighting a Newport. He blew the smoke through his nose. Exhaling. He was good at that.

Ike looked at Crime and nodded his head. Cold blood killer, he thought as he exited the booth.

BALTIMORE

Tia and Jackie were walking in as Toya and Jada seemed to be on their way out.

"Where ya'll going?" Tia asked. "And why ya'll so dressed up?"

"We going to drop this off at the spot and then we were thinking of going to the bar," Jada answered. "We tried waiting on ya'll but it seemed like ya'll were never coming back."

"We were out shopping for another location. You wouldn't believe it but we might have just hit the big times. In fact, I'm a need you all to get whatever coke we got left, take it to the spot, give it to the workers and have them deliver to this new location," Tia said, giving them the address.

"Tee, what are you hollerin' about?" Toya asked confused as to what was going on.

"We got a goldmine and I'm gonna need Red and his cousin to switch locations."

"But what about the current location?" Jada asked.

"We'll still use that spot. Keep Nee-Nee over there. Give her all the cook- up we got and let her know we no longer got coke unless they want weight," Tia instructed.

Jada and Toya looked at each other. Tia had completely lost her mind. "Tee, we don't have that much work left to handle two locations unless you and Jackie also found a key lying in the dirt," Jada said.

"Don't worry about that. Rich is on it right now," Tia said.

"Alright, Tee. If you want to do it that way, let's do it. But I think Nee-Nee may get a little upset seeing that boozka don't make the same profit margin as powder," Toya added.

"I see you looking out for your protégé," Tia smiled. "Okay, I get it. So that she doesn't feel left out, just increase her take on every packet she sells and also let her know that if she get any weights, she gets an extra ten percent. Fair?" Tia asked.

"Fair," Toya was pleased with the decision. Nee-Nee with be alright with that.

"So, ya'll comin' wit us or not?" Jada asked.

"Comin' with ya'll where? Oh, naw. I'm gonna stay back, I gotta make a few calls. By the way, did Kaisia call?"

The crew shook their heads.

"What about Rich?"

"Naw, nobody called," Jada said and turned to Jackie. "What about you? Are you gonna hang out tonight?"

Toya gave Jada a look. She couldn't believe the heifer was asking Jackie to join them!

"I don't got nothin' else to do but I gotta get dressed."

"Alright. Check it. We're gonna drop this stuff off and come back for you."

Jackie nodded and headed upstairs. Toya gave Jada the look of death.

"Oh, hold up, Jada. Here's the number for the runners to call when they get the shit to the new location. Tell them to call when they are on their way. The owner of this number gets his two and a half off the top. He already paid," Tia said. If it was a booby trap, they'd know soon enough.

Toya was already out the door when Tia handed the paper to Jada.

"This shit is on fire," Jada grabbed the paper.

"Yeah," Tia said.

CHAPTER TWENTY-ONE

SEAN SAT IN HIS OFFICE GOING over ever profile of the Dynasty co-defendants one by one. So far, he'd identified only one prospect who he suspected might cooperate. The case had Sean stressed and he knew it was going to get worse. Not only were the defense attorneys making it hard for him to interview members of the Dynasty crew, but the investigation itself rested entirely on information from an informant, who Sean found out had been murdered a few weeks before. Though he couldn't say for sure that the murder was connected to the case, he suspected it was. If it wasn't, why was precinct 28th not cooperating? He'd requested details of the murder but all the precinct had given him was a description of the murder scene. The body of the deceased was found in a local park by a group of kids enroute to playing night pool. Homicide reports stated that the body was stuffed into multiple plastic bags. Cause of death was suffocation, which the autopsy ruled was inflicted elsewhere before the body was dumped in the park.

The deceased was identified as an African America male, mid-twenties to early thirties, six feet tall and weighing 275 pounds. Sean had spent a good amount of time going over the deceased's rap sheet. As expected, he had many priors but the one that stood out, the one that grabbed Sean's attention was the criminal's passion for moving controlled substance. He was arrested for having 425 grams of cocaine with intent to sell, a serious charge. Sean focused on the affidavit that said the deceased had plea bargained to avoid jail time. He did not agree with plea bargaining as he could not fathom how one felony could be compromised for another. As an ADA, he was committed to bringing justice to the masses, but he was not willing to let anyone who broke the law go free.

Sean looked up at the clock above his desk. It was 12:30 in the morning. He should go to bed but he was obsessed with this case. Just a few more minutes, he thought, as he rifled through more paperwork. For some odd reason, he felt somehow connected to this case or was it that he needed to show those in the DA's office just who he was - a brilliant attorney. That would mean he needed to find a way to get to the mastermind behind the Dynasty. Sean stretched his arms over his head and was about to get up when his cell phone rang.

"Yeah, I'm sure about that," Tia said. She had finally gotten in touch with Rich after trying to reach him for two straight hours. "You heard from Kaisia?" Tia had been trying to reach her too, on both her cell and home phones. Though she had told Kaisia to remain indoors until they returned, knowing her, she was out in the streets . Cooped up with her baby father for weeks was probably driving her crazy.

"Nah, I've been meaning to check in but I've been on the move. But everything is set up."

"You straight?" Tia knew Rich was sitting on Thirty Thousand from the money they'd sent through Western

Union. Though it was risky, she wanted more than a bird. If shit went wrong they were all still sitting on a bundle from the stick-up as nobody had splurged except Jada who'd purchased Ten Thousand Dollars' worth of furniture for her crib. They couldn't risk transporting so much coke so it was best to do the deal. "Rich, we'll be back out there by Sunday so go ahead and cop the three."

Tia heard the door and walked from the kitchen into the living room. Toya and Jada were walking in, and she pointed to the phone at her ear.

"Who's that?" Jada asked.

"Rich."

"Word...tell him my money better be right or else he's gonna have to bring his ass down here by himself and make it back." She laughed pulling off her boots and rubbing her feet. She had to change these muthas. Cute but she couldn't dance in them all night.

Tia rolled her eyes and continued talking with Rich. Jada gave her the evil eye for not relaying her message.

Toya was listening to Tia. At the mention of Kaisia's name, she indicated she wanted to know what was going on. Tia shook her head to let her know Rich hadn't spoken to her.

"So," Tia was saying, "when was the last time you talked to Kay?" her voice had an edge of worry.

"Man, I been busy in and out and about. But I'd say 'bout four or so days ago. I tried calling her today but ain't nobody picking up. I figured I'll check in later. But she told me she and Ty were on good terms so who knows what them freaky deeks are over there doing! Could be new love all over again. She was playing house making dinner and shit just waitin' for him to come in."

As Tia listened to Rich, she tried to calm herself from thinking bad thoughts. Four days! That wasn't like Kay. And why hadn't she called them? But if something had happened Rich would have known. She knew that girl still loved Ty though she acted like she couldn't stand him because he was constantly running from his responsibilities as a father. Deep down, Tia knew Ty was a good person and he did provide for Dakota so if they were getting their freak on it would be a good thing, she hoped it brought them closer. Always a silver-lining. When they were an item they were like rubber and glue, Tia couldn't imagine what this new turn of events would bring. They would probably stick together like white on rice. But, doubt crept in. Wouldn't she have called? Shit, they had been so busy she probably got tired when nobody was available to answer her calls. Tia found herself making up all kinds of excuses for the lack of communication but truth be told, she was worried. Something just didn't feel right in her gut.

Tia didn't let on about her worry to Rich or to Toya, who was watching her. Toya knew her so well that she would detect one false flinch. She couldn't afford for the crew to worry, especially if her worry turned out to be nothing.

"Alrigth Rich, I'm bouncing, but do me a favor and keep trying to contact her and tell her to call me. I'ma keep my cell live. And change of plans, we'll be back Saturday evening instead of Sunday." Tia hung up the phone and watched as Toya got off the stool and walked out of the room.

Tia rubbed her temples. A bitch of a headache was starting and spreading fast. She looked at the clock 12:25, and buried her face in her hand. Didn't seem like there was going be no party tonight, not the way Toya had left the room. Damn, this shit was getting to be too much. She needed to talk to somebody who could take her mind off all this and one who could begin to understand her struggles. The only person who came to mind was Sean. She wondered if she dared to call him at this hour. She looked at the phone in her hand and pressed the on button. The screen lit up. She punched up his number and put the phone to her ear.

Sean answered the phone midway through the first ring. Whoever was calling at this time of night must have something important to say. He looked at the caller's number. Tia?

"Hello, Stranger?" Sean said.

"Is it too late to call?" Tia asked.

Sean scanned his emotions. He was a bit pissed since it was over a week since he had heard from her but elated that it was her voice on the other end of the line.

"No, it's an okay time." He said still trying to figure out this mysterious woman. He had strong feelings for this woman but she wouldn't let him behind her mask and he had no idea what she felt about him. Was this going to be a relationship or an on-and-off again sexual encounter with no accountability on their parts? He was not interested in the latter. Why didn't she trust him to share what was behind the pain and sadness so obvious in her eyes?

"I mean if you were asleep or going to sleep I can call you back later."

I've waited every minute of every day for you to call since the last time we spoke. Now you telling me you'll call back? That's what he really wanted to say but instead Sean said, "Look, Tia. I am not going to lie and say I don't miss you, because I do. I'm also not going to lie and say I haven't given a lot of thought as to where this is going. If it were going somewhere I imagined I'd have heard from you way before now. Though we've known each other only a few months, I think you know how I feel about you. The question is, do you feel the same way about me? When we are together, I feel like you care about me but when we are apart it seems like I am completely an afterthought. But that's only what I think." Sean surprised even himself. He had never, not once, said those words to a woman.

"Sean, what do you want from me? I'm not ready for the life you think we should have. You don't even know me?" She had never uttered words so far from the truth. She was so ready to embrace his feeling. She wanted to tell him that despite everything, her heart belonged to him but that she also knew that in the end that love would hurt him beyond words and cost him more than he was willing to pay.

"Tia," Sean snapped. "Why do you do that? Why do you try to hide yourself from yourself? I am not asking you to commit to me nor am I expecting you to melt because I have told you my truth. My feelings are mine and by choice I have chosen to share them with you. You pretend that you don't know how I feel but it's your self-centeredness and ego that prevents you from trusting me. Why can't you trust me, Tia?"

Tia was silent. Tears were clinging to her lids and she couldn't find the words. Did he know that the love he offered was what she had been looking for her entire life? If only she could go back to a place where she could come to him without all her baggage, did he think she wouldn't do it?

"Look, Tia," Sean continued. "I don't know what happened that makes you so hard on the inside but I want you to understand that maybe my only function in your life is to love you unconditionally. To give you the best I have to offer. If you chose to accept my feelings, I wouldn't expect anything from you but your best, which would include your trust. So, Tia, I won't ask you to choose between me and what's going on in your life. All I ask is for you to give what I've said some thought and keep us in your mind."

They both lapsed into silence but did not hang up their phones. The moment was both intimate and fearful. Sean was Tia's salvation. She knew that but she didn't know how she'd get from here to there. Sean was silent because he dared not continue. He was at least glad for the distance between them because he was feeling very emotional.

"Tee, what's up? Why you looking like somebody just slapped the crazy shit outta you?" Jada asked opening the refrigerator to grab a soda.

Tia covered the phone and hurried into the other room.

"Who was that?" Sean asked.

"Oh, that was just my crazy girlfriend, Jada. She's just being nosy."

Jada walked into the room where Tia was. She peeped the situation. "I got something better to do but if I tell, ya'll will be calling me all kinds of slut!" She whispered to Tia, poking her in the head.

Tia brought her finger to her mouth.

"So that's the notorious Jada you've told me about?" Sean asked.

"Yes, that's her." Tia looked at Jada and smiled. She was glad she'd interrupted the moment because it had gotten real heavy, real fast. The mood was back to normal.

"So," Sean said. "Why are you calling?"

"Actually, Sean, I've been meaning to call but I was so caught up in enjoying my time away from the city that the days just slipped by. Are you mad at me?" she whispered so Jada, who was headed back upstairs, didn't hear her being mushy.

"At first I was. Yes. But I guess that was just my ego speaking and my being spoiled. To be honest I was more worried about you than I was mad."

"Well, I am glad to know I was missed. It feels really good. But I tell you what, I'll spoil you and call tomorrow. I'm sorry Sean I should have called…but know that I am fine."

"Are you enjoying yourself or at least getting the rest you need?"

"I haven't done much resting but it's a good time. It's pretty quiet and restful though. Maybe too quiet. Anyway, enough about me. How's work treating you?"

"Same ole…same ole. Good guy, bad guy drama. The sooner we take the dirt off the street, like magic, twenty more garbage cans appear. It's a never-ending story for our people. But I've got to do what has to be done so I guess there is a benefit to the never-ending cycle. Don't ask me what it is."

"I'm sure there is," Tia said. If he only knew that she was turning over garbage she wondered what he'd say. She really ought to let this go but somehow she didn't seem to be able to.

"What does that mean?" Sean asked.

"Well, really nothing. I'm just being silly. But look at it this way, if you left the old dirt there're be twenty-one garbage cans instead of twenty."

"Ha," Sean said. "You are so right."

"So, do you have any good cases you're working on, or do they just give you the DWIs and traffic tickets?"

"You got jokes," Sean laughed loudly at Tia's attempt at comedy. "In fact, I am working one of the biggest cases of my career."

"Oh, Mr. Big Shot. And what might that be?"

"I don't know if you're familiar with the case. It was all over the papers and in the news last year. Matter of fact, it was in Harlem."

Tia tried to pick her brain to see if she knew what he was talking about. The only big case she remembered was a basketball player being gunned down. "I'm terrible at following current events. I don't know."

"Have you ever heard of the Dynasty Drug Crew? They were notorious in Harlem and it was such big news when it went down, it was hard to miss even if you weren't in law enforcement."

"Oh snap," Tia said hurriedly, "Sean, hold on a minute, I gotta run to the little girl's room. I'll call you tomorrow." She dropped the phone so fast, it cracked the headset. All the color drained from her face.

"What the hell?" Toya said as she came into the room. "You look like you've just seen a ghost!"

CHAPTER TWENTY-TWO

BALTIMORE

TIA NEEDED AIR. She went out to the front porch, dazed at the news that Sean was the prosecutor in Kato's case. What lesson was this life trying to teach her? Of all the people on earth, how? Why? Tia looked up at the night sky. Maybe the stars might spell out a message for her that showed her a way out of her cluttered and complicated life. She closed her eyes as a light breeze caressed her face, hoping that it would blow away some of the stark reality that was her life. When she finally opened her eyes, the emptiness and silence of her surroundings only served to heighten her despair and loneliness. How would she ever get from here to there?

When Tia left the porch, she resolved that the unknown, at which she was a master, was her domain. She was great at tackling obstacles but this situation was above her abilities. How would she tell Toya that she was in love with the man who was going to prosecute Kato? Toya would never understand, yet she should tell her. What would she do? What could she do? She had to keep this a secret. She had been growing more and more attached to the feelings Sean evoked in her and it was at that moment that she understood how much in love she was. She could no longer deny it. For the first time in her life, Tia felt vulnerable and exposed. She locked the doors. Tonight, at least, she was safe from having to face Toya.

The following morning, Tia did her best to be normal. When she went downstairs, Toya and Jada were playing casino, a card game that Toya had learned from her many visits to Kato. Jada was shuffling the cards as though she could will them to fall her way.

"Damn, Bitch, you're mixing them cards like you really can escape this whipping," Toya was laughing. She always won and she had just done beating Jada 12-10.

"Here, Bitch...cut!"

Toya cut the cards knowing she had no intention of letting Jada win or she wouldn't hear the end of it.

Just as Jada was reaching for the cards, the phone rang. She sprang up and answered it. Toya took advantage and peeked at the top card. It was the ten of diamonds which meant two extra points for Jada. She placed it at the bottom of the deck.

"Cheating again," Tia said stepping into the room.

"Sush," Toya smiled. "Where you going this early morning?" Toya was asking when they heard a blood curdling scream. Both Tia and Toya raced to the kitchen only to see Jada balled up on the kitchen floor, the wall phone hanging off the hook.

At first, they though Jada was playing the fool as usual but then they noticed real tears rolling down her face, they both rushed to her side. "What's going on Jada?" Toya brushed her hand over her face. She seemed to be in shock.

"They killed her. Oh, my God," Jada wailed. "They killed Kay."

Tia felt as though her heart would jump out of her chest. Toya was standing with a blank stare on her face as though she was trying to comprehend what Jada had said. Time seemed, all of a sudden, to be moving in slow motion as Jada continued to repeat. "They killed Kay. Why they kill Kay?"

"Hello, hello," the sound was coming from the phone. She picked up the receiver and put it to her ears. All she heard was heavy breathing which she realized was her own.

"Hello, Hello." It was Rich's voice.

"Hello," Tia said, feeling as though she was having an out of body experience. She needed that other person inside her to take control because as she listened to Rich, inside she had fallen apart.

"Tee, they killed Kay. They murdered Kay," his voice was cracking under the strain of delivering such tragic news.

The phone slipped from Tia's hand. She sat on the floor as rage coursed through her veins. She began banging her head trying to will Kaisia's face into her mind. She banged harder and harder when she could not conjure up a single image of her friend.

190

"Stop it, Tee," Toya was trying to hold back her friend whose anger had brought forth a brute strength they'd never seen. She was beating bruises into her face. Soon Jada joined Toya in holding Tee but they were struggling to control her. Toya ran to get something to restrain her while Jada pinned Tia to the floor.

"Get the fuck off me!" Tia yelled twisting and kicking in an attempt to break free. "I can't see Kaisia's face! I can't see Kaisia's face!" she kept screaming but it all came out as senseless screams.

"Tee," Toya had managed to restrain her friend and she was now cradling her in her arms. Jada was sitting in the corner rocking back and forth her arms wrapped around her knees. "Tee," Toya said again softly. "Please don't make me have to do this alone. I am not as strong as you. I can't hold on to all this by myself. You and Kaisia were my rocks when Kato got locked up. You carried me through the storm. I need you to be strong again right now. Kay would want you to be strong. We gotta be strong for Kay."

Jada now came over to where Tia and Toya were huddled. The women held each other and as their tears mingled, they vowed to revenge their friend's murder. Suddenly Kaisia's and Dakota's faces flashed into Tia's mind. It was as if Dakota was standing right next to Tia. Her beloved friend was gone. What on earth would happen now?"

The phone was still hanging from the wall. Tia picked it up. "Rich you still there?"

"I'm here Tee."

None of the women slept. They were paralyzed by the horrible details of their friend's death. At 9:30 a.m. the following morning, Tia called Jackie and told her to come over to the house. She didn't go into details but told her she'd explain once she got to the house.

Tia, Toya and Jada immediately got to packing. When they finished, Toya and Jada went to get the whips gassed up. Tia's plan was to be on the road by 11 a.m., if not sooner.

Tia had spoken to Rich five times since he'd called with the horrible news so she could get more details and understand what had happened. During one of the calls, Rich reported that they killed Ty as he was entering his apartment, blew his face off, then killed Kay with a shot to the head.

Tia didn't know if she hadn't understood that Ty was dead or if Rich hadn't said it earlier. It was another blow. Immediately, her mind went to Dakota. Tia was scared to ask because if the little girl had met the same fate as her mother and father, she would not be able to live with that. Tia braced herself but she had to know. "What about Dakota?" Her voice was deadly calm.

"I don't know but when Homicide got there, Dakota was not in the apartment. Maybe she was with her Grandma. I'ma gonna find out," Rich had promised.

"Who found the bodies?" Tia asked, taking charge.

"Ty's neighbor. She was passing by his door and realized it was slightly open. She knew Ty would never keep his door open for any reason so called out to him and when she got no response, she pushed the door open and the stench of..." he trailed off.

"That's enough," Tia didn't let Rich finish. She already knew the ending.

"It's all over the news. They interviewed the neighbor who found them and she too didn't say anything about a little girl in any of her interviews. I'ma check in with Kaisia's mom," Rich repeated.

Tia already knew that Dakota's grandmother didn't have her. The killer had taken her to extort money or to bury her. "Look, Dakota is missing and I don't want to think we'll..."

Jada had cut Tia off. "I don't need to hear it." She got up, grabbed her bag and walked out of the house to the whip to put her bags in the trunk. She slammed the door so hard, Tia and Toya had to clear their ears.

Tia was just zipping up her bag when Jackie walked through the door. She was about to speak when she saw in Tia's eyes that something was wrong. Very wrong.

TRENTON, NJ

Crime paced his bachelor apartment trying to figure out why he'd risked everything by bringing his victim's daughter to his home when he could just have easily left her behind. She wasn't even old enough to be a witness. He'd done what he had to do. Killing was never personal, it was a way of life that he enjoyed. He'd respected the bitch's loyalty and felt some remorse that he had to kill her. That could be one reason he now had a smarty pant kid on his tail. Crime sat on the barstool he'd pulled into the living room and replayed the scene in his head. When the little girl had stepped out of the room and stared so deeply into his eyes, it was as if his victim's soul was reaching out to him and he felt challenged and exposed. The kid was an exact replica of the woman whose brains he had blown to bits. As he turned to leave he felt rooted, captivated by the little girl whose eyes he felt burning a hole in his back. Crime faltered. His first mistake. He'd looked back. His second. He understood her loss. He knew exactly what she was feeling as his own mother had been murdered in front of him when he too was just a child. Though he was a hardened man, he had a heart for lost and lonely children. Maybe his own loneliness and pain contributed to him wanting to rescue her from the pain and loss she would experience with no one to care for her.

Crime's eyes wandered to the mini-bulk that was now resting on his couch. She'd been sleeping for a long time, almost as if she was too scared to open her eyes. The first few nights had been hell for all she did was cry for her mother and a few times for her father. Crime who had a few cribs around the city and Jersey opted to take her to his most secluded place in Trenton, New Jersey. Though the place sat on a few acres, he had gone through the trouble of having it insulated with the latest in soundproof materials and mounted a state-of-the-art security system complete with CCTV cameras. This was his major stash house where he kept a large amount of cash and an array of guns that he sold.

Crime got up from the stool and stood over the little girl. He watched as her tiny chest heaved up and down as she inhaled and exhaled. She looked just like a little African doll. Crime shook his head both to shake sense into it as well as to clear it so he could formulate a plan. No matter how similar their life journeys were, he could not allow himself to get attached. His lifestyle demanded his full attention. She had to go.

Crime reached behind his back and pulled out a nickel plated 9-millimeter Beretta. He cocked it against his hip and aimed it at Dakota's forehead but for the first time in his life, a conscience rose up. His will was weak. Crime knew that once he took her life and spilled the blood of an innocent child, there would be no turning back for him. No redemption ever. Crime willed his mind blank and wrapped his index finger around the trigger. He could feel the indented metal waiting for his command. Sixteen bullets. He only needed one to do the job. He closed his eyes and aimed the gun. When he opened them again it would all be over. He took one last look and once again found himself staring into the very eyes that had captivated him ten nights ago. Crime quickly put the gun back in his wait. He kneeled beside his captor and brushed her cheek with the back of his hands. He smiled down at her and was surprised when she smiled back at him.

"What's your name?" the soft, tiny voice of his captor asked looking up at him. Her voice turned Crime's heart to mush.

"I'm Uncle C. Crime realized that they'd been together for almost two weeks and he didn't know her name. His heart warmed again at her attempt at an introduction. He also figured she'd probably be more apt to accept a relative over a stranger.

"If you're my uncle, why don't I know you?" asked Dakota staring at Crime with wonder and curiosity.

"Because I was away," Crime replied. She was too smart for her age. He hoped his away statement would squelch her inquisitiveness. But that only started a series of questions he could not answer so he decided to change the subject.

"So, Beloved, are you hungry?"

"My name is not Beloved. It's Dakota, silly."

Crime smiled at her. Her wit and sharpness was refreshing. "Okay, Miss Dakota, what would you like to eat?"

SOMEWHERE ON I-95 N

Tia and Jada rode in silence. It had been a little over an hour since they left Baltimore and Tia was thankful that traffic wasn't heavy. Jada was slumped down in the passenger side her face swollen from tears. Tia checked the rearview to make sure Toya was still behind her.

Tia looked over at Jada once more. She was the one most likely to fall apart, though she'd been the one to hold it together when Tia had completely lost it. Still, Tia was most worried about Toya. This could throw her over the edge. She had a lot on her plate and though she was trying to be hard on the surface, everybody had a cracking point. She hoped this was not it for Toy. There was no way in hell she could ever tell her about Sean. Not ever. That would certainly be overload.

Tia called Rich to find out news about Dakota.

"Nothing new. I went over to Kaisia's mother's house. She's a wreck. There are lots of family members and friends with her trying to comfort her best they know how. She does not have Dakota."

"We're about two hours or so away. I'll hit you up once we get into the city. Keep your ears to the ground and call me if anything changes. We've got to find Dakota."

"Alright," Rich said. Tia was confident Rich would do everything he could to find out what had happened to Kaisia and Dakota.

They entered New Jersey and Tia checked once again to see if the crew was in-formation. Jackie had offered to ride into the city with them but Tia had told her to stay in B-More and hold down the fort. They would rejoin her after the funeral service. Tia wasn't quite sure that would be the case but she told Jackie they'd holla if their plans changed.

Tia picked up speed and continued on to New York.

CHAPTER TWENTY-THREE

Ebony AND TWEET WERE SITTING in Ike's den when Tweet told her the news. She was stunned. Kaisia was like a second mother to her and Tia's best friend. Ebony's heart broke for her sister and grieved for Kaisia. For the next few hours, the girls remembered the moments they'd shared with Kaisia with fondness and sorrow. Ebony longed to see her sister. Kaisia's loss underscored just how much they had both supported her. She felt a twinge of remorse.

"Tweet, remember the day Kaisia came to school and pressed that girl I had a beef with?"

"Yeah, I was shocked when she copped out so fast in front of the whole school. I remember."

"And remember when we went school shopping at Queens Plaza and we wanted to get those DKNY matching baubles and Tia and Rich said we'd already cost them too much?"

"Yeah," Tweet wiped tears from her eyes. "And Kaisia told us to wait until we were about to leave the store then threw the baubles in the cart?"

"Your brother and my sister's heads were real fucked up when we got in the car with the baubles on. Remember how they fell out laughing?"

Ebony sniffled. "I can't believe it, Tweet. How can Kaisia be gone?"

"I know. Do you think Kay got killed because of Ty?" Tweet asked.

"Why would I think otherwise? Everybody knows that Ty was out there in that life. Niggers get jealous quick."

Ebony wondered why Tweet had asked the obvious. Was there more to Kaisia's death? Ebony immediately thought of Tia. None of it made sense. Kaisia and Ty had long broken up. If someone wanted Ty, they could have killed him a long time ago. Why would they wait until he was back with Kaisia? Come to think of it, why was Kaisia even at Ty's house? If Kaisia's death wasn't about Ty, and Kaisia and Tia were best friends, could her sister's life be in danger? Ebony gasped and looked over at Tweet. She couldn't even imagine how she would endure losing her sister. She couldn't even fathom a world without her and though they weren't on the best of terms, she knew that would all blow over. At the moment, Ebony desperately wanted to see her sister.

As she stared at Tweet, it dawned on Ebony that her own safety could be at stake being Ike's girl. She had never thought of the dangers connected with this life until now and now that she realized what could happen, she no longer felt safe in Ike's house. She couldn't pretend either that she didn't know what he was doing.

"Did you know that Ty and Kay were back together?" Tweet interrupted Ebony's rumination.

"No. When did that happen?" Ebony asked.

"I don't know, that's why I asked. I thought maybe you'd heard something. I mean, if they were really together I'm sure Rich would have said something."

"I'm saying maybe Kay didn't want everybody up in her business, including your nosy brother and my sister. Besides, that's her baby father. Maybe it was just a coincidence and she'd just taken Dakota over to him. Matter of fact, where is Dakota?" Ebony's eyes got wider than saucers.

Tweet sat up straight. Hell, how could they have missed that? Where was Dakota? Why wasn't anybody talking about Dakota? "Ebony," Tweet turned to her friend. "I'm just gonna come out straight and say it. I think some funny shit is going down and I think your sister and my brother know more than we are lead to believe. I just feel that."

Ebony didn't mention that the thought had crossed her mind. She thought back to the last time she'd spoken with Rich. He was the one who kept her up to date on her sister. He'd told her that Tia had gone out of town for a little R&R and that Toya and Jada had gone too. She understood why Rich hadn't gone as he couldn't afford to leave Tweet's reckless-ass by herself, but why no Kaisia? The invincible five rarely went too many places without the other. Maybe that's why Kaisia had gone to Ty. She was trying to get him to keep Dakota so she could join Tia. It made more sense now than Kay and Ty getting back together. Ebony knew Kaisia despised Ty. Instead of sharing her thoughts with Tweet, though, she kept quiet. Ebony figured if Tia was in any way connected to whatever was going on, it was best to leave the connect out. Why add fuel to the fire? Plus, if she did tell Tweet, although she was her best friend, Tweet was capable of opening the gates of hell by mistake and Ebony just wasn't ready to risk her sister's reputation on he-say, she-say nonsense.

Tweet was looking at the painting of a mother and child that hung over Ike's desk. It was an odd painting for a guy unless he already suspected Ebony was pregnant. But no, it'd been there since she and Ebony started coming to Ike's. Maybe he had no mother too. Tweet wondered if all their destinies were tied together because they had no mothers. Was Dakota doomed to the same fate as all of them? Tweet looked from the painting over Ebony's head to Ebony, who was now sitting behind Ike's oak desk in his Italian leather chair. One of the reasons they'd become as tight as friends was because they shared the same story. They were both motherless and their elder siblings were trying as hard as possible to fill in for that loss, yet the bond of mother and child could never be replaced. Poor Dakota. Tweet's mind lingered on the little girl. What would happen to her? She figured that most likely, her grandmother would take her but Tweet knew that regardless of what happened, she was going to miss her mother because there could never, ever be anything like having a mother around. Tweet's heart reached across the distance to Dakota, wherever she might be.

Ebony sensed Tweet's eyes on her but continued to stare out the window. She felt drained and sad. She could no longer engage in this conversation, especially if she had to think about her sister who she was missing dearly. But how could she go crawling back when she had acted like a woman and moved out? Right now, she didn't feel like a woman. Her life seemed so uncertain. How could she find her way back to her sister without being a punk-ass coward? And how could she stay with Ike knowing the dangers of his lifestyle.

"Damn," Ebony said. "We've been sittin' here for two hours. I need some air." She rose from her chair and walked toward the door. Tweet followed.

The trio arrived in the city at 2:45 p.m. beating the Saturday traffic. As they hit the Lincoln Tunnel, Tia tried calling Rich but the cell signal was too weak. Besides, Jada was still sleeping as soundly as a baby, oblivious to reality. Tia tried to call Rich again as they hit West 4th and Spring. The phone rang four times and again went to voice mail. Why wasn't he answering? He knew they'd be back by now. She left a voicemail telling him they were back and to holla when he got the message.

Finally, Jada stirred in her seat as if she knew they were almost home.

"You finally gonna wake up, huh? You alright?"

Jada covered her eyes from the sun. "What time is it?"

"Time to wake your ass up. We home. Jay, you gonna be able to handle this? You were shaking in your sleep."

"Yeah, I'm good."

Tia was relieved because she knew she needed every soldier in tip top shape to bring justice for Kaisia's death and, more importantly, to find Dakota and bring her home safely. If she was still alive, they would find her, Tia vowed.

The light at 114th Street turned red and Tia stopped. The place was familiar but it now, all of a sudden, seemed different. Yes, she thought, nothing will ever be the same without Kay. The light turned green and Tia pulled off into the Harlem traffic.

BROOKLYN DA'S OFFICE

Sean left the judge's chambers drained. He spent the morning debating motions filed by the DA's office and the defense and Sean began to appreciate the enormity of the case. He'd walked into chambers hopeful and confident and walked out feeling like he was fighting a losing battle.

Needing to get out of the building, Sean walked down Chambers Street feeling much like a man with the whole world on his back. The whole damn case narked him to no end. It was a pomp and circumstance case anyway and he knew it. He'd been given the case that weighed heavily in favor of the defendant because the DA wasn't about losing and getting trashed especially since he was planning to run for mayor in the upcoming elections. This case was getting on his last nerve and he deserved it for taking the case when he knew the DA's true motive!

Sean stopped at his usual newsstand to get a copy of the *Daily News*.

"What's good, Sanjeer?" Sean chatted for a few minutes with the Indian attendant who'd been there for years.

"No news is good news, Mr. Adams." He gave him the change from his $5.00 bill.

Sean glanced at the headlines. Yes, he thought, no news was good news in his world. Nicole Simpson murder still dominated the headlines. Sean had been following the developments much like any curious citizen but his take was a little different from the media glut. The general population will quickly judge and convict anyone based on media propaganda. The media was so powerful that sometimes cases had to change states just to get a fair trial. For the media, these sensational stories were a windfall but for the accused, it could adversely affect the outcome of their trials. Media couldn't care less about the why and the who, because the "P" in profit was the game they played.

Sean always used these kinds of cases to study how the media can be used to influence judgment. He understood the tactics they used to make O.J seem like a brutal monster and Nicole, an innocent victim. The color polarization was a side show on its own. He knew that if he were to have a chance of winning the Dynasty case, he was going to have to understand the social, political and emotional strategies that he'd need to employ to impact its outcome.

Sean waved goodbye to Sanjeet and ducked into the small café next door that carried the best hash brown in the city. He took his usual corner seat. The waitress, not his regular, approached to take his order. His usual waitress would have put his order in the moment she saw him walk in the door. It was all good for he could do with some extra time away from the office.

Sean watched as the waitress walked over to the order terminal. Damn, for a white woman the girl had some junk! That probably meant she was mixed with something. She wasn't attractive or anything but in a pinch, she could do. Sean immediately caught his thoughts. He was missing Tia. She had not called back after she abruptly hung up on him. That's what was wrong with him. Tia Davis. He was confident that after their emotional conversation, she'd have called again but not a peep. She was a hard woman to fathom. Sean loved a challenge and though he had really developed genuineness feelings for her, at this moment he wasn't sure that he would keep trying.

The waitress placed Sean's order in front of him and flashed him a smile. Sean smiled back, glad for the distraction from his thoughts. With fifteen minutes to spare, Sean opened the newspaper and scanned the headlines. God, another tragic story in Harlem. A couple gunned down inside their apartment. And they were so young. Sean hated that. Every time there was a borough killing, it was always the young who died. The young woman in the black and white picture was very attractive. What a waste of a life! As he expected, there was no suspect or witness. That was always the case in the 'hood where snitching was worse than death. Disgusted, Sean closed the paper and reached into his pocket for a Twenty Dollar bill. He paid the waitress and left her a generous tip.

HARLEM

Tia pulled into the parking lot of the St. Nicholas Houses. She'd finally reached Rich and they were all meeting at the Honeycomb. Tia and Jada exited their car and walked over to Toya's car.

"Ya'll wanna get something to eat before Rich gets here?" Tia asked.

"I don't care one way or the other," Toya said.

"I could go over to MaMa's Fried Chicken and get a bucket," Toya put her duffle bag back on the trunk.

"Yeah, we could do that. What'd you say Jada? We'll all go together."

"On second thoughts, Tee," Toya said, "you just go on in and rest a while. I'll run over with the car. Take Jada with you. She's in no shape to handle this right now."

Tia agreed. Jada was an emotional wreck. They needed to be inside. "Okay, but give me your duffle bag. It'll make it easier for you to bring up the chicken."

Toya handed Tia her bag and got back in the car when Tia came running back. "Let's walk. Jada's gonna go on up."

The women sat on the hood of the car and watched as Jada entered the building. Toya was happy to be home. B-More was definitely not her speed. Plus, she's missed Kato. She was planning to go up and see him at tomorrow. She didn't even know how she was gonna bring up Kaisia. She had been wracking her brain on the drive back and was glad she'd driven in by herself. She'd cried practically the entire time home. After today, there would be no time for tears.

"Ain't it some shit how life goes on?" Toya says to Tia.

"Yeah. Ain't it a bitch."

"Look at all them strangers going up and down 8th Avenue oblivious that Kay is dead. This is the street that holds all our memories, good and bad, and now she's gone and these fuckers don't even know." Toya's eyes moistened.

"Can't do that shit, Soldier," Tia slapped her on the back. "We're in combat mode. You ready?"

Toya nodded and the women headed up to 8th Avenue.

Tia and Toya walked through the projects with their 9-millimeter hand guns concealed in their handbags. They studied every face they saw, and every young child Dakota's age. They were taking no chances. Schooled in the ways of project life, they move swiftly and stealthily through looking for any sudden movement that could mean danger. They didn't recognize too many of the people in this project. As they came to the exit on 7th Avenue, they noticed a group of about eight guys posted by a white recycling bin. When they were about ten feet away, Tia and Toya noticed that a couple of them turned to look in their direction as they approached. Under normal circumstances, Tia would have chalked this up to a group of niggas being niggas but nothing was normal after Kaisia's death. Tia reached into her handbag and gripped her palm around the cold metal of the Glock. Toya had already removed her gun and placed it in the kangaroo pocket of her sweatshirt. As they came closer, the entire group of boys seemed to be watching them. Toya kept her eyes on the big, dark skin brother who seemed too grimy for his own good. She knew she could remove the top of his dome from where they were and still have fifteen billets to play with.

As they continued walking toward the group, a brown skinned brother sporting a white T-shirt, denim shorts and white on white Air Force Ones stepped over to block the entrance. Tia grip was firm on the Glock. She could discharge in seconds and if it went down right now, they had a good chance of airing over half of them out before they even heard the first shot.

Brown Skin licked his lips as Tia and Toya got closer.

"Nigga, stop frontin'. You ain't tryin' to holla, is you?" the dark-skinned brother asked.

Toya watched him with deep concentration. He stepped right up to them. Tia and Toya stopped dead in their tracks, in preparation to make somebody's child a memory. It's true: the women were beautiful. No ordinary, average chicks and it could be that the group of brothers were just trying to get the attention of two beautiful females who could be the ultimate booty call.

"Ya'll two ladies look like ya'll want some company. Can I walk with ya'll?" Dark Skin asked, stepping between them.

"Excuse us, please," Tia said, refusing to move until he stepped back from them.

"I'm saying, Ma, why it got to be like dat and shit? Just holla at a boy for a while. You won't be disappointed," he grinned. He stood his ground because these wicked lines of his had been used on many unlucky females who'd crossed his path.

Toya had already made up her mind that she didn't like his grimy ass. Now he was tryin' to add insult to the injury with his ignorant ass. "Didn't my friend say excuse us?" Toya was irritated.

A few of the guys that were with him came over when Toya screamed at him. His posture and mood had gone hostile and his homies circled in.

"Bitch, first of all, I'm not talkin' to ya yellow ass, but if want some attention, I be with you in a second. Until then, hold ya breath while I holla at ya homegirl."

His posse broke out into oohs and aahs as they cheered him on. Homeboy was grinning from ear to ear. Tia, realizing that the whole thing was nothing more than what was, a nigga tryin' to holla', said. "Toya, come on."

As the women stepped pass Dark Skin, he grabbed Tia by the wrist. Tia snatched her wrist away and smacked him. For a second, his homeboys fell silent then only a second broke out into laughter.

"Bitch, is you fuckin' crazy?" Dark Skin said trying to save face and regain his crushed pride.

"Fuck you," Tia said and turned her back to him and kept walking. Toya and Tia had gotten a couple of feet when a bottle crashed in front of them. Being that it didn't hit them, they ignored it and chalked it up to a hot headed, immature nigga who got his feelings hurt. As they stepped out of the projects and onto the Avenue, a Snapple bottle brushed pass Tia's face. Toya didn't wait for the third bottle. She spun around gun in hand. Tia did likewise and pulled the pistol from her purse. Toya fired the first shot followed by a torrent of gunfire. The skies were mid-dark but the sparks from both pistols lit 7th Avenue up like the 4th of July. When they stopped firing, Tia was able to look clear across the Projects from 7th to 8th Avenues. Tia and Toya walked back towards the projects with guns by their sides. Dark Skin was lying on the ground bleeding from a leg and chest wound.

"Ya'll bitches better kill me 'cause if I see ya'll again, it a problem." They were sure he regretted not having his gun at home 'cause he'd have dropped some bitches.

Standing on either side of him, Tia and Toya looked down at the fool. "Don't worry, Handsome, you won't see us again," Tia said as she and Toya emptied the remaining slugs in their clips into his chest.

CHAPTER TWENTY-FOUR

As TIA AND TOYA HURRIED BACK through the Projects on their way to the parking lot, they saw Rich and Jada coming toward them. They still had their guns at their sides and they noted, so did Rich and Jada.

Rich was the first to spot them and as they met up Tia said, "Turn around and go back toward the parking lot."

Rich and Jada did just that and Toya and Tia followed leaving enough distance so no one would know they were together. The project had emptied out and cop sirens were roaring in the background. Only when they reached the parking lot did Tia look around to make sure nobody was watching as they tucked their pistols in their waists.

With red and blue lights coming from 7th and 8th Avenues, the Projects began to come alive with nosy people trying to figure what had gone down.

Rich and Jada waited for Tia and Toya to make it to the lot. Rich was unsure of what just took place but he knew that whatever it was they would not be returning to the Honeycomb.

"Follow me, Toy," Tia said. "We're going to my crib." She said getting into the driver's side of the car.

"Naw, Tee. Your brother might be there," Rich said. Why don't we go to my crib? My sister is over at your sister's spot. We'll have privacy there."

"I-ght, get in. Let's go."

Tia's nerves were shot. She had never felt so out of control in her life. She wasn't even sure what had just happened. My god, she thought, they'd been back in the city for only forty-five minutes and already they had murdered a man; a man who probably deserved it but she wasn't in the habit of taking lives unnecessarily. She was tense, her emotions heightened because of Kaisia. She could blame all this on that and she could accept it, but what scared the hell out of her was the cold bloodedness with which they had killed the man, how devoid of emotions she felt. And if she were to be truthful, there was a sort of power and even an enjoyment behind her brutal act. They had to get out of this business. Things had gone too far. Her crazy actions could have jeopardized Toya. What was she thinking? What she knew for sure was that it was going to be a long, long night, and already she was feeling fatigued.

NEWARK, NJ CRIME'S PLACE

Shit was getting crazy. It had already been almost three weeks since he'd iced her parents and over a week since Crime had been cooped up in the New Jersey house with Dakota all day and all night. He barely stepped out onto the balcony to smoke a Newport and he was a chain smoker. He kept watching the news to see if they would mention anything about a little girl. Nothing so far. He wondered if she had family outside of her mother and father. If she did, why wasn't anyone looking for her? Crime looked down at the little head that rested on his lap. They had become close these past few days. She asked about her mother from time to time but it surprised Crime that most of the time she was peaceful and attentive. If he had kids, not that he cared to or would, they would have to be like Little Ms. Dakota here. As he sat looking at the little girl, he wondered whether there was a soul connection. Why had he spared her life? Crime couldn't believe that he had so much in common with someone so young.

He was also just a child when he witnessed his mother's murder. At her age, he was also mesmerized by guns. When Crime had tried to watch the Lion King 2 movie with her, thinking that all kids liked that sort of thing, he had quickly found out differently. Not only wasn't she not interested, she had seemed more interested in the 9-millimeter Glock Crime had tucked into his shoulder holster. At first, Crime had tried to brush off the questions by gently telling her that it wasn't a toy but she had shocked him when she had said she knew what it was because her mommy had two. Her curiosity and natural innocence had prompted Crime to remove the pistol from the holster, take the clip and extra bullets from its chamber and hand it to her to see her response. Dakota had held the gun with both hands because it was too heavy for her. She had gazed at it then looked up at him.

"Do you shoot people?" she had asked. Crime couldn't believe she had even known what it was much less its purpose. She had stared at the gun as though mesmerized.

"Yes," Crime had said because he couldn't lie to her. He actually hated liars. Well, for starters she was smart and witty.

"Why do you shoot them?"

"Because it's my job." Crime had replied, feeling completely comfortable engaging in conversation with Dakota.

"Can I shoot people too?" she had asked, staring directly into Crime's eyes, the eyes that had spared her life.

Crime had sat next to Dakota and had looked deeply into her eyes. He had stared at her for what had seemed like eternity for he had realized that in the mesmerizing eyes that had been staring back at him was a steeliness, an edge that convinced him he was looking in the eyes of a natural born killer.

HARLEM

Rich flipped on the light switch as soon as they walked in and the stark darkness in the apartment came to life, the only noise the rumbling of the refrigerator. The living-room of Rich's two-bedroom apartment was covered in plush wall-to-wall carpeting with large black and gold hexagonal shapes. Three large traditional African masks adorned the far wall and African art in a kaleidoscope of vibrant colors covered the walls, making the apartment look like a gallery for African art and gave the house an elegant finishing touch. The gold and black motif continued into Rich's bedroom where the highlight of the room was the marble lined in-floor Jacuzzi. The canopy-style bed boasted a black and gold comforter which matched the drapes. An air conditioner whirred and kept the room at a very comfortable temperature.

Everyone picked their corner of the room to chill. No one spoke for a few minutes, then Tia broke the silence. "We can't go back to the Honeycomb, at least not for a while. In fact, St. Nicks is a dead issue."

"Tee, what the hell happened back there?" Jada asked.

"A group of guys assaulted me and Toya. It all happened so fast I am having trouble myself making sense of all this."

"Unfortunately, we laid one of them down," Toya said.

"Did ya'll know them? Did you suspect they may be connected to Kaisia?"

"Naw, we didn't know them. It was more of a spur of the moment thing," Toya said.

"What do you mean spur of the moment? How could you kill a mutha fucker in a spur of a moment in broad daylight? Ya'll were only gone for a few minutes, Toy. Fuck! I don't know what's happening to us." Jada was getting emotional all over again.

Toya who'd been sitting on the bed got up and walked over to the bedroom window. "How the fuck would you know how long we were gone. You've been in a fuckin' coma for two days to even realize what the fuck is going on around you!"

"Toy, why the fuck you always gotta come out your face with me? I've been lettin' a lot of shit slide that's been coming my way out of that stank mouth of yours."

Tia felt the tension boiling over but she felt powerless to do anything. What could she do? She was herself in deep shock. Rich looked at Tia who was staring at the floor, like she was waiting for a sign, and realized she was going to be useless. He knew he had to do something to break up the confrontation as Toya spun around from the window and advanced to where Jada was sitting. Jada, who was a few inches taller than Toya and build more solidly, immediately jumped to her feet.

Toya wagged her finger In Jada's face. "Bitch, you don't dictate shit I do!"

When Jada brushed Toya's hand away from her face, she became further aggravated. Rich jumped in between them to break up what looked like it was about to become a cat fight. "What the fuck wrong with ya'll? Why the fuck ya'll beefin'? Come on, we're fuckin' family here. Jay, if a nigga got laid out because he played himself, so fuckin' what? That's life. He made a choice and the choice he had to live with called death. All we have is us yet ya'll really all tryin' to come to blows over some bullshit. It ain't all about that and we know. So, let's call it what it is. Matter of fact, fuck it. We might as well all rumble up in this bitch so we can get down to business." Rich stepped aside. "Go ahead, but whatever you break you gotta buy back, Bitches."

Tia laughed. Toya looked from Rich to Jada and returned to her place at the window. Jada sat back on the bed.

"Listen ya'll, our nerves are frayed. It's been a rough few days but we've come this far because we all have something nobody seems to cherish more: each other. One of us is gone and we feelin' it but I wish Kay was here to see how ya'll bitches are actin'," Tia said.

At the mention of Kay, the room fell silent.

"I got some smoke if any of ya'll want to get right," Rich pulled out a drawer and held up a bag.

"I think we all need to be a little bent tonight," Jada said.

"Also, I spoke to Kay's moms. The wake is tomorrow over at Bentley's Funeral Home on 145th and St. Nick."

Tweet couldn't stand being cooped up in Ike's house any longer. First of all, she was never in one place long enough to feel crazy and though the house was stifling, it was more the fact that Ebony, since they found about Kaisia's death, had pretty much withdrawn. And, she didn't seem to be coming out anytime soon. Tweet wasn't sure what exactly caused the sudden change in Ebony but she was in no mood to be anybody's shoulder tonight. Besides, Ebony'd know where to find her if needs be. Tweet listened to hear if there was any movement behind the bedroom door. Nothing, so she grabbed her stuff and headed out.

Foolhardy as it was probably too late to walk through the desolate Colonial Park at this time of night, Tweet took her chances to avoid the hordes of people on the Avenue. The night air felt refreshing. When she exited, she was on Bradhurst Avenue. Tweet crossed Bradford and headed down the hill towards Edgecombe Avenue. The Jamaicans were out in full force tonight selling weed. Tweet didn't look in their direction or make eye contact but she it was hard to miss the loud-ass Jamaicans in their multicolored gear. She wondered how an earth they were so successful at what they did especially since they did their dirt right out in the open. She'd heard that even New York Cops didn't fuck with the Rasta men. She was just glad that as she passed none of them tried to holla at her. Tweet got to 143rd and Edgecombe about to turn the corner when she heard someone calling her name. She turned to see Joy walking toward her.

"Tweet, what's up?"

"Bitch, what's good?" Tweet replied. It'd been a while since she'd seen Joy.

"Ain't much, but damn where you been? I thought some rich nigga kidnapped you and took you out of the 'hood."

"I wish that was the case." Tweet loved the idea of being out of the 'hood and having money. "Anyway, I've been around but I just recently had a death in the family."

"Damn, sorry to hear that. Is there anything I can do?" Joy offered.

Tweet wanted to look at the bitch cross-eyed. *I just said I had a death in the family. What could you do to bring her back?* Instead she said. "Naw, I'll be alright. Anyway, what's been up with you?" Tweet checked out homegirl's getup. She was rockin' that Prada hard. She wondered what her latest trick was. That was the reason she liked Joy because they were both top of the line operators who knew how to hustle niggas, except she didn't have to give up the pussy as fast as Joy. From the look of things, it had paid off. "So, who's your new friend? I see they takin' good care of you."

"You don't know him." Joy answered too quickly.

The bitch, Tweet thought. But she knew that's how the game was played. You don't give away your source or other bitches will be scheming to take away your goods.

"Did you hear about Rob?" Joy asked.

"Which Rob? I know fifteen Robs," Tweet said, ready to end the friendly street meeting.

"Rob from St. Nicks projects that got money with Lye and Doug on 7th.

"Oh, black-ass Rob that use to fuck with Crystal. I know him. Why? What happened?"

"The nigga got murdered tonight right in his own project and guess what, they said some bitches did it. That's the rumor anyway. But I think that's some bullshit 'cause you know how grimy that nigger was."

Tweet knew exactly how grimy Rob was because she used to talk with one of his people. One day she'd gone into the projects looking for her guy and ran into Rob. When she'd asked Rob where his man was he'd said he was up in his crib and that he'd was on his way back up after copping some smoke so she could come up with him. At first Tweet had told Rob to just tell his man to come downstairs but Rob insisted that she come upstairs. When Tweet got up to the apartment, his man wasn't there. All Rob wanted was to try and feel her up. She was lucky that someone came to the apartment and she was able to get out. To this day, she felt if she hadn't escaped he would probably have raped her with his grimy-ass mutha fuckin' self. Good the nigga was laid down. "Shit happens." Tweet said.

"Word," Joy said and gave Tweet a pound.

"Listen, Boo, I'm out and about but make sure you get up with me this week. I heard they just opened a new club called 40/40 and I've been dying to see what it's about," Tweet said.

"Been there and it's all that, but you know I'll ride with you up there. I'll holla this week and check in with you." Joy said.

"I-ght then. Peace." Tweet gave Joy a hug and continued down Edgecombe.

THE BRONX

Crime didn't quite understand why he felt compelled to drive around the East Tremont section of the Bronx at 2:35 a.m. with this little girl in his car. After a week of being cooped up, they needed air but this was a little too much air. Not only were they out late but they were crusin' one of the worst sections of the Bronx. Soundview was notorious for murders and druggies and although he didn't grow up there, he'd always hated how dark and hopeless the area was for anyone living that reality. Crime looked out the window at a bunch of guys hanging out on the corner. One wearing a throwback New York Knicks jersey and matching cap, was sitting on a dumpster. Another guy was talking on his phone and another three were in a group not too far away. He just knew they were up to no good. These reckless mutha fuckers were a menace to society who always ended up hurting someone innocent--someone who just couldn't escape the reality of the

214

ghetto. His mother was recklessly murdered by a group of young, stupid niggas just like the ones he was observing. Crime made a U-turn and parked directly across the street from where the group was hanging out.

Dakota was also looking across the street but when Crime followed her eyes, he saw that she was looking at an older lady. She turned to face Crime. "Are we going to see my Nana?"

Crime had never heard her mention the name before. He figured Nana meant grandmother and that she was indeed talking about her grandma. He thought back to an older woman he saw being interviewed on the news. Maybe he should find her and drop the kid off anonymously. "No, we are not going to see your Nana right now."

Dakota turned away from him and looked back at the woman walking into the projects. "Listen, do you want to help me do something?" Crime asked, hoping to take her mind off her Nana and the past. What good was it to remember the past? It would only mean a long and painful future life.

Dakota turned to face him. "Yeah."

"Okay, but first you have to make a promise not to tell nobody our secret."

Dakota bobbed her head in agreement. She smiled at Crime and again the eyes bore into him. She seemed to like the idea.

"I'm a big girl, right? Mommy told me if I can keep secrets I am a big girl." Kay had told Dakota that when she had walked in on her removing two guns from her purse. Dakota had kept the secret until she saw Uncle C had guns too, it hardly seemed a secret.

Crime reached into his waist and pulled out the Glock 9.

"Are you going to shoot somebody?" Dakota asked looking steadily at the gun in Crime's hand.

Was he crazy? Crime questioned his logic but if his instincts were right, he had the making of the perfect assassin on his hand. Maybe he was giving her too much credit or he was seeing what he wanted. Maybe she was just an innocent girl whose life he'd finally fucked up. Maybe he should find her

Nana for real as bringing her up would be way out of his league. Then again or maybe she would be his protégée.

"Kill then all," Dakota said narrowing her eyes as she turned her gaze to the group that Crime was focused on.

All Crime's doubts vanished as he stepped out of the car, leaving the engine running. He walked over to the passenger door and opened it so that Dakota could step out. He took her hand as they crossed the street headed in the direction of the group. An eye for an eye, Crime thought as they approached. He knew very well that it was not this group of thugs who killed his mother but they would kill somebody else's mother. They would doom another him and Dakota to life as an assassin, hating the world for its cruelty and allowing the highest bidder to take advantage of their dead emotions.

The streetlamps overhead, those that weren't broken, cast an eerie feel over the barely lit avenue and was the only source of light. Crime measured his stride so Dakota could keep in step with him like a shadow. For as far as the fools on the corner were concerned, they could be a father and daughter going home. Except the guy who was sitting on a dumpster, not one looked up. Crime did not look in his direction and Dakota didn't take her eyes off them.

When Crime and Dakota came within a couple of feet from the targets, Crime released Dakota's hand and removed the Glock from his waist, placing it between him and Dakota. Dakota did not flinch even as the lowered gun was at the level of her head. Crime and Dakota were about foot away when he raised his gun and fired twice hitting the guy on the dumpster in the chest. As he fell to the ground, Crime continued to fire hitting all but one individual who was standing in the group of three. The guy tried to run through the projects but was cut down as the slug tore through his head. Crime watched as he fell to the grass.

Dakota and Crime walked over to the guy who'd fallen from the dumpster who seemed to have been moving. Blood oozed from his mouth and body. He was trying to say something and Dakota started at him at him as his eyes pleaded with her to spare his life. Dakota looked up at Crime.

Crime pointed the gun to his face and fired once. The impact of the bullet hitting flesh squirted and splattered blood, a sprinkle hitting Dakota who used the sleeve of her dress to wipe the blood from her face. Crime tucked the Glock back into his waist and put out his hand to Dakota. Like a parent reaching for their child's hand when crossing the street, Dakota placed her hand into Crime's and together they crossed the street back to the car

CHAPTER TWENTY-FIVE

"WE HAVE TO FIND OUT whose spot it was that we hit in order to know who's behind this, which means we gonna have to hit the streets hard. We've got to be diligent. We can no longer be merciful to our enemies. This is serious business as whoever it is may have kidnapped Dakota to get to us." Tia said, looking at each person. "We will use every means of retribution to avenge Kaisia's death. I mean to lay down the lives of each and every person who is responsible for her murder and possibly her daughter's."

Everyone agreed that Kaisia's murder deserved justice and that they were willing to lay down their own lives to make sure that street justice was exacted. What worried them was they had no idea where to start. Rich had been beating the streets since the murder yet not one of his sources had a single lead. They were clueless. Not even the rumor mill coughed up anything and that was very odd. Rich found that especially odd since in all his dealing in the street somebody always knew something. To Rich, it all added up as a personal hit rather than an act of retaliation. Rich wondered if anyone else saw it as he did.

"I'm suspecting that Kay's cousin was murdered because they figured out that he was involved with setting up the hit and with his life on the line, he might have exposed Kaisia. We can start there and find out who else he was fuckin' with. They may know something," Tia offered.

"What I want to know," Toya said as Tia sat next to her. "Is how the fuck we all got so deep in this shit?" Toya thought of all the times she'd encouraged Kato to just walk away from the game telling him that nothing good could come out of this kind of life. He'd always answered, 'you have to be in my shoes to really understand that it's not that easy.' Now that she had walked the distance, his words became more real. She also knew that she would never leave her friends alone with this reality. She was no coward and they had pledged to the motto. They have pledged an Oath to Honor Kay's death. Toya had been in the game long enough to know that once they made the move they were planning, there would be no turning back. "Tell me soldiers," she said. "What do we gotta do to bring the wolves outta hiding?"

Tweet stepped off the elevator feeling exhausted. The walk from St. Nicholas Place to Lenox Towers had drained her, but she was happy to be back home. Tweet dug out her keys and hurried down the hallway. She'd expected the apartment to be empty but as she pushed open the door she saw that the living room light was on. Tweet closed the door softly because she didn't want to disturb Rich. It was unusual for him to be home at this time. She tip-toed down the hall toward her bedroom. A light peeked out from under Rich's door and the bathroom light was on. She was about to knock on his door when she heard a female voice, one she immediately recognized. Tweet put her right ear to the door and tried to hear the words that came from inside Rich's bedroom.

"We have to do this right. I'm gonna contact Jamaican Stan because we are going to need the proper artillery to execute our next move. Jada, you gotta find us two hoopties, nothing that can be traced back to any of us. Try to get dark colors and nothing flashy. Rich, check the morgues and see if any little girl aged six to nine years has come through." Tia didn't like assuming that Dakota was dead but she had to accept all possibilities until she found out otherwise and with whom they were dealing.

"I'm just sayin'," Jada said. "If they do have Dakota, wouldn't they try to contact somebody, if not us? Her grandmother has been all over the news pleading for her return."

Tia had thought about the very same thing countless times. In order for the killers to have known who they were, Kaisia would have had to reveal that information and she was sure Kay would never have done that.

"Let's just say they do contact us. It's not like nobody knew we were Kaisia's friends. But how would we know they weren't setting a trap and that Dakota isn't already dead?" Toya asked, hoping and praying her latter statement was nowhere near true.

Tweet kept her ears glued to the door. All her suspicions about them knowing more than meets the eyes were being proven right. Poor Dakota, Tweet felt a deep pain in her heart for the little girl. No matter what, her innocence and childhood had been shattered or cut short. An innocent victim caught up in random bad luck. Tweet always had a feeling that Rich was involved in more than credit card scams and boosting. That alone couldn't have afforded them the top of the line apartment or the unlimited money that seemed to be flowing around there. She listened closer to hear if they mentioned anything about why Kaisia was murdered. Nothing. If they had it might explain what they were into. Tweet stayed plastered to the door.

"I think C-Black knew Fat Steve," Jada said.

"Who's C-Black?" Tia asked. Nobody seemed to recognize the name.

"You remember C-Black. He's the kat who gave me half of the money we used to cop them burners from Stan," Jada replied.

"Oh, yeah," Tia said. "But how do you know that he knew Fat Steve?"

"Because one day we were uptown around Drew Hamilton and there were some guys standing by the ramp. C-Black went and hollered at them. Anyway, Fat Steve was there and although C-Black didn't say anything to him they gave each other that look like, what's up. You know that shit niggas be doin.'"

Tia perked up. She believed this could be their first break. "Alright then, find out all you can about who he fucks with, especially who he gets money with and find out who's he dealing with out of the Bronx. If he starts getting suspicious, fall back. Oh, yeah, before I forget. The same day I called ya'll about Kay my connect off of Broadway is willing to deal Fifteen Thousand a bird just as long as we cop four and better, also..."

Tia stopped Rich by raising her hand and putting her fingers to her lips so everybody got the message. The room fell silent and they all looked at Tia trying to understand what was wrong. Tia pointed to the bottom of the bedroom door. There was a shadow that blotted out some of the light revealing that someone might be there. Quietly, they got off the bed. Quality paid for itself, thought Rich as his Sealy mattress, unlike the cheap shits with squeaky spring, did not make a sound. The intruder was not alerted as Tia tip-toed over to the door. Rich opened his chest of drawers and retrieved his .44 magnum. Toya and Jada pulled out their pistols and Tia already had hers as she approached the door. Whoever the unwelcomed soul was, it would not be their lucky day as the posse closed in on the door. Rich was now at the door, his gun aimed at the mid-section of the frame.

Tweet could not believe she was hearing all this shit. It was like one of them urban novels. Shit. She wondered if she should tell Ebony but immediately knew that was not a good idea. It was best to let Ebony continue to believe that Kaisia death was the result of being in the wrong place at the wrong time. Ebony, with her innocent-ass self wouldn't be able to deal with any of this. Tweet adjusted her ear. The conversation had quieted down but she was hoping it would pick up again. This was juicy information.

Rich wrapped his arm around the door knob and waited for Tia to give the signal. Tia watched the shadow under the door trying to get a sense of how many people might actually be out there. The shadow seemed to move from time to time but it was trying to stay in one place as if the person on the other side of the door wasn't sure when to strike. Tia gave Rich a nod and he snatched open the door so fast backing up to take aim, he froze when he saw the person on the other side of the door.

Four guns were aimed at Tweet. She had a look of abject terror on her face as she found herself staring down the barrel of four guns. Her face had paled like ghost and her heart was beating so fast she thought she was going to collapse right then and there. Sweat poured from her forehead and her lungs were struggling to catch air. Tweet thought about moving but her feet would not obey. She stood looking at the four people behind the door, her mouth gaped wide open as the look of terror spread over each of their faces. "It's me." Tweet's voice was so small, she thought she'd died and was having an out of body experience.

The Posse lowered their guns. They stared at Tweet and couldn't believe their eyes.

"What the fuck?" Rich dropped his gun on the carpet and rushed over to Tweet who looked like she was about to faint at any minute. He grabbed her by the shoulder, shaking her more out of shock that anything. "What the fuck are you doing here?" He screamed, pulling her to him. "You alright?" He asked embracing her so tightly, he could have just asphyxiated her.

Tweet was crying now, her lips quivering with fear as she tried to speak. Toya, Tia and Jada flopped down on the bed. Toya covered her face with her hands. "We could have killed her," she whispered, her nerves now completely shot. Tia and Jada got up and walked over to where Rich and Tweet were standing. Tia pulled Tweet into an embrace and started stroking her hair.

"Tweet, you alright?" she asked.

Jada leaned against the wall shaking her head. "This day is turning into a mutha' fucker!"

Rich stared at his sister. He could have killed his own sister. "Tweet," he said, "what are you doing here? I thought you were staying with Ebony for the week?"

Tears were rolling down Tweet's face. "I so sorry, Rich. I...I just wanted to come home and be with you."

"Okay. It's okay now," Rich said walking his sister to her room. "It's okay," he said as he set her down on the bed. I know that was a shock, so rest for a minute."

Tia and Jada had followed him into Tweet's room.

"Tweet," Rich sat beside his sister. "I need you to be honest with me. What did you hear?"

Tweet looked at Tia and lowered her eyes for it was Tia she had heard talking mostly and she was scared to repeat it. Rich could tell by her look that his suspicions that she'd heard too much was right. Tia, too, had picked up on the body language.

"Tweet," Tia joined Rich and Tweet on the bed. She placed her hand on Tweet's leg. It was a friendly gesture but she flinched. "Listen to me, ain't nobody going do nothing to you. We are family here. You are like a sister and I love you deeply but it's real important that you tell us what you heard."

Tweet felt all eyes on her. She nodded in agreement.

"Alright. Did you hear everything we said?" Tia asked.

"When I came in, I was trying not to disturb Rich but when I say the light under his door I was about to knock when

I heard your voice. Tee, I didn't mean to listen. I swear," Tweet said as she started to cry.

Jada handed Tweet some tissue from the nightstand.

"Tweet, you can't take back what you heard. What's done is done so I'm just gonna ask you to believe me from this point on. When I said we loved Kaisia and Dakota very much and that is the reason we have to find out who did this and we would do the same for you, do you believe that?"

Tweet nodded her head again. "I know that Tee, but why did they kill Kay? She was a good person and didn't fuck with nobody."

"I don't know Tweet but we'll find out. But I'ma need you to do me a favor. You can't ever reveal nothing you heard tonight to nobody. There may be a chance that we could still bring Dakota home even if it's a shot in the dark. It's a chance we have to take. Do you understand?"

Tweet nodded again. Tia kissed Tweet on the forehead. Tweet knew that if she didn't keep this secret, this might just be the kiss of death.

"Come on," Rich said. "Get some rest."

Tweet held onto her brother's hand and he put his arm around her. "It's gonna be okay," Rich said. He feared his sister might have just grown up a bit.

Tia, Jada and Toya left the room. Jada sidled up to Tia and asked, "Do you think she'll be able to hold all that?"

"I think she will because she loved Kaisia as much as any of us, but I'm afraid that the information she now has may be a burden, and may scar her. I hope she is as strong as she appears to be."

Back in the living room each of the women was lost to their own thoughts. Toya who was nursing a serious headache decided that she'd go see Kato right after Kaisia's wake the next day. She really wanted to talk to him and seek his guidance. She wasn't sure how much she could or should tell him. She didn't want to add any more burden to him than he already had with his trial coming up the next month and all.

Jada was thinking about Kaisia and Dakota. How the fuck can life change so drastically in the blink of an eye? All the "what ifs" and "maybes" of the situation were driving her crazy. The one thing she was sure of was that if they went down the road they were planning, none of them would come out being the same people who'd gone in. For the first time in Jada's life, she understood her mortality. At the moment, an overwhelming feeling took over and she missed Kay terribly. They'd taken it for granted that they'd all be around. Now Kay was gone. You never really know how to appreciate someone until they were no longer around.

Tia watched the blank TV screen seeing only her reflection. She closed her eyes hoping that when she opened them she would be back home, like Dorothy in the "Wizard of Oz", back to the warm and welcoming home where her mother was in the kitchen cooking dinner, Tone and Ebony would be doing homework and she'd be running to catch the phone which would be Kaisia calling to tell her about Ty's trifling ass and the dumb shit he'd just done. But when she did open her eyes, the woman who looked back at her through the TV screen was almost unrecognizable. Her face was hard and cold. All their lives were a mess.

She looked at Toya and wondered why a love as deep and real as hers and Kato's wasn't allowed to flourish? She then thought of Sean, a sure star-crossed love. Why did she have to develop feelings for him? He must be worried again. She'd promised to call and hadn't. Neglecting him should make him back off and spare her the pain. But she missed his voice and deep inside she wished she could call him and ask him what to do with the crazy life she and fallen into. It was never going to work between them because Tia knew she had to tell Toya that the man she had fallen in love with was the man that might put her love behind bars for his natural life. Toya was her friend, a comrade, a soldier and above all, a sister. There was no way she could keep this secret and she wasn't about to take that chance for no man. For a split, second Tia entertained the thought that if she could convince Sean not to prosecute the case then she'd not have to say anything and that such a decision might make it easier for her to be with him. Just as soon as she cleaned up her act. She also knew that was futile.

When Rich walked back into the living room, his swagger was a little shaken. "She's asleep," he said slumping down beside Tia. "She was so scared."

"Rich, don't worry about Tweet. She's strong and loyal, and her heart is from the same mold that pumps blood through yours. Besides, she would have found out one day. Her and Ebony are young women now and they aren't stupid. They'd have figured out something sooner or later. This bitch of a life catches up with any and everyone who play it. We are no exception." Kaisia crossed Tia's mind as the uttered the words.

"You're so right, Tee. I was just hoping to be long gone from this game before she found out."

"Win some, lose some. We weren't as lucky," Tia said sympathizing with Rich. She too never considered this life as a long-term option. It was the option she had but when she finished school and had a nest egg, she planned on going on the straight and narrow. Never in her life did she think they would be faced with a situation like they were in. Kay was dead and they wouldn't be able to let it go until they understood why. Now the once five, now four kids from motherless homes wondered if when they got in the game they had created a blueprint for their futures.

It was 5:45 a.m. and the light outside the window announced morning was on its way. "Listen ya'll, I gotta go home and get some sleep," Toya rose from the couch. We need to be ready for..." Toya stopped herself because she didn't want to think of Kaisia's wake.

"Me too," Jada jumped up.

"Yeah, ya'll right. We better get some rest." Tia said stretching her arms above her head. "Rich, I'll be by your house to pick you and Tweet up."

Rich agreed and walked them to the door, hugging each one as they left. And then there were four, he thought.

225

Tia turned back to the door. "Have Tweet call my sister to find out if she's going to the wake. If she is, have her meet ya'll here so we can ride together."

"Don't worry Tee, everything gonna be alright. We just have to stay focused."

Tia smiled. "I know."

CHAPTER TWENTY-SIX

WHEN TIA WOKE UP she could still feel the emotional and physical tiredness in her bones. She sat on the edge of the bed trying to process that today was the day they finally said goodbye to Kay. She rubbed her eyes to focus her vision catching a whiff of the funk from her armpits. When was the last time she'd taken a bath or shower? Whenever her armpits said she was past the expiration date. Funny how life just kept rolling, stinky armpits and all. Tia slipped out of her thongs and white nightshirt and padded to the bathroom. She stood under the steaming hot shower and let the water beat against her skin. The pulsing and pounding water was not enough to ease all the tension or the fact that today, in a few hours she would have to see one of her closest friends lying in a casket, no more to this world. Tia felt her tears mix with the steaming water and she didn't try to be strong. She let the flood gates of her eyes open. She hadn't told her friend all the things she wanted to, like how much she respected and looked up to her; how much she'd admired the way she had moved forward with her life when Dakota was born and that she was an amazing mother. Tia hadn't told Kay either how much she had appreciated that she was a shoulder that she could count since everyone else's head rested on hers. Only Kaisia understood. She didn't tell her in words either just how much she loved her. Tia's tears were coming harder and harder as she turned her face upwards. As the hot water beating down pelted her body, she said a prayer for her friend and her daughter Dakota. She said a prayer for the remaining four, asking God to guide them and help them put her friend to rest.

When there were no more tears Tia turned off the water, grabbed a towel, wrapped it around her body and went back into her bedroom. She rifled through her closet pulling out a Black Christian Dior dress. She chose a pair of black pumps and packed them into a carry bag. She had two stops to make before the wake, both vital in their mission to find Dakota and exposing the faces behind Kaisia's death, so she donned a gray ENCY sweat suit and a pair of Air Max. Tia pulled the Glock from under her pillow and held it in her hand. She squeezed the cold barrel trying to decide if it was gift or a curse. So far, it'd been both.

She thought of Kaisia again. If she could whisper something worthwhile to her, she was sure she'd hear. Tia dropped to her knees and prayed:

Dear Lord, I can't have the blood of anymore of my friends on my hands. Please give me the strength to see this through. If you allow me to do this for Kaisia, Lord, I promise I will walk away and lead my friends onto the path of what's right. Forgive us our sins for we have had a hard life and everything we did was out of love.

Sean's Apt. Lower West Side

Sean should have been at work but for some reason his body refused to cooperate. He just couldn't make himself get out of the bed. Maybe he was coming down with the flu, but he didn't feel achy. Of course, the lethargy usually hit before the rest of the symptoms. He tried to get up once again but was unable to budge from the tiredness in his body. He looked at the clock. It was 9:45. If he decided to go to work, he would be close to four hours late. Today needed to be an R&R day, one he really needed. He could use a full vacation but every time he'd attempted to get a little time, work just seemed to pile up. He'd take one when the Dynasty case was over. Sean grabbed the phone and dialed his office. To his relief, his back-up Rebecca was there and on standby to cover for him. He was living right, he thought! He'd give her a raise the first chance he got. She was good people.

Sean looked out the window. The day looked clear and bright, which was good. He pulled off the covers and made another attempt to get up. He had no trouble this time. Now that he knew he didn't have to go to work, he wondered if his tiredness was just plain laziness. He wasn't that kind of man. A grin spread across his face as he stuffed his feet into his slippers and headed to the kitchen to make coffee. By the time he took a quick shower his coffee would be ready and he'd spend the day relaxing. He would not look at a single thing to do with the Dynasty case. As he reached the bathroom door, his cell buzzed. Sean stepped back into his room hoping it wasn't Rebecca with bad news. If that was the case, she would get no raise!

He looked at the number scrolling. Tia.

"Hello." There was silence at first then Sean heard a soft cry. "Tia, what's wrong? Are you alrigth?" Sean's voice expressed concern.

Tia immediately regretted her moment of weakness and wish she'd just hung up. But just hearing his voice had done wonders to calm her frayed nerves.

"Tee, hello. Tee. Are you there?"

"Yeah, I'm here."

"What's wrong? I mean you don't sound too good."

"I'm fine. Really. Well, not fine. I'm not sure how I am. I had a death in my family," Tia felt the hot tears threatening to fall all over again.

"Oh, Tee, I'm so sorry to hear that. What can I do to help? Do you need anything?" Sean asked.

Tia wanted to say yes, Sean. Right now, I wish you could just hold me and let me know the world will be alright. Instead she said, "I'm alright. I just wanted to call and let you know that I'm back in the city. I came back yesterday she lied but with all that's going on, I got caught..."

"Tia, you don't have to explain. I understand. Right now, my only concern is you."

Tia needed to hear that. She felt relieved and sad at the same time. Here was a man who really cared about her and she cared deeply for him too but would she ever be able to fully reveal who she really was and the fears that plagued her?

"Tia, remember what I said the last time we talked. I am here for you. All you have to do is trust me."

How could she forget the conversation? It was the very day she had gotten word of Kaisia's death. "Look Sean, I gotta go but I will see you soon. Today is Kaisia's wake and...for the whole week I'll probably be with the family to do what I can." Tia knew she was never going to be able to see Sean again.

"Kaisia?" Sean thought about the name Tia just mentioned. She talked about Kaisia all the time but another bell went off in his mind but at the moment, he wasn't able to recall where he remembered the name from. "Is she the one with the pretty daughter you always talk about?"

"Yeah, she is the one," Tia realized immediately that she might have slipped up.

"I didn't know she was sick, Tee. You never mentioned that." It was the furthest thing from Sean's mind to even imagine the real circumstances behind Kaisia's death.

"She wasn't sick, Sean. She was murdered."

The silence on the line was palpable. What was this world coming to? Harlem was a hot bed of craziness. Sean had been a child of the ghetto and he remembered that crime was a major factor of his youth but back then, even criminals had a code of ethics: protect women and children. Now crime was rampant. Regardless of who you were - old, young, women, children - nobody was safe. His concern for Tia was heightened.

"Sean, I have to go," Tia hurriedly said. I'll call you later."

Sean heard the words and wished there was more he could do to comfort and protect her. "Alright, Tee, but listen, if you need anything, I'm home all day. In fact, come over if you want. I mean that."

"Thank you, Sean. Don't worry about me. I'll be alright. I have to hang up now and get ready. I'll call." Tia clicked off the phone just as Sean was saying, "Tia, hold on." She didn't hear the last part of what he was going to say. "I just want you to know that I love you."

Tia stood holding the phone. If only he knew how much I love him, she thought as the hopelessness of the situation caused her to collapse on the bed.

CHAPTER TWENTY-SEVEN

Ebony HAD JUST GOTTEN off the phone with Rich,
agreeing to go to the wake with the family when Ike walked
through the door. Ebony hadn't heard the front door but
when she saw Ike standing in the hallway, her heart leapt. She
flew from the bed and into his arms, kissing him passionately.

"Why didn't you call to let me know you were coming
back today?" Ebony asked when they parted.

Ike had taken the red eye out of Ohio. There had been
major complications and he had to burn. "I was trying to call
but reception at the airport wasn't too good. The phone kept
cutting off. Let me take a shower and I'll show you how much
I missed you," Ike said as he dropped his bags and walked into
the bathroom. He really didn't have time to play house
because other things required his immediate attention but he
had to play it cool. One of his spots that opened up was
raided by the Feds and two of his workers were knocked
down. Ike hadn't bothered to wait around to find out what
had gone down, he gathered the money they had made and
skipped town. What the fuck had gone wrong? He needed to
go see Ice to inform him. He knew that Ice would look into
the matter. What the fuck was up with his shit these days?

Ike stepped out of the bathroom, his tooth brush still in
his mouth. He walked over to the dresser and dropped his
Rolex in the drawer, went back to the bathroom and finished
brushing his teeth. "So, what did you get up to while I was

away?" He stood naked in front of Ebony. He'd hit it quickly and get on the way.

Ebony was sitting on the bed, her feet tucked under her. You have no idea, she thought. She looked up at Ike. He knew the drill. Whenever her legs were crossed, something was bothering her or something had happened. He was getting to be quite the observant fiancé. "Okay, Boo, what up? You're ignoring my shit." He pointed to his dick.

Ebony cast her eyes down and began twirling the blanket between her fingers. Ike lifted her head with his index finger. Ebony looked directly into Ike's eyes and then turned away. Ike took a seat next to her preparing to hear the drama.

"Eb, you're worrying me with this silence. I mean whatever it is you can tell me. I got your back. You know that." Ike sat staring at Ebony. The worse thing that could happen was that she'd fucked some other nigga while he was gone. His temper was rising and his patience was wearing thin. "Ebony, you are buggin' right now with this silence shit."

Ebony knew that when Ike called her by her full name, he was annoyed. She was scared. What if he left her? She was more scared of losing him than anything else in this world and she wasn't completely sure that he would be ready for the news she was about to drop on him. Should she wait? She'd been so excited when she found out she was pregnant but now with a little time to think, she wasn't sure Ike was as interested in starting a family right now. But it's too late. Ebony took a deep breath and looked directly into Ike's eyes. The eyes never lie and she would be able to see his first reaction to what she was about to say. Ebony took Ike's hand, placed it on her thigh and covered it with her own.

Ike took her hand, cautiously, for he had watched a couple episodes of Jerry Springer and Maury to know that whenever a female had something to tell you that was not in your favor, they always grabbed your hand first.

Ebony moved their hands together to her stomach. "Ike, I'm pregnant."

Ike jumped up releasing Ebony's hand. "Whose is it?" Ike shouted.

Ebony looked at Ike dumb founded. She couldn't understand what he was talking about. All she could do was stare at him.

"Eb, I gave you everything…wait. What did you just say?" Ike had jumped the gun and thought she was telling him she was leaving him. Funny how the mind can come up with its own drama. "Did you just say you were pregnant?"

"That's what I said, Ike. I'm pregnant."

Ike threw his arms around Ebony so fast they both tumbled backwards on the bed. Ike scooped her up in one quick movement and lifted her into his arms. Ebony pounded his back shouting, "Put me down!" Ike slid her to the ground. He leaned against the dresser and feeling overwhelmed with joy.

"You're not upset?" Ebony asked as she stood before him.

"Baby Girl, why would I be upset?" He took her face between his hands, "You've made me the happiest man in the entire world." He pulled her into him and wrapped his arms around her waist. "Boo, I love you crazy. From the moment I laid eyes on you, all I thought about was having a family with you. Now you've made that dream a reality."

Ebony wrapped her arms around Ike's neck and pulled his head down. When their lips met, it was the most tender kiss she had ever experienced. Ebony didn't believe she could ever love anyone more. Ike backed them up and gently pushed her on to the bed, "Well, my future wife and mother of my child," he whispered against her ears, "isn't it time for the baby to meet his daddy?" He pushed her legs apart with his knees.

Ebony laid on Ike's chest as her breath metered. Ike was stroking her hair thinking about some of the changes he'd have to make in their lives. He needed to get the house in Long Island squared away, and with a child on its way, he'd have to limit his activities. The risks were greater now and he had to ensure the safety of his family first and foremost. Ike knew he just couldn't leave the game all together and even so that would take time but he had to move towards retirement. He needed to put some of his money in real estate. He'd been doing that anyhow but he'd speed up the process now. He'd see what Ice found out, but they'd probably have to put on ice their idea for the string of nightclubs, he grinned at his cleverness. Maybe Long Island was too close; Atlanta was better. He always had his eye on Atlanta as his retirement spot. Maybe he should get something out there and move Ebony there once the baby was born. That would give him time to finish conducting and concluding unfinished business.

Everything was so simple when Ike was around, Ebony thought. She had to face the reality of their lives now. She knew Ike was in the game and his lifestyle was dangerous. Prison was the least of their worries. In the game, people died. She didn't want to be a widow or single mother and she knew, with every breath of her being, that she could not leave the man she loved. She wondered if her love was strong enough to make him want to leave. She could ask him but he had to want to leave the game on his own. And even if he said yes, it would take time for him to get everything in order. Ebony closed her eyes and prayed. She hoped too, that having a child would be more reason for him to want to leave the game sooner than later. "Shit! What time is it?" Ebony bolted up and hopped out of the bed.

Ike also jumped up his eyes following Ebony's figure darting around room. "Eb, what's up? Why you in such a hurry? You going somewhere?"

"Oh, Ike I forgot to tell you. A close friend of the family was murdered and I am going to the wake." She threw clothes from the closet.

Ike threw the bedcover off and walked over to Ebony. "Honey, why didn't you tell me?"

"I was too caught up with trying to figure out how to tell you I was pregnant and, then you had to meet Junior," she smiled, "and it slipped my mind."

"Oh, Baby, I'm sorry." Ike put his arms around her. "What time is it? I'll drive you."

"No need. I'm going with Tweet. I'll just cab it over to her house. You rest. I know you tired." She kissed him.

"Can you call your friend and tell her you'll be ten minutes late?" he asked as he cupped her ass.

"Honey, I can't be late. It would be so disrespectful. She was like a sister to me." Ebony now had tears in her eyes.

"It's okay, Baby. Baby don't cry. It's gonna be alright...I promise."

"Ike, I wish you could have met her. She was cool, nothing like Tia...but I guess she didn't have to parent me like Tia. But she had a child, too. Why would someone kill her? It don't make no sense. Tweet said she was just at the wrong place at the wrong time...but..."

Ike pulled her closer. He didn't have an answer for the senseless murder. Some people deserved death but he hated when people got caught up in other people's drama. Like Ebony, innocent as all get-up, could get caught up in his. He had to get out of the game. It was the one thing about the game he despised. Sometimes the innocent suffered the wrath of the guilty.

"Kaisia was a second sister to me. I just can't believe she is dead and they can't find her daughter. Dakota was my baby doll too."

Ike froze at the mention of the name. Could it possibly be? Naw! He pondered how small the entire world could be. Ike hoped and prayed the name was just a coincidence but somehow, he knew Ebony's Kaisia was the same Kaisia he'd ordered executed. How the hell did he get caught up in this shit? His heart raced a million miles a minute. He had to find out what was going on and the first person he had to call was Crime.

Tia picked up Jada and then stopped at the flower shop and ordered a dozen white roses - Kaisia's favorite. She paid extra to have them delivered to the funeral home. Rich had sent flowers but Tia wanted something special between her and Kaisia. Rich had also delivered the cash they had collected to Kaisia's mother so she could pay for the funeral in cash and not be burdened by the expense. They also gave her Kaisia's share of the money, Sixty Thousand in cash. Kaisia's mom had tried to refuse the money but they had convinced her that it was money all of them had been saving for a trip around the world. Rich lied that they had been saving it for years and since Kaisia was the first one to go on an out-of-the-world tour, it was only right that she should have the money. Plus, he added, it will help her with Dakota.

Tia pulled up in front of Rich's crib. She grabbed her carry bag and headed upstairs. Tweet answered the door. Rich was in the back getting ready, Tweet said. She'd change when he was done. By then, Toya and Ebony would have arrived.

On the surround sound speakers, Mary J Blige and Faith Evans were crooning *Love Don't Live Here Anymore. Hell no,* Tia got up and changed the station to Hot-97. The doorbell rang and Tweet went to answer it. Toya and Ebony walked into the living room.

Tia sat where she was while Jada rose to meet Ebony encircling her in her arms. Tia looked at her sister and a gulp caught in her throat. She'd changed so much. She seemed more mature, and more beautiful than ever. Tia and Ebony eyes made four and they both saw each other's tears. Ebony smiled and when Jada let her go, she went to stand before her sister.

"I'm so sorry," Ebony said bending down to embrace her sister.

"Me too." Tia hugged her sister as though she would never ever again release her. "Me too."

"Where's Tone?"

"He'll meet us there." Tia said.

Rich walked into the living room. He was wearing a charcoal black double-breasted blazer, black silk shirt, grey slacks and a black derby with a white feather, a neatly-folded white handkerchief in the breast pocket of his jacket. Black snakeskin belt and shoes completed the attire. He was dapper.

Tia quickly went to the room and changed. She returned as Rich asked, "Is everybody ready?"

The posse nodded and headed out the door.

CHAPTER TWENTY-EIGHT

NEW JERSEY

"WHAT DO YOU MEAN YOU'RE BUSY? I'm fuckin' pay you good money." Ike was shouting into his cell phone.

Crime hadn't expected Ike to be needing him anytime soon but things had changed and he couldn't leave Dakota alone so he had to pass on whatever Ike was offering. Crime couldn't believe how the little girl had changed him. He'd never passed up a bank roll in his life, especially one that paid top dollar. But he wasn't in the single life anymore, he had responsibilities Ike could never know about. Crime had saved a nice amount of money. He'd never taken the time to count his stash but he knew that he was probably a millionaire a few times over, off the books. Passing up the offer was not a big thing as Ike was one of his best customers and he owed a lot of his fortune to him. Crime hated owing people things. He looked over at Dakota who was sitting on the rug playing Grand Theft Auto on the iPad that he'd bought her when they went shopping for new clothes and stuff. As always, she impressed Crime with her sense of style and coordination as his little champ picked out her own clothes. She had far better taste than him for sure. He smiled when he though back to how he'd tried to buy a Barbie doll outfit he was sure she'd love, like all little princesses but she had checked that, taking the outfit and dropping it on the floor.

"Crime, I need you." Ike's voice brought him back to the present. "I may have the rest of them bitches who hit my spot. We can probably get them in one shot," Ike said, annoyed that he felt like he was begging to give away his money. It was probably a job he could handle with one or two of his little soldiers but he needed a professional to do the job right.

"Ayo, Ike...check it. Give me a few hours to think about it. If...."

Ike cut Crime short. "We don't have a few hours. Either you're not hearing me or you're pretending to be incapable of understanding me."

"Listen Bro, if you can't deal with my terms then find someone else. Simple as that. Like I just told you I got other things going on right now. You're not the only person with problems that need to get handled." Crime watched as Dakota shot at the cops.

Ike wanted to give Crime a piece of his mind but saw no point in offending him. He also realized that he didn't have a choice but to accept Crime's terms for now, but he vowed that after this was taken care of, Crime would never see another dime of his money. "Alright, Playboy, you got that. Just holla at me soon." Ike hung up the phone before Crime could answer. Fuck him, he said to himself.

Crime looked at the bitch in his hand. Did that mutha fucker just hang up on him? He walked over to where Dakota was sitting. He sat and leaned his head back against the couch trying to think about what he was going to do with her while he was gone. He knew he was going to end up having to take the job. Truth be told, he was missing the thrill of his occupation and it would be doubly fulfilling if any of the bitches were as loyal as their friend. Crime raised his head and said to Dakota. "Do you want to go on a little ride with me?"

Dakota stopped moving the controller in her hand. "Yeah," she smiled.

Crime knew he couldn't take her with him, that would just be too cruel. He could think of only one person in the world he'd trust her with - his friend Denise. They'd been friends since their public school days. Crime considered her a sister. She was the only one who really knew him and didn't judge, plus she was loyal as hell. He made a call.

NEWARK, NJ

Crime sat in the back yard of his friend's house in Newark, New Jersey watching Dakota and his friend's 7 year-old son play in the grass. Denise, a beautiful 5' 6" mid-weight woman with a brown complexion handed him a glass and sat across the table from him.

Crime refused the drink. He didn't drink when he was working. "Sha," she began. "I'm gonna take it that this girl is family, no questions asked. But tell me, Sha, what are you going to do with a child in your life with the lifestyle you lead? Children are high maintenance. It's impossible to do both in your situation. Sha, you know I love you very much and I'm not going to be the one who tells you what to do with your life but do you see the little girl over there?" she nodded in Dakota's direction.

Crime hadn't taken his eyes off Dakota even when Denise was talking. He couldn't, for the life of him, fathom why she was so dear to him. He'd even thought of giving up the life to be her father! What the fuck was all this about?

"That little girl is gonna need you so if you're gonna take her on as your responsibility, you will in the long run have to make some sacrifices," Denise was saying.

Crime briefly looked at Denise weighing everything she'd said against his own thoughts. He knew, without a doubt, that in their short time together he had attached himself to the little girl as her father. Maybe, they were each other's salvation because for the first time in his life he loved someone. That was how strong his feelings were for the Accidental Princess who came into his life. "Denise," Crime finally said. "I feel where you are coming from and I do plan to do right by her. If not, I would never have taken on the responsibility. I haven't got it all worked out yet but you know me better than that. I don't know why, but I would die for that little girl there," Crime said.

Denise reached out and held Crime's hand. "I believe you will do just that, Sha. The hard part will be living for her." Denise squeezed the hand she held. "Anyway, Big Head, go take care of what you got to take care of. She's gonna be alright here with me and Day-Day."

BENTLEY'S FUNERAL HOME, HARLEM

Tia pulled up behind Toya in front of Bentley's Funeral Home. They parked in the reserved family-only spots. Tia recognized many of the people standing around who had grown up with Kaisia. She was surprised to see three different news teams on hand and wondered why. Kaisia was just another dead woman in the jungle of Harlem. Then she thought about Dakota. That must be reason. Jada was the first to step out of the car. Tweet, Ebony then Toya followed her. They joined Rich, who was already waiting. A reporter seeing them park in the family spot pushed a microphone in Tia's face. She pushed it away and went into the parlor. The posse went straight to Kaisia's mother and hugged her. They then hugged assorted individuals, some they hadn't seen since high school.

People were shameless. Toya pointed out a woman who she knew didn't like Kaisia because of Ty. Others were dressed as though Kaisia's wake was the goddamn runway. Toya wanted to go over and beat the shit out of the fuckin' ghetto bitches.

They all signed the remembrance book and headed down the aisle. Tia spotted Tone and smiled. Tone smiled back but his face lit up when he saw Ebony beside Tia, holding her hand. The group saw Kay's mother and the relatives who were comforting her and headed for the row right behind them. Each of them greeted Kay's relatives, gave her mother a hug and expressed their regret at her loss.

After a few minutes, the group got up and together walked to the open casket that held their friend. The mahogany casket was lined with white satin. Around it were huge floral displays. The funeral home had placed the white roses Tia had ordered directly at head of the coffin, and one white rose in Kaisia's hands which were folded on her chest. Tia looked at Kay. She couldn't believe she was dead. She looked so beautiful and peaceful. She was wearing a white dress and gloves, her hair crowing her shoulders. Oh, she was so beautiful, Tia thought as she felt tears escape. She placed a hand over Kaisia's cold hand and quickly pulled back. Though she knew Kay was dead, she expected somehow that her hand would be warm. She knew in her heart that this was goodbye but she wanted Kaisia to be alive. Her cold hand forced her to accept that she was not coming back.

"Oh Kay, you didn't deserve this. You were always too good for this life and I'm gonna always blame myself for getting you involved in this shit when I couldn't even protect you and Dakota. We are gonna make this right Kaisia. We are gonna. Believe that." Tia bend down and rested her hear on the side of the casket. "Kay," she wailed. "I am so sorry. Oh, my God, Kay, I am so sorry," Tia felt her knees buckling as Rich reached over and held her up.

"It's alright, Tia. Come on. Let's go back now. Let Toya and Jada say their goodbyes." Rich lead her back to the pew.

Jada and Toya stood in front of the coffin. They could not believe Kaisia was in that box, that she was gone from their lives forever. Toya stroked Kay's hair. "Don't you worry, Kay," she whispered, "we gonna kill every last one of them niggas who did this to you. Don't worry, Boo. We're sending you company soon so you can kick their asses." Toya's voice was so soft that only Jada and, she hoped, the dead could hear.

Jada kissed the cold forehead of her friend for the last time. "I love you, Kay," was all she said.

Tweet and Ebony stood side by side. They were crying so hard that their tears made like track lines through their foundation. For the first time since her mother died, Ebony, who was a little girl then remembered the day she had stood over her mother's coffin saying goodbye. As she stared at Kaisia, it seemed that Kaisia's face transformed to that of her mother's and then back again. Why? Why in her short life was she burying two people who she loved so dearly?

Tweet was so scared she almost peed her pants. All she could think of was that her brother and the rest of her aunts were next. Instead of seeing Kaisia's face she watched the collage of Rich's, Tia's, Toya's and Jada's face appear before her. If they were part of the reason Kaisia was dead, would they be next? She couldn't breathe and she didn't care who was watching as she bolted down the aisle and threw open the doors of the parlor. She had to get away.

Rich was about to go after his sister when Ebony tapped him on the shoulder. "Don't worry about her, Rich. I got her. Go pay your last respects."

Rich looked at Ebony, nodded and walked towards Kaisia's casket.

Ebony scanned the streets looking for Tweet. She spotted her sitting on a nearby stoop, her face buried in her hands. Ebony quietly sat beside her, saying nothing. She watched as cars went by - life in motion oblivious to the fact that someone dear to them had departed this land of the living. She watched as Tweet's body racked with sobs and wondered why she and Tia were taking Kay's death so much harder than anyone else. She could understand Tia's grief as Kaisia was her closest and oldest friend of the group, they had been inseparable at times, but Tweet was acting so strange almost as though Kaisia's death was her fault. Ebony felt there was more to her grieving than met the eye but she wouldn't press the point. She'd give Tweet time before she tried to find out what was going on.

Ike and Crime sat across the street from the parlor. They were dressed all in black, not to pay respects to the deceased but to be less obvious. They had smoke grey tints to conceal their identity. They watched as several people exited the wake. Many were milling around on the street. Ike wasn't sure what or who he was looking for but he was sure they would find it here if anywhere.

"Ayo, Dawg," Crime was impatient. "Who we supposed to be looking for? I'm saying even if the broad or broads she was down with show up, we still don't know what they look like. Man, there are alotta people up in this joint. How we gonna be certain we have the right set of bitches?"

"You're right. This whole shit we're doing right now is based on assumptions at this point but we ain't blind and dumb." Ike spotted Ebony walking with someone and strained his eyes to see who was beside her.

"I don't remember nobody giving a description of those bitches so I don't see how blind and dumb applies." Crime was annoyed.

"We got deduction, Bro. Not a full description but we know it was two chicks. No, let me take that back: it was two chicks and a dude dressed like a bitch.

"So, you're telling me that you expect some homo to come through here dressed in drag with a couple of bitches on his arm? And you're gonna tell me too that you have a special homo detector to top it off to zero in on some bitch ass nigga rockin' some thongs? Crime was deadly serious 'cause he hated wastin' his time. He wasn't a what if guy, he was certain about everything he did. This felt like some novice shit and he wasn't feelin' it.

Ike gave Crime a burning look. He had a strong desire to tell him to get the fuck out, he got this. The nigga was getting too fuckin' cocky and he recommitted to the promise he made to himself that after this the mutha wouldn't see another dime of his cake. Ike turned his attention back to the person beside Ebony. He could see better now as they reached closer to the SUV. Ike blinked a few times and looked closer. He was shocked. Although he'd seen Tia in pictures, he never thought two sisters not in the same age bracket could look so much like twins. Apart from the fact that Tia was a bit curvier and a shade lighter, the women were identical.

Ike continued to stare at Tia and Ebony but Crime had zeroed in on a single face of someone he hadn't seen in ages. In fact, he hadn't seen her since he was just Shorty coming up in the game. Crime stared at Toya as if he was seeing a ghost. He'd known her all too well when he was younger, although she probably never knew he existed. More than nine years before, Crime had taken his first contract hit. He was to take out a guy called Tue'Gee and another name Kato, but Kato had lived. He'd never worried about that because the homeboy never knew where the shot came from and the kat was locked down facing wild numbers. Crime knew that Toya was the one responsible for murdering the man who'd hired him to hit her man. Crime had always respected Shorty for that for he had always dreamed of having that kind of loyalty from a female. Crime had kept tabs on her for a few years but after he'd gotten deeper and deeper into the game, he had lost track of her. Now here she was like an apparition. Crime was still staring at her when Ike asked, "Playa, what's up? I see you looking in that direction like you see something that interests you. If so, put a nigga on, it may be useful."

"You see Shorty right there. The one with the black and white dress on?"

Ike nodded as his eyes focused on where Crime was looking. "Yeah, I see her. Why. What's up?"

"That's not your average Shorty right there. She's about her business and believe me when I say this, if she's here she has reasons and anybody who fucks with her is on the same shit she's on...trust that," Crime said. His admiration for her talents went deep. Maybe...

"Crime, what the fuck are you talking about? Fuck this riddle bullshit. Tell me the deal with the bitch!" Ike had had enough of Crimes bullshit.

Crime looked Ike dead in the eyes. "She's a silent assassin."

Ike spun his head around to look at Toya. She was as pretty as the get up she wore, but this time he looked pass the dress and pretty face. He intended to squeeze this one slow.

Ike and Crime sat silent. They continued to observe the group that was around Toya. Tia was in that group. Ike wondered if Ebony's sister was somehow involved in all this shit. It wouldn't matter because he wasn't about to show an ounce of mercy. Besides, if he hit the bitch and got rid of her, Ebony may have some peace and he needed his baby mother to be peaceful.

CHAPTER TWENTY-NINE

ONCE THE WAKE HAD ENDED, Tia and Toya decided they wouldn't follow the mourners back to Kaisia's mother's house. They had other business to attend to. Tia gave Rich the key to the truck and told the rest of the posse to make their appearance as planned.

She climbed into Toya's car. Rich and Jada knew well the moves that Tia and Toya were making as they had discussed it the day before. Ebony wasn't close enough to hear the conversation between the four friends but she thought it was odd that Tia and Toya were not going to Kaisia's mother's house. She knew something was up. Tweet was watching the group from the public mailbox that she was leaning on. She hadn't said a single word since running out of the parlor.

"In four hours," Tia said to Rich, "let's meet at my crib. I'm gonna call when we're on our way back from Jamaican Stan."

"Tee, what you want me to tell Kaisia's mom if she asks about Dakota again?"

"Rich, just do and say whatever pops into your head, just don't say anything that will make her panic. I know we can't keep telling her Dakota is over at a friend's house but I don't have an answer yet. We need to make a move quickly though before the police gets involved."

Ebony was trying to read lips but she wasn't able to so she walked over to the car where the posse stood. As soon as she approached, all chatting ceased. "Tee, listen. I'ma go'on back home. I don't think I'm up to going to Kaisia's mother's house."

What fuckin' house? Ain't your house. Tia looked at Ebony a barely there smiled on her lips. No point starting a fight just when they were trying to get back on solid ground. She wished they could have spent more time together and put everything out on the table concerning them but today wasn't gonna work. Tia still didn't approve of that Ike mutha fucker. He was too old for Ebony but she admitted that she might have overreacted and blown the whole ordeal between them out of proportion. Tia looked her sister up and down. She seemed tired. She could understand. The emotional toll of today had taken its pound of flesh from all of them. "Alrigth," Tia said. "Rich will drive you home."

"Naw. Me and Tweet gonna take a cab back home." She hadn't even checked whether Tweet wanted to come back to the crib but Tweet was holding onto something and Ebony needed to know what all that was about.

"You sure? It ain't no problem. You're only five minutes' drive from here and it's on the way." Rich said.

"Yeah, I'm sure. Kaisia's mother really needs to have people around her who were close to her daughter. Even five minutes could be too long. So, it's alright. Tweet and I will take a cab. We'll be fine."

Rich hugged Ebony. She was a wise girl sometimes. He went over to Tweet and hugged her too. Jada hugged the two girls and climbed into the SUV. She wasn't happy about any of this shit. Tweet running out of the church and all. She hoped Tia was right about her.

Tia watched Tweet real hard. Was she going to be able to keep their secret? The woman who looked back at her was not the same girl she was before she got information she shouldn't't have. Like Jada, she wondered. Tia spun her head as she felt eyes staring at her and made four with Ebony's.

Ebony smiled and waved. She wasn't sure why she was staring at her sister. Maybe she should not have left home.

Maybe she just wanted to be a little sister again. She loved Ike but she also loved her sister. Anyway, it didn't matter because she couldn't reveal her feelings now. She was no longer a child. She was a pregnant woman who had to manage her life from here on out.

"Hey, Ebony," Tia said to her sister. "Did you talk to Tone?"

"Yeah, briefly. He left early but I told him I'd call him later tonight."

"Yeah, he really hates funerals. Ever since Mommie…" Tia allowed the sentence to trail off. "Anyway, Eb, listen up. I want to talk to you but I have…"

"Don't worry about that now, Tia. Go take care of whatever you have to do. I'll call you tonight 'cause I really need to holla at you too." Ebony said.

"Alright, Eb. I'll be looking forward to hearing from you." Ebony leaned in and hugged her sister.

Ike and Crime watched the going on with the posse they had come to focus on. Ike saw Ebony and Tweet get into a cab and figured out they were heading back to the crib. He turned his attention back to Toya and Tia. They said a few more words to their companions and then drove off in the all Black Ford Explorer.

"Peep game, Playboy?" Ike said to Crime. "I'm gonna get out here and catch a cab back to my crib but I want you to follow them bitches. I want to know their every move and where they are at all times."

Crime nodded his head.

Ike stepped out of the car and slammed the door behind him. He wasn't feelin' Crime as he walked to the end of the block to catch a jitney.

Tia turned down St. Nicholas Ave. heading toward 8th Avenue. They needed to change clothes 'cause there was no' point drawing too much attention to themselves. People dressed like them didn't go see Stan.

Crime pulled out behind the Explorer keeping a respectable distance so as not to alert them to his presence.

He finally lit a Newport. A heavy chain smoker, Crime hadn't even thought about cigarettes after he saw Toya. She had his full attention. If he'd known that she was involved in this shit he'd have taken the job for free. He owed the bitch one.

Crime continued to follow the car until the women pulled into a parking space on the left side of the street at 133 between 7th and 8th Avenues. He drove past them and parked out of sight, at the corner of 7th Avenue, to await their reappearance.

Ebony and Tweet didn't talk on the way home. Something was really wrong because Tweet was not someone who would ever shut up. When they got to Ike's crib, Tweet went directly to the living room, kicked off her shoes and climbed onto the couch. Ebony went into the bedroom and changed into all white Phat shorts and a tank top. She pulled out the bobby pins that held her up-do and washed the make-up off her face. She detoured to the kitchen and got them something to drink. At first, she thought Tweet had fallen asleep but as she got closer, she saw her eyes were wide open and filled with tears. Ebony put the drinks down and knelt by her friend who had rolled herself up into a ball.

"Tweet, what's wrong? You haven't been yourself all day. I know this is hard to take but you are really having a harder time that I'd thought. What's going on?"

Tweet sniffled and a tear escaped. Ebony used her thumb to wipe away the tear which caused a cascade of tears to roll down Tweet's face. "Tweet," Ebony pleaded. "Talk to me. Is all this about Kay or something else?"

Tweet turned her back to Ebony. Ebony was not about to let her off that easy. If it were her, Tweet would have pestered her to death. "Okay, Tweet, listen up. I think this has something to do with Kay and whatever it is, my sister is knee deep in it. Maybe Rich too. Talk to me if you know something."

Tweet didn't answer.

"Look, I just want to be able to protect my sister and your brother, if what I'm saying makes sense. I know you loved

Kaisia Tweet, but she is gone now and nobody can bring her back. If our family is involved and you know something that can protect them from harm's way, you have to tell me."

"They wanted to protect her," Tweet said between sobs.

"Tweet. Who they?" Ebony tried to get Tweet to turn around so she could better understand what she was saying.

"They said she wasn't supposed to die and Dakota may be dead too."

"What? Ebony jumped to her feet. "Tweet, what the fuck you sayin'?" There was no way her sister was involved in with this. She wouldn't do a thing to harm Kaisia or her own goddaughter, Dakota. Something was real fishy and it was beginning to stink to high heavens. Dakota's dead? That could never be. "Tweet," Ebony pulled at Tweet's arm forcing her to sit up. "What are you telling me, Tweet? I don't understand." Ebony was yelling. "For fuck's sake snap out of this shit and tell me straight. Did they kill Kaisia? Did my sister kill her?"

Tweet stared blankly at Ebony. She wasn't sure what to answer. They might not have pulled the trigger but in her mind, they did something that caused her death.

"Who killed them, damn it? Got dammit, Tweet, who the fuck killed Kay?"

Tweet grabbed her shoes and ran out the apartment almost knocking over Ike as he was just walking through the door.

Ebony was on the floor crying. Ike rushed over to her and lifted her off the floor. She was kicking and screaming and flailing her arms. Ike lifted her and carried her into the bedroom.

"Put me down." Ebony was screaming so hard, Ike tightened his grip.

What the fuck was going on here? Got damn didn't he have enough troubles out in the streets? "What the hell is going on, Eb?" Ike asked.

"Ike, I said put me down. You are fuckin' hurting my arm."

Ike put her down but kept a firm grip on her arms. He pinned her against the bedroom door to gain leverage. Ebony was still kicking a flailing and one of her knee blows landed in Ike's groin. Ike immediately let go of her, doubled over and cupped his groin.

"Oh, Ike. Are you alright?" Ebony jumped into action. "Baby, are you alright?" She came over to where Ike was doubled over on the floor his hands between his legs. "I'm sorry, Baby, it was an accident."

Ebony flew across the room as Ike's backhand connected with her face. Ebony felt the sting of his hand and touched her face where his blow had landed. She rested against the dresser. This day was just too fuckin' much but how dare that mutha hit her. "I didn't mean to fuckin' hit you." Ebony yelled glad that she was across the room. Ike had climbed onto the bed. He felt like someone had knocked the air out of him, as a paralyzing, mind-numbing pain spread throughout his body.

Ike sat up on the bed as the pain subsided. His right hand still tucked inside his pants. He couldn't believe he had hit his beloved. It was protective impulse but shit, he had to learn to control his temper. He'd hit the mother of his child and that was not okay. Ike rocked back and forth on the bed to dissipate the last of the pain. "I'm sorry, Beloved, but what's wrong with you? You almost made me a fuckin' eunuch!"

"I am sorry, Baby," Ebony got off the floor and went over to Ike.

"I sorry too, Baby, real sorry. That was just a reaction."

Ebony pushed him back on the bed and took off his pants. Some fuckin' reaction hitting your baby mama. She filed the information. "Let me see, Boo. Let me try to make it better." Ebony reached her hand into his jockeys and began massaging him. "Is that helping baby?"

Ike nodded and as Ebony continued to massage him, he felt his other head begin to rise. "Ain't that a bitch," he smiled at how quickly lust can replace pain. Or maybe they were the same thing.

"So, Boo," his voice deepened as she brought him to full life. "What was going on in here? Why was Tweet rushing out the door crying? Why were you screaming at her? Form where I stood, I thought you were about to kill her or something."

Ebony began trying to tell the story as she understood it. Ike just listened wondering how she got the story so twisted up. He was just glad her sister was no wiser as to who killed her friend and who would kill them if it was proven that they had hit his shit. But there was a new development that caught him off guard and concerned him. If the child was there when the hit was carried out why didn't Crime mention it? Apart from the fact that Crime was getting too big for his britches, it was not in Ike's nature to hurt children, regardless of the situation. "So did anyone call the cops about the little girl being missing?" Ike asked. It would be bad news if the police was involved. First, he needed no heat attention and second, it would be harder getting rid of the broads. He didn't need no long, drawn-out shit on his hands.

Ike moved Ebony's hand harder. " Baby," he croaked. "Stay away from everything and everybody until I figure out what's going on. I don't need you caught up in some bullshit."

"But Ike, that's my family. I just can't turn my back. If something is wrong, I need to help." Her hand stopped stroking his phallus.

"Don't stop, Baby," Ike moved her hand up and down. "I'm not asking you to turn your back. I'm just asking you to give me a chance to find out what's going on. Maybe I can help her too."

"Do you think you can help her, Ike?" Ebony's voice was excited.

Ike looked at the woman he loved and realized how innocent she really was. Ike had no intention of helping them. His intentions were far deadlier but he couldn't think right now. He needed her to ride the dick in her hand. "Baby," he said, pushing her head down, "help this man right here," he said spinning her around and pulling off her tight, tight shorts.

Crime drove two cars behind Tia as they came off Broadway crossing over into Washington Heights. They made a right on 163rd Street and he could see they were checking for parking spaces. He parked behind a yellow Jetta as soon as he turned the block. They pulled into a parking space six cars up ahead.

"Do you want me to wait in the car?" Toya asked.

"Naw, you're coming in with me cause you gonna need to help me carry this shit out."

"Alright," Toya stepped out of the car.

Crime saw one of the women exit the car and said something to the other who then exited and they both headed for a brownstone. They were dressed in dark colors. Nothing out of the ordinary but if one was in the life they avoided dark colors at it attracted too much attention. Maybe they weren't in the life and Toya had just blown away a mutha fucker who messed with her man. Even if they were, in the game, two fine looking women like them wouldn't be suspect.

Crime was familiar with the neighborhood as he had a lot of business in these parts. Even the very block rang a bell but he couldn't remember why.

Tia and Toya climbed the steps to Stan's brownstone. Tia had called ahead from her crib to let him know they were on their way so he'd expect them. She'd told him she'd knock twice as she was now doing. She scanned the area because Washington Heights was known for bullshit. Although they both carried heat, Tia wasn't trying to take any chances in this sketchy neighborhood.

Toya looked around too, but for a completely different reason. She had the strangest feeling that someone was watching, even back at the funeral parlor. She trusted her intuition 'cause that mutha had saved her skin a few times. She kept her hand on her piece inside her jacket pocket.

Crime was half-watching. His mind had strayed to Dakota. It had been over eleven hours since he had left her with Denise. He missed his princess. He couldn't believe that the unconditional love he'd sought his whole life was coming from a pint-sized little girl. He also couldn't believe how attached he had become to her in such a short time. He could no longer imagine life without his mini-sidekick. When this was all over, Crime promised himself, he'd take his little princess and they would go somewhere far away and never come back. He was ready to become a father and he knew he'd be a good one.

Crime glanced up as the door opened to the women. He couldn't see the occupant but he kept wracking his brain trying to remember why the place seemed so familiar. Crime was just about to recline in his seat when a head popped out the door and scanned the street. Crime bolted upright. He recognized the face immediately and remembered why the place was so familiar. That was Stan. He was sure of it. The only thing different was that his dreads were longer. "I'll be a mutha!" Crime said aloud. That's the rat-bastard who got him his first city bid on an attempt. Ain't this some shit! He thought that bitch-ass had gone back to coconut grove land to hide out. Payback is a bitch and this bitch-ass nigga was gonna feel it at its worst. Crime picked up his cell and called Ike.

CHAPTER THIRTY

Tia EXAMINED THEIR PURCHASES. Toya admired the Chrome Desert Eagle one of Kato's favorite guns.

Tia was asking, how much for this one Rude Boy, but Stan was so taken with Toya's ass, that Tia had to walk up to him and tap him with the gun and repeat her question.

Stan quickly put back on his 'baadasss' business face. "Star wa ah gwan? Mi see yu got some fire power ya, man." He kept ogling Toya's rear end.

"Never mind that, just hit me with the price so we can raise up on this bitch."

"Chuh, 'yu wah left a Dread hungry?" Stan looked at Tia and sucked his teeth. "Me give it to you for Fifteen Thousand."

Tia looked over at Toya and moved right in. Since he liked her ass so much she could try a thing. "Listen, Playa, we're just tryna get a little cash ourselves. Can you let it go for me for Eleven straight and I promise you that on the re-up we'll spend no less than Twenty-Five Gs with yo?" She positioned her ass for a good look.

"Baby Gal, seen. Send your brethren here home and we can talk business."

"Boo, you know I can't do that but I tell you what. Why don't I give you my home phone number and me and you get up later. Right now, let's handle this 'cause we need to handle a thing." She stood close to Stan her tight fabric jeans suggestively hugging her camel foot.

Stan grabbed Toya by the waist, unabashedly staring between her legs. "Write de numba pon this ya paper while a brethren count out de money." He inhaled Shorty's essence. That thing down dere was as deadly as the Desert Eagle, he could tell.

Toya grabbed the paper and stepped off to look for a pen.

"You are too fly," Tia sidled up and whispered while Stan got the goods.

"You aren't so bad yourself. You counting that cake real fast." Toya began to write down a phone number.

"That's cause I know your ass was in trouble. Stan's one clever nigga."

When Tia finished counting the money, she gave it to Toya who took it to Stan in the room where the Dessert Eagles were kept. "Here ya go, Rude Boy," she flashed him a wicked smile. "Everything alright?"

"Yea, everything ire."

As the women prepared to leave, Sean grabbed Toya by the waist. "One second, Star," he reached for his cell and called the number on the paper. Tia eyed Toya and kept a straight face. Tia knew she had written down some bogus number.

"No answer."

"Of course not," Toya was been fast on her feet. "What you expect? You holding me hostage," she pointed to him holding her waist. "You think me can be in two places at the same time?"

Stan smiled and released his grip. "Game you cell."

"I just lost the mutha. I get a new one tomorrow. When you call tonight I give you that too."

"You caaan give it to me in person," Stan winked.

"You bet." Toya ran her hand down the beast of a man's chest. "Can we go no now"

"Walk good." Stan stepped aside and the women exited.

When they were outside and out of view they began laughing their asses. Tia was laughing so hard she choked on her own saliva. "Good thing you're fast on your feet," Tia said when she recovered. "We did good with the purchases."

"Anything for Kay but I gotta run home and get in the shower to wash that nigga's smell off me." Toya grimaced.

"I get that. That man tried to inhale your coochie. You should've seen your face." Tia was laughing again.

"You got jokes. That's funny, huh? No wonder you wanted me to throw on these tight-ass pants. You knew what was going to go down. You just used a bitch."

"Ayo, on some real shit though. I would have sworn up and down that you'd given that nigga clown a fake number."

"Something told me homeboy wasn't gonna let me outta there without checking it out. I did think about it at first but I gave him the number to the Honeycomb since we ain't ever gonna use it again."

"Damn, Girl. You really think quick on your feet. That's gonna be one pissed off Jamaican once he start calling and get no answer all the time. And when it's disconnected he'll come looking for you."

"Yeah. Well he'll eventually get the message."

Crime watched the women crack up and wondered what was so funny. Too bad they were such beauties. He watched the stealth's scan the street. He was sure these were the bitches they were looking for. They were definitely in the game. He watched Toya stop before getting into the truck and zero in on her surroundings. She'd check out the Dominican couple in their twenties or so and even the young boy, no older than thirteen, carrying a bag of garbage to the front of his building. Crime respected the women. They were on point and obviously seasoned assassins. Checking out the kid showed that they were not novice because in the game thirteen was no protection. He knew some deadly thirteen year olds in the game. Toya finally checked out the group of hustlers by the bodega before opening the car door. The other beauty jumped into the passenger's side. Crime didn't miss the bags they carried either. He wondered what was in the bags but he really didn't care. What he cared about was that the faggot nigger Stan had lived on this earth way too long. He was past his expiration date today. Crime tapped a Newport from the cigarette box, placed it between his lips and hunted in his pocket for a light. He watched as Toya pulled off and then called Ike.

Ike was getting his freak on when the phone rang. He considered not answering it but he had too much shit going on in the street. Hold up sweetheart," he slapped Ebony's butt. She was riding him like a thoroughbred. "Yeah," he said breathing hard.

"I think these are the bitches you looking for. I followed them to Washington but ain't nothing happening here. " Crime lied. He was ready to be done with this job. I have to bounce too cause I have another job. "

"A'right niggaz. Good look out. I'll take it from here. Go ahead and conclude the business." Ike knew where to find the bitches. He was good.

Crime hung up the phone not bothering to tell Ike what the other business that needed his attention was. He stubbed out the Newport in the car ashtray and reached under the seat for his 9-millimeter Ruger. He screwed on the silencer and put the Ruger into his waist. Crime left the car door unlocked and walked up the block. He was a brownstone away from Stan's when a Latino guy about 29 or 30 stepped in front of him.

"Papi, I hot today. I got boy. Chu boy got everything. Straight pure Pik and for you I give you a good deal." He was in full hustle mode blocking the path.

Crime tried to brush past him without acknowledging any interest whatsoever in what the hustler was selling, but Latino just mirrored his move and blocked his path. "Listen, Home Team. I'm not interested," Crime said.

"Papi, listen I got chu. Just tell me what you want. I got eveythin' you want, aye. Yeah. You look like chu like to party, sí?" said Latino with a wide grin. He seemed proud of his salesmanship.

Crime was irritated and aggravated. He was tempted to spray the brains of the pest in front of him all over the curb. He just couldn't risk drawing attention away from his mission. "Alright. Listen, I'll cop you but first I gotta go see my man, if you wait here I'll be right out in like five minutes. He lives right there." Crime pointed to Stan's brownstone.

"Sí, Papi. I'll be right here when you come out." Latino said. "Remember, don't see nobody else. I got chu." He stepped aside.

"Don't worry, I'm coming back to see only you. Nobody else." Crime walked on and up the steps to Stan's crib. He knocked on the front door twice. He'd seen the bitches do that. He pulled his gun from his waist and kept it at his side and donned his New York Yankee fitted cap, which he pulled over his eyes. Crime listened as hurried footsteps approached. He stepped to the side wedging his pistol between his right leg and the door and positioned himself so Stan could only see his side view.

"Wah a gwan star?" Stan looked through the peephole.

"I want to cop a Twenty," Crime remembered that Stan always sold weed even when they were young.

"Put your money in ya so," he flapped the mail slot in the door.

Crime reached into his pocket a pulled out a bill, he didn't even know how much, and dropped it into the slot then lined up the barrel of the silencer on the edge of the mail slot. He knelt and peeped through the slot as he heard dreadlocks bend down to retrieve the money.

As Stan was retrieving the money, he noticed that the slot hadn't closed properly. He looked closer and bent drown to investigate why the slot was jammed. He lifted the slot and found himself looking in a pair of sinister eyes.

"Wha the blood clot?" Stan seemed stunned that someone's eyes were peering through his mail slot.

"Stan, my man, did you inform on anybody lately?" Crime asked as he pulled the trigger.

Stan tried to release the slot but it was too late as his face exploded and splattered all over the cream carpet.

Crime walked calmly down the steps. The Latino guy was, as he promised, waiting for him. He was running up to Crime who still had the smoking gun at his side. Crime quickly re-stashed his Ruger. He stopped and smiled at the guy, looking him dead him the eyes. This man probably came to America for a better life.

"Papi, what you need?" the Latino man fell in step beside Crime.

"Yeah, let me get an ounce of that boy," Crime said, and watched the man's eye light up at the mention of an ounce. "How much is that?" Crime asked, reaching into his pocket and purposely dropping a wad of cash on the ground. The Latino bend down to retrieve the money for Crime but when he came back up he felt something cold and hard pressed to the back of his head. Then there was darkness. Crime looked down at his latest victim as smoke rose from his head like a chimney. Crime took the money out of the dead man's hand. "Life in America is tough, Amigo," he said as he walked calmly to his car.

Ike called an emergency meeting with his crew that he knew for sure, would bust their guns, if needed. Time was running out and he didn't want to wait. Any longer and the police would complicate things. He was going to start hitting them one by one. He'd sent Ebony and Tweet on a little vacay. He needed her to stay away for a few days while he investigated and since she trusted him, she knew he'd send her somewhere safe. Jamaica was a good spot. This shit would wrap up in no time.

"Listen up," Ike was saying to his crew. "Those bitches hit my spot and must be dealt with immediately. *And,* like I said before, anybody who gets in the way will also become victims. Wrong place at wrong time and shit." Ike had all the Intel he needed from his street informant so he knew where everyone lived. He'd even found out that the one they called Rich was Tweet's brother and a fag. Everything added up nicely. Ain't life a bitch the way it rolls. The bitch called Toya was the hardest one to find out anything about but once he made the Kato connection flood gates of information opened. Ike had heard about Kato even before he came home from the Feds. He was a street legend and deadly. No wonder his missus was so stealth. Ike didn't have to worry about him because he was locked up looking at mad time. He wasn't going to worry about that shit 'cause when and if the time came, he'd deal with him too. "Alrigth. The bitch Jada is being dealt with as we speak but them other bitches are on ya'll and I expect this shit to go down without any of it coming back this way," Ike warned.

After the meeting Ike went to see Ice. "Listen, Ice, you don't have to do this if you don't want. I mean I can always get one of my niggas to take the bitch out."

"Daddy, you know I'm not in this half way. Besides, I know this bitch personally and I probably have the best chance of getting closer to her than any of your soldiers. Look at it as a favor paid. That Ohio shit was bogus." Ice stuck out his right hand.

"A'right, Playa," Ike smiled and took Ice's hand. "Soon as this is done with we'll all get right back to business. Ohio don't know who they fuckin' with." He walked toward the door.

Tia dropped Toya off at Rich's crib. Toya insisted that she should go home and get some rest and not bother to come up to Rich's. She would handle what needed to get handled and then she too was gonna go get some rest. Tia agreed as they pretty much hadn't slept since their return from B-More. Not that she trusted that she could sleep but it would be good to be still. With so much on her mind, especially Dakota, Tia was certain that sleep would not find her. Regardless of the situation with Dakota, none of it could be good. She was either dead or the killer had kidnapped her. Tia waved goodbye to Toya and headed out. Without even being conscious she turned the car in a direction that did not lead to home. She knew where she was going but not what she would do once she got there.

Sean sat back from the laptop he'd been staring at for hours. He passed a hand through his hair and cupped the back of his neck. The more he searched for a nugget that could help him convict Kato Pascal, the more he hit a brick wall. The DEA had really made a big mistake. How the hell could they have fucked up the wire-tap? Sean had already listened to over eighty-seven phone conversations, house meetings and private discussions but not one had implicated Kato or suggested that he was even the head of the Dynasty Crew. All they had on him was good for three years' max, and he'd probably be out in fifteen months. He had to find something solid. The FEDS were of no help either. When he'd call to find out if they had ever investigated Dynasty, he had been ceremoniously dismissed. He was going to win this case. He just had to. But he felt like he was going backwards. Damn, he was beginning to hate the case but he was not a man to quit.

Sean leaned back against the sofa and stared at the screen. There had to be something he'd missed. He kept staring at the screen as if by magic the answer would appear. Hypnotic staring and whir of the computer was somewhat relaxing and Sean felt his lids get heavy. The buzzing of the intercom jerked Sean awake. He looked at the clock. 1:45 a.m. He rose and rubbed his eyes to make sure he was seeing right. Who on earth would be ringing his doorbell at this hour? Sean padded to the kitchen where the intercom was mounted and pressed the speak button. "Yes?" He said into the contraption.

"Sean, it's Tia. Can I come up?"

Sean immediately pressed the buzzer to let her in. He pulled his robe around him, slipped his feet into his bed slippers and went to stand in the doorway to wait for her. He heard the elevator climbing.

Tia exited the elevator and made a right turn. As she turned the corner, she saw Sean standing in his doorway waiting for her. She hesitated, contemplating turning back. She had made a grave mistake.

"Hey," Sean said. "Don't leave."

How the hell did he know I was thinking about leaving? The man is so in sync with me, Tia thought.

Tia walked over to Sean and rested her head on his shoulder. She looked so sad, that all Sean could do was wrap his arm around her and pull her closer.

"I didn't know where to go. I just couldn't be home by myself." He felt tears against his neck.

"Baby," he kissed the top of her head. "You came to the right place."

By the time they hit the other side of the door, half their clothes were off and trailing to the bedroom. Tia's needs were great and heightened by her loss. She wanted to feel the living. Sean matched her desire for he had missed her so very much and he was so glad she was beginning to trust him. Their love making was torrid, demanding and healing. Tia rolled next to Sean, her body satiated and relaxed. Sean eased his hand under her neck and cupped her to him. He stared at the ceiling, the aroma of love as intoxicating as the sex they'd just had.

Tia rested her face on Sean's chest. She moved her hand back and forth across his soft, curly hair. "I shocked you, huh? What went through your mind when I just showed up at your door?"

Sean kissed her forehead. "I thought about how much I missed you and that if you'd left I would surely have died."

Tia laughed and tweaked his nipple. They were so in sync that Tia wished he could just read her mind. That way he would understand everything without her having to say it. How would she ever be able to explain to this man, in words, what she thought about telling him in her mind? She tested the waters.

"I'm so sorry I barged in on you. It's just that today I felt so lost and so angry. I saw my dearest friend in a casket and Sean the only thing I could think was about hurting the people who'd hurt her."'

"That's normal, Tia. Really. It's only natural that we want justice in a situation like this. Our anger and frustration makes us want to do unto others but that's why there is the law. Plus, your friend would never want you to jeopardize your life and future on revenge."

That answered it then, Tia thought. His words were not of someone who would understand her code of honor. She would never be able to explain it to him or reveal who they really were. She would never be able to tell him that Kaisia was not just a friend and sister but a comrade in the game. A loyal and faithful soldier and that they had taken an Oath of Honor. Killing the enemy was to keep up her end of the bargain. Tia sat up and swung her feet over the bed. She felt naked and cupped her breast as she picked up her clothes and made her way to the bathroom.

She returned fully dressed and sat on the bed to find her shoes. Sean began massaging her shoulders. "What did I do? Tia, I know there are things you wish you could tell me but don't know how to say them. I am okay with that until you are ready but don't shut me out. I don't expect you to reveal your whole life to me. I'd like to think we have all the time in the world. The one thing I ask is don't let doubt stand between us. I am a patient man. When you are ready to let me in, I'll be right here."

"Sean, I may never be ready. When you tell me that I seem like a shell at times, you are right. I am a shell. I don't mean to suppress my feelings, but I do. I am so afraid to promise what I can't give and in the process hurt you...someone I could love very much. I am afraid to commit to anyone when my own life is so uncertain and there are so many things in my path that are not clear. How do I find happiness? How can I be so selfish to just take what I need and have someone I love get hurt?"

Sean swung his legs over the side of the bed and sat next to Tia. He was such a handsome man both in body and spirit and she loved him for that. Sean took Tia's hand and squeezed it.

"Tia," he said looking at her closely. "That's what love is. It's two imperfect people coming together, each standing in the shadow of the other. They pile their worries into one big basket and work together to empty the basket. In doing so, they gain each other's strength and wisdom and find a love so strong it cannot be broken. Love is all and you can't hurt the person you love. Hurt is fear and love is love, pure and simple."

Tia didn't want to break down again. Enough of that for one day but this man was melting her heart. She had to be extra careful and that meant not seeing him again. The though scared her to death. She hoped one day she might find the kind of love he spoke about but in this lifetime, with the lifestyle she had chosen, that was prohibited. She had danced with the devil and their love was not permitted. Tia smiled and squeezed his hand back.

"Before I met you, I never thought of love. The love you speak of was not an option for me. I have loved deeply but that love has been reserved for my family and the few close friends who know and understand me. They would never judge me or turn their backs on me. I know it's a different kind of love Sean, but maybe it's enough for me. You require a different love and I don't know how to give that. You've known me for only a few months and yet you see the baggage I carry. Only when you truly see my baggage can you declare that you love me."

Sean didn't say a word. He got up from the bed and walked over to the closet. Tia's eyes followed him and her heart sank. She didn't want to give him up but what choice did she have? She had already chosen, a long time ago. Sean riffled through the closet and returned to the bed with a box and sat next to Tia. He placed the box on the bed, removed the lid and pulled out a handful of pictures and some news articles. He spread the pictures and the articles over the bed. The pictures were old and yellowing and showed a bunch of people sporting Afros, bell bottoms jeans and Chuck Taylor shoes. Sean picked up one of the pictures and handed it to Tia. It was a picture of four young boys no older than about thirteen in b-boy pose. Three wore leather MGM jackets and the fourth a Jeans jacket with an inscription on the pocket. She looked closer and recognized Sean as the kid with the jeans jacket.

"Life is about choices and circumstances lead to choices. I grew up right here in the projects with these boys. He pointed to one of the kids to the right of him. That's my cousin "D" and his friend. The one to the left of me is Keith. He was older than us by two years. We looked up to Keith because he was the man...experienced in everything: sex, clubbing, reefer and even the fast life. He was the opposite of the rest of us but we admired and respected him. Keith wanted everything fast and he wasn't willing to settle for less. While we were looking up to him, he was looking up to the guys on the street who had the finest women, clothes, cars and money. We would all talk about our plans for the future and how we'd make it out of the ghetto. We had a pact but Keith got caught up in crack. He started saying he'd get back on track once he made some fast money. We believed him and he remained a part of our group. Then he started coming around with all kinds of new things - gold and diamond cable chains, double wide four-finger rings with his name engraved and a brand spankin' new car. We were sure that since he got what he said he wanted, he'd be back. We were kids and we listened to him and never saw the bigger picture. He hid everything from his family and only us knew what he was up to. Somehow, though, I think they figured it out but chose to look the other way."

Sean handed another picture of Keith to Tia. He looked so different that Tia couldn't believe it was the same guy. He was decked out in full leather with gold all over his chest and hands and leaning against a car. She figured it was about five years later and was surprised when Sean said it was the same year as the first picture. Damn, Tia thought, the street aged him fast.

"He was only fifteen in both those pictures," Sean said.

"I was thinking it was about five years later," Tia admitted.

"My father used to tell me that age wasn't physical, it was mental. I still believe that to this day. In Keith's case, the streets drained his youth. It stole his innocence and reduced him to a product." Sean handed Tia a tattered newspaper clipping. Tia opened the fragile paper carefully and stared at the man who was the poster child for Americas most wanted. The caption of the article read, "4 Dead in Turf Drug War." Tia's spine straightened involuntarily. Keith Washington of Harlem was arrested Thursday night for the brutal murders of his rival along with his rival's wife and two children ages 9 and 11. Tia took a deep breath and folded the paper. How well she knew this life.

"This is the last picture I have of Keith," Sean handed her the picture of a man who looked like a stone cold addict.

He seemed so far away Tia didn't dare say a word. What could she say anyway? She had to say something, so Tia said, "So what happened to him?"

"He's dead," Sean said. "He was murdered in Attica. That was Keith's choice and it lead to a life of sadness and short lived gain. D became a doctor, Chuck is a music producer and I became a lawyer. I've always felt so badly that we didn't do anything to try harder to steer Keith back to the fold but the street was bigger than us. I sometimes felt we let him down by being silent."

How could she forget? Sean was an A.D.A. and she was a murderer and a master at the game. "You know Sean, I don't think you can make other people's choices for them," Tia thought of Ebony. "You can't blame yourself."

"I know that intellectually, but my heart wishes I could have. You know what's funny?"

"No, what?"

"He was murdered trying to get some young girls out of harms' way. I had to believe he was trying to find his way back because the Keith we knew and loved would never have killed a single soul. But crack doesn't discriminate. Even then a kernel of his values showed up when he tried to save that girl. That's what I chose to remember."

Tia helped Sean gather up the pictures and put them back in the box. Karma was a bitch, she thought, as she watched him return the box to the closet. She would never have been able to tell that her A.D.A. was a product of the mean streets and that her life was not that far from Keith's. She had planned to get out of the game once she had her degree but now with Kaisia's death, it seemed she'd gotten deeper and deeper and deeper.

As he walked her back to the door, Tia saw the Dynasty Case spread out on his desk. Lord she wished she could trust him. After she did what she had to do, maybe she would try.

Jada had stayed after Toya left to help Rich finish up what had to be done. It was three in the morning when she finally got home. Rich had wanted her to spend the night but she really want to be in her own bed. It had been a challenging few days and she desperately needed to chill. Jada walked down the hallway with her apartment key in hand. She knew the drill. As she turned the corner she jumped with fright as a man stood directly in front of her.

Ice had been waiting for Jada since he'd left Ike. Ike had informed him that she was probably not returning tonight but he knew Jada and knew for sure she would return to her home. She had a thing about sleepovers.

"Nigga, you scared the shit out of me," Jada punched him in the arm. "What the fuck you doing creepin' and shit at this time of morning'?" She brushed pass him to unlock her door.

Ice realized he could put her lights out at that very moment. What a waste? he thought. She was one helluva looker, with a slammin' body and the juiciest clamp he'd ever hit. The world would lose a master but he was goin' to hit that pussy one last time.

"I just got here. I tried calling you but got your voice mail," Ice walked into the apartment behind her.

"Yeah, I guess I didn't turn it back on. I cut it off when I was at a wake today. I guess you really horny?" Jada said coming to stand in front of him. She grabbed his cock. "How you know I wasn't with another nigga, coming up here uninvited."

Ice, who was standing by the window, pulled the curtains and then followed her to the bedroom. He watched her undress and licked his lips at the sight of her bare ass in her purple thongs.

"If you were with some other kat you know he would be just a place holder until the real thing showed up." He stood behind her and palmed her ass. He snapped off her bra and turned her to face him. Her firm breasts sprung loose and Ice stared at the nipples that had never suckled a baby. She had the darkest nipples he'd ever seen. He covered one with his lips as he murmured. "You act like you don't miss a nigga." He sucked hungrily. He liked the bitch...a lot. She was just his kind of kinky.

Jada moaned. She missed this nigga. His sex was like the bomb but she liked playing hard to get because he only showed up when he was horny and it made their sex more interesting. "Well, I was able to occupy my time while you were missing in action. I have a ten-inch dildo and some friend who like to watch me play with it," Jada said between moans.

"But I bet all your friends at once and your toy couldn't make you cum like I make you cum." He slipped a finger into her wetness.

Jada smiled back at him...the sly mutha fucker had the biggest grin on his face and bulge in his pants. Jada unzipped his pants, pulled out his manhood and brushed her face against it. She kissed the tip and just as he was trying to push her head further, she stood up. "Let's take a shower," she said grabbing his hard-on and heading to the shower.

The water that sprayed them was warm and as enticing as the sex they were about to have. Jada lathered her hand, kneeled and began washing his dick. She teased and pulled and massaged while Ice played with her tits. Jada cupped his balls and ran her tongue over his shaft before she curled her lips over his pulsating dick.

Ice grabbed the top of her hair to control the rhythm. "Yeah, baby, I like that…do that shit," he moaned pinching hard on her stiff nipples.

"You like that, Baby?" She swallowed him all the way up to his pubic hair.

Ice moaned louder and Jada sped up her action until she felt his pre-cum, she abruptly stopped.

"Ah, Baby, don't stop."

"You don't think I'ma let you off that easy."

Ice pulled her to her feet, lathered his hand and washed her, his hand sliding back and forth until he felt her bud rise. They washed each other then stepped out of the shower. Wet and slippery Jada climbed on the bed, positioned herself on the edge and opened her legs. Ice got on his knees, spread her wide open and buried his head in her fur. Jada opened wider and wider as his tongue brought her to full erection. She grabbed his head and began grinding her hips. "Got damn, nigga, you got it going on. Ohhhh, shit!" she was rising off the bed. Ice stuck a finger in her as he continued to tease her womanhood. By now, Jada was writhing, her cum was explosive, covering the inside of her legs.

Ice released her as he watched her spew all over his face. In one quick move, Ice flipped her over onto her knees and entered her from behind. The bitch was moving like an ocean in a tropical storm.

"Daddy, do that thing," she muffled her cry into the bed covers. Ice was stroking and she was moaning softly. Ice quickly pulled out then slipped into her anus, and put his finger into her wetness.

"Oh, God!" Jada moaned her cry of ecstasy louder and louder.

OH, SHIT, BITCH I' CUMMIN, OHHHHH SHIT!" Ice yelled as he collapsed on top of her. When their breathing was normalized, he pulled out and lay next to her. No woman had made him this crazy.

"I really needed this," Jada said, resting her head on his chest.

"I know, Bitch. I'm the only one that has what you need."

Jada eyes began to close. She was tired. So very tired. She was so glad Ice came by. It was just what she needed, she thought just as she fell asleep.

Ice lay beside Jada staring at the ceiling. He looked at the clock. 5:35 a.m. He needed to be out of there before the world woke up. He looked over a Jada to make sure she was still asleep. Ice quietly got out of bed and started putting on his clothes. Once he was dressed, he got a wash cloth and began wiping away fingerprints. Everything he had touched in the apartment. They wouldn't be able to ID his sperm, so that was that. Once he felt satisfied, he removed a pair of leather gloves and unplugged the phone at both ends. This was the way to kill her. He didn't want to spill blood or disfigure the beautiful body. "Sorry, Baby." As he was trying to wrap the cord around her neck, his knee hit the bed and she bolted up. Jada was disoriented and couldn't remember where she was. She felt something wrap around her neck and realized there was an assailant in her house. Ice must have left the door open by accident she thought fighting off the assailant. The more she fought, the more the cord cut into her skin. Jada swing the pillow which caught the assailant off guard and he loosened his grip. She yanked herself, falling off the bed and onto the floor. The assailant put a knee in her back and began to tighten the cord again.

Unnoticed, she reached under the mattress where her pistol was. She couldn't die like this. Her hand connected to the pistol when she heard her assailant say, "BITCH, DIE!"

Ice! Jada recognized the voice. She couldn't believe it was Ice who was trying to kill her. She couldn't believe that nigga-ass bitch was her assassin. Jada had no idea where her will and strength came from. Her desire and determination to kill him was stronger than ever. Jada curled her hand around the gun handle.

Ice was tightening his grip when he heard a gunshot followed by a bright flash. He felt a burning sensation spreading through his stomach, fell backwards and brought his hand to his stomach. He looked at his hand which was covered in blood, as the second shot ripped through his upper chest. Three more shots hit to his chest and Ice fell to the floor, dead.

Jada slid to the floor panting for breath and then passed out.

When she regained consciousness, Jada was staring at the body of the dead man in her bedroom. Hysterically, she dashed to the phone and called Rich, then Toya. When Rich and Toya arrived, the blood around Ice's body had coagulated. He was lying face up on the hardwood floor of Jada's bedroom. Rich was thankful that the area rug was on the other side of the bed and was spared from blood.

THE BRONX

It was 9:15 a.m. when Tia woke. She jumped out of the bed as it she was hit by a volt of electricity. She was supposed to have met her peoples at her house. Tia looked quickly around the room for her clothes. She saw that Sean had folded them and put them neatly on a chair beside his dresser. She walked over to retrieve them and noticed a single red rose sitting on top of a card. Tia picked up both items. She brought the rose to her nose, closed her eyes and inhaled its soft, sweet fragrance. She opened the card and read the inscription.

Baby, I knew that I wouldn't be here when you returned from your peaceful slumber, I wanted to leave behind a scent of myself to remind you that what we share is beautiful in all aspects and I want you to know and realize that my shoulder and time are always available for you. Hope to see you tonight. With love, Sean.

Toya refolded the card and placed it beside the rose on Sean's dresser. Her heart felt full, her feet light as she grabbed her clothes and headed towards the bathroom.

Toya called Tia and informed her that they had a situation though she didn't go into details. She asked her to meet them at Jada's.

Rich gave everyone a pair of rubber gloves. He then got a bottle of bleach while Toya and Jada got a full-size area rug from the living room to wrap the body. Rich vacuumed the rug and proceeded to clean down the entire apartment with bleach. Toya removed Ice's boots, gloves, jewelry and wallet for his pocket and threw them into a garbage bag. Rich removed all the bed sheets, pillow cases and everything else that needed to be thrown out, pulled a Hefty garbage bag from his back pocket and dumped them into it.

"Rich," Toya said. "We need your help."

"What ya'll need me to do?"

"Help us roll this nigga up in this rug."

While Jada and Rich held the body, Toya got the duct tape around the rug at the corpse's head, torso, stomach and feet.

"That should do it." Rich got up walked back to his Hefty bag duties. "Dumb bitch-ass nigga," he said. "Take that mutha fucker outta here so I can clean up this mess."

Toya and Jada dragged the body into the hallway. As they were laying the body down, the doorbell rang. Rich pulled out his .44 magnum and went towards the door. Toya pulled out two Glocks. Rich had taken apart Jada's gun, cleaned it and flushed some of the parts down the toilet.

They crept to the door as quiet as cat burglars. Each stood on the opposite of the door.

"Who is it?"

"Tia."

The stealth lowered their pistol and Rich opened the door. Tia walked in and they locked the door behind her.

"What the fuck happened?" Tia's eyebrows went up when she saw the rug in the hall. She wasn't a weaver but she knew a dead body when she saw one.

Jada walked into the bedroom and began laying down towels over where Rich had cleaned. She looked at Tia, her eyes sad and angry.

"Who was it?" Tia had grasped the picture by now.

"This nigga named Ice who I was dealing with," Jada shook her head in disbelief.

A nigga you were dealing with, Tia wanted to ask but it was not the time. They had more pressing matters to attend to, so she grabbed some gloves and began cleaning up the mess.

"What we gonna do with this body?" Jada was still somewhat in shock.

"We gonna need to get it to the truck. The front of the building is packed with wannabe gang bangers so the front door isn't an option in this broad daylight. We could use the side entrance but there's no parking space back there to pull the truck into. We can't do much till it gets darker anyway."

"Tee, none of those are options. This place always have people swarming around. We can't risk anyone seeing us. That would surely tie our hands. Around here you never know who could be watching," Toya said.

"You're right. I didn't think about that. Let's take those options off the table for we can't run the risk of being a.m. bushed carrying a body. It would make us open targets if the rumor mill got to talking." Tia got up and threw a bunch of bloodied towels in the Hefty bag Rich was holding.

"So what we gonna do now?" Jada was pacing. "We can't leave the nigga in my crib."

"Jay, we know that. We gonna remove the body today. What the fuck? This nigga is more trouble than he was worth."

"We gonna have to go over the roof," Toya said.

Everyone turned and look at her.

"Go over the roof. Then what?" Rich asked.

"Jay, isn't there an abandoned building two buildings down from here?"

"Yeah."

"All the buildings' roofs are connected. We have to get the body over there and leave it there."

"We don't have another choice ya'll. That there is the only solution."

"Let's finish cleaning up this place," Rich said. "When things quiet down, we'll dump that nigga's ass in the trash where it belongs."

Late into the night the posse made their move. It was a good thing Jada was on the top floor, and the stairs to the roof was just outside her door.

"Jada, that mutha ain't have no alarm, right?" Rich said.

"No. But sometimes them niggas be up there smokin' reefer so I need to make sure it's clear before we make a move."

Jada tip toed up the stairs and looked around. She signaled that all was clear and held the door open. Rich and Tia took the body out while Toya trailed with her Glock cocked. There were only eight steps to the roof. They moved steadily, their bare feet making very little noise. Tia hated heights so she looked straight ahead into the darkness. When they got to the third building they realized that there was a seven-foot gap separating it from the other two.

"Got damn!" Tia said. Her heart sunk. The only way to get over was to jump and she wasn't about to do it. "How we going get the body over there?" She kicked the body they had gently laid down. "Somebody gonna have to jump."

"I could jump but there are two problems with that. First, jumping would cause a noise. Second, how we gonna get the body over there?"

"What difference will a thud make? The building is empty. We gonna have to swing it across then you follow and drag it inside."

"Okay. Let's do this," Toya said.

Tia and Toya took one end of the rug and Rich took the other. "We gonna all swing together and on the count of three, we throw the mutha." Tia said.

"One, two, three," Tia whispered and the rug went flying into the air landing on the roof of Building Three. Rich, was the best high jumper in high school, got a running start. Shit, everything comes in handy, he thought, as he leapt into the air and landed safely on the roof. He grabbed the rug and dragged it into the abandoned building. He was back in no time and the posse retraced their steps to Jada's crib.

The house was spotless and Rich had bagged up everything and placed them outside of Tia's bedroom door. They would take them down to the truck when they left.

Tia stood by Jada's window. She didn't open the curtain but took a quick peek to scope out the street. How the fuck did all this happen? She turned to Jada and said, "Do you know who the nigga was dealing with? This had to be a hit, she was sure of it. Maybe that's why the nigga had stepped to Jada in the first place. But he didn't have to step to her to do a hit. There was a lot more and they needed to know what.

Jada tried to recall what she knew about Ice. Besides being a good fuck, she realized she didn't know much. "I don't really know much about him and who he fucks with. I know that he's getting paper, lots of it, knows damn near everybody who was somebody and he just opened up a club called Paradise a few months ago.

"I heard of that spot, but I don't know from where. I definitely heard of it though. It's supposed to be the new hot spot."

"That's a start. Me and Toya are gonna go through there and make some trouble. Jay, you know where the nigga live?"

Jada nodded her head. "I have his driver's license."

"You and Rich go over to the nigga's crib and see what's there. Don't do anything grand just go and see what you can find. Be careful 'cause if this was a hit job people will be looking for him."

"I got his keys too," Jada said.

"What days that mutha is open?"

Toya pulled out her phone and called the number. "It's open now."

"Jada, you gotta lay low. You can't say here. Check into a hotel downtown. Whoever sent the nigga might send more. Plus, when they don't hear from him they'll start looking and the first place might be here." Tia pulled some bills from her purse.

"I'm good," Jada said.

"Pay cash."

"Ya'll ready to get up outta here?" Toya asked.

"Yeah, let's get the fuck up outta here," Rich said.

"And let's get this party started 'cause I'm go see Kato tomorrow."

CLUB PARADISE

Tia pulled the truck up to the valet. She jumped out and handed the key to the driver. "I'm paying you ahead of time and a bit extra 'cause I need my keys back and I need you to park it right there." Tia handed him a Hundred Dollar bill. Mr. Park quickly parked the car and brought the keys back.

"Enjoy, Homeboy." Tia took the keys and put them in her bag. As Tia and Toya walked away, he checked them out. Tia was in a tight cat-suit, belted with a silver and red Chanel that cinched her tiny waist and matched the red and silver boots that hugged her well-toned legs. Beside her, Toya was rocking a brown suede skirt, a low-cut beige blouse that showed off her bosom, and tied-up strappy heels. Her brown suede bag was slung across her torso.

They crossed the street and looked in awe at the line that snaked round the block and out of sight. The women had no intention of standing in line so they had to get their game on. As they were formulating their game plan, a limo pulled up and a light-skinned brother stepped out. He was in his mid-twenties and dressed in a designer suit. If Tia had to guess, it was a Michael Kors. When the club goers got sight of him, they went wild. He must be somebody important, Tia thought. "You know who that is?" She asked Toya.

"Not a clue."

Five other guys stepped out of the limo behind him, dressed also in designer duds.

Tia stood on the sideline. She too was dressed to the nines and noticed the light skin guy checking them out. Even the bouncers were ogling them. They made their move. Light Skin stepped onto the red carpet and Tia flashed him a smile and a coquettish look. He smiled back. Tia and Toya stepped onto the red carpet right behind Light Skin as though they were part of his entourage. She watched him hug one of the bouncers as he and his entourage stepped into the club. Tia and Toya followed close behind but one of the bouncers stopped them.

"What's your problem?" Tia asked, pretending to be offended. Before the bouncer could respond, Light Skin stepped up.

"I got them, Play. They're rollin' with me tonight."

The bouncer smiled and nodded his head and let the women pass.

The club was fly. The plush interior boasted a huge dance floor, a DJ booth overhead, a stage and a wrap-around bar. It put Tunnels, Tia's favorite spot on 23rd Street, to shame.

Light Skin asked them if they would like to join him. He walked them through the dance floor to the VIP section. The five men who Tia had thought were his friends were actually bodyguards and they took up their posts nearby.

"What are you drinking?" Light Skin asked.

"Oh, order for us," Tia smiled then she and Toya excused themselves to go to the ladies' room. She grabbed Toya's hand and they made it back through the dance floor. When they were on the other side, Tia said, "Toya, I'm gonna head over to the bar to see what I can find out. You go talk to a few people to see what you can find out. Meet me back here in ten so we can get up outta here."

Toya nodded and the women headed in opposite directions.

BROOKLYN

Rich and Jada, both in disguise, sat in the car in view of Ice's apartment on Clinton Avenue in Brooklyn, an area of modern condos. Ice's was in a six-story building. The area was pretty deserted except for a few passersbys now and then.

Jada was the first to exit the car. As planned, Rich would wait until she was across the street and in the building before he got out. He didn't want any connection, if he could help it.

Jada walked to the door of the building. A security guard was inside reading the paper. She pulled out the keys that had been in Ice's pocket and was glad the guard wasn't paying too much attention as it took her three tries to find the right key. She opened the door and headed to the elevator. The guard was probably not a regular and figured since she had a key she actually lived there. As Jada exited the elevator on the third floor, the apartment was right in front of her. She let herself in quietly after a few tries since there were seven keys on the key ring. She did not turn on the lights but she had her gun drawn just in case the nigga had some bitch up in his crib. Jada listened for any sound. None. Once she was sure no one was there, she turned on her flashlight so she could ID the buzzer, then called Rich so she could buzz him in. "If the guard stops you for any reason tell him you going to 3D. He don't seem like a regular so it'll be okay."

She flashed the light around. The place was simply furnished. Nothing lavish. A regular bachelor's pad. She'd wait for Rich to ring the buzzer and decide if they should turn on the lights.

CLUB PARADISE

Tia ordered a shot of Hennessy and set it before her. She had no intention of drinking. It was just a front and a reason to hang out longer at the bar. She took a seat. She was glad to see that the bartender was female as she would be able to juice conversation out of her much easier. Tia watched her serve a few more drinks before coming back in her direction. Tia dumped her Henny on the floor then signaled the bartender.

"Let me get another shot of Hen, Dog." Tia smiled. "And do you mind if I ask you where you got those badasss shoes from?" Tia stifled a laugh, for to be honest, they were the ugliest pair of shoes she'd ever seen. So purple 70's get-up shit.

"Oh, these?" the bartender said as she lifted her foot to be further admired. I got these on vacation in Jamaica a few months ago. In fact, I think I am the only person in New York with them."

As it should be, Homegirl, 'cause them things are hideous! "They are cute," Tia lied. "And I have the perfect outfit for them too," She winked.

The bartender placed Tia's order in front of her. "Yeah, you can pretty much wear them with anything."

"Hey, listen, maybe you can help me. I'm waiting for a friend but he hasn't show up yet. He's a regular here. You probably know him. His name is Breed." Tia said pulling a name out of a hat. She knew no one called Breed.

The bartender shook her head.

"He told me that if, for some reason, he was unable to make it, to check Ice or his man."

"I know Ice. He owns the spot but he's not around today. I never see them too much so I don't know who his man could be."

They talked for a few more minutes before Tia excused herself.

Toya walked up on a group of girls by the bathroom smoking a joint. "Ya'll want to sell some of that?" Tia acted like she'd known them for years.

"We only have a little bit but we'll let a bag go for $25.00," said a big ass girl. Tia immediately thought of Big

Mama. The brown skin girl was so chunky her legs, beneath the too tight jeans skirt, blended together and looked like one single thigh. Man, Toya thought, and the bitch was bringing even more attention to herself wearing the brightest red lipstick.

Toya knew home girl was trying to get over but she went along with it. "I'll take watcha got, but will it be alright if I stood over here with ya'll and blow this?"

Big Mama looked at her friends and shrugged her shoulder.

Toya took a couple of toots off the joint and passed it around. The weed heads would like that. Sell their shit and cop a smoke too.

A young girl, no older that seventeen, was standing beside Toya pointing out the status of several different niggers that passed. She seemed like the one with the information.

"That one is mine," Big Mama said as School Girl ran down his dossier. Each of them were laying claim to their prey for the night.

"By the way," Toya asked. "Do anyone of ya'll know what's the deal with the owner of the club?" She was looking straight at Miss Talk A lot.

"Who Ice? That nigga is fine as hell. He off limits though. I wish I could slide up on that," said one of the girls, dressed like a stroll-ho said.

"Yeah? Do you know him?"

"Who don't know him? That nigger got it going on, shit! If he want he could have his choice of coochie up in here, but he don't play. I know one thing for sure, he could definitely get some of mine." Said Hoochie Mama making a cowgirl call and high fiving her friends.

"You got that right. He's the truth but you gotta see his man. Now that nigger is the real deal. In fact, I heard he's the real owner of this spot," Miss Talk a Lot said.

"I don't think I've ever seen his man either," Toya took the joint that was being passed.

"He comes through here and there, but the couple of times I've seen him he always had his bitch on his arm. Joy, what's home girl's name?"

"Her name is Ebony and why do she have to be a bitch? Ya'll just jealous 'cause none ya'll bitches got a man."

Toya looked at the redbone sister who was talking. She'd seen that face before.

"Damn, Joy, why it gotta be like that and shit?" Big Mama asked.

"Because I know her and she's good people. Plus, ya'll bitches stay scheming on what's not ya'lls. Anyway, excuse me," Joy said pushing pass Toya.

"Damn, the way she acting you'd think that it was she who's fuckin' Ike," Miss Talk a Lot scoffed.

That got Toya's full attention. She spun her head to look at Miss Talk a Lot. "Who you say her man is?"

"I don't know who Joy is fuckin' with." Hoochie Mama said.

"Not Joy. The other one, Ebony." Toya asked casually.

"Oh, Ike."

BROOKLYN

As they guessed the guard was no problem and Jada and Rich were rapidly searching through Ice's place. They searched bookshelves, and cabinet drawers and closets. Neither came across anything that would reveal who contracted him. In fact, there was so little in the apartment that Jada wondered if Ice really lived there. Not even a family picture, to do lists, or a pot in the whole place. This may not be his true residence, Jada thought. It was a decoy. She knew many men who kept extra apartments as decoys.

Jada was now pushing a button on the keyboard but the laptop screen remained blank. She had no idea what his password would be.

"Look. I think we done here, Rich. This nigga was either the smartest nigga in the world or the loneliest fuck. We can't even find a fuckin' phone number."

"We didn't listen to the phone massages," Rich said as he saw the blinking light. The obvious is not always obvious, he thought, as he walked over to press the play button. He turned the volume down.

"You have three messages," the thing spat out.

Message One: "Yo Ice, what's up? I tried callin' ya cell but you ain't pickin up. Holla at me when you get this."

Message Two: "Yo Dawg, it's been like four hours since I've heard from you. I need to hear from you to find out if you took care of that thing so I can take care of what I gotta take care of. Holla."

Message Three. "Ice, I'm ready to send somebody over to that bitch's crib. If I don't hear from you like in 30 minutes, the troops are gonna move in."

End of messages.

Rich checked out the time stamp of the last message. Fifteen minutes ago. Thank God they were out of there. And they needed to get up outta of here too 'cause this was the next place they were coming.

"That sounds like the person we may be looking for but he didn't leave a name so it could be just about anybody."

"Hold up. Let me try something quick." We gotta get out here too, Jay."

Rich pressed *69 and the phone on the other end started ringing. "It's ringing," he mouthed to Jada.

"Hello," a female answered.

Rich altered his voice and said, "May I please speak with Ice?"

"You mean Ike?" The female asked.

"Ike. No, no I said Ice."

The woman again tried to correct him. Rich's heart fell to his feet. It was Ebony's voice.

"I got the wrong number," Rich said and hung up the phone. He turned to Jada and said. "We have to contact Tia and Toya fast. That was Ebony on the line. The hit man is Ike!"

285

CHAPTER THIRTY-ONE

"THIS SHIT IS GOING DOWN TONIGHT. We're gonna hit that faggot nigga first." Ike was furious about all the misses of everything lately. He looked at the trigger-happy youngsters he'd hand-picked to carry out his orders and the bitch-ass niggas had failed. He needed a professional and though he hated the fact, he'd called Crime.

Ice, too, was fuckin' missing so Ike had sent out a couple of people over to Jada's apartment but they came back empty handed. Not only was Ice missing but the bitch-ass Jada was missing too. Shiiit! They might have run off together. Ike knew Ice was hitting it but Ice wasn't the type of guy who got attached or reneged on an agreement so Ike had to assume something went wrong.

Ike and his crew were, as usual, in the back of the Bodega, which Ike had ordered to close early because he wanted no interruptions.

"Let me make it clear. I want those bitches dead by tonight!" Ike shouted, spit spewing everywhere. "Fuck this up, and there's going to be more than four fuckin' funerals before this day is out."

Everyone shuffled in their seat and was glad for the distraction when some guy they'd never seen walked in.

"I see you'll started without me," Crime stood at the back of the room.

Even the so-called killers were intimated just by his deadly look. Ike was the only one who seemed unconcerned by Crime's presence.

"Nigga, I called you over an hour ago!" Ike raised his voice, to show that he was in control and no one was exempt from obeying his orders.

Crime looked over at Ice and smile. A deadly smile. He should spray the fucker's brains all over the nice leather chair he was sitting in. "Something came up," Crime said coming further into the room. "Besides, you're on my time." Crime informed, with every intention of letting Ike know that he wasn't anybody's puppet.

If Ike had been one of them light niggas he'd have turned red, instead veins began popping out of his forehead.

Crime took a seat on a folding chair. Ike glared at him and swallowed the bitter taste in his mouth. He was going to have to take care of this uppity nigga soon, for good. He was going to tolerate his shit tonight because he wanted the bitches dead, by any means necessary. Ike stood up and walked around his desk. "Ya'll know what you have to do so ya'll go handle the damn thing."

When the young assassins had departed, Ike went back around his desk and took a seat.

"So what's the word?" asked Crime.

"You tell me, Dawg."

Crime looked at Ike and wondered what could possibly be going through his head. He was becoming a real problem. All that money and power got him stuck on himself and believing he was invincible. He must be smelling his own piss and forgetting who took care of all the dirt that got him in the position he was in now. "So you got your young assassins. Why you need me?"

"For look out in case those bozos fail. But Crime, why didn't you tell me about the little girl?"

Shit. Crime knew he wouldn't have been able to hide Dakota for long. Someone was bound to start looking for her. Crime just wondered why Ike hadn't brought it up before.

Crime was formulating his explanation when Ike started speaking again.

"You know, I don't get down like that," Ike shouted, banging his fist on the desk. "I didn't order you to kill a child."

Crime was relieved to find out that Ike was under the impression that the little girl was dead and he saw no foul in letting him believe that. "Dawg, you paid me to take care of the bitch and I gave you that service. The girl was a witness."

"A witness? She was only FIVE OR SIX. What could she have possibly told the cops?"

"Nigga," Crime leaned into Ike, "you don't fuckin' tell me how to do my job. Its time Nigga, you understand your position. You're a fuckin' drug dealer, nothing more. I don't tell you how to push your product so make it your business to never again tell me where to put my bullets!" Crime shouted, bringing his face close to Ike's.

"NIGGA, WHAT THE FUCK IS THAT SUPPOSED TO BE? A THREAT?"

Crime stood upright and smiled. "I don't make threats. I make owners of funeral parlors very rich. Our business is done here." Crime headed toward the door.

Ike, in one sweep knocked all the items on his desk to the floor.

Tia sat on the couch in Rich's living room staring at the array of guns spread over the coffee table. "I can't believe that nigger was under our noses the entire time," Tia said, still trying to comprehend the information that Ike was Kaisia's killer and was now plotting to kill them all. By the time Rich had called, they had already put two and two together from the information Toya was able to pry out of Joy. They had plied her with drinks and drilled the information out of her in a way that would never understand how it happened. When they learned that the spot they'd hit in the Bronx was Ike's, it all became crystal clear why they hit her but how did they even find out?

"It's a small fuckin' world," Jada said shaking her head. She was loading bullets into clips.

"Come tomorrow this nigga's gonna be remembered." Toya was also loading bullets.

Rich came into the living room dressed in an all-black fatigue suit and black chukkas. "I called Tweet. She's over at a friend's house so I told her to stay there for a couple of days."

Tia had also called Tone to see if he could stay over at his girlfriend. She told him she was having company at the crib that night. She hated that this mutha was upsetting everybody's life but she needed Tone safe and far away from any drama-shit that might go down. Now that she knew who the enemy was, there would be no mercy.

"We could take the nigga at his crib," Jada said, rubbing her neck. Shit had moved so fast she couldn't even appreciate the fact that someone tried to murder her. The mark on her neck reminded her but she didn't have time to grieve.

"That nigga ain't stupid. I'm pretty sure that he knows the heat is on him especially since his goon never checked in and never will again." Rich began loading bullets. They needed to hurry because he just felt shit was gonna go down.

So, what the fuck we gonna do? Wait for the nigga to hunt us down? Tia was madder than hell. "I can sit around waitin', not for nothing. I ain't gonna be nobody's hangover. We're gonna have to hit the nigga first."

"We can't hit him at the crib. My sister is there." Tia said. She still couldn't believe how small the damn world was. How in hell did Ebony end up with a man whose spot they hit and who was trying to kill her own sister. What a fuckin' comedy of errors and shit. Now her sister was sleeping with the enemy and her first love had to die.

"And we can't call to tell her to come over because that would make him suspicious and put her at risk." Rich added.

"SO WHAT NOW! "Toya shouted. "Are you tellin' me that the he's off limits because he's fuckin' Tia's sister? That nigga murdered our friend and her child. Now you'll want to think about personal reason why we shouldn't twist that coward?"

"Ain't nobody saying that he won't get his but Ebony is caught in the middle," Jada said calmly trying to de-escalate the temperature in the room.

"How in the fuck is she caught in the middle of somewhere she wants to be? Besides, how certain are ya'll that she's unaware of what's goin' on?" Toya looked directly at Tia.

Tia tried to understand how Toya was feeling but her last comment erupted all the anger and frustration she had been feeling. "Bitch," Tia stepped to Toya. "What you say? I would fuck you up right here if you don't keep my sister's name out of your mouth right now!" Tia yelled.

Rich quickly intervened, grabbing Tia in a vice grip.

"Don't hold her. Let her go, Rich." Toya removed her pistol from her waist and set it on the table. "This Bitch needs some sense knocked into her fuckin' head. Alright Miss High-and-Mighty wantin' to be some kind of leader and shit. It's time to be a leader and let me tell you one more ground-breaking thing: Toya can move without a thousand mutha fuckers behind her."

"This is really what you think this is about, huh Toya? You think I'm trying to stand on the stretch line and point fingers? If that is what this is about, why don't you step up to the plate, Bitch!"

"Just chill ya'll." Jada shouted over the din as she stepped in front of Tia and blocked Toya.

"Tee, it's not that and you know it. You know that I don't get down like that, especially with my people, but there is a problem. You are letting your personal relationship with your sister put us all at risk. You are thinking only about her. What about us? What about Kaisia and Dakota?" Toya said, tears glistening in her eyes.

Tia stared at Toya. Everything she said was true. She pulled free of Rich and flopped down on the chair. She looked at Rich and then at Jada. She could see they agreed with Toya, and they were right. Ebony made her choice the moment she moved out, but how could she? Tia had given up her life for her and the rest of her family. Tia got up and walked over to the window and scanned the streets. They were in danger as it was being in Rich's crib. Tried as she did she couldn't shake the feeling that what Toya had said carried a lot of truth. She felt like she was slipping. But if Ebony knew more than what appeared on the surface and was protecting her man, why would she sacrifice her friends for Ebony's love?

"Tee, I know how much you love Eb. We all love her, but the fact is she is caught up in this shit one way or the other. The longer we sit here and on this info, the greater the chances are for them to get us. Just being here right now is risky. We gotta make some decisions. If we strike now we have the upper hand," Toya said softly. "Step away from that window," she added.

They both knew their nerves were on edge, and faced with their lives being on the line too had made the pot boil over. Toya's tenderness when she told her to step away from the window proved it was just anger boiling over.

"Jay," Tia said, "are the heats ready?" They had to do what needed to be done. If they didn't, Tia knew that Toya would act on her own accord and you put her life in even more danger. She had to protect both her sisters. Her family was no less important than Ebony. She hoped she could save them both.

Ike was in a bitch of a mood when he walked into the apartment. He walked into the bedroom and headed directly to the bathroom without a word to Ebony who was lying cross the bed reading Sister Souljah's, The Coldest Winter Ever. Ebony looked up as he stormed pass her. She immediately knew something was wrong. It was rare that he never spoke to her when he came home. She heard the water running. Why was he in such a hurry to shower? Did he have some bitch on the side? Ebony wondered.

Ike walked back into the bedroom a few minutes later, stark naked but instead of coming to claim her, he headed straight to his dresser and pulled out a silver-plated gun from the back of one of the drawers and marched back to the bathroom. This was really abnormal. Ebony hopped off the bed and walked into the bathroom. Ike was stepping into the shower. He looked at her and pulled the curtain. Ebony pulled back the shower curtain and glared at Ike. The gun he'd retrieved was on the window sill within his reach.

"What the fuck is going on? What's all this shit about, Ike?" Ebony asked.

Ike held his head under the water as it ran over him. He ran his hand down his face and attempted to close the curtain. Ebony jerked them back open. "I don't have time for this right now, Eb."

"Time for what, Ike? I don't fuck with you about what you doing on them streets, that are your business but when you bring the shit home, that's our business!"

Ike lathered up his body and let the water beat on him. He stepped out of the shower and Ebony moved to the side allowing him to grab a towel. Ike began drying himself off while ignoring that Ebony was standing in front of him.

"Ike," Ebony said. "Why the fuck do you have to, all of a sudden, take showers with guns? Nigga, you ain't no cowboy."

Ike snickered and brushed pass Ebony. He got the gun from the window sill and walked back into the bedroom. Ebony was fuming. She followed him. "Nigga you hear me talking to your dumb ass. WHAT THE FUCK IS THE GUN FOR?" She locked eyes with him through the dresser mirror.

"Eb, it's for our protection, that all," Ike said nonchalantly.

"What the fuck you mean our protection? Who the fuck would be after me that I would need protection?" Ebony eyes expressed both anger and fear.

Ike spun around to face Ebony. "You act like you don't know what I'm into in them streets. Do you think every day is peaches and cream? Shit is hectic right now that's all. It's part of the game. I'm just trying to protect my family."

Ebony began shaking. What the fuck had she gotten herself into? Something in the way Ike said "protecting our family" didn't sit right with her. Ebony began backing away. When she felt the edge of the bed against the back of her legs, she sat down. Her eyes were so sad that Ike walked over to her and knelt on the floor.

"Baby, I would never do anything to intentionally put you or our unborn child in danger, but you have to understand this is the life I lead."

"Ike. I want you to leave this life. You can't do this forever. We have a baby on the way and I can't be a mother and a widow. I can't bear the thought that you could die or be locked up for the rest of your life. I'm not built for this, Ike. We owe it to our baby, Ike," Ebony touched her belly.

"Eb, I not gonna leave you stranded. In fact, I have everything all set for us. We outta here after I handle this one last thing. I'm outta the game after that, I promise. Have faith in me."

"Oh, Ike," tears rolled down Ebony's cheek. "You promise?"

"Yes. Can I hear you say you have faith in me and will trust me to do what's best for us?" Ike cupped her face. He wasn't sure that anything he said was all true but he knew that was what she needed to hear and he had to hurry up and get outta there. One thing he knew for sure was that he had to give it serious thought because if he continued, he would be dead or in some white man's cage.

"Okay, Ike." Ebony toughed her head to his and nodded her agreement. "I love you Ike and I don't want anything to happen to you or us." Ebony was a bundle of nerves and she couldn't shake the feeling that something bad was about to happen.

Ike kissed her forehead and stood up. He grabbed the gun off the dresser and padded to the dresser and returned it to its place. Ebony walked up behind him and removed the gun and placed it back on the night stand. Ike looked at her and nodded. She'd be alright.

Jada, Rich, Toya and Tia all exited Rich's crib one after the other. They scanned the surroundings for the activities of the people around. Toya watched two guys who were having a conversation in front of a car. Her antennae went up and she nodded at Rich who turned his gaze on a group of guys across the street throwing dice. Toya was also checking the group to see if anything didn't fit right. Jada walked a little further looking up and down the block for anything out of the ordinary. Once they were satisfied, they began a steady walk in the direction of the parking lot.

They stayed alert because the further they walked the darker the street got as some of the street lights were broken. So far, nobody had popped out of the shadows. Nobody noticed as three of the guys playing dice stepped away from the game. Two walked side-by-side, the other stayed on the sidewalk.

The parking lot was just a few feet away. Jada turned around once more and caught sight of the two guys' crossing over to where they were. Jada watched and walked on. The two guys continued on a straight path toward them, Jada's alarm went off when the other guy on the other side of the street hurried his pace to keep up with the two guys approaching. "IT'S A HIT YA"LL," Jada yelled, reaching to her waist and drawing her gun. In a split second, all hell broke loose as the sound of gunfire thundered through the night air.

Rich ran behind a parked car and began shooting at the attackers. Toya sprinted behind a mailbox and let roar both her Glocks. Tia ran across the street and held a single gun battle with the lone assassin. Jada fired her .45 from a parked car. The night sky appeared to be on fire from the flashes from the gun sparks. Bullets ricocheted off everything. Windows were broken, cars were shot up, car alarms went off. Toya stood up and began shooting random shots watching as the gunmen dove for cover. Rich covered Toya and began to shoot at the car where one of the gunmen was hiding behind. Tia quickly reloaded her clip and continued firing. Jada slid along a parked car up the avenue. Tia held the gun to her chest as if to contain her galloping heart. She sprinted like a Cheetah across the street and saw Rich and Toya take cover.

Sweat dripped off the bridge of her nose. Tia was sprinting back across the street to where Rich and Toya were when Rich saw the lone gunman step into the open street to get a clear shot of Tia. He opened fire and sprayed the street with bullets in the direction of the lone gunman. Rich saw him fall backwards as two bullets connected to his chest.

"Where is Jada?" Tia asked as she tried to catch her breath.

"She's still out there. Over there," Toya pointed her gun in the direction she'd last seen Jada.

Toya looked in the direction and saw Jada leaning against a park car. Tia panicked for she couldn't tell if Jada was dead or alive. The distance between them was too far. Tia broke cover and walked down the street towards Jada as if her flesh was made of steel. Tia fired at her assassins who were trying to hit a moving target. Rich and Toya, seeing their friend in danger, stood up. Toya walked behind Tia firing into the streets while Rich walked directly into the street firing.

Both guys stood up from behind the car they were crouched and began firing, but one was luckier than the other. Jada who'd been on the other end of the car stood from her post and had a clear shot from behind. She fired a bullet to the back of one of the guy's head which snapped forward as he dropped to the ground. Tia made it over to Jada just as they heard the sound of police sirens in the distance. The surviving gunman fired one last shot before running from the scene. Tia and Jada stood up and began running to the parking lot with Rich and Toya right behind them.

Tia had just pulled off the block as the police cars began to flood Lenox Avenue. Even though they were out of the scene, Toya drove with caution because it was too late to be pulled over by the police and their work wasn't done. If shit has come home to roost, Tia knew they would hold court with the Po-Po in the streets because none of them was trying to do life in prison.

Tia checked the rare view mirror to make sure they were not being tailed. Nothing. Not even an unmarked car that detectives usually drive in the 'hood. She stopped at the red light on 135th and Lenox right across from Harlem Hospital. "Everybody alright?" Tia asked. Rich and Toya nodded but Jada who was slumped down in the passenger's seat, made a groaning sound. Tia looked hard over at her friend and realized she looked a little pale. "Jay, are you alright?" Tia asked.

Jada looked up at Tia and nodded her head, but even that seemed to cause her some pain. She flinched as she attempted to gesture about something. Tia reached over and removed Jada's arm from where she had folded them against her chest. Tia heart jumped as she saw blood all over Jada's chest. "Oh shit! Oh shit!" Tia screamed. "Toy, Jada's hit!"

"What?" Toya and Rich shouted at the same time. They leaned over and saw the splotch of blood over Jada's chest.

"No, Jay," Toya cried.

Car horns blared behind them and Tia pulled over in front of the hospital. Thank God, they were right there at the hospital. "Let's get her inside," Tia said.

"No," Jada stopped her from opening the door. "What sense does that make? The cops will be on us and they gonna lock us up." The pain on her face was severe.

"It don't matter, Jay, we need to go in there and get them to fix you up," Toya whispered.

"That would be stupid. Then we'd all be roommates Up North."

"But we'd be together." Toya insisted.

"Tia," Jada smiled at Tia. "Take charge."

"Jada, we'll do whatever you want us to but know we are down with you."

"Ya'll don't worry about me. It's probably a flesh wound. Didn't I just blow away a mutha trying to kill me?" Jada tried to laugh but winced.

They all smiled. Jada still had her sense of humor, even in pain. Shit. The girl was made of steel.

"Let's just go and take care of that nigga so Kaisia and Dakota can rest. And if shit happen I don't wanna tell them we didn't try. We remember?" She coughed a bit.

"Okay." Tia said. "But as soon as this shit is over, you're going to the hospital. We don't have to go to one in Harlem. Just hold on. This shit will be over soon and you'll be okay." Tia looked at Jada one more time before pulling off.

Ike was a busy man but the woman had his nose wide open. Instead of heading out the door as was his intent, he had just finished making love with his woman, soon to be wife. His cell phone buzzed.

"Hello."

"What?" Ike jumped out of the bed and moved to the living room. "What the fuck you mean ya'll missed?" He lowered his voice.

Ebony got out of bed and tiptoed to listen to what Ike was saying. She was concerned about her uneasy feeling. Maybe it was not as bad as she thought. She tiptoed back to the bed when the conversation seemed to be ending.

"Listen, be at the spot in an hour and have the rest of them niggas there with you," said Ike.

"The others dead."

"What? Pussy-ass bitches!" Ike cut off the phone.

"Baby, what's wrong?" Ebony asked, concern in her voice.

"It ain't nothing I can't handle, but listen, I'm gonna have to step out for a few and I want you to stay inside and don't answer the door under any circumstances."

"But Ike…"

"Listen, Ebony, just do the fuck what I asked you to. No fuckin' twenty-twenty questions right now," Ike shouted. Shit, he had to get her to understand but he felt bad for shouting at her but he had not time to pamper her right now. The iron-ass bitches were still on the out there. He was determined they wouldn't live past tonight.

297

When Ike left, Ebony remained rooted to the bed. She pulled her knees up to her chest and folded her arms across her belly. She rocked back and forth. She didn't feel well.

Tia entered St. Nicholas from 150th Street. The block was completely dead. Not a single activity on the street. She drove down the one-way street in search of the red building which brought back ill memories. She thought about Kaisia as she cruised the street. They were together the last time she was here. How the fast fuckin' life changes!

Toya and Rich were in the back, their pistols on their laps. Tia spotted the building. She pulled to the curb and stared at the entrance. She took her pistol from under the car seat and felt the heft of the Heckler and Koch before cocking it back.

Tia looked over at Jada. "Jay, we're here." Jada was slumped over, her head resting on the window. Tia slid her hand into her friends. "She's gone ya'll. Jay is gone." Tia squeezed her friend's hand for the last time.

Rich stopped breathing and Toya jumped forward to see what Tia was talking about. "She can't be." Toya dropped her head and tears fell everywhere. Rich reached over and touched Jada's cheek. "It's still warm," he said, disbelieving the evidence. He wiped his eyes as he rubbed her face knowing this was the last time he would be able to feel her warmth.

Tia squeezed the handle of the machine gun she was holding to maintain control. She could lose it now or lose focus. She leaned over and kissed Jada on the cheek and stepped out of the truck. She turned out all the lights and left the truck with Jada lying back out of sight. When Toya and Rich hit the sidewalk, there was just one thing on their minds: MURDER. Maybe Two. Vengeance.

Ike felt for the pistol in his waist. He hated to leave Ebony in the state she was but this was his life. The night was humid. Ike stepped out of the building and wished that he was doing this shit for the last time. He had enough paper; he should quit while he was ahead. Ike patted his pocket and was about to turn around thinking he'd left his keys only to hear them jingle in his back pocket. He was so focused on his keys, he never noticed the people unloading from a truck.

www.ingramcontent.com/pod-product-compliance
Lightning Source LLC
Chambersburg PA
CBHW020943260626
47169CB00006B/1792